WHERE NO ONE CAN HEAR YOU

JE ROWNEY

LITTLE FOX
PUBLISHING

Other thriller books by this author

I Can't Sleep
The Woman in the Woods
Other People's Lives
The Book Swap
Gaslight
The House Sitter
The Work Retreat
The Other Passenger
Waking Up in Vegas
Xmas Break

Find out more about the author and her books at
http://jerowney.com/about-je-rowney

If you enjoy reading this book, please remember to leave a review. Reviews help readers find new books and help authors to find new readers.

Dear Reader,

As the author of "Where No One Can Hear You," I want to ensure you can make an informed choice about your reading experience. This novel contains several themes and situations that some readers may find disturbing:

- Sexual assault (not graphically depicted but referenced)
- Violence against teenagers
- Traumatic injury and medical procedures
- Child abuse and exploitation (referenced)
- PTSD and trauma recovery
- Parental abandonment
- Descriptions of blood and injury
- Serial predator/killer themes
- Missing persons

This story focuses on healing and recovery but engages with these difficult topics in service of an authentic portrayal of trauma and resilience.

I encourage you to prioritise your wellbeing while reading. The novel includes moments of hope, healing, and connection alongside its darker elements.

Take care,
JE Rowney

Nulli soli, omnes uniti.
No one alone, all together.

PROLOGUE

Blood feels warm when it's leaving your body. Like bathwater. Like summer rain. Like tears.

Mine trickles down my neck in steady pulses, each beat of my heart pushing out more of my life. I can feel it pooling beneath me, sinking into the cracks of the road.

The night air chills my skin as I lie in the centre of the desolate highway, but I don't close my eyes. I can't. Closing them means giving in.

Please see me.

Please find me.

The words come without sound. My throat is too ruined for voice. But I keep mouthing them, tasting copper with each syllable. The tarmac beneath my cheek has lost the day's heat, cooling rapidly as darkness falls, but my body is cold everywhere except where the blood flows. My hands are bound behind my back, the fabric cutting deep into my wrists. I flex my fingers, feeling the slick warmth between them, but there's no give, no chance of freeing myself.

Above me, the last traces of twilight are fading, a final ribbon of deep purple surrendering to black. Night skies look different when you're lying on your side, chin pressed to your shoulder in a desperate attempt to stem the bleeding from your throat. Stars appear one by one, distant and cold. I always thought they were beautiful. Now they feel cruel. Too remote, too indifferent, as if the universe is mocking me with its vastness while I grow smaller.

The darkness deepens, the purple edge of horizon now just a memory. I can barely see the trees that line the road, their shapes merging into a solid wall of shadow. The temperature drops with each passing minute, the night air biting at my exposed skin, making me shiver where the warmth of my blood doesn't reach.

I focus on the emerging stars, not the ache in my body, not the sticky wetness beneath me. My vision blurs and contracts, darkness creeping in from the edges like spilled ink. The world shrinks to nothing but the slow, uneven throbbing of my pulse, each beat pushing more life out of me, onto the cold road beneath.

I don't know what I believe in, but I send a prayer into the night.

Send a car, please.

Send someone. Anyone.

Not anyone. Someone good.

I can't die here. Not alone on this empty road with no one to hear me.

As if summoned by my fading thoughts, I hear it.

A sound, distant at first, but growing. The unmistakable rumble of an engine cutting through the silence.

My heart stutters, pushing more warmth down my neck. A car. Someone's coming.

I am here.

Please see me.

Please find me.

The rumble gets louder, and suddenly all I can think about is how much blood has pooled beneath me, how it's matted my hair to the tarmac. A sick sense of shame floods my thoughts. I must look disgusting. A mess. Whoever finds me, because they will find me, will be covered in my blood. Their car will be ruined.

The strange things that run through your head when you're dying.

My mind floats.

I never ate at a real restaurant.

Not the kind with candles on the table, where someone pulls out your chair and refills your glass before it's empty.

Not the kind where the menu is heavy in your hands, pages thick and smooth, full of dishes I wouldn't know how to pronounce. We always meant to go. Mum said maybe for my birthday, somewhere nice. Not Paul, just the two of us. I was supposed to dress up. Order something I'd never tried before.

I have to make it to seventeen.

I've never seen the ocean, either. Not in real life. It was on my list: stand in the waves, let the salt burn my lips, collect shells in my pockets. But I never made it.

I think about my bedroom with its purple blue wallpaper. I think about the socks kicked under my bed, the notes I scribbled in the margins of my biology book, the cherry lip gloss I left open on my desk. My mum will find it all. She'll sit on my bed and run her hands over my unwashed sheets, press her fingers to the mirror where I last checked my reflection.

She'll press her face against anything that smells of me, just to keep me around a little longer.

I hope she knows I was trying to be better.

Then I realise I'm drifting.

I can't close my eyes.

I force my eyelids up with every ounce of remaining strength, blinking hard against the darkness that wants to claim me.

The engine sound grows closer. Headlights pierce the darkness, twin beams cutting through the night like searchlights. I try to move, to make myself more visible, but my body feels so heavy. The fabric around my wrist cuts deeper as I struggle, and the fresh taste of old pennies fills my mouth.

If blood is still flowing, that means my heart's still beating.

That means I'm still alive.

A different kind of fear grips me.

If they don't see me...

It's okay, I tell myself.

It's okay.

The car crests the hill. For a moment, the headlights blind me, brilliant against the complete darkness.

They'll see me.

They'll help me.

But then...

The car swerves.

Tyres crunch on gravel.

It keeps going.

I don't understand.

Why didn't they stop?

Maybe they didn't see me properly. Maybe they thought I was something else: a deer, a shadow.

The next car will stop.

Someone has to stop.

Someone has to save me.

So I can save her.

PART ONE

CHAPTER ONE

We're on the edge of winter and spring. One of those days where the sun fights to warm the town, but the wind still carries a razor-sharp bite. Out here, on the gravel track behind the sports stadium, we are exposed. Twenty-three girls in black shorts and yellow pique polo shirts, all but me in trainers that cost more than a weekend abroad.

It's indoor sports only until March, but today, Bagley has decided to break us in. Hockey, netball, track, and whatever fresh hell she dreams up. We stand in a loose line, bare arms prickling against the wind.

For once, my heart isn't hammering with the familiar dread of team selection. No dwindling line of rejects, no being picked last.

Just cross country.

The word '*just*' catches in my throat like a lie. Off campus, along the track, around the reservoir.

Sarah's shoulder brushes mine, steady as always. The wheezing in her chest builds slowly, a quiet rebellion against what's coming. She's not made for this. Neither of us are. We're shorter, softer. We could pass for sisters with our mouse-brown hair, always loose unless, like today, we're forced to tie it back.

Bagley has been our physical ed teacher for four and a half years. In all that time, I've never liked her. Sometimes she shows up in a t-shirt boasting about marathons she ran years ago, but now, she's just another middle-aged woman clinging to faded glories. Today, she wears her sweatpants and school hoodie, logo bold and proud, the motto underneath cracking with age. *Nulli soli, omnes uniti*. No one alone, everyone together. Another lie.

She raises her whistle.

"Reservoir run. Let's go, ladies."

And she sets off, leading the pack.

The group surges forward like a tide, and we're caught in the undertow. Sarah matches my pace, breath coming in short bursts that echo my own. We know how this goes. The slow fading behind. The growing distance. The quiet shame of being last. Not picked last this time, but last all the same.

Ahead, the others glide over the track, bodies moving in unison, their yellow shirts blurring into the grey morning like watercolour bleeding too thin. My lungs burn, my heart pounds, my muscles demand more oxygen than my body can give.

If I were an animal, I'd have been picked off by predators before I learned to walk. If I were a predator, I'd have starved in the first winter. But I am neither hunter nor hunted, just a girl failing at the simple act of putting one foot in front of the other.

The first stretch takes us down the path where the smokers gather at break times. Just far enough away that the only thing visible of the school is the top of the sports hall, its sloped metal roof like the Anderson shelters we built models of in history class.

Sarah nudges me. I snap back to the present. The last of the group is out of sight. No marker at the back. No one to check in on us. The school only cares about its athletes, the ones who win. The rest of us don't matter.

"You okay?" I ask Sarah. Not that I'm trying to make this about her. I know she is only hanging back because of me. Asthma or no asthma, Sarah could be up there with the other girls.

She's not. She's at the back here with me. When I slow, she slows. When I put my hands down onto my knees and bend, breathing hard and heavy, she stops too.

"Yeah," she replies. She tilts her head to see my face.

It's cold enough that my cheeks are already red.

"They could have waited," Sarah says, tilting her head to look at me.

We are alone. Left behind. Forgotten.

I am invisible.

"Yeah." My breath is steadier now. The thudding in my temples is fading.

The route on the far side of the reservoir opens up onto a narrow track. No sign of Bagley or the rest of our class. Sarah pauses, and my heart sinks. I was hoping that she would take the lead here. I have no idea which way we should go.

There's another thought that I bury: two girls like us shouldn't be alone like this. It's a dumb thing to think. We live in a quiet, pretty town where nothing bad ever happens. Still, I can't help but look around me, convinced that someone or something is lurking, waiting to pounce.

"Did Bagley say...?"

I turn my thoughts to the reality of the situation we're in, and look up the hill. It's barely a road. Wheel tracks have cut into either side of a grassy clump down the centre. Loose rocks litter the two lines and I'm sure if I tried to run up there, I would lose footing, turn my ankle. That same path runs downwards, in the general direction of the school. But even sadistic Bagley wouldn't want to risk her star pupils injuring themselves on this precarious ground.
Straight across the path is tarmac. Grey cold, but flat, stable.

"I..." Sarah's eyes follow mine, then she turns. Up. Straight across. Down. "Depends how savage she's feeling." She forces a smile.

"Must be uphill then," I joke. Logic tells me it's the road most travelled: tarmac.

Sarah's taking a breather, her arms folded, back bent, leaning on her knees.

"We can sit for a minute?" I ask, as though it's for her benefit. My chest is burning. Lifting my legs becomes more difficult with every stride, although we've been maintaining a fast walk rather than any kind of run for the past few hundred metres.

She looks at her watch.

"We shouldn't," Sarah says. "Another half hour and they'll all be going home."

We should be going home. That's what she's implying.

Fast walk back to school, slow walk back home after. We've been making our own way, together, since we met five years ago.

"Sure," I say, hiding my disappointment.

It's colder now, out here where the wind whips down from the hills. Moving will keep us warm, getting back to the changing room will keep us warmer.

I try to talk to Sarah as we semi-run ahead, onto the tarmac road.

"You'd think someone would stay at the back. To, you know, keep an eye on us," I manage between heavy breaths. That thought of not quite being safe out here tries to raise its head again.

Sarah shrugs. Either she doesn't have the energy to argue, or she just doesn't care. Usually, we talk nonstop. But out here, in the cold, words seem pointless.

The road is uneven beneath my feet. Cracks, loose gravel. My foot catches. The moment stretches, too long, inevitable.

Then I go down hard.

Pain flares instantly, sharp and bright, as my knee grates against the rough surface. A sickening heat spreads through my leg, followed by the slow, creeping burn of torn skin. My palms take some of the impact, but my knee takes the worst of it.

Sarah's breath catches. "Shit. Amanda..."

I don't answer right away. I'm stuck in that strange limbo between shock and pain, where the body is still deciding just how bad the damage is. The world shrinks to the sting of air hitting raw skin, the dull throb beginning to pulse in my kneecap.

Sarah crouches beside me, her fingers ghosting over my shoulder before she hesitates. She knows I hate being fussed over, but I also know she won't just let this go.

"Let me see," she says, voice tight.

I shift, wincing as I drag my leg forward. Blood wells, dark and thick, carving its path down my shin before dripping onto the tarmac. The scrape is deep, ragged. Tiny bits of gravel cling to the open wound.

Sarah pulls the hem of her polo shirt over her hand and presses it lightly to my knee. "We need to clean this. Can you walk?"

I nod, even though I'm not sure.

"Yeah. Just give me a sec."

She hooks an arm under mine, steadying me as I pull myself upright. The movement sends a fresh jolt of pain through my knee, and I grit my teeth against the sharp inhale that wants to escape.

Sarah watches me closely. "Don't be a hero. If you need a minute..."

"I'm fine," I cut in, though I know I'm not.

We start moving, slow and uneven. I put as little weight on my injured leg as possible, but every step is an exercise in endurance. The school feels farther away than it should be, the route stretching into an impossible distance.

We don't talk much after that. The silence between us is thick, heavy with unspoken worry. The temperature has dropped, the earlier bite of wind turning into something meaner, something that cuts deeper.

The school looms in the distance. Dark. Silent.

I glance at Sarah. Her face mirrors my growing alarm. "What time is it?" I ask, my voice thin.

She checks her watch. "Shit." A long pause. "We're late. Really late."

I frown. We weren't moving that slowly. Were we?

Sarah tugs at my arm, urging me forward despite my aching knee.

"Do you think they've locked up already? I need to get my bag." Sarah's face is pale with panic.

"We need to get changed," I say, almost out of breath. "I can't go home like this."

We limp toward the entrance. The door groans open.

Inside, the silence is worse. Thick. Wrong.

Footsteps echo across tile. Slow and deliberate.

Sarah's fingers grip my wrist, tight enough to leave marks.

We freeze.

We are not alone.

CHAPTER TWO

My stomach plummets as Principal Donaldson steps into view, her tall frame blocking the corridor ahead.

In five years, I've never been summoned to the principal's office. I'm not a troublemaker, but I'm not exceptional either. I'm average, practically invisible.

But the moment I see her, arms folded, her face shadowed in the flickering light; I know that's about to change.

She doesn't speak. Just watches.

The silence stretches, tightening around my ribs.

My knee throbs. Blood trickles down my shin, but the sting is nothing compared to the slow coil of tension in my spine. There's something about the way she looks at us, about being alone with her in this empty school, that makes my skin prickle.

"Miss Gray. Miss Fairchild." Her voice is calm. Too calm. The kind of voice that makes you second-guess your own instincts. "You're late."

Sarah shifts beside me, her grip on my arm loosening.

"Amanda fell," she says with an undisguisable quiver. "We..."

"Why didn't you come back sooner?" Donaldson cuts in, stepping forward.

"We..." I start, but stop.

I don't know how to explain it. How the run took longer than it should have. How, even without the fall, we would have been late. How we were left behind. By Bagley. By the others. It sounds like I'm blaming the PE teacher, and of course I am. I just don't want to do that. Not right now.

All I really want to do is to get changed and get home. It's Tuesday. Pizza night. And I need to be anywhere but here.

"We got turned around," Sarah says quickly. "Went the wrong way after the reservoir."

"They..." They left us. I want to say it. I should say it. But I don't.

Donaldson doesn't blink.

"Hmm."

Her gaze flicks to my knee, to the sluggish drip of blood onto my sock. I brace myself for the usual concern, the predictable: *Do you need the nurse? Are you okay?* That's what a principal should say.

But she doesn't.

She just stares. Like she's looking through us.

"Fine," she says finally. A pause. "Come with me."

Sarah and I exchange a glance, a silent conversation passing between us.

We don't want to. But we don't say no.

Because you don't say no to Donaldson.

We follow her down the corridor, the sound of our footsteps swallowed by the hush of the empty school. I feel Sarah tense beside me, her discomfort rolling off her in waves.

Donaldson leads us past the darkened classrooms, past the abandoned reception desk, and stops at a door at the very end of the hall.

Her office.

She pushes the door open. Gestures for us to go inside.

"It's late," she says, voice still steady. "And I'm sure you both want to go home. Let's get on with this."

Donaldson takes a seat behind her heavy outdated, out of place wooden desk. She doesn't invite either of us to sit, so my legs, near numb, have to keep me standing a little longer.

I can hear Sarah's breath, and it makes me more conscious of my own.

The silence is otherwise only broken by the sound of Donaldson's sausage fingers clattering over her keyboard. She's looking up our student records.

"Gray, Amanda," she says out loud without raising her gaze.

Her hand reaches for the phone with the kind of muscle memory that comes from years of having to call students' parents.

She dials and clicks the phone to speaker.

She wants me to hear Mum's disappointment first hand.

It rings.

And rings.

And rings.

After an eternity, the answerphone clicks in.

Mum's voice, distant and disembodied.

My throat catches.

Donaldson doesn't wait until the end of the message; she hangs up.

"Your mother doesn't seem to be answering," she says, as if she doesn't know how voicemail works.

Donaldson looks back at the computer screen, scrolling.

"No contact details for your father?" she queries, peering at me over the top of her monitor.

I shake my head, and Donaldson makes a humming sound that carries so much meaning that I feel tears prickle.

"Fine," she says again. "Fairchild, Sarah."

The tapping of keys, dialling of phone number repeats.

"Joyce Fairchild." Sarah's mum answers on the second ring.

"Joyce Fairchild," Donaldson repeats. "I'm afraid I'm going to need you to come down to the school and collect your daughter."

Joyce starts to ask if everything is all right, but Donaldson cuts her off.

"Sarah and her friend absconded from school on their cross country run this afternoon. Of course we sent out the search party. Heaven knows where the two of them were hiding."

The truth is being stretched so thin that I'm sure it could snap.

"They sauntered back in here a few minutes ago."

"Is she... are they okay?" Joyce asks again.

"Mrs Fairchild. Your daughter..."

There's a flurry of noise from the other end of the line. The phone crackles. Joyce's voice is muffled. I picture her pulling on her coat and hear the jangle of car keys.

"I'll be right there," Sarah's mum says.

The line goes dead, and Donaldson lets out a frustrated breath.

Beside me, Sarah is silent, her gaze tilted towards the worn orange-brown carpet. I can see her eyes move as though she is tracing the swirls. I should do the same. I should shut up and look down.

But I don't.

"We were lost. She...they just left us." I can feel the indignance rising. Does she really think this is our fault?

Donaldson's glare burns through me.

My voice withers. I am done.

"Detention. One week. Both of you."

Again, my eyes flick to Sarah, but she doesn't look back. She's somewhere else, in her mind, and I wonder where. When I stare at the same shitty carpet, all I see are dark stains.

Staying behind after school for a week with Sarah doesn't feel like much of a punishment. It's not like I do anything or go anywhere. My empty social schedule is not going to suffer.

It's not like anyone cares.

Then it hits me.

Paul.

Paul is going to be pissed.

I'm already a grade A pain in his ass, but now I've proven to him I'm some kind of deviant mess up.

He was right about me all along.

In the swirls of the carpet I see his face, the faux sorrowful shaking of his head as he wraps his arm around Mum, comforting her.

My throat constricts. I want to cough, but instead I swallow hard. Sometimes it's best to keep quiet.

"Nothing to say?" Donaldson's voice is a dog bark.

I have so much to say, but nothing that will help.

I hear the sharp intake of breath as Donaldson revs up to snap again, but it's cut short this time.

The door cracks open.

Donaldson locks eyes.

"Sarah, darling," Joyce Fairchild sweeps in, pulling her daughter into a tight embrace.

"Mrs Fairchild! Your daughter..." Donaldson starts.

"My daughter has *asthma* and shouldn't be *forced* to run cross country."

"Mrs..." The principal stiffens.

"Mrs Donaldson," Joyce says. "I trust this isn't going to happen again. If anything had happened to," Joyce looks from Sarah to me, "either of these girls..."

She leaves the sentence there, unfinished. However much Donaldson might have got a kick out of seeing the two of us limping back to school, it could have been a lot worse. Two sixteen-year-old girls.

"You have a duty of care," Joyce says, picking up Sarah's rucksack, pulling a neat handkerchief from her pocket and running it over her daughter's face. "it's okay," she murmurs, her voice snap changing from protective lioness to soothing mother. "It's okay. Let's get you home. Okay?"

Sarah brings her eyes up from the floor and nods once in silence.

"Amanda?" Joyce turns to me. "You need a ride?"

I have to look at Donaldson before I reply.

"Uh..." I can't even ask whether I should accept.

Donaldson wafts her hand dismissively.

"Take her," she says.

Joyce puts one hand on my shoulder and a rush of warmth thrills through me. Not that metaphorical warmth of love, but a physical wave of security.

I wonder for a split second what it would be like to be Sarah. To have a mother and father that live together, that stayed together.

Sarah's hand reaches out and her fingers interlock with mine. It's only when she touches me, I realise I am crying.

"It's okay," she says, in the exact same tone that Joyce used to reassure her.

Instead of making my tears stop, her words open the floodgates.

But not until I have turned away from Donaldson.

Not until she can no longer see my face.

CHAPTER THREE

Sarah sits in the back of the Audi with me. I keep my hands folded over the rucksack in my lap, but her right hand is flopped out beside me. It's an offering, I know. I could reach out and hold onto it, but I don't. I've already taken enough.

She should be up front with her mum. She should be chatting away about her day. She shouldn't be burdened with me.

Joyce Fairchild's eyes are fixed firmly on the road as she drives toward our neighbourhood, but her lips are moving along with the song on the radio.

Take me home country roads.

I've heard Mum listen to this one, too. Not recently. I can't remember the last time I saw her flick through the records in that heavy cardboard box that says Bells Whiskey on the side but has only ever contained Mum's prize vinyl collection as long as I can remember.

There's no music in our house anymore.

West Virginia, Mountain Mama. I mumble it under my breath. I can't sing, not now, but I want to feel the words. I want to remember what it's like.

Joyce must have heard. She looks into the rearview and gives me a tight-lipped, friendly smile.

If I had been alone, would Donaldson have kept me there in her office until she could reach Mum? Would I still be there now?

I wouldn't have been alone.

Sarah shifts in her seat beside me.

The town speeds past her window.

The next song comes on the radio.

Joyce pulls up the car in the space where Paul's flash piece of shit usually sits. Wherever he is right now, he's not here, and I couldn't be more relieved.

"You going to be okay?" Joyce says into her rearview.

I nod and clear my throat.

"Thanks," I say. Thanks for the ride. Thanks for stepping in. Thanks for rescuing us.

Joyce wafts away the word like unwanted smoke from a cigarette.

"You want to hop in the front, Sarah?" Joyce asks.

Sarah looks at me. "I'm okay."

Joyce casts her eyes over me one last time as I push open the door and step out onto the pavement. The streetlights are starting to come on, even though the sun hasn't set. It must be five thirty, later maybe.

"Thanks," I say again because I don't know what else to say.

Sarah ducks down to see me better from the other side of the backseat.

"See you in the morning," she says, smile beaming.

I give her a salute, and blush at the sheer nerdiness of it, shrinking inside myself until she raises her hand and returns the gesture.

Joyce calls through from the driver's seat. "If your mum wants to know where you've been, you just get her to call me, okay? I'll straighten things out for you."

"Thanks, Mrs... Joyce. Thank you."

She winds down the window and heads off.

Sarah waves through the rear and salutes again, still giving me that reassuring, loveable best friend forever smile.

I should feel tense, terrified maybe, but I don't. I feel Sarah's warmth. Joyce's too, I guess. My best friend is so lucky to have a mother like that. A family that loves her, that cares.

I stop on the pavement.

The house is wrong.

I know it as soon as I reach the gate. No porch light glowing against the deepening afternoon shadows. No warmth seeping through the front door. No smell of pizzas cooking.

It's Tuesday and on Tuesday we always have pizza. Even Paul couldn't change that.

Donaldson couldn't reach her, and as I walk up the path, I know why.

Mum's not here.

My key scrapes against the lock, a harsh sound in the quiet neighbourhood.

Inside, the house is silent, holding its breath.

The stinging of the graze on my knee hasn't let up yet, but the blood has dried to a dark crust. There's still some road in there. I need to clean it. I need Mum to clean it, but she isn't here.

"Mum?" I call, just in case, even though I already know that I'm alone.

My footsteps echo across the hardwood floor as I make my way to the kitchen. It's not quite dark enough to turn on any lights, but it's heading in that direction.

I'm heading for the sink, but I stop in my tracks.

The bright yellow Post-it note on the fridge stands out like a beacon.

Mum's hurried handwriting slants across it like windblown rain: Important appointment with Paul. Grab whatever you want for dinner. Love you.

I stare at the note until the words blur. The kitchen feels massive around me: too big, too empty. For eight years -

half my life - it has just been the two of us. Mum and Amanda against the world.

Eight years since Dad left and became nothing more than a faded photograph in an album that neither Mum nor I ever open. Our life with him, the life before is a story I stopped telling myself years ago.

Just the two of us. That's all we needed. We were fine. We were fine until Paul happened.

Now it seems like Pizza Night has become Paul Night, and little old Amanda can just take care of herself from now on. Six months of Paul, and I am nothing.

I am invisible.

The digital clock on the microwave blinks 5:48. I'm late, very late, but apparently there's no one here to notice.

Without thinking, I rip the note from the fridge, crumple it in my fist and lob it toward the trash can. It bounces off the rim and skitters under the cabinet. It can stay there.

"Thanks, Mum," I mutter in the petulant tone she hates.

I drop my rucksack onto the chair, then pull open the fridge door and stare inside. Without looking at anything in particular, I let my eyes scan, not taking in the contents. Truth is, I'm not hungry.

I want the dressing down for being late.

I want to be sent to my room for getting detention.

I want to be yelled at, even though I've done nothing wrong.

I want Mum to be here.

I want pizza.

I want pizza night.

I want to be a child.

I want to be wanted.

I am invisible.

I try to slam the fridge door shut, but it closes slowly, the rubber edging bouncing together softly.

I can't even be petulant successfully.

Screw this.

I grab my bag and almost pull the chair over in the process.

"Okay," I say to nobody, and give the chair the extra force it needs to bring it crashing to the floor.

I thought it would make me feel better, but with no one here to see it, it's such a ridiculous gesture.

I walk towards the door, change my mind and go back to right the chair. It'll only be Mum that has to do it if I don't.

When everything is tidy, I exhale and take the stairs two at a time, up to my room.

In my bedroom, I don't even bother undressing before sliding under the covers, slipping in my earphones and pulling the duvet back up around me.

I stick my playlist on shuffle. I don't care what comes on because I'm not listening. I just want to mask the silence of this house.

I think about Sarah, going home to her family; her mother, father, brother. Even though Oliver is older than her, he's not the mean, shitty kind of big brother. He's polite to me when I visit. He's just a decent guy in a decent family. And no, I don't have a crush. This isn't that kind of story.

They'll be sitting around the table now. No television. Talking about what they've done today, and I'd put money on the fact that it won't all be about Sarah *absconding* from school.

Thinking of the word forces a silent rage in me.

Absconding. Shit, we were left alone by freaking Bagley. We were left alone by the other girls. I let myself think, just for a minute, about what I would have done if I was Claire or Sally or one of the other alpha girls in the class. I probably wouldn't have noticed that the stragglers were missing either. It's not their fault. This isn't a mean girls set up, it's a lack of, what was it Joyce said? Duty of care.

Absconded. Get shit on, Donaldson.

I haven't changed out of my gym kit. I haven't cleaned the wound on my knee. I couldn't care less.

As my thoughts wander, I casually pick at the scab that's formed over the graze. A small rough chunk of gravel pops out, into my hand. Blood oozes from the space left behind, but it's dark, thick.

I ignore it, duck under the cover, and close my eyes.

CHAPTER FOUR

I wake up when I finally hear the door open downstairs.

Mum and Paul are talking; I hear the murmur of voices, but don't catch any traces of the conversation.

"Amanda, honey?" Mum calls.

"She's been home," Paul says, as though he's Sherlock or something. "The note's gone."

"Amanda?" Mum's voice has a shrill, tense tone.

"She'll be fine," Paul says. His voice becomes muffled, as though his mouth is pressed against something.

Mum laughs, and I pull the covers up further over my head. I don't want to hear. I don't need to hear.

I feel the slight movement of the house as she comes up the stairs and opens my door.

"Amanda?" she says. It's never Mandy, Manda, Mand. I've always gone by the full three syllables of my name. "You okay?"

There's no use pretending I'm not here. I know she can see the shape of me.

I make the kind of grunt that could mean that I'm fine, that I've just woken up, that I want to be left alone.

I want it to mean all of those things.

I hear the pad of her soft flat shoes across the wooden floor. She's about to pull back the cover.

Smile? Frown?

I have a split second to decide whether I want to be a bitch about being left alone.

"Hey, hon," she says, drawing the duvet from my face and leaning in towards me. She kisses my forehead, and my decision is taken from me.

I smile.

"Hey, Mum," I reply. All thoughts of abandonment wash away. She is here.

"I'm sorry," she says, before I even bring up the subject, "about pizza night."

I nod. She's got more to say, and I don't want to interrupt.

Behind her, in the doorway, I see Paul. His tall dark annoying figure leans against the jamb.

"You can tell her," he says.

"Paul. I... I thought we agreed," Mum says, her head spinning to look at him.

He waves his hand. "Go ahead," he says.

"What?" I've tensed up again. I pull up into a sitting position, forcing Mum to jerk back.

"What?" I repeat.

"Good news," Paul says, stepping into my room. I don't remember him ever being in here before, and I don't like it. I don't even want him in the house. He can at least stay out of my space.

I say nothing.

"Paul," Mum says. "Let me."

"There's going to be a new addition to the family," he smiles, but the smile is for Mum, not for me. She isn't smiling back, though. She looks pissed.

And stupid as I am, my mental image conjures up a puppy. A furry, sweet addition to the family. I wanted one for so long, after Dad left. Mum said with just the two of us, there was no way. We couldn't. Perhaps one good thing could come from Paul being here. Would they let me pick one out, or had they already chosen? The appointment. That's where they were. They...

I look at Mum. I look at the way she looks at Paul. I look at his smarmy disgusting smile.

And I know.

We are not getting a puppy.

"Mum?" The word falls out of my mouth.

She nods.

"You're going to have a brother," she says, trying to make it sound like good news.

"Isn't that just the greatest?" Paul steps behind Mum, in my room, and puts his hands on her shoulders.

"Mum?" I say it again.

"I... we wanted to have the scan, to wait to make sure everything is all right before we told you. That's... that's where we were earlier. I had to go after work, you know. Last appointment of the day. They fit us in..."

She keeps talking, but the words drift over me.

A brother.

I don't know how to feel.

My blood has been replaced by ice water. I can barely feel my own body. I'm not really here.

I think of Sarah, staring at the orange-brown carpet, and I pick a spot on the wallpaper, just behind Paul's head, and I stare. I didn't choose it, the wallpaper. The pattern's a watercolour mess of purples and blues, like a bruise that spreads across the entire room. I stare and I stare until my mind is blank. Until I'm thinking of nothing at all, and Mum is saying my name over and over until Paul takes her hand, leads her out, and turns to look at me like I'm the worst thing that ever happened to him.

And I stare and stare at the wallpaper.

I lose myself in the colours.

And I feel nothing.

The house is silent. I slept too early and when I wake it's only just after five.

My gut rumbles. I missed dinner. Probably burned off ten thousand calories on that cross country shambles.

Mum is pregnant.

I can't believe it wasn't even the first thought I had this morning.

Mum is pregnant, and not only does that mean that I'm going to have a brother, but also that Paul is here to stay.

I want to qualify that thought with *for now, at least*, but I've been without my dad for eight years and much as I despise Paul, I don't wish a fatherless existence upon my future brother.

Brother. Just one word. It hasn't crossed my mind to think of him as my half-brother. I mean, I went to sleep pretty soon after I found out about him, but it's not like I lay awake cursing his future existence.

I wanted a puppy, but I got this.

So why am I so mad at Mum?

Because I am.

And even though I don't want to let the thought surface, I already know that I am mad because Mum is *my* mum and I am selfish, stupid and, despite what I might project, I am a child.

I know the house as well as I know my own insecurities. I don't need to turn on the light to make my way across my room. I'm tidy enough that I don't have to navigate around junk to get from my bed to the door. No tripping over my bag, no stumbling on my trainers.

Stepping out, I tiptoe across the landing, past Mum and Paul's room, which was once Mum and Dad's room, and push down on the bathroom door handle.

It's locked.

"Hold on." A whispered voice from inside. There's an edge to it I can't interpret.

"Mum?" I press my face towards the door.

"Go back to bed," she says with forced cheerfulness.

I upset her last night. I didn't react to the baby news in the way she wanted me to. I was an idiot.

I lean back against the landing wall and construct an apology. I'll tell her I'm sorry, that I'm happy.

Because I am.

Not about Paul, but about having a brother.

About *Mum* being happy.

Isn't that all I want?

"Amanda," Mum's voice is louder now. "Go back to bed."

"I need to pee."

"Amanda."

I tense against the discomfort in my bladder.

I open my mouth to protest again.

And I back down.

It was never like this, before.

CHAPTER FIVE

When I hear Mum leave the bathroom and shuffle back to her room, followed by mumbled conversation that I can't pick up on, I finally get to empty my bladder. Afterwards, I try to go back to sleep but I fail. I could go downstairs, get cereal, pretend it's morning, but really, it's all too much effort.

The last thing I want is Paul coming down and laying into me for disturbing them, keeping them awake, whatever little thing he would find to pick at me for. I'm already going to be in enough shit because of today. Detention is detention, whether or not I deserved it. Donaldson didn't bother leaving a message, and I guess Joyce hasn't called Mum, because we haven't had The Talk yet. Sometime today it's going to catch up with me and I'm going to have the dressing down again.

I'm a disappointment, I know.

I know. I know.

I flip over, press my face into the pillow, block my mouth and nose, and force out a long breath. A silent scream of frustration. Soundless in the lightless room.

It doesn't make me feel any better.

I was invisible before Mum decided to bring another little person into our home.

What's it going to be like when she has a cute little newborn to focus on?

But that's not what's bothering me the most, and I know it.

It's the thought I can't escape from. Paul is here to stay.

It's not like I ever thought that Dad would come back. I have no clue where he is. I don't think Mum knows or cares either. Somewhere in the back of my mind, though, there must have been some hope lingering that one day it would be the three of us again.

That's never going to happen.

It never was.

Paul.

It's not like he's even a bad guy. That's not it. He's never raised a hand to me. He barely raises his voice to me. He's not bothered about me at all. That's the crux of it.

And I'm worried that the lack of concern, the lack of care, the lack of love is going to seep into Mum. Two colours too close to each other, bleeding at the edges.

I used to be enough for her. Now I am nothing.

I am invisible.

I've repeated those words to myself so many times since Mum met Paul. I've thought about having them tattooed, a constant reminder to myself of my worthlessness, as if I need it.

Sarah rings the doorbell at quarter past eight, the same as she does every morning.

Reaching out to hug me goodbye, Mum says, "See you tonight. Maybe we can have Pizza Wednesday this week?"

I pause. I haven't told Mum about my detention.

"It wouldn't be the same," I say. There's no resentment in my voice, no bitterness, but I can see that my words still sting.

"Oh. Okay." Her defeated tone hurts me as much as my words hurt her. Is this the way we are now?

I push myself into the hug, breathing in her familiar scent, and force myself out into the grey morning where Sarah waits.

My knee throbs with each step down the path. Sarah launches into a story about something her brother did last night, her voice bright against the dull day. I try to focus on her words, but they slip past me like rain. My mind keeps circling back to the bathroom this morning, to Mum's voice through the door. To the way she didn't want me there.

"Earth to Amanda," Sarah nudges my arm. "You haven't heard a word I've said, have you?"

I shake my head. "Sorry. Just..."

"Still thinking about yesterday? Because Mum meant it - she'll sort it out with Donaldson."

"No, it's..." The words stick in my throat. I watch a car pass, focus on the sound of our feet against the pavement. My knee sends sharp protests with each step.

"What's wrong?" Sarah's voice drops lower, concerned now. "Did something happen with Paul?"

A laugh escapes me, harsh and hollow. "You could say that."

We walk in silence for a few steps. A group of year eights pass us, their voices too loud for the morning.

"Mum's pregnant," I say finally. The words fall between us like stones.

Sarah stops walking. "What?"

"That's where they were yesterday. When Donaldson couldn't get hold of her. The scan." My voice sounds distant, like it belongs to someone else. "It's a boy."

"Oh my God," Sarah whispers. She reaches for my hand, but I stuff both of mine into my pockets. If she touches me now, I might shatter.

"Amanda..."

"It's fine," I blurt. "It's good news, right? Everyone loves babies."

"When did they tell you?"

"Last night. While you were having your nice normal family dinner, I was finding out I'm getting a brother." The bitterness I've been trying to swallow seeps into my voice.

"Paul couldn't wait to tell me. Couldn't even let Mum do it her way."

We start walking again, slower now. My knee aches, but I barely notice.

"This morning," I say, the words tumbling out now that I've started, "I tried to go to the bathroom, and she was in there. She wouldn't let me in. Just told me to go back to bed. Like I was annoying her. Like I was in the way."

"I'm sure she didn't mean..."

"She's probably got morning sickness. I should have realised. Should have left her alone." I kick a stone; watch it skitter across the tarmac. "That's what I'll have to do now. Leave her alone. Give her space. Let her focus on the baby and Paul and their perfect new family."

"You're part of that family," Sarah says softly.

"Yeah," I say, my voice barely audible. "Until I'm not."

The words hang between us, heavy with all my unspoken fears. That Paul will replace Dad completely. That the baby will replace me. That the colours of our new family will blend and spread until there's no space left for the shade that is me.

Sarah doesn't answer. There's nothing she can say that would make it untrue. Instead, she walks closer, her shoulder brushing mine with each step. The silent contact says what words can't: I'm here. I'm here. I'm here.

But for how long? Everyone leaves eventually. Even best friends. Even mothers.

Even me.

CHAPTER SIX

The detention slip weighs down my pocket all afternoon. It's just a piece of paper, but it feels heavier with each passing hour, like it's made of lead instead of cheap school stationery.

My thoughts circle, and by the end of the day, I've given myself a headache. I should tell Mum where I am. I should have told her this morning that I would be late home. After last night, though, I didn't know how. What would I even say? That I got detention for something that wasn't my fault? That Donaldson didn't believe us? That somehow, despite everything, I'm the one being punished?

Mum and Paul are happy. They don't need me creating problems. Chances are they won't even notice I'm not home.

The detention room is on the far side of the building: a classroom stripped of anything remotely interesting. Just empty walls, scarred desks, and the slow, torturous ticking of a clock that seems determined to move at half-speed. The lucky teacher who gets to watch over us is Mr Perkins. He doesn't even look up from his crossword puzzle as we file in, just points to the whiteboard where he's scrawled "NO TALKING" in aggressive capital letters.

I wonder if he gets paid overtime for this, or if he does it because he likes to see us all sitting here, not even watching over us as we read in silence.

Sarah and I sit next to each other, exchanging glances whenever Perkins isn't looking. She shouldn't even be here. She could have thrown me under the bus, told Donaldson it was all my fault we couldn't keep up. She didn't even have to lag behind. She could have let me make my way back on my own. But that's not Sarah. She'd never leave me to face anything alone.

I lift my book strategically higher, creating a barrier between Mr Perkins and my face. Behind this literary shield, I lock eyes with Sarah and dramatically mouth 'KILL ME NOW,' followed by our universal signal for absolute boredom, the single finger dragging across my throat. I add a silent, theatrical yawn so exaggerated my eyes water.

Sarah's shoulders start to shake, and I watch the telltale crinkle appear at the corners of her eyes: the same one she's had since we met, the private signal that she's about to lose it. She presses her lips together, but a small snort escapes before she can clap her hand over her mouth.

The sound cuts through the silence like a gunshot. Mr Perkins's head snaps up, pen freezing mid-air, his eyes narrowing behind those wire-rimmed glasses we've nicknamed 'the soul-searchers.'

"Something amusing about Shakespearean tragedy, Miss Fairchild?"

Sarah straightens immediately, the smile vanishing from her face. We've perfected this routine over years of passing notes, sharing looks across classrooms, communicating in our silent language that no one else can translate.

"No, sir," she says, voice small and compliant.

"Then perhaps you'd both benefit from silent reflection on why you're here instead of causing more disruption."

We lower our eyes to our books simultaneously, another well-practiced move. Just two more girls learning the art of swallowing words, of quieting ourselves when authority demands it.

The clock crawls toward four-thirty. When Perkins glances at the time and waves his hand dismissively, Sarah and I are out of our seats before he can change his mind, not even looking at each other until we're safely in the hallway and the detention room door clicks shut behind us.

Sarah falls into step beside me as we leave school, our footsteps naturally syncing. She doesn't push me to talk about detention, just walks quietly, her presence steady and familiar. That's Sarah. Always there, always knowing exactly what I need without me having to say it.

We pass the closed-down corner shop, its sun-bleached posters still clinging to last year's Christmas specials, three months out of date. From the dusty windowsill, a fluffy grey cat watches, its tail twitching in a steady beat against the worn wood. Sarah makes a soft clicking sound at it, the same way she does with all animals.

Everything feels slightly off-kilter today, like someone's shifted all the furniture two inches to the left. The timing is all wrong, but Sarah's shoulder occasionally bumping into mine keeps me anchored.

We pass the playground, and I glance toward the woodland path that snakes behind it. Some days, Sarah and I take the longer route, but not today. I'm already late, I can't have Mum worrying about me.

I check my phone, but she hasn't messaged.

"Do you think your mum called mine about detention?" I ask Sarah.

She shakes her head. "If Mum had called Abby, she would have texted me straight away to warn you." Sarah frowns. "It's weird she hasn't even checked where you are. That's not like her at all."

The sick feeling in my gut intensifies. She's right - Mum always texts to make sure I'm home safe. Always. Even with Paul around, even when she's at work, she checks in.

"Maybe she's just busy," I say, not believing it.

Sarah gives me a look but doesn't argue. We've never needed many words between us. That's the thing about best friends - sometimes just existing together is enough.

When we get to my house, I get an unexplainable urge to ask Sarah to stay. If we weren't already late, perhaps I would, but Joyce will already have made dinner. Mum likes to know when anyone is coming over, and by anyone, I mean Sarah, because Sarah is the only person I would ever invite.

My shoulders sink as I reach the gate, and Sarah must either sense it or see the hangdog look on my face.

"It'll be okay," she says.

I'm not sure what *it* is. The evening ahead? Mum and Paul having a baby? Telling Mum about detention? My entire life?

"Sure," I say, faking a smile.

Sarah waits for a moment, as though she doesn't want to leave me, either.

"I'll be fine," I tell her. "You go. Honest, go on."

"See you tomorrow," Sarah says, hitching her backpack higher on her shoulder. "Text me later?"

I nod, watching her walk off up the road towards her house. She turns to wave before disappearing around the corner, and suddenly I feel very alone.

The house looks normal, which is the first lie. Mum's car is in the driveway alongside Paul's BMW. It's only just after five, so either he was working from home, or he's bunked off early again. Either way, it's disappointing.

"Hello?" I call, dropping my bag by the door.

"In here," Paul's voice comes from the kitchen, strained in a way I can't quite place.

I follow the sound to find him standing at the counter, mechanically making tea, his movements precise but somehow distracted. He barely glances at me when I enter.

"Where's Mum?" I ask.

"Bathroom," he says tersely. "She's been in there a while."

Something in his voice makes my stomach tighten. "Is she okay?"

"Morning sickness, probably." He shrugs, but the rigid set of his shoulders betrays his concern. "Though I don't know why they call it that when it lasts all day."

I remember last night: Mum's voice through the bathroom door telling me to go back to bed, the way she wouldn't let me in.

"How long ago did she go in?"

I should have used the toilets at school, but all I wanted to do after detention was get out of there. The more I think about it, the more I need to go.

He glances at the clock. "I don't know. Is that the time? Shit. Half an hour..."

Paul moves toward the stairs, and after a moment's hesitation, I follow. Something about his sudden urgency makes the knot in my stomach tighten. We stop outside the bathroom door, where a thin slice of light shows beneath.

"Abby?" Paul knocks softly. "You okay in there?"

Silence stretches for several seconds before Mum's voice comes through, thinner than normal. "I'm fine. Just... give me a minute."

But she doesn't sound fine. Her voice has that forced steadiness people use when they're trying not to worry others. Paul and I exchange glances, a rare moment of silent agreement.

"You've been in there for plenty of minutes," Paul says, his voice gentler than I've ever heard him speak to her. "Let me in, Abby."

"I just need..." Her voice cuts off abruptly, followed by a soft sound that might be a suppressed sob.

Paul doesn't wait for more. He turns the handle, finding it locked. "Abby, open the door." The panic in his voice makes my heart race.

"I'm coming," she says, but her voice is fainter now. I hear movement, then the soft click of the lock.

The door opens just a crack at first, then wider to reveal Mum standing there in her new blue dress. The one Paul bought her last week, the one she said was too young for her. Her face is ghost-white, almost translucent against the bathroom's harsh lighting. One hand grips the sink for support. The other presses against her stomach.

"I think something's wrong," she whispers, and only then do I notice the small, dark spots on the white tile of the bathroom floor. Blood.

Paul's eyes follow mine, and I see him gulp hard.

He moves instantly, his arm around Mum's waist.

"Hospital. Now. Christ, Abby, why didn't you call me?"

Mum shakes her head, though the movement seems to cost her. "It's probably nothing. Just spotting. Lots of women..."

"I don't care what lots of women do," Paul cuts her off. "We're going to the hospital."

She looks past him to me, her face softening with concern despite her own pain. "Amanda, honey..."

As he guides her into the hallway, they have to sidestep me. Paul turns to me, his face a mask of barely controlled panic.

"You aren't helping, Amanda. Just stay out of the way."

I freeze, his dismissal stinging more than I expected. But as they reach the stairs, Mum suddenly sways, her hand clutching more tightly at her stomach.

"Mum?" I say instinctively, ignoring Paul completely. "What's happening?"

"Amanda, please," Paul's voice rises, tight with fear. "Just stop with the questions!"

Mum makes a small noise: perhaps pain, perhaps distress at our bickering. Paul's face transforms, fear crystallising into anger as he finds somewhere to direct it.

"This is what happens when you stress her out," he snaps, eyes burning into mine. "Are you happy now?"

Each syllable slams into me, sharp and unforgiving.

"I didn't..." But they're already moving down the stairs, Mum's steps unsteady, Paul's arm tight around her waist.

"She doesn't need any more to deal with right now. Get her coat," he orders over his shoulder.

I rush to the hooks, grabbing her old denim jacket. The one she wore before Paul started buying her clothes. When I return, they're already at the front door.

"Mum?" I try, reaching for her hand.

Paul steps between us. "Look what you've done." His voice drops to a hiss. "Look what YOU have done."

But I can't look. I don't want to see the pain on Mum's face.

What I want is for Mum to tell me it's not my fault.

What I want is for her to hold me and tell me everything is going to be okay.

I step toward her, the words on my lips. *Everything is going to be okay.* I can't speak. I can't bring myself to say them, because I don't know if they're true.

As I stand hesitating, Paul raises a hand in a bold pink stop sign. I teeter on my heels, uncertain, unsteady.

"Mum. Say something," I whisper.

She says nothing. She clutches the place where my brother lies, and her large round eyes lock with Paul's. Not mine. Paul's.

She doesn't look back. Doesn't say goodbye. Paul snatches the jacket from my hands with a look of disdain. He bundles her into the passenger seat of his BMW and slams the door.

"Go back inside," he says as he rounds the car. "We'll call."

The engine roars to life. I stand in the driveway, watching until the car disappears around the corner. Only then do I realise I'm shaking.

I look down at my hands.

This is what happens when you stress her out.

I stumble back inside, pull the door closed behind me, and turn the lock. I'm on my own, for now.

In the hollow silence of the house, Paul's accusation echoes. Did I cause this? Logic says no, but guilt doesn't listen to logic.

I find myself drawn back to the bathroom, where those small dark spots still mark the floor. I should clean them up. Should do something useful. Instead, I back away, pulling the door closed as if that can contain what's happening.

I retreat to my room, each step feeling heavier than the last. I sit cross-legged on my bed and stare at the wallpaper until the bruise-coloured pattern starts to swim, watching how they seem to pulse and spread in the fading light. Purple bleeding into blue, blue seeping into shadow. Like a blood stain. Like the life draining from my brother before he even has a chance to exist.

Are you happy now?

No. No, I'm not happy. I'm terrified. I'm guilty. I'm alone.

I am invisible.

I am nothing.

My phone buzzes with an incoming call.

Sarah.

I should answer. I should tell her everything.

But what if talking about it makes it real? What if my words somehow make things worse, like everything else I do?

I turn it face-down. I don't deserve her concern, her friendship, her comfort. Not when I've already caused so much damage today.

I squeeze my eyes shut, but the pattern follows me into the darkness. My body feels distant, disconnected, like it belongs to someone else. Maybe it does. Maybe if I'm quiet enough, still enough, I can disappear completely.

I don't turn on the lights when night falls. Don't change out of my uniform. Don't check my phone again.

The bruise-colours fade to black in the darkness, but I keep staring at where I know they are. Counting. Breathing. Becoming nothing.

It's safer here, in the silence. Safer not to speak, not to move, not to breathe too loudly.

Because look what happens when I exist too much.

CHAPTER SEVEN

The kitchen is a cold, monochrome void in the morning light. Shadows stretch long across the tiled floor. I catch my reflection in the window. Hollow-eyed, pale. Hair tangled and stiff from sleep. Yesterday's uniform hangs from my frame like a discarded skin, creased and stale. I should care. I should shower. I should at least change.

But caring takes energy I don't have.

Instead, I stand motionless, as if stillness could stop time, could erase what is happening, could turn back the moment before everything went wrong.

Fifteen missed calls. Twenty-seven texts.

Sarah.

The guilt claws at my stomach, sharp and merciless.

I ignored her because I couldn't bear to speak it into existence. Because I can't stand to hear my own voice confirm what I already know.

That this is my fault.

The doorbell rings.

The sound cuts through me like a blade, freezing me in place. I don't move. If I stay still, maybe she'll go away. Maybe I can pretend I don't exist.

But the silence doesn't hold.

The bell chimes again, insistent this time.

Sarah.

I could lie. Say I was asleep. Say I lost my phone. Say anything except the truth.

The truth is that I disappeared because it's what I do. It's what I always do.

I force myself forward, each step like moving through wet cement. My muscles resist, instinctively trying to pull me back into the shadows. It's like my body knows something my mind doesn't want to admit; stepping into that light means being seen. Really seen.

The door creaks open.

Sarah stands on the doorstep, her face tight, her breath sharp against the morning chill. She takes me in. Yesterday's uniform, tangled hair, the dark circles under my eyes.

For a long, unbearable moment, neither of us speaks.

Then, finally, "What's going on? I thought you'd blocked me." Her voice is thin, stretched tight.

She reaches a hand out towards my hair.

I don't know what to say, so I say nothing.

Of course I hadn't. I never would. Not talking to Sarah would be like losing a part of myself.

"You look like shit," she says, not holding back. "What's happened?"

I turn my eyes away. I can't stand the weight of her worry.

"I'm sorry," I say. The words feel useless, meaningless.

I wrap my arms around myself, holding everything in.

Sarah exhales, a slow, unsteady breath. "Amanda... what happened?"

I hesitate. If I say it out loud, it becomes real.

But the words slip out before I can stop them.

"Mum's in the hospital." My voice is barely more than a whisper. "There was blood. And Paul said..." I swallow hard. "He said it was my fault."

Sarah stills. "What?"

"He said I stressed her out. That I..." I shake my head. The memory of Paul's voice, low, deliberate, accusing, presses against my skull. "And then they just left me here."

Sarah's face drains of colour. "Amanda..."

"They didn't even call." I let out a brittle laugh, the sound wrong in my throat. "Paul said they would call.

But...” My voice cracks. “What if something’s happened to the baby? What if...”

“Have you tried texting her?” Sarah asks.

I tense under her hands. “Paul said to stay out of the way.”

Sarah makes a sound somewhere between a scoff and a sigh. “Paul’s an arse. And he was panicking. This is your mum we’re talking about.”

“I know, but...” I trail off, not sure how to explain the complicated fear that’s keeping me silent. Fear of making things worse. Fear of finding out something I don’t want to know. Fear of being blamed again.

“Just a simple message,” Sarah suggests. “Nothing dramatic. Just ‘Thinking of you, hope everything’s okay.’”

I reach for my phone, turning it over in my hands, feeling its weight. “What if she doesn’t answer?”

“Then you’re no worse off than you are now.”

With a deep breath, I type out a simple text: **Morning. Just checking in. Hope everything’s okay.**

My thumb hesitates over the send button.

I click it and Sarah pulls me into a tight, fierce hug. The sudden contact knocks the breath from my lungs.

“Why didn’t you tell me about all this?” she whispers. “You shouldn’t have been alone. Why didn’t you answer last night?”

“I didn’t want to say it out loud.”

Saying it makes it true. And I can’t let it be true.

Sarah pulls back but holds onto my hands. “Listen to me. *This is not your fault*. No matter what Paul says.”

I try to believe her. I want to believe her.

But the image of my mother’s blood on the bathroom floor is burned into my skull, and I can still hear Paul’s voice.

Look what you’ve done.

I shake my head. "You don't understand."

Sarah's jaw tightens. "Then make me understand."

But I can't.

Because the truth is, I don't know where to begin.

Should I try to tell her I feel responsible for my mother's pain?

Or that deep down, I suspect he's right to blame me.

I swallow hard, forcing the breath back into my lungs.

Sarah speaks again. "Promise me something?"

"Anything."

"No more disappearing acts. Even if you can't talk about it, just... let me know you're alive?"

I squeeze her hand. "Promise."

"Paul's an idiot," Sarah says with such conviction that I almost smile. "And whatever happens, you're not alone. Okay?"

"Okay."

"One more thing." Sarah looks serious, and my heart skitters. Have I done something else wrong?

"What?"

"Let me fix your hair, at least. You look like you've been dragged through a hedge."

I touch my tangled mess of hair self-consciously. "That bad?"

"Worse." She pulls a hairbrush from her bag. "Turn around."

I let her smooth out the knots, her gentle tugging oddly comforting. For a moment, I can pretend everything's normal.

"There," she says finally. "Now you just look sleep-deprived instead of completely feral."

I smile, and feel the warmth spread through me.

Outside, the morning air is crisp, the sky a clear, pale blue that feels at odds with the turmoil of the past fifteen hours. Sarah links her arm through mine as we set off down the street.

"She's going to be fine," Sarah says again. "And so are you."

I want to believe her. Want to believe that not everything that goes wrong is because of me. That Mum and the baby will be okay. That Paul's accusations were just fear finding a target.

"Thanks," I say, meaning it for everything: the hairbrush, the text suggestion, the unwavering certainty that things will work out.

Sarah bumps her shoulder against mine. "What else are best friends for?"

As we walk toward school, Sarah chats about weekend plans and homework, normal things that make the knot in my chest loosen just a little. The spring sun feels warmer now, almost comforting.

"Oh, by the way," she says, "Mum wants to know if you're still coming to the mall with us on Saturday. New shoes, remember?"

The invitation catches me off guard. With everything happening with Mum, I'd forgotten about our plans. "I don't know if I should..."

"You should definitely come," she insists. "Mum's been looking forward to it. Besides, might do you good to be out of the house. Give Paul and your mum some space with everything going on."

I nod slowly. She's right. I'd probably just be in the way at home.

"Okay. Tell Joyce I'll be there."

"She'll be thrilled," Sarah says, her smile brightening. "She says you're the only one who stops me from buying hideous clothes."

"Someone has to save you from yourself," I reply, and for a moment, everything feels almost normal again.

We take our usual route past the shuttered corner shop. I'm half-listening to Sarah's story about her brother's latest girlfriend drama when something near the edge of the woods makes me pause.

"What?" Sarah asks, following my gaze.

I study the tree line where shadows shift and sway, one of them moving in a way that seems... wrong somehow. Not like branches in the wind, but purposeful. Almost like a person.

"Nothing," I say, shaking my head. "Just shadows playing tricks on me, I think."

Sarah loops her arm through mine again. "Lack of sleep will do that. Come on, we're going to be late."

I let her pull me forward, dismissing the uneasy feeling that briefly crawled up my spine. After all the stress about Mum, my mind is probably just searching for new threats. Finding patterns where there are none.

Besides, we've walked this way hundreds of times before. Nothing ever changes in this town.

Nothing ever happens here.

CHAPTER EIGHT

Freedom comes at exactly 4:30, when Mr Perkins finally dismisses us from detention again. The hallways are already empty, the usual after school chaos replaced by an eerie quiet that makes our footsteps echo against the polished floors.

"God, I thought that would never end," Sarah says, her voice bouncing off the lockers as we make our way toward the exit. "Did you see Perkins's face when my stomach growled? I swear he almost exploded."

I manage a weak smile in return, but my mind is elsewhere, circling the same anxious thoughts that have plagued me all afternoon.

We push through the heavy double doors and step outside. The afternoon has turned cool while we were trapped inside, the sun already dipping toward the horizon, painting everything in amber and long shadows. The school grounds are deserted except for a janitor emptying trash bins near the bike racks.

The air is sharp, the late sunlight stretched thin.

Nulli soli, omnes uniti.

The words carved into the stone above the doorway mock me.

No one alone, all together.

Except sometimes you are alone, even when someone is standing right beside you.

Sarah walks close, her bag slung over one shoulder, her head tilted slightly as if she's waiting for me to speak. I don't.

"Any update?" she asks softly.

I pull out my phone, showing her the message that arrived during detention. Not from Mum, but from Paul:

Still at hospital. Tests and observation continuing. Will probably be here late.

The last instruction is so typically Paul: concerned with practicality rather than emotions, treating me more like a roommate than family despite four months of living under the same roof.

"That's it?" Sarah's forehead creases. "That's all he said?"

I nod, sliding the phone back into my pocket. My fingers curl tight around it, nails digging into my palm.

"He couldn't even tell you if she's alright," Sarah says, anger flashing across her face. "Or if the baby's okay."

"Classic Paul," I mutter. The man who swept into our lives, claiming space that wasn't his, now potentially father to my half-brother if the bleeding hasn't...

I push away the thought. I can't let my mind go there.

Part of me had hoped for a message from Mum herself, some small proof she was well enough to think of me. But there's been nothing except Paul's clinical update, devoid of anything that might actually comfort me.

"Have you tried calling Abby?" Sarah asks.

"Three times. It goes straight to voicemail."

Sarah watches me carefully, like she's trying to read between the spaces in my silence. Then, with a gentle smile, she says, "Want to take the cut-through? There's no point rushing home if they're not going to be there."

I hesitate. Our usual route home is predictable: fifteen minutes along the main road, past the shuttered corner shop, through the playground, then onto my street. Safe. Routine.

But today, routine feels suffocating.

Sarah must see something in my face, because she hesitates before adding, "I thought maybe we could pick some flowers for Abby."

The way she says my mother's name like we're talking about a person, not just Mum, makes my chest tighten.

"She... she'd like that," I say, the words slow, careful.

"The bluebells will be out," Sarah continues.

The mention of them sends a ripple through me. A scent I haven't thought about in years: something soft, something safe.

Mum used to wear a bluebell perfume, back when things were different. Back when it was just the three of us, when we were a family. The bottle had a delicate, floral design, the colour of faded sky. Dad used to buy it for her.

After he left, she stopped wearing it.

Or maybe it didn't hit the same when she had to buy it for herself.

I swallow against the thickness in my throat.

"She likes bluebells."

"We should have an hour or so before it starts to go dark. Plenty of time."

"It's not like there's anyone waiting," I say, the bitterness in my voice surprising me.

Sarah, though.

"Won't Joyce... your mum... be worried?"

"It's fine. Mum and Dad are off at some *thing* tonight."

"Thing?"

Sarah makes a noncommittal sigh.

"Mum's told him they have to start having date nights. Apparently, I'm old enough to stay home on my own now. I have no idea why they didn't think my responsible adult brother wasn't able to keep an eye on me before, as if I need it, but..." she shrugs.

It's not even a joke. Oliver *is* a responsible adult, as sensible and straight as either me or Sarah. He left school, went straight into college. He works weekends at the pool and I'm sure he helps little old ladies across the road whenever possible.

I still don't have a crush. He's just a good guy.

If *I* had an older brother, perhaps Mum and Paul could go out more. Not that I like to think of Paul anywhere with Mum, but I would so much rather she was at some *thing* with him rather than being where they are now.

Am I going to have a brother at all?

The thought sends an icy wave through me. What if she loses the baby? What if something worse happens? What if I never see her again and the last thing I did was complain about pizza night being cancelled?

"I'm sorry," Sarah says, reading my mind. "I shouldn't..." Her voice trails off. "You want to just get back? You could... we could go up and visit her?"

I think of Paul's voice and shake my head.

"Bluebells," I say. "Let's go before it gets too late."

School fades behind us as we take the narrow cut-through along the fence line. The metal bars are streaked with rust beneath peeling green paint, and as I squeeze past, flecks of it brush onto my sweater.

It's probably still cold enough that we should be wearing coats, but neither of us is. We don't roll the top of our school skirts over like some of the girls, but we're far enough into the year that the hems sit just above our knees. Slouch socks, black shoes. We all look the same.

We shuffle along in single file, Sarah ahead, until the path forks. Our route home carries on, dead ahead. The fork to the left meanders downwards, through the trees.

Turning off, we follow the smaller path until it breaks out into a clearing. The grass is pale, patches of brown here and there, long, overgrown. Trees line the edges of this arbitrary area. It feels far more isolated than I remembered, like stepping into a pocket of wilderness hidden within our suburban landscape.

Sarah doesn't wait. She steps ahead, turning back just once. "You okay?"

I nod, though I'm not sure if it's true.

She doesn't press. She just keeps walking.

Out here, away from the familiar route, away from school, the world feels thinner. Like the edges of reality are fraying.

I inhale, searching for it.

That scent.

Bluebells.

And there it is. A whisper in the air. A hint of something that doesn't belong in this moment, something that feels like a memory folding over itself.

Sarah slows as we reach the gate. The latch is stiff, reluctant. She lifts it, and the metal groans in protest.

We step through.

The path ahead is narrow; grass and wildflowers shift in the breeze. It's not a long walk, but it feels different from the streets we usually take.

A breath of wind carries the scent again. Faint, but unmistakable.

I think of Mum.

Of her standing at the bathroom mirror, pressing a fingertip to her pulse point, dabbing perfume along her skin. The way she used to do it before nights out with Dad, back when her hair was still long, back when she still wore that silver bracelet he gave her.

Back when she smiled more.

I haven't seen that bracelet in years.

"Over there," Sarah says, pointing to the shade beneath the trees. The bluebells stand tall, their heads tilted toward the ground as if in quiet reverence.

I step forward before I can overthink it.

The smell is stronger here.

I kneel, reaching for the stems. My fingers brush against the cool leaves, the damp earth. The flowers come free easily when I twist them at the base, their delicate stems bending under my fingers. They look so fragile in my hand, their blue bells almost translucent in the fading light.

Sarah watches but says nothing.

As always, she lets me move at my own pace.

I gather a handful, careful not to crush them.

When I inhale, the scent floods through me, pulling me somewhere else, somewhere distant.

I smell Mum.

I don't know what I expected. Comfort, maybe. A piece of her, something solid to hold on to.

Instead, all I feel is loss.

The way things used to be. The way they never will be again.

I close my fingers around the stems, grounding myself in the pressure, in the realness of them. They feel so delicate, so easily broken. Just like the careful balance of our lives before today, before the blood, before the hospital.

Sarah shifts beside me.

"I think..." Sarah's voice catches. "She's going to be okay."

"And the baby?" I ask after a moment. My voice is hoarse, thin.

Sarah exhales. "I don't know. But... sometimes people bleed, and it doesn't mean..."

She trails off. We both know she doesn't have an answer.

Maybe no one does.

I twist the flowers between my fingers, watching as one of the tiny blue bells detaches and drifts to the ground. So easily damaged. So fragile.

Maybe, when I get home, Paul will already be there. Sitting at the table. Wearing that same expression, the one I can't read, the one that makes my stomach turn.

Maybe, this time, he'll have something to tell me.

Something I don't want to hear.

A sudden wind rustles through the trees, sending a shower of fresh petals from the higher branches. For a moment, I feel a prickle at the back of my neck, as though we're being watched. I glance over my shoulder, seeing nothing but shadows stretching longer between the trees.

Just nerves. Just my mind jumping at ghosts because of everything else today.

I turn back to the flowers, ignoring the feeling of unease that settles over me like the approaching dusk.

CHAPTER NINE

The late afternoon sun stretches our shadows across the grass as we kneel among the bluebells, fingers working methodically at their stems. The conversation drifts like dandelion seeds - harmless, weightless things. A new Netflix show I can't stop watching. A song Oliver played for her last night that "you absolutely have to hear." Neither of us returns to the topics of Mum in the hospital, or the baby, or the humiliation of being left behind on the cross country run. It's easier to float on the surface than sink into the undertow of what matters.

I don't know this is the last normal conversation we'll ever have.

Our backpacks rest against the oak tree at the edge of the clearing, Sarah's phone tucked inside with that song she's dying to play for me. She'll never reach for that bag.

The shadows grow longer, darker, as we work.

The wind picks up, making the bluebells shiver on their stems. A cloud passes over the sun, and for a moment everything looks different - darker, stranger. But then it passes, and we go back to our gentle conversation, blind to how quickly everything can change.

I notice him before Sarah does. She's pulling one of the tallest bluebells from the root, the white at the bottom of the stem still intact. As I freeze, she looks up at me.

"What's up?" she asks. Her smile has faded even before she follows my gaze.

I feel it before I can name it: a primal warning that crawls up my spine, raising goosebumps on my forearms despite the mild air. My mouth goes dry. I've felt this before, walking home alone after dark, or when a car slows beside me on an empty street. That ancient animal instinct that whispers *danger*.

Funny, my mind goes to the contents of my backpack. Nothing of value. Like my natural reaction to a stranger is one of mistrust.

We must have been out here for a good three quarters of an hour and not a single other person has passed by. Not until now. If there had been a constant stream of foot traffic, I'm sure we wouldn't be looking at each other like this now.

He's walking slowly, methodically, turning his head from side to side. Not the casual scanning of someone enjoying nature, but the deliberate search pattern of a hunter. Something in his hand catches the fading light, but from this distance, I can't make out what it is.

Sarah stands upright and nudges me.

"Stop staring!" She laughs, but it's full of the same nerves that I'm feeling.

I'm holding enough of a bunch of bluebells to fill the vase Mum always uses. We can stop now. We should stop now. The blush of sunset is spreading across the horizon. The bare trees are becoming black silhouettes against deepening purple. In the next half hour, forty minutes maybe, the daylight will have faded completely.

"Let's go," I say quietly, even though he's too far to hear us.

Too far, but also to get home, we need to walk past him.

I'm being overly dramatic, I tell myself. It's just tension from everything with Mum. Just the stress of the day making shadows into monsters.

Everything with Mum. Is that what I've reduced it to? She's in hospital. She's... I don't know. I don't know what's happening. I need to go home. I need to talk to Paul.

Sarah nods and strides over to her bag. I turn to follow, but before I step away from the spot, I hear the man's voice.

"Hey!"

I gulp in a mouthful of air. A high-pitched ringing starts in my ears. My gut clenches as if bracing for impact. Sarah is already ten paces from me.

"You haven't seen a dog."

The way he says it is more like a statement than a question. It throws me off. His voice is controlled, too even, like someone trying to sound normal.

"W-what?" I sound more nervous than I intend. My voice is childlike, pathetic. "A dog?" I add the last two words just so I can say something else, make myself sound more authoritative, less weak. Also, I want Sarah to hear me. I want her to come back.

She stops.

The man approaches.

He's not so tall. Not as tall as Paul. Perhaps not even as tall as Mum. He's wearing one of those red and black check lumberjack jackets, thick and fleecy with a tear along the right pocket that's been clumsily repaired with thick black thread. His face is covered with dark stubble beneath the red glow of his windblown cheeks. His cracked lips are drawn out in a smile, a crooked row of teeth just visible, like he doesn't quite want to show them off. But it's his eyes that make my stomach twist: pale blue, almost colourless, watching us with an intensity that doesn't match his casual posture.

The thing I saw in his hand but couldn't make out is a tan leather dog lead, worn at the edges, with a distinctive brass buckle that catches the dying light.

A dog. He's looking for his dog.

My tension softens, just for a moment. That makes sense, right? People walk dogs in the woods all the time.

"Little thing," he says with a smile that doesn't meet those pale eyes. "A cockapoo. You know what they look like?"

I nod, even though I'm not entirely sure. It makes no difference. We haven't seen any kind of dog, or any kind of human for that matter. It's just been me and Sarah this whole time.

While he talks to me, Sarah moves back over and positions herself by my side. He doesn't look at her, he's looking at me.

"Hurt yourself, there," he says, pointing the lead down towards the grey speckled blood patch on my knee.

He's already moving towards me, stooping down, peering close. Not asking permission, not maintaining the distance a stranger should.

A stench of stale cigarette smoke wafts from the jacket, mingled with something else: a sour odour that makes my nostrils flare. It's one of those fabrics that holds a smell, and I can't help but think that this one hasn't been washed for some time. I stumble back a step as he looms in, my heart hammering so loud I'm sure he must hear it.

The apprehension returns, jolting my muscles into a rigid tension. My mother's voice echoes in my head from years ago: "*Always trust your instincts, Amanda. If something feels wrong, it probably is.*"

"We... our parents... I mean, I..."

The man takes a step back, away from us, and I'm suddenly dizzy. I reach out towards Sarah, afraid I'm about to fall.

He lifts his hands in a *harmless see? nothing to worry about* gesture. The lead still looped around his left wrist sways gently with the movement. But I notice how his fingers twitch slightly, how his weight shifts forward onto the balls of his feet, like a runner waiting for the starting gun.

"You need to get home," he says, his eyes flicking between us, lingering a second too long on my face. "Someone's waiting for you."

The words are innocuous. It's a statement. It's fact, or at least any other day it would be fact. Tonight, this evening, I don't know. I doubt Paul will be home, and I know Mum won't be. All that's waiting for me is the microwave and whatever I can find to feed myself. His eyes study my face as though he's looking for tells.

And I realise with sickening clarity what's happening.

I know right then, as he stares at me, that we're in serious trouble.

He knows, somehow, that there's nobody waiting for me.

No one misses me.

No one will raise the alarm if I don't arrive home.

Sweat buds on my forehead despite the cooling air. Time seems to stretch, each second expanding into an eternity of suspended terror.

"Sarah," I say, reaching out a hand for hers, never taking my eyes off the man.

"Sarah," the man repeats, the name sounding wrong in his mouth, contaminated.

He steps closer.

I step back.

Sarah grasps hold of me, and in that one movement I know she feels it too. The wrongness. The danger vibrating in the air between us.

We have to get out of here.

"I'm sorry," she says, a tremor in her voice that she can't conceal, even though I know she is trying to. "My mum's making dinner. I've got to be back by..."

Before she can finish the sentence, the man lunges forwards and pushes her.

Everything happens both too fast and impossibly slow. A single flat palm against her chest that knocks the breath out of her. Sarah's eyes widen in shock, her mouth forming a perfect O of surprise. Her fingers, warm and alive, torn from mine as she falls backward. Her body crumpling as it hits the ground, bluebells crushed beneath her weight. The soft thud of impact. The tiny gasp that escapes her lips.

In the split second before instinct takes over, I have a choice.

Fall with her. Stay with her. Hold on.

Or save myself.

My instinct is not to fall with her.

My instinct is to protect myself.

And I let go.

CHAPTER TEN

There's one of him and two of us, but he's already positioned himself over Sarah, one leg on either side of her, looking down with an expression of detached curiosity. Like she's an insect he's pinned to a display board.

Bring your leg up, I think. Kick him there.

But Sarah is frozen, her eyes wide and unblinking, her body rigid with terror.

"Quiet," the man says. One word, delivered with calm authority.

I could run.

Right now, I could run.

The thought forms with crystalline clarity: the path behind me is clear, unobstructed. If I sprint now, I might make it to the main trail. I might find someone to help.

Her name forms on my lips, but my voice has abandoned me. My throat constricts, air passing soundlessly over paralysed vocal cords. I can't speak. I can't say anything.

My thoughts spin through every possible move I could make: a wheel of fortune cycling through rapidly diminishing options. Each one ending with Sarah hurt. With both of us hurt.

Or worse, much worse.

I could run.

I could run and find help. I calculate the distance to the main path, the additional minutes to reach the road. Too long. By the time I brought anyone back, it would be too late.

I could scream.

Someone might hear, even at this distance. My chest expands, lungs filling with air in preparation.

"You shut the hell up, Maggie." His voice is ice cold, calm, and aimed at me.

"I'm not..." The protest dies on my lips as confusion swirls through my mind.

"You heard me," he says, and I see Sarah shake her head. One slight movement.

He stares at her. Not with rage or intensity, but with the empty gaze of someone looking through a window rather than at a person.

"She's not going to be a problem," he says.

Me. He means me.

Sarah shakes her head again, more definite this time.

"Say it."

His tone hasn't changed: still conversational, still empty of emotion. Somehow that's more terrifying than if he'd shouted.

Sarah licks her lips, and I can almost feel the dryness of her mouth. The desert her throat has become. My own tongue feels glued to the roof of my mouth, useless and swollen.

I could run.

Twenty seconds at a full sprint might get me far enough away. But Sarah would remain. Sarah, who lagged along with me on the run. Sarah, who stayed with me when I was injured. Sarah, who never leaves anyone behind.

I stand my ground.

"She's not going to be a problem," Sarah says.

Her voice cracks. The words are barely audible.

Even here in the silence. Here, away from the road, away from people, away from our regular life on our regular route. Even here, her words are so fragile they're almost lost in the still air.

"Say it again." The man picks up his leg and puts his foot down on her chest, pressing down with increasing weight.

I see the way Sarah's breathing shallows, and panic spikes through me. She already struggles to catch her breath when she's anxious. If he presses any harder...

It hurts her.

I know it hurts because a sound escapes her that I've never heard before. Not quite a scream, not quite a whimper, but something primal and wounded that carves itself into my memory.

I know it hurts because her eyes turn back toward me, and in them I see a message as clear as if she'd shouted it. Run. Run. RUN.

I know it hurts and there's no way I'm leaving her here.

"I'm not going to be a problem," I say, the words tumbling out, desperate to draw his attention away from Sarah.

And I want to say more. I want to say please, please, please don't hurt her again. Let her breathe. Don't... whatever you're thinking of doing... don't do it...

But as soon as that thought forms, as soon as my mind heads in that direction, I know I can't say anything else. I know I can't think those thoughts.

Because Sarah and I are alone out here, with him.

No one knows where we are.

And no one is going to miss me.

"Get on the ground."

Sarah's already down. There's no way she's getting up, not with his boot on her school shirt. He's talking to me.

Before it registers, he's telling me again.

"Get on the ground, Maggie."

Without looking at him, without breaking eye contact with Sarah, I lower myself. My movements feel distant, mechanical, as if someone else is controlling my body from a great distance.

"Turn around."

I'm sitting. I press my hands into the earth, rotating. Dead leaves and twigs crackle beneath my palms.

And all I can think is why, why, why? The word repeats, a broken record of incomprehension. Why us? Why here? Why now?

What is he going to do that he doesn't want me to see?

I have to stop thinking.

"Please," I say. I try to keep my voice quiet and polite, but it comes out like a mouse squeak of a word. My heart thunders so loudly I'm sure he must hear it pounding against my ribs.

"Maggie." The name again, spoken with a familiarity that makes my skin crawl. "I'm not going to tell you again. I swear to God if you open your bitch mouth one more time, your friend here is going to get it."

And his tone is so calm, so flat, that again I freeze. Apart from the constant tremors that are shaking my body, the tears that I can't hold back and the pressure in my legs, those tense sprung muscles I'm fighting against, the ones that want to run, run, run, apart from all of that I am stone still.

He is slow, taking his time.

No thought of hurrying. No fear of being caught here, with us.

I hear the ripping of fabric.

Frantic sounds now from Sarah, not words.

Then footsteps.

His heavy boots come towards me.

His hand is on my back.

He pushes me forward.

My legs are in front of me.

I can't move in the way he wants me to.

He tips me to the side, and for a split second, I see Sarah. She's flat on her belly in her shirt and knickers.

No skirt. No skirt now.

He's tied her hands together, behind her back, with the dog lead.

There is no dog, I think, and I don't know if I'm thinking about Mum and the baby and the puppy and the colours on the wall in my bedroom as I realise he's gagged her and now something's going into my mouth, fabric, in and around and I try to shout for the last time but there's no way, I can't make a sound as he pulls it tight behind my head.

None of my thoughts make sense. They're just a garbled whirl of things I might never see, might never see again.

He rolls me onto my stomach too and is there any point in me kicking? Should I thrash out with my arms, or will that make him mad? Will he hurt me more if I fight? Will he hurt her more? Because if there's any chance at all that some stupid shit I pull could wind up with her getting hurt more, I can't do it. I can't risk it.

I am still as he binds my wrists with more of the fabric he's cut from the bottom of her skirt.

Cut.

He has a knife.

He has a knife.

He cut her skirt. He has a knife.

My mind makes the connection, and I immediately try to unthink that thought.

Because that thought can't lead to anywhere good.

He sees me looking at Sarah, and with one swift movement of his leg, he kicks me around like a rag doll so I'm facing away.

"You don't need to see this, Maggie," he says.

My face is against the mud now. Ahead of me, six feet away, maybe less, the bluebells hang their heads as a final piece of fabric is wrapped around my face, covering my eyes.

He's so close to me, as he ties off the makeshift blindfold. I can smell that stale cigarette and dried-in body odour cocktail, and it makes me retch.

Then he's gone. Back to her.

And now there's no chance of running.

I hear Sarah yelp. It's a short sharp noise, like a dog would make if you stood on their paw.

It takes everything I have not to turn around. Not out of any kind of morbid curiosity, but out of love. I can't sit here with my back to my best friend while he hurts her.

But that's exactly what I have to do.

"If you're going to make noise like that, missy," he says, "I'm going to have to take you where no one can hear you."

Take us. The words register with fresh horror. He's not just attacking us here. He plans to move us somewhere else. Somewhere even more isolated. Somewhere...

Behind me, I hear movement; a thud.

"Plllsss," Sarah says from beneath her gag. The word is small, choked, broken.

Please.

Not a request. A prayer without hope of answer.

Sarah's plea shatters something in me. My best friend, my sister in all but blood, and I can't do anything to save her. I've never felt more useless, more broken. All I can do is sit here, back turned, while he...

Another thud.

Above me, a wood thrush trills its evening song, sweet and pure. A gentle breeze rustles through new spring leaves, carrying the scent of bluebells. Everything about this moment should be peaceful. But beneath these gentle sounds, I hear the terrible reality.

Behind me, Sarah's breathing changes. Quick, shallow gasps give way to muffled sobs that sound as though they are shaking through her entire body. The sounds of her distress fill the clearing, each one cutting into me like the knife I know he carries.

"I can't do this if you won't shut up."

I part will her to keep fighting, part will her to do what he says, so maybe, just maybe, he'll stop hurting her.

But then the air shifts with movement. His footsteps retreat from her.

Is it over? Is he done?

The relief is momentary, vanishing as his boots approach me instead.

Twigs snap beneath his weight as he crouches beside me. I can feel his presence, smell the cigarettes on his breath, sense him studying me through the blindfold.

A finger traces my cheek, the touch almost gentle.

Intimate.

Terrifying.

"You're being so good, Maggie," he whispers, his mouth close to my ear. "Always so quiet. So obedient."

I fight the urge to vomit, to scream, to jerk away from his touch.

Sarah's breathing shudders in the background, her pain a counterpoint to his twisted tenderness.

"Calm down," he says in what I fear might be his most soothing tone. "I'll fetch the truck."

My eyes widen behind the polyester blindfold. It's not over. It's only beginning. He's actually going to abduct us.

I hear it as he walks away: the rhythmic jangle of keys, the casual whistling that starts up as though he's simply running an everyday errand.

Sarah's sobs grow quieter, more controlled, as if she's trying to listen too. Trying to understand what comes next in this nightmare. The whistling fades into the distance, but the promise of his return hangs in the air, heavier than the scent of crushed bluebells beneath us. The truck means somewhere else. Somewhere worse. Somewhere truly out of reach.

Somewhere no one can hear us.

CHAPTER ELEVEN

I hear his footsteps fade to silence, but can't be sure that he has left. Straining my ears, I try to focus on the sounds around me. I zone in on what I can't hear: no truck sound, not yet; no heavy feet on the track. No whistling.

He wants you to think he's gone.

It's possible. I don't know this man. I certainly don't know how his mind works. What kind of person wanders around the woods waiting for girls he can tie up and take to his truck?

The type of person who would walk to the edge of the clearing, stand and watch, wait for one of you to give him a reason to hurt you.

He wants you to think he's gone.

My thoughts are not helpful, but the logic checks out. Still, I can't not try to communicate with Sarah. I need her to know I'm here. I need her to know we are still together in this.

"Srrrh." I try to say her name, but the gag muffles it into nonsense.

There's no reply.

Bile rises in my throat, thick and burning, and for a moment all I can think is that I'm going to choke on my own vomit because this gag is in my mouth and I'm about to bring up the last meal I ate: a dry tuna sandwich and a carton of milk from the cafeteria, the taste of it already curdling at the back of my throat.

Is that going to be the last meal I ever ate?

I know I'm panicking, and I try to slow my breathing. I try, but the acid taste is in my mouth, the lingering salt of cheap canteen mayonnaise mixing with bile, and there's no way to be rid of it. I gulp back the bitterness. I suck air through my nostrils. I push it back out, slow and steady. At least I think the words slow and steady as my breath stutters from my nose.

Slow.

And steady.

Saliva fills my mouth, and I push it out, feeling the dampness against the crepe texture of Sarah's skirt.

Joyce will be mad.

I let the thought fade away.

My gag cuts into the corners of my mouth, but what about Sarah? Hers must be pressing against her lips, her panic stealing the air she needs. She needs full breaths. Deep ones. If her chest tightens... Oh God, if she has an asthma attack now...

My wrists burn where he bound them, the fabric of Sarah's skirt digging into my skin. I try to move my fingers, just to make sure I still can. They respond sluggishly, pins and needles spreading through my hands.

My chest rises and falls heavily, but the rhythm steadies.

You're wasting time.

Am I really going to wait here for him to come back and take us to wherever it is he plans to take us in his truck?

The worst-case scenario just escalated from what he could do to us here to what he could do to us in a place of his own choosing. And that seems like a hell of a lot worse.

What are my options?

I could rub my face against the floor until I free myself of the blindfold and gag, get to my feet, run over to Sarah.

We could get away.

But I can't be sure that he has gone.

What if he *is* testing us?

And if he's still here, if he's even nearby and sees us, just exactly how are we going to outrun him?

At least Sarah's asthma gives her an excuse. All I have is my pitiful lack of fitness and general uselessness.

If I get out of this, I swear I'm going to work on myself.

If we get out of this.

Sarah. Her name fills my mind, pushing against everything else. Sarah, who I heard sobbing. Sarah, who made those sounds I've never heard before.

"Srrrh." I force the sound again.

"Mmmph," she replies.

Sarah is here. She is conscious. That's all I know.

Behind the darkness of the blindfold, I can only form a mental image of her. Bound and gagged, the same as I am.

But without her skirt.

The bile rises again, and I swallow hard.

Even now, even here, I have to have some kind of control.

I've called out to her twice. She's responded. He hasn't told us to shut up. He hasn't shouted, hasn't threatened.

I think he has gone.

"Srrrh. Yughky?"

The gag mangles my words. *Are you okay?* Stupid question. Of course, she's not okay. How could either of us be?

"Whrrweuhoo," Sarah replies.

I have no clue what she's trying to tell me or ask me.

"Whrr we uh oo," she repeats, spacing her words, or at least the sounds of words.

What are we going to do?

I shuffle on the ground. The earth beneath me has turned cold as the sun begins to set, leeching warmth from my body. Beneath me, the long grass is flattened. It's not hard enough for me to gain any kind of friction to help me release the bindings on my wrists. I move my head instead, like a nodding dog, scraping against the ground, trying to free myself. My movements are frantic, and I bang my head against the ground. Wincing, I try again. Steady now, using my whole body to shift against the...

But it's already too late.

"Truuud!" Sarah muffle-shouts, but I've heard it too.

The growl of an engine coming closer.

It's not a road, the path that runs through the woods here. I've never seen a vehicle here. But he must know the area well. He knows how to drive to where we are.

Make a mental note of that.

The voice in my head has a point. Anything that might help later. I must try to remember.

He knows the area.

He was ready for us.

I realise with stomach-dropping clarity that this was planned.

The truck was already there. He was here, with that dog lead, looking for someone. Hunting for prey.

We have to get out of here.

I know now, as the sound of the truck's engine dies in the hum of the ignition being switched off, that it's too late.

He's whistling again as he walks towards us. No song that I can recognise, just it's-a-lovely-day-to-go-a-kidnapping tune.

The smile on his face is obvious, even though I can't see it.

The footsteps stop, but the whistling doesn't. It changes pitch as Sarah yelps.

"Neugh!"

"Hush now," the man says, amusement lacing his voice. Then a grunt, before going back to the whistled soundtrack of our abduction.

The sound seems to physically touch me, like fingers dragging across my skin. I curl inward instinctively, my muscles contracting painfully after being stretched in the same position for so long. My jaw aches from clenching against the gag, teeth grinding together so hard I can hear the sound inside my skull.

Behind the blindfold, there is only darkness.

The fabric against my eyes is rough, already damp with tears and sweat. My skin feels clammy, the cool early evening air raising goosebumps along my exposed arms and legs.

I focus on a mental image of the bruise-coloured wallpaper in my bedroom. Something to ground me. Something to hold onto.

I wonder if Sarah has gone to her own safe place, too. I wonder if there's any such thing anymore.

"Get up," he says.

I think he's talking to me, but when I try to rise, he says, "Not you, Maggie, not yet."

Not yet.

So, soon?

I picture Sarah getting to her feet as I hear the shuffling behind me. She doesn't speak, doesn't protest.

"I don't have all day," he says, and there's a thud followed immediately by a small yap of a cry.

Footsteps recede. Him and her. Away, but I can't tell which way. Along the path we were walking? Back? Forwards?

I lie still, listening.

Has he taken her and left me here?

I could run.

I hear the words repeat in my head, but they sound ridiculous. Of course I couldn't.

What if she's gone now? What if...

I stop myself and close my eyes. Darkness within the darkness. The wallpaper pattern. A sick meditation.

Who the hell is Maggie?

My eyes shoot open, but to no avail. I am alert. I am thinking. I am still blindfolded.

And I try, try, try to recall if I've seen anything in the news, heard anything on the radio. Maggie. Margaret.

I come up blank. If there were any missing girls around here, my mother would be a damn sight stricter about knowing where I was, Paul or no Paul. And Joyce? Joyce wouldn't let Sarah out of the house at all if there had been anything like that.

Joyce.

What am I going to say to Joyce if he has taken Sarah and I just lay here like a ham ready for roasting?

Maybe you won't have to say anything.

The voice in my head isn't comforting. It's ominous.

What if neither of us are going home?

"Maggie. Come on, now."

His voice again.

And for a moment, I'm almost glad.

Because it means wherever Sarah is, I'm going too.

CHAPTER TWELVE

There's no walking. He picks me up, throws me over his shoulder in a fireman's lift and strides forwards. I think forwards, but I don't know what direction that really is. The world tilts and spins, blood rushing to my head as my stomach lurches. His shoulder digs into my abdomen with each step. The blindfold rubs up against him and I catch glimpses of the ground moving beneath us. Patches of scrubby grass, then gravel, then dirt. Everything's blurry through my tears and scrambled, like my brain can't process which way is up.

His hands clamp around my thigh, fingers digging in hard enough that I know there will be a bruise. A reminder, even if I survive. The casual strength in his grip makes me want to vomit. I don't think he's even exerting himself carrying me. I must be weightless to him. Just another piece of cargo.

He walks. He carries me. And when we get to where he wants to be, he leans against glass and metal, supporting my weight as he pulls open the door of his truck.

My body jolts against his, and as he adjusts his grip, the blindfold rises slightly again, rubbed against his foul-smelling jacket. I see red, more red. The red of his jacket, the red of the truck.

Remember. Remember this.

There's no more time to see anything else.

It's all I get before the blindfold is forced back into place. A rough hand grips my face, fingers pressing into my cheeks hard enough to make me wince. He's checking that it's secure. Checking that I can't see.

"You know the drill," he says, his voice almost gentle, as though he's talking to someone he knows well.

Someone who's done this before.

Of course I *don't* know the drill, but apparently Maggie does.

Maggie, whoever she is.

Maggie, who's probably dead somewhere just like Sarah is going to be if I don't...

I cut off the thought. I can't afford to think like that now.

If it does me any good to go along with this Maggie role, then I'll play along. I lean forward, trying to feel my way, trying to act in a way that makes sense to him. What would Maggie do? My heart pounds so hard I'm sure he must hear it. He guides me, pushing me down into the seat. The door slams, sealing me inside. Trapping me.

The inside of the truck smells of oil and that same cigarette stench as his jacket. That and an underlying rank scent that I can't place. Something rotting. I try not to breathe too deeply. My body trembles as I shift, feeling warmth next to me.

Sarah

I know it must be her. She's not moving much, but she's here. I can feel her presence. It's the only thing grounding me. My hands are bound behind me. Hers must be too. I want to reach out, to let her know she's not alone. But all I can do is move my foot, sliding it carefully across the floor until it brushes against hers.

She flinches, then presses back. A tiny movement. A tiny reassurance.

My mind races as I try to remember every detail. Every little thing that might be helpful later, if there is a later. That's another thought to add to the nope list.

Something in the back rattles. Chains, maybe. Tools? I make a mental note and then try not to think any further about what chains and tools could be used for. Nope, nope, nope.

I want to speak, of course. Want to say something to Sarah. To let her know I'm here. We're together. No one alone.

The engine roars to life, the truck shuddering beneath us.

I hear the man shift in his seat. Then his voice, sliding between the cracks of my fear like something oily and thick.

"You shouldn't have been out there, Maggie. Ain't I told you that?"

I'd love to be able to place his accent, but he sounds like a mash up of trashy horror movie actors. Maybe this isn't his real voice at all. Maybe this is all for show, a character he thinks he's playing. He doesn't sound local, that's for sure.

He repeats himself, louder this time.

"I said, 'Ain't I told you that?'"

"No." I try to say the word, but the gag translates it to *Neugh*.

He laughs. A real laugh. Deep, amused, like this is some kind of inside joke.

"Well, now you know."

I don't know how long he drives for. I try to work out a way to measure the distance. I count seconds as they tick past, but there are too many. I lose track. My thoughts wander to the possible outcomes of this truck ride. None of them are good. Each and every one ends up on the nope list.

I try to focus on a plan to get away, but every idea I have seems to mean that one of us is left behind.

That's not going to happen.

Nulli soli, omnes uniti.

We can't talk to each other, can't communicate. I wonder what Sarah is thinking about, whether she has been counting the seconds and adding to a nope list of her own.

My hands dig into my back with every bump on the road.

The road is fairly smooth.

The occasional bump.

Trees scrape the top of the truck as we travel.

I add these details to my mental list of things that might help later, even though it probably describes most of the main routes in the area.

I listen for anything else that might be useful.

Later.

After.

I'm sure I've heard that the sense of hearing becomes clearer when you're deprived of other sense. I wish I was deprived of smell, because the bastard at the wheel is chain-smoking, and I hate it. It's the least of my worries, though. Dying in a distant year from second hand smoke inhalation would be a perfectly fine option right now.

I hear tyres turn on road.

I hear my own laboured breathing.

And nothing else.

Nothing useful.

Nothing until the click of the indicator, the crunch of gravel beneath us, rather than tarmac, and then a smooth bumpiness that I think must be mud or grass below.

Not much further on, the truck stops.

My heart stops with it.

The man sighs, stretching like he just pulled into his own driveway after a long day. Like this is routine. Like this is normal.

Then he speaks.

"Here we are, Maggie. It's that time again."

The gentle way he says it makes my skin crawl. Like a father telling his child it's bedtime. Like a waiter announcing a special. Like someone, somewhere, has heard these exact words before.

And suddenly I know - really know - that somewhere out there is a real Maggie who heard these same words.

She heard these words.

She felt this same terror.

And she never made it home.

Whatever *that time* is, I'm pretty sure that I don't want to have any part of it.

And I'm also pretty sure that I am about to.

CHAPTER THIRTEEN

He opens the door at Sarah's side first, and I feel her body move away from me. The warmth of her disappears.

"Urgh," she says.

Before she's pulled from the vehicle, I jab out my foot towards hers, making one final contact.

Then I inhale, trying to steady myself. Trying not to freak the frick out about what's about to happen.

It's that time again.

Nope, nope, nope.

How do I get out of this?

No.

How do *we* get out of this?

I sit, waiting for him to come and open my door. He's left the one on Sarah's side open. The breeze blows through, colder now on my legs.

I sit, waiting.

I wait.

I wait.

I can't hear any trace of footsteps. I can't hear any signs of struggle. I can't hear anything apart from the sounds of my own body. There's nothing to suggest we are near houses. No television sounds, no conversations to overhear. Other than that, there's a faint trace of static in the air, and silence.

No. Not static. Just audible, running water. The white noise of a river? A stream? It's so faint it might as well be a puddle. Still, I try to set the memory in my mind.

The door opens, and I almost fall out of the truck. It's not so high that I have to climb down, and I store that thought. He tugs me, but gently.

"Come on now," he says. There's smoke on his breath now, fresh from a cigarette in his left hand. I don't see it, but I feel the bend of his arm, hear the soft fizz of his inhalation as he sucks on it.

I misstep on the uneven ground. There's a small dip, a channel of some kind. My foot goes straight into it, my ankle turning.

"Easy," he says, as though he's herding a cow rather than directing a girl. He jerks me up before my weight falls onto my ankle, and I'm almost grateful.

Almost.

We walk, but not far, his arm around my shoulders, directing me.

"Nearly back."

Back to somewhere I've never been before and hope I never come to again.

But maybe there is no *again*. Maybe everything I have experienced in my life I've experienced for the last time. No more pizza night. No more detention. No more picking bluebells in the woods. No more Sarah. No more Mum.

The thought chokes in my throat, and I let out a small sob. I try to keep it quiet because that pain is for me, it's not for him. I don't want him to know that he is making me feel anything.

"Here we go." His voice is so steady, it feels like this is routine for him.

Maybe it is.

Calmly, without warning, he presses on my shoulder.

"Down, now," he says, dropping me to the floor.

It's damp. We didn't go through any doors, not even a gate. We are still outside, but further away from home. We aren't in the cut-through. We aren't in the bluebell grove. I don't know where we are, but I don't want to be here.

I can't steady myself with my hands behind my back, so I flop to the side and lie in a near foetal position. There's no point trying to sit. He doesn't tell me to try.

My shirt wicks up the moisture in the earth in no time, moisture pressing against my skin. My legs are exposed, straight against the ground where flesh touches soil. My skirt is hitched up, and I want to smooth it down, cover the top of my thighs, but then I think about the gag in my mouth, of Sarah in her panties.

Sarah screams, and I know he has gone back to her.

She's nearby.

There's a pause. The soft rustle of fabric, a weight settling onto the ground with a muted thump. A methodical shifting of movement. My stomach turns; he's preparing for something. I don't want to think about what, but I know. Back at the clearing, he stopped because she was making too much noise. But here, where no one can hear us... here he can do whatever he wants to her.

To us.

"I could take that gag off, now," he says. "No one can hear you." He pauses for a moment and laughs. "I like you better this way, though."

No.

I kick and pull myself up. I can't lie here and do nothing. I can't let this happen to Sarah. I want to say *take me instead*, no matter how the thought of that freezes my blood.

Take me instead because she is special, she is kind and sweet and caring and so full of love and support and affection and she has always been there for me, and I love her, I love her, I love her.

"Get down, Maggie," he says. His voice is glacial: flat, calm, cold.

I'm not Maggie, and I don't get down.

"Get DOWN, Maggie," he says again. He changes the emphasis on the word, but there's still no emotion.

"Neurgh!" I yell through the band of Sarah's school skirt.

I'm up and I'm running towards him, and I'm going to stop him. I charge like a bull, aim my weight at his legs. Without thinking it through, my inner voice tells me to take him down.

"Srrrh!" I shout as I almost reach him.

"Niiiifffhhh!" Sarah yells back.

And as she says it, I feel it.

Before I even reach him, I drop to the floor.

My useless arms, tied behind me, try to reach upwards, try to touch the place that's throbbing now. My useless brain trying to catch up, to work out what has happened. Knife.

The blade opens my throat before I even feel it. One second, I'm running, the next I'm drowning in copper pennies. My body knows I'm dying before my brain catches up. Blood hot, then cold, then hot again as it pumps out my life onto the damp ground.

"I wish you hadn't made me do that, Maggie," he says, as though he means it.

I can't put pressure on the wound. I drag up the idea from somewhere, from television probably, that it's what I'm supposed to do.

I try to ignore the other fact that having your throat cut is a surefire way to end up dead.

Pressure. Pressure. I dip my chin towards my chest, feel the top of my spine stretch as I push down as hard as I can.

All I can think about is how to stop myself from dying.

And then Sarah starts to scream.

I can't see what he does to her.

I hear the sound, dulled first by the piece of black polyester in her mouth, and then, I picture, by his hand pressing over her face.

Bite him. Kick. Do anything.

If I move, I'm almost certain I will die.

I will Sarah on, and then I hear his voice.

"You be a good girl, and you won't end up like Maggie."

And the noises from Sarah stop.

No.

No, please.

Keep fighting.

But the next sound I hear is a pained yelp, and I know what he is doing. I hear flesh against flesh, but Sarah, after that one sharp sound, is silent.

The man's breath comes out in grunts. Over and over. The movement of skin on skin intensifies. Faster, and I think harder, but I don't want to think about it at all. I don't want to think, but how can I not? How can I block out the evil?

The bruise pattern on my bedroom wall fills my mind, but as I float, I realise it's not that at all. It's a shadow falling over me. It's a purple red blue darkness. The colours are seeping into each other. The night is falling.

I'll never see my brother.

ssrrrh

PART TWO

CHAPTER FOURTEEN

The brightness is overwhelming. Needles of white light stab through my eyelids, making me flinch away. I try again, more cautiously this time, letting my eyes flutter open in tiny increments.

Hospital. The word forms before I even process the details: the antiseptic smell, the steady electronic beeping, the too-clean surfaces gleaming under fluorescent lights. But underneath that sharp clinical smell, something else lingers. Something metallic that makes my stomach clench as memory flickers...

No. Not yet.

My head feels wrong, heavy against the pillow but somehow floating, like I'm not quite attached to my body anymore. Medication clouds everything, making the world swim at the edges. A monitor to my left maps my heartbeat in steady green peaks. A tube runs from a transparent bag into my left arm, dripping clear fluid into my veins.

Don't pull on that one.

The thought surfaces from nowhere.

But that's not the tube that terrifies me. Something invasive protrudes from my throat, held in place by straps around my neck.

Sarah.

My voice is blocked by the plastic invasion in my throat. My right hand flies up, finding bandages and medical tape where I remember blood. So much blood. I try not to think about what lies beneath.

All I can think about is Sarah.

My free hand flaps weakly, searching for a call button. Someone needs to know I'm awake. Someone needs to tell me where Sarah is, that she's okay, that she's alive. I must have told them about her when they found me. Before the tube but after the... After the... I must have...

But I can't remember. The timeline shatters like broken glass when I try to grasp it. Sarah being pulled from the truck. His voice. Blood filling my mouth. Then... nothing.

How did I get here? Who found us? And Sarah... Sarah... Sarah...

The monitor's steady beeping accelerates as panic claws up my chest. As my heart pounds harder, the monitor shrieks in response, its professional calm fracturing like everything else. Like me.

She has to be here somewhere. Another room. Another floor. She has to be.

The walls are too white. The lights are too bright. Everything is too clean, too sterile, too controlled. Nothing like the damp earth where I last saw her. Where he...

No.

The monitor wails as the room fades. I need to know. I need to find her. I need...

Sarah.

When I return to consciousness, the clock on the wall reads 3:17, its red digits almost lost in the intense light of the room. Afternoon then. But which day? How long have I been here?

I try to push myself up so I can see more of my surroundings, but my arms tremble with the effort. I'm cautious of the lines, the tubes, the wires. I move so slowly, but even that slight movement sends fresh pain shooting through my neck. The bandage and tape pull against my skin as I sink back into the pillow, defeated.

A whiteboard hangs on the opposite wall, just visible if I turn my head carefully. "Your nurse today: David." Below that, vital signs and numbers that mean nothing to me. No other name. No indication of where Sarah might be.

She has to be nearby. They wouldn't separate us.

Footsteps squeak past in the hallway with that distinctive hospital shoe sound. For a moment, the steady rhythm transforms into heavier boots on damp earth, and my heart rate spikes. I try to steady myself, instinctively attempting to control my breathing, but the tube in my neck makes it impossible. My breath comes in mechanical, shallow pulls that I can't regulate. Another thing he's taken from me: even my own breathing is no longer under my control.

My hospital gown is thin cotton, printed with faded blue diamonds. Someone changed my clothes. Someone washed away the blood and dirt. I try not to think about my ruined school uniform, about Sarah's torn skirt.

No.

Focus on now.

On getting help.

There must be a call button somewhere. My right hand explores the bed rail, finding smooth plastic and metal, but nothing that feels like a button. The effort leaves me exhausted, my arm flopping back onto the scratchy blanket. Even my fingers feel weak, like I've been lying here for days.

I catch a flash of blue scrubs as a nurse walks by, but he doesn't look in. I try to call out, but my damaged throat produces only a rasp that dissolves in the antiseptic air. The smell reminds me of cigarette smoke, and suddenly I'm back there, his breath hot against my ear as he...

No.

The monitor beeps faster again. I close my eyes, trying to shut out the memories, but they leak in anyway. Blood in my mouth. Sarah's muffled scream. The thud of boots.

She has to be here. They must have found us both. I wouldn't have left her there.

But when I open my eyes, I'm still alone in the too-white room. The clock now reads 7:19. Each minute stretches like old gum, sticky with questions I can't voice. My throat aches with words I need to say, with Sarah's name trapped behind damaged vocal cords, behind plastic and bandages.

Something glints in the dim light: there, half-hidden by the blanket. A small controller. The call button. Relief floods through me, until I try to reach it. My arm feels like it's moving through wet concrete, each inch an impossible distance.

Not enough strength. Not yet.

Just like before, when Sarah needed me.

Time blurs. The clock keeps changing, but the numbers mean nothing. My world has shrunk to this: the steady drip of medication, the hum of fluorescent lights, the endless circle of my thoughts as I try to piece it together.

The last thing I remember clearly is the feeling of my life draining out onto the ground. Then just... fragments. My mind skips like a scratched record when I try to push past that moment.

Was there a siren? Voices? The sensation of being lifted? I can't hold on to anything solid, can't string the pieces into a story that makes sense.

Sarah.

If I am here, she is here.

Because the alternative, that someone found only me, that I somehow got help while leaving her behind, is impossible. I wouldn't have done that. Not ever. Even bleeding out, even dying, I wouldn't have left her.

An ambulance wails somewhere outside, its blare fading into the distance. The sound fills my head with red and blue lights, with urgent voices and hands pressing against my neck. But the memory stops there, fragmented and useless. Nothing about Sarah. Nothing about how I got from there to here.

Wherever *there* was.

Wherever he took us.

Wherever there was no one to hear us scream.

My throat burns with unshed tears. The call button is still there, mocking me with its proximity. This time when I reach for it, I manage to brush it with my fingertips. The effort costs me and black spots dance at the edges of my vision. My arm shakes uncontrollably.

Just a little further.

The clinical smell is getting stronger, or maybe I'm just more aware of it. It reminds me of the metallic scent of blood. He was checking my pulse. He thought I was dead. But Sarah...

What happened after that?

Why can't I remember?

My fingers close around the call button. The plastic is warm from being trapped under the blanket. I try to press it, but my hand is trembling too badly. Tears roll down my cheeks, stinging where they meet the edge of the bandage.

I need to know. I need someone to tell me she's okay. I need...

The button clicks softly under my thumb.

Somewhere, a gentle chime sounds. Footsteps approach, lighter than his, faster. A shadow appears in the doorway.

I try to form Sarah's name with my lips, but only a silent sob escapes.

The door opens.

CHAPTER FIFTEEN

A woman in lavender scrubs steps into the room, her face brightening when she sees I'm awake.

"Hello there," she says softly, already moving to check my vitals. "I'm Jen, one of the nurse team here."

I try to speak, forgetting for a moment about the tube in my throat. Nothing comes out, not even a whisper. The tube makes sure of that. My hands flutter up toward my neck in frustration, but Jen catches them gently.

"No touching the trach tube," she says, guiding my hands back down. "I know it's uncomfortable, but it needs to stay in place while you heal."

Trach tube. It has a name.

My heart pounds against my ribs, a frantic rhythm that the machines betray with a quickening beep. Tears of frustration burn in my eyes.

Jen's hands still on the chart she's checking. For the briefest moment, her gaze flickers. I'm not sure if she's feeling pity, concern, or whether there's something worse behind her expression.

"Let me get the doctor," she says, not meeting my eyes. "They'll want to know you're awake."

No. I need her to stay. My fingers scrabble weakly against the blanket, trying to get her attention. There's something else, someone else, I need to know about. The memory struggles through the medication fog.

Jen frowns, taking a step closer. "Are you feeling sick? Pain in your abdomen?"

I shake my head weakly, frustrated. Press my hand against my stomach, try to make a rounded shape. The effort leaves me dizzy, the room tilting slightly. The air is suddenly cloying, thick in my useless throat.

Her forehead creases, and for a second, a look of horror crosses her face.

"Pregnant?" She almost leaps to my notes, flipping through them, eyes scanning frantically.

I move my head as much as I can bear to. Left to right. One slight expression of *no. No, not me. Mum, Mum, Mum.*

I see her exhale, her fingers tightening on the clipboard. Her brain is working, I can see it, but she doesn't reach for my hand. Doesn't offer comfort.

"Oh, your mum?" she says, with a smile of something that looks like relief. "Of course. Don't worry, I'll get the doctor," she says. "And then we'll give your mum a call. She's been here every day, waiting for you to wake up."

She says it so casually, like she's telling me the time. Been here every day? But Mum is in hospital herself. Unless...

How many days have I lost?

The words echo in my head as the nurse disappears down the hallway, leaving me alone with questions I can't voice and a throat too damaged and stifled to even try.

My eyelids are too heavy to keep open. Every blink lasts longer, the harsh white light fading in and out. I fight it; I need to be awake when someone comes back. I need to know...

But how? How?

A burst of noise from the hallway. Trolley wheels squealing. Someone calling for Dr Miles.

Stay awake. I have to stay awake.

But the drugs are stronger than my will. The ceiling tiles blur and swirl. My limbs sink into the mattress, and the beeping of the machines fades.

I dream of Sarah's hand being torn from mine.

When consciousness creeps back, the light has changed. Sunset paints the walls orange, softening the stark lines of the hospital equipment. But it was evening. It was dark.

Something warm presses against my right hand.

Fingers intertwine with mine.

I know before I turn my head.

Mum.

For a moment, I think I'm still dreaming.

Her face is pale except for dark circles under her eyes, and she's wearing one of her teaching dresses - the blue one with tiny flowers that she saves for parents' evenings.

She hasn't noticed I'm awake. Her head is bent over what looks like paperwork in her lap, but her hand stays wrapped around mine.

I try to squeeze her fingers. It takes three attempts before my muscles obey.

Her head snaps up. "Amanda?"

I want to smile, to reassure her, but my face feels frozen. My throat is sandpaper, splinters and plastic. My eyes burn. All I can do is blink against sudden tears as she leans closer.

"Oh, baby." Her free hand hovers over my face like she's afraid to touch me. "You're really awake this time."

This time?

She must see the question in my eyes. "You've been drifting in and out." Her voice cracks. "But not... not really here."

I need to know how long. Need to ask about Sarah. About the baby. But when I try to make a sound, Mum presses her fingers gently against my lips.

"Don't try to talk yet. Please." Two tears roll down her cheeks. "Just... just let me look at you."

Her fingers brush my hair back from my face with such gentleness that more tears spill from my eyes.

The last time I saw her, Paul was taking her to hospital. To this hospital? I'm not even sure where I am. I never got to visit her, and now here she is, visiting me.

I'm sorry. I want to tell her, but my voice has been taken.

I open my mouth, but she shakes her head.

"No," she says, simply. "You can't speak yet, love."

Are you okay? Is the baby...? Are you still...?

With trembling effort, I lift my hand toward her stomach, my eyes questioning.

"Oh, sweetheart." Mum follows my hand with hers. "Don't worry about me. I'm fine."

I must look unconvinced because she adds, "The baby's fine, too. It was the amnio. They said that's what caused the bleeding. Everything's okay now." She squeezes my fingers. "It seems like such a long time ago."

She speaks about it like it's ancient history, but in my mind, it was yesterday. Paul's face white with panic; blood on the bathroom tiles. How many yesterdays have I lost?

"I just have to get some rest and try to avoid stress."

Mum's eyes flick to the elevated numbers on the digital display screen, then back to my face.

I turn my eyes downwards, but she smiles, trying to reassure me.

"Sorry," she says. "I just.... I don't know how to deal with this, so.... I'm sorry."

It's difficult to smile; the skin on my neck tightens as my facial muscles contract and a ripping pain shoots into my throat.

As I wince, Mum's expression becomes an agonising grimace. She doesn't try to hide her panic at seeing me in pain.

"Nurse!" she shouts, fumbling for the call bell.

"Can we get a nurse in here?" she yells. "Anyone?"

A tall man strides into the room, silencing the call alarm. His expression remains neutral, unimpressed. The name tag clipped to his uniform reads: David Spinner, Senior Nurse.

I simultaneously recognise him and don't recognise him. It's as though I saw him in a dream and now he is by my bedside.

"She..." Mum explains. "Her neck... she.... she's in pain. Can you do something?"

The man nods and stands to my right, peering at the dressing as though he can see through it.

"I can bump up the morphine infusion," he says.

He's already leaning towards a pump on the opposite side of me, that name tag dangling dangerously close to my face.

Mum sits back, then stands out of his way.

"Yes," she says.

No, I think.

I try to reach out for Mum's hand again. Try to get the message across that I don't want more drugs. I can't fall asleep again. I have to know that Sarah's okay. I have to know that they found her. That she's here.

"Rest now," she whispers. "I'm here. You're safe."

Safe. The word echoes strangely in my head. How can I be safe when I don't know what happened to Sarah? When I can still feel his hands, still hear him calling me Maggie?

But the medication is pulling me under again, and Mum's warm hand in mine feels like an anchor to reality. The last thing I see before darkness claims me is her face, lined with worry and something else. Something that looks like guilt.

CHAPTER SIXTEEN

Days bleed into nightmares, reality dissolving like watercolours in rain. Everything runs together: memory, dream, truth, lie. I surface through layers of darkness, never quite reaching the light.

White ceiling. The constant rhythm of machines measuring my life in electronic pulses. A nurse's shadow falls across my bed, her movements quick and birdlike as she suctions the tracheostomy tube. Something about her reminds me of that day in the woods. Swift movements, darting eyes, the sense of being watched. The tubes in my arm writhe like snakes beneath my skin. I try to move, but my body betrays me, weighted with lead and terror.

The hospital gown scratches against my skin, a constant reminder of where I am. The thin mattress crinkles beneath me with every shallow breath. The smell of disinfectant burns my nostrils, making me think of cleaning day at home, when Paul insists everything must be spotless.

Darkness.

Mum's fingers stroking my hair, just like when I was little. The familiar scent of vanilla coffee on her breath washes over me, bringing memories of Saturday mornings and pancakes, before Paul, before everything changed. I try to reach for her hand, but my arms won't cooperate. Her touch is tentative, almost fearful, as if I might shatter under her fingers like delicate glass.

Darkness.

Is it Tuesday yet? I don't think I can manage to eat pizza.

Darkness.

Alone. The clock on the wall reads 3:47. Or 2:47. The numbers swim and dance before my eyes, refusing to stay still. My head feels stuffed with cotton, thoughts slipping away like fish in murky water. Someone moans in pain from another room, the sound echoing down the hallway. The night shift nurses whisper outside my door, their conversations just quiet enough to be unintelligible.

Darkness.

Unfamiliar shoes clicking on linoleum. Hushed voices. Charts being checked. Someone mentions "vitals" and "stable," but the words float past me like autumn leaves. A blood pressure cuff tightens around my arm, its squeeze a distant discomfort. Someone adjusts my IV, the cold rush of new fluids making me shiver. My skin prickles with goosebumps, and I hear someone call for another blanket.

Darkness.

Paul's aftershave. Strong. Toxic.

My eyes flutter open to find him sitting alone beside the bed. No sign of Mum. His presence feels wrong. He leans forward, his voice unexpectedly gentle, so unlike his usual commanding tone.

"She's just gone to the loo. Can't hold it in now."

He smiles like he's made a joke, and then sits back again, like he doesn't know what to say to me. The chair creaks beneath his weight.

His shirt is pressed perfectly, control in every crease. Even here, he maintains his immaculate appearance, not a hair out of place.

I wonder how many times he's been to see me.

I wonder if she makes him come with her.

Then, out of nowhere, so quietly that I barely hear him, he says, "They're doing their best for Sarah."

The first words anyone has spoken about her.

Relief floods through me, warm and swift. The monitor beside me beeps faster. My hands move instinctively toward the tracheostomy tube, as if I could somehow remove it, somehow force words past the plastic in my throat.

Where? How? When? The questions burn inside me, impossible to voice. I try to catch Paul's eye, to make him understand, somehow. I need to know more, but the medication is already pulling me under, down to a place where questions don't matter.

Darkness.

Mum again, this time with Paul following behind her like a dark sentinel. Is this the same day?

He's wearing a sweater now. Casual. Time has passed.

Her eyes are red-rimmed, her hands trembling as she fusses with my blanket, avoiding my gaze. The baby bump beneath her dress seems more pronounced than I remember.

She keeps glancing at Paul, as if seeking permission to speak. Her fingers twist the tissue in her hands until it shreds, little white pieces falling like snow onto the floor. She opens her mouth several times but closes it again, words dying before they reach her lips.

Darkness.

A different nurse. New medications dripping into my veins, cold tendrils snaking through my body, making everything fuzzy around the edges. She checks my bandages with gentle hands, murmuring something about healing nicely. Her name tag reads *Linda,* but the letters keep rearranging themselves like puzzle pieces. Her touch is professional but kind, reminding me of Sarah's mum, Joyce, and her warm hugs.

Darkness.

Alone. The ceiling fan spins lazy circles, hypnotic as my thoughts spiral. Sarah's face floats in my mind, but not how I want to remember her. Not laughing as she helped me stumble through cross country, always patient, always waiting, always the strong one, despite her asthma. Not the hundred thousand moments of her quiet strength, pulling me through life like she pulled me through that run.

No. I see her there in the dirt, moments before the blindfold. The terror in her eyes. The way she tried to tell me something through her gag when he dragged her away. I hear it all again: the quieted sounds, her struggle for breath, my own heart thundering as I lay there helpless, throat pouring blood into the earth. His grunts. Her whimpers.

I couldn't even scream for her. Couldn't move. Couldn't stop what he was doing to her. Just had to lie there, dying by inches, while he.... while she...

I don't remember. I won't remember.

My heart rate quickens, but the wailing of my mechanical babysitter is nothing compared to the sounds that echo in my head. Sarah. My best friend. My protector. And at the moment she needed me most, all I could do was bleed.

Darkness comes again, but it brings no peace. In the darkness, Sarah is always reaching for me. And I can never, ever reach back.

CHAPTER SEVENTEEN

Eventually, the darkness doesn't come as often, and I know they must be weaning me off the strongest medications. Reality seeps back in like water under a door: cold, unstoppable, terrifying.

Each time I surface, I stay longer.

Think clearer.

Remember more.

I wish I didn't.

They removed the tracheostomy tube yesterday. I remember fragments: the doctor's careful explanation, Mum's anxious fretting, the strange sensation as they deflated something called a cuff.

The final removal felt like drowning in reverse: sudden pressure, panic, then the shock of breathing normally again.

Now every breath feels wrong, like my body has forgotten how to do it naturally. The hole where the tube sat is covered with a dressing, tender to touch. But underneath that discomfort is something else: a strange emptiness where the tube used to be. Like my throat is finally my own again, even if I can't make it work yet.

The doctors warned me it would take time before I could speak. Said the damage to my vocal cords needs to heal, and the stoma, the hole where the tube was, needs to close. Forcing sound too soon could cause permanent harm. But being free of the tube makes me want to try anyway, even though my throat still feels like I've swallowed broken glass. The agony has dulled to something almost bearable. Almost.

When I swallow, I can feel the pull of healing tissue, the forming scar tight and angry. Every breath reminds me of that night, of blood soaking into earth, of Sarah's terror.

I try to count the days since that night, but they blur together in a haze of pain and medication. How long have I been here? A week? Two? Time stretches and contracts like a rubber band. Sometimes an hour feels like a minute, sometimes a minute feels like a day. Only Sarah's name remains constant in my mind, a steady pulse beneath the fog of medication.

The nightmares are getting worse. Last night, Sarah's screams mixed with the beeping of my heart monitor until I couldn't tell which was which. I woke gasping, my damaged throat seizing with the effort of trying to cry out. The taste of copper flooded my mouth, and that's when I knew I couldn't wait any longer.

Without the tube blocking my throat, I might be able to say her name.

I need to know where she is. I need to see her.

The day shift arrives at seven. Medication rounds at eight. Vitals at nine. David always comes to check my IV around ten.

He's all efficiency, no small talk. When he speaks to Mum, his words are measured, clinical.

"She's doing well."

"Everything is as we would expect."

"No, I can't tell you when she'll be able to talk again."

With the doctors, I'm reduced to numbers. David talks to my consultant, Dr Miles, in his calm, steady voice. Pulse rate. Blood pressure. Pain scale. I listen as they discuss my case like I'm not even here, like I'm just another set of data points on their charts.

But every day at ten, Nurse David leans in close, concentration furrowing his brow as he adjusts the drip rate.

Close enough to hear a whisper.

I practice in silence when they're not looking, shaping my mouth around her name until my lips know it by heart. Sarah. The 'S' like a secret. The 'ah' soft as a sigh. The 'rah' rough in my ruined throat. Over and over, testing the movement, feeling the pull of damaged tissue.

One word. That's all I need. One word to break this conspiracy of silence. One word to make them finally speak to me.

Today, the clock on the wall seems to move in slow motion. Eight o'clock. The medications make me float, but I fight to stay alert. Nine o'clock. My vitals are steady. Nine forty-five. I hear David's voice in the hallway, discussing another patient.

Soon.

It's almost time.

David isn't like the other nurses. They bustle and chat, their movements quick and casual. He moves like someone who's being watched, every gesture measured, deliberate, accurate. Sometimes though, I see his hands linger too long on my chart. His eyes stay fixed on my face, like he's waiting for something. I see a side of him that really, genuinely cares about me.

Today, I'm going to give him what he's waiting for.

I've been saving my saliva, ignoring the cotton-dry ache in my mouth. Each swallow is like razor blades in my throat, but I need the moisture to form the sound. One word. Just one word. I've never needed anything so desperately in my life.

I know the doctors said I shouldn't, but every cell in my body tells me I should. I need to ask about her.

I've learned to read the hospital's language. The soft-soled shuffle means morning meds. The click-click-click means doctors doing rounds. The squeak of David's shoes is different: a precise rhythm, like a metronome marking time until our moment arrives. Eight steps from door to bed. Three to the IV stand. One final step that brings him close enough to hear a whisper.

In and out of my medicated haze, these are the facts that have become fixed in my mind. Watching, counting, waiting.

I know before he arrives, before David appears in the doorway. Each step brings him closer to the IV stand. Closer to my one chance.

I focus every particle of my being into my throat, into my tongue, into my lips. The machinery around me fades away. The pain recedes. There is only this moment, this breath, this word burning inside me like a coal.

He reaches for the IV port, leaning in close. The angle is perfect, his ear nearly level with my mouth. Now. Everything I am contracts into this single second. My damaged vocal cords strain like violin strings about to snap.

"Ssssss..."

Fire explodes through my neck. Tears spring to my eyes. No. I won't fail. Not now.

"...aaahhh..."

Heat radiates from the healing stoma as air escapes through both my mouth and the partially closed hole in my throat. The sound is barely audible, more breath than voice, but David's head snaps up.

"...rrrrruh."

David freezes. The world stops spinning.

"ssssrrrrhhhh."

The almost word hangs in the air like smoke. Tiny. Fragile. Malformed.

I wasted my chance.

I failed her again.

"Stop. Don't try to speak yet," David says quickly.

I need to talk. I have questions. I have so many questions. The attempt was more draining than I expected. My throat spasms, pain radiating from the healing stoma up through my jaw. Tears roll down my cheeks as I try to breathe through the agony.

He softens, and says, "Hey, we'll get the speech therapist along to see you, okay? You'll be speaking again before you know it. But not yet, Amanda. Not yet." My frown doesn't placate him. He gives me a tight-lipped smile and, with kind eyes, continues, "You're much more lucid today. More present than you've been. Maybe we could try the whiteboard again?"

Again?

He must see the confusion on my tear-stained face because he adds, "You weren't ready before. The medication..." He pauses, choosing his words carefully. "You weren't quite with us."

A whiteboard, or apparently *The Whiteboard*, appears in front of me, with a marker, already uncapped. My hands shake as I grip it, but I force myself to focus. Only one word matters.

The tip stutters over the shiny surface as I try to remember how to form letters.

Each movement takes more effort than I used in trying to say the word. This time, though, this time I'm not going to waste my shot.

The letters are hard won, but I win them.

Sarah?

The question mark is crooked, desperate. My first real communication in weeks - the only thing I need to know. I tap the whiteboard where her name is written, once, twice, my finger leaving smudges in the ink.

Please.

Please tell me.

David studies the word for a long moment, his expression carefully neutral. His eyes track my tapping finger, but he doesn't respond to my silent plea. Instead, he straightens, snapping into his professional persona.

"The police will want to speak with you," he says finally. "Now that you're more alert. Do you think you're up to it?"

He can't just ignore my question. I furiously point at the board, hands shaking as I write again:

Where is she?

The letters are bigger this time, urgent. Each one takes an age to write; I'm exhausted by the time I dot the question mark. I tap them harder, the marker squeaking against the board as I underline them twice.

David's hand moves toward my IV. "You need to stay calm."

I knock his hand away from the medication port, surprising us both with the sudden movement. No more top ups. No more sleeping. I need to know.

I shake my head and jab at the board.

He sighs, stepping back. "Amanda, I'm not authorised to..." He stops, reconsiders. "The police will explain everything. But first, you need to be stronger. You need to be ready."

I grip the marker tighter, flip the board with unsteady hands, and write one last time:

Ready now.

My fingers ache from the effort, but I hold his gaze. I won't let him sedate me again. I won't let him brush this off.

I close my eyes momentarily, drained from the effort of writing, my throat burning from the attempted sound. But unlike before, I fight to keep the darkness at bay. I force my eyes open again, focusing on the whiteboard where I've written *Ready now.*

David studies my demand as though he's trying to work out the best way to respond.

"I'll speak to Dr Miles," he says finally, backing toward the door. "And your mother. But Amanda, you need to understand... the police have been waiting to talk to you, but we needed to be certain you were... stable enough."

He pauses in the doorway. "Try to rest," he says, his voice gentler than before. "And please, don't try to talk again."

As the door closes behind him, I clutch the whiteboard tighter instead of letting it slip away. I focus on Sarah's name, tracing each letter with my finger. The sensation grounds me, keeps me present. *S-a-r-a-h.* Five letters that mean everything. Five letters no one wants to discuss.

I picture her in another room, maybe on another floor. Recovering like me. Or maybe she's already been discharged. Maybe she's at home, waiting for word that I'm finally awake.

But something doesn't add up. If Sarah is okay, why won't they just tell me? Why did David's eyes fill with something that looked too much like pity when I asked where she is?

A memory surfaces: Sarah's hand being torn from mine. I remember it, but somehow, I'm also not quite sure whether it actually happened.

I remember clearly, though, her screams fading as consciousness left me. The weight of my failure pressing me into the damp earth.

I can finally feel something stronger than the drugs coursing through my veins.

Determination.

I stare at Sarah's name on the whiteboard, my finger tracing each letter over and over. The police want to talk to me? Good. I need the police. I need someone to answer my questions.

And this time, I'm not going to let anyone silence me.

CHAPTER EIGHTEEN

Something feels different now. The world is sharper, clearer. It's like emerging from deep water; sounds and sensations are finally reaching me undistorted. I've been drowning in medication for... how long? Days blend into each other in my memory: fragments of voices, hands checking vitals, needles sliding into veins. But today I can hold on to a thought without it slipping away.

Every sensation feels razor-edged: the pressure of the pulse oximeter on my finger, the steady drip of the IV marking time. The pain medication still flows through the syringe pump, but it's not enough to dull everything anymore. Not enough to make me retreat into that comfortable haze where nothing matters. It's enough to keep the throbbing in my neck under control, but not to keep me under control. Not anymore.

And that tube in my throat is gone.

The door opens and a woman with close-cropped grey hair and glasses perched on her nose enters, carrying a folder.

I've not met her before, that I remember.

"Amanda? I'm Kate Elliott, the speech-language pathologist," she says, moving to my bedside with brisk efficiency. "Nurse David mentioned you tried to speak. Not even twenty-four hours post-decannulation. That's quite ambitious."

She pulls a chair closer to my bed, her movements efficient but not unkind. Her eyes fall to the whiteboard in my lap, to Sarah's name scrawled in shaky letters.

"Looking for someone," she observes. "Your friend?"

I nod, relief flooding through me at being understood. I tap Sarah's name again on the board.

Kate's expression softens slightly. "David mentioned you've been asking about her. Your mother is on her way in, and I understand they're contacting the police as well."

It's still not an answer, but I feel a rush of gratitude toward David. He didn't just ignore me after all.

Kate leans forward, adjusting her glasses. "Let me be clear, Amanda. You are not physically ready to speak. Your tracheal stoma is still healing, your vocal cords have been traumatised, and forcing vocalisation now could cause permanent damage." Her voice is firm but not unkind. "But I understand the urgency you're feeling."

She opens her folder and pulls out a glossy pamphlet, setting it on my tray. "These are exercises we'll start with. Breathing techniques first, to reestablish proper airflow. Then, once the stoma begins to close more, we'll move to gentle humming exercises."

I stare at the pamphlet, frustration building in my chest. Weeks. It will take weeks before I can properly communicate.

I don't want to hum; I want to scream.

Kate seems to read my thoughts. "I know it feels impossible to wait, especially when you have something urgent to say. But there are other ways to communicate in the meantime." She taps the whiteboard. "Your fine motor skills will improve with practice. And I'll bring you some communication boards with common phrases to make things easier."

She demonstrates a breathing exercise, having me place my hand over my diaphragm. "Like this. Slow and deep. Helps your body remember how to breathe normally after the tracheostomy."

I follow her instructions mechanically, my mind still fixed on Sarah. On the empty space where answers should be.

"I'll be back this afternoon to start our first proper session," Kate says, checking her watch. "I'd like to speak with your mother too, once she arrives. She needs to understand the recovery process."

As she finishes, I hear a commotion in the hallway. Rushed footsteps, familiar voices. Mum. And Paul.

"Perfect timing," Kate says, moving toward the door. "I believe your family is here."

Mum bursts in, her face flushed like she's been running. Paul drifts in the doorway behind her, a dark shape at the edge of my vision.

"She tried to speak?" Mum's voice cracks. Her eyes find mine, wide with worry and fear.

"Mrs Gray," Kate begins, extending her hand. "I'm Kate Elliott, Amanda's speech therapist. Yes, she attempted vocalisation, which is why I'm here."

"Is she... will she be able to...?" Mum doesn't finish the question.

"Recovery takes time," Kate explains in that same firm-but-kind tone. "The tracheostomy was only removed yesterday. Her vocal cords need to heal, and the stoma needs to close more before she can safely attempt speech."

Mum's hand finds mine, squeezing too tight. "That's... that's good though, right? And she wrote?" She gestures to the whiteboard in my lap. "That's progress, too."

But there's something wrong in her voice - a tremor that doesn't match her words. Like progress isn't something she wants to face. Like progress means questions.

"It is progress," Kate confirms, "but we need to proceed cautiously. I've explained to Amanda that pushing too hard could set her recovery back significantly."

I watch Mum's face carefully. The relief that flickers there when Kate mentions weeks of therapy before speech.

The way her eyes avoid the name on my whiteboard. The nervous glance she exchanges with Paul.

They don't want me to talk. They don't want me to ask about Sarah.

Why?

Kate continues explaining the recovery process, but her words fade to background noise as I study my mother's reactions. Something isn't right. Something beyond the trauma, beyond my injuries.

What aren't they telling me?

Beyond that question, I notice things I was too medicated to see before. Through my window, daffodils bloom in the hospital garden, their yellow heads nodding in the breeze. The last time I was outside, I was walking past trees with bare branches, searching for early spring bluebells with Sarah. The sunlight streaming through my window feels different, warmer, like the world has moved on without me.

Kate glances at her watch. "I should mention that I'm not the only one who's been waiting to speak with Amanda," she says carefully. "The police have been checking in regularly on her condition. We need to let them know she is trying to communicate. It's been six weeks. They need to try again."

Six weeks? The words sink in, slow and suffocating, like drowning in air. I've lost six weeks.

It's the end of April already.

The memories come now, surfacing like bodies in dark water. Fragments I'd forgotten until this moment: A whiteboard (The Whiteboard?) falling from trembling fingers, the plastic clattering against sterile rails. My heart monitor shrieking as panic clawed up my throat, nurses rushing in with sedatives. The consultant's face swimming above me, mouth moving with words I couldn't grasp.

Time dissolving between each attempt until I couldn't tell if hours or days had passed.

I remember now. Or rather, I remember not remembering. Those first attempts at consciousness, where reality slipped through my fingers like morning mist. The crushing weight of darkness whenever I tried to think about that night. More recently (last week? The week before?), staring at the empty board while voices murmured encouragement I couldn't seem to hear.

How many times had they tried to reach me? The memories blur together, different days, same result. Every attempt ending with my retreat into the safety of unconsciousness. But today feels different. Today, the fog has lifted enough to let me think, to let me remember.

My mother's voice is filled with protest. "But she's been so confused, with all the medications... You said yourself she needs weeks before she can speak properly."

"She doesn't need to speak," Kate explains. "The whiteboard communication is enough. She's lucid and responsive. We've been reducing the morphine, and she's managing on the standard basal rate. Attempting to talk, despite my professional disapproval, shows her determination to communicate."

A sharp knock at the door interrupts their discussion. I vaguely recognise the medical team that's been overseeing my recovery: the consultant, Dr Miles, with two other doctors.

"Mrs Gray," Dr Miles says with a nod to my mother. "I see you've met Ms Elliott." She turns to me, her expression warming slightly. "Amanda. I understand there's been significant improvement today."

Kate steps back, allowing Dr Miles to approach my bed. "She's communicating through writing," Kate confirms.

"And attempted vocalisation, though I've advised against further attempts at this stage."

The mist that's floated around my mind for weeks is finally lifting. Each breath feels sharper, each thought clearer. I can think about that night without drowning in darkness. I need to tell them everything.

I motion at the board.

Turn it over.

Read the question.

Read her name.

Tell me where she is.

They just keep talking. About me, around me, but not to me.

"The early stages of recovery were difficult," the consultant says, flipping through my chart. "Between the trauma, the pain medication, and the psychological shock, communication wasn't possible. But Amanda's latest psychological evaluation is promising; it suggests she's both able and willing." She sounds like she's delivering a lecture, reciting my medical history like a script.

She taps the whiteboard where I scrawled 'Ready now.' "The important thing isn't just that she managed to say a word. It's that she's trying. That shows significant progress. I agree. Amanda wants to communicate."

"And the trauma team believes she's ready to try," Dr Miles adds. At least she looks at me when she speaks, though there's something cautious in her voice, like she's stepping through a minefield. "We'll have support in place... for whatever comes next."

I nod, remembering the psychologist who'd visited yesterday with her clipboard of careful questions. *How would you rate your anxiety on a scale of one to ten? Are you experiencing flashbacks? Nightmares?*

I'd answered as truthfully as I could, knowing what was at stake. They wouldn't let me talk to the police otherwise. I'd passed the test, despite being honest about the nightmares, but the psychologist's parting words still echo: "*This is just preliminary, Amanda. Once you're physically stronger, we'll need to do the real work.*"

I squeeze Mum's hand, hard. I've been trapped in silence for six weeks while he's out there somewhere. My free hand moves frantically, miming writing.

I point again at the board.

I *am* ready.

But Sarah. Sarah.

Where is she?

"We'll continue using the whiteboard," Kate says firmly. "Amanda needs to rest her vocal cords, even though she would clearly like to start using them." She smiles at me like an aunt that's just slipped me a sweet I'm not allowed. "I'm confident that she can write what she needs to say. And of course I'll bring the communication boards."

Paul steps forward, his hand finding Mum's shoulder. "After everything she's been through... couldn't we wait? Just a few more days?"

I shake my head violently, ignoring the pull of scar tissue. Don't they understand? Every day we wait is another day he's free.

The consultant watches my reaction carefully. "I can see Amanda is eager to communicate with the investigators. That's a good sign."

Mum's hand trembles in mine. "But she's *not* ready. She needs more time to..."

I gesture more urgently for something to write with, grabbing towards the board. The movement sends pain shooting through my neck, but I don't care. I need them to understand. I need to tell them everything: about his voice, about the dog lead, about Sarah's screams...

"Perhaps," Dr Miles says, noting my determination, "we should let Amanda decide if she feels ready."

Paul's fingers dig into Mum's shoulder. "Abby..."

There's a warning in his voice that makes my skin crawl. The single word carries enough weight to make my mother's shoulder curve inward, away from me.

But I'm already nodding, my eyes locked on my mother's face. She wants to protect me, just like she always has. I understand that, but he is out there. They haven't caught the man who did this to me, to us, and it's up to me and Sarah to give them everything we can so they can find him.

Maybe she's already given them a statement. Maybe her recovery has been faster than mine. But even as I think it, something shifts in my chest, a cold certainty I'm not ready to face. If Sarah were able to speak, would they really be so desperate to hear from me?

The consultant's expression doesn't change, but her voice carries a new edge of authority. "I understand your concern, but this is a police matter. They need to speak with Amanda while her memories are still fairly fresh."

Memories. The things I tried to remember and the things I have tried to forget. They are fresh: knife-sharp and burning. All the details preserved like insects in amber. His voice. The dog lead. Sarah's pain...

Everything up to a point. And then...

"Detective Barnes has been checking in regularly," Kate says.

"They could be here tomorrow morning if we let them know Amanda is ready," the consultant continues. "Give you all time to prepare."

Everyone's looking at me like they're waiting for something to break. Mum and I stare at each other. I can't read the expression in her eyes, or maybe I just don't want to. But it doesn't matter. I can finally help.

Sarah should be the one telling them everything. But if she can't, then I will. I'll remember every detail, every word, every moment, and I'll make them listen.

CHAPTER NINETEEN

Kate, the speech therapist, returns as promised in the evening, after everyone else has gone. She's brought her folder of techniques and a gentler approach, in contrast to her brisk morning introduction.

"Let's start with some basic breathing techniques," she says, demonstrating how to place my hand on my diaphragm. "Breathe from here, not your chest. This method reduces strain on your throat."

The exercises seem pointless, with so many unanswered questions hanging in the air, but Kate is persistent. When she sees my frustration building, she sets her folder aside.

"You're desperate to communicate," she says. "And I can help with that, even before your voice returns."

She brings out a whiteboard, larger than the one David gave me.

"The police will be here tomorrow," she explains. "You'll want to be prepared. Writing can be as exhausting as speaking when you're recovering from trauma."

From her therapy bag, Kate produces several laminated boards, each filled with words, pictures, and symbols arranged in neat categories.

"Communication boards," she explains, laying them across my lap. "This one's for basic needs: pain levels, comfort, medical concerns." Her finger touches a simple outline of a human body on the first chart.

The dead eyes of the generic figure stare at me from the laminated card. It's a blank canvas, waiting to map my trauma. I shiver involuntarily, imagining pointing to where his knife sliced through my neck, where his hands held Sarah down. The clinical simplicity of it, this paper person with no face, no voice, just areas to indicate pain, feels both necessary and horrifying.

"This one has emotions and sensations," Kate continues, moving to a second board. "And I made this one after speaking with Detective Barnes; terms that might help during your interview tomorrow."

I scan the police interview board: LATER, STOP, NEED BREAK, alongside emotions like AFRAID, ANGRY, SAFE/UNSAFE.

The reality crashes over me like a wave. Tomorrow, I'll sit in this bed, surrounded by police, struggling to write and point my way through the worst experience of my life. I'll have to describe Sarah's terror, the sound of her screams going silent, the feeling of my own blood soaking into the earth, all without a voice. Without any way out for the words rushing through my head, except through these inadequate tools.

How can I possibly make them understand by pointing at cartoon faces and scrawled notes? How can plastic boards and dry-erase markers possibly get across how his voice changed when he spoke to Sarah? Or the particular shade of rusty red his truck might have been in the fading light? Or the exact way Sarah called out to me before everything went dark?

My hands tremble, the enormity of tomorrow's task suddenly overwhelming. The police need details to find the man who did this to us, but what if I can't give them enough? What if I forget something crucial because I am too exhausted from writing, too frustrated by pointing at generic emotion cards?

"There's a letter chart on the back here too," Kate says, turning over one of the communication boards to show me a brightly coloured alphabet, neatly captured in squares.

It reminds me of kindergarten, learning to read, and Kate must see it in my expression.

She gives me a kind smile. “It seems incredibly simple, doesn’t it? But I’ve worked with lots of people who have found it useful.”

I can’t bring myself to look convinced.

“Here. Try it. All you have to do is point to the letters.” She puts the board beside me on the bed.

Of course, I know which letters to choose.

S

A

R

A

H

And she’s right. For this simple word, this simple word that means everything, pointing is easier than writing.

Kate doesn’t flinch like the others. She simply nods.

I’m not going to get any answers from her, either, it seems.

Just in case, I tap the question mark.

“We.... I,” Kate stumbles and turns her eyes away. “I don’t have any information about Sarah, I’m afraid, Amanda,” she says. “I know she’s important to you. But tomorrow, the police will need you to tell them everything you know about *him*. About what happened. Can you tell me what you remember?”

I stare at the boards, feeling tears pool in my eyes.

I want to throw the boards at her. Want to force my damaged throat somehow to scream Sarah’s name until someone answers me. But Kate is steady, patient, waiting.

“Look,” she says gently. “Let’s get some notes written down.”

I don’t want to do anything. I want answers.

“And, I’ll try to find something out, okay?”

I prod the letter S again.

“Yes. I promise. I’ll try to find something out.”

It's the first step forward I've had since Paul told me they were doing all they could for her. I have to trust Kate. I have no other option.

She hands me a tissue, and when I've wiped my eyes, takes it away again, replacing it in my hand with the black marker.

The vast blankness of the whiteboard intimidates me; how will I ever fill it with the details of that day? Where do I even start? With the woods? The man? The knife? My mind jumps between fragments like a scratched DVD, never playing the entire scene in order.

I raise the marker over the board, my hand trembling slightly. Kate waits patiently, not rushing me. Finally, I press the tip to the smooth surface and write the first thing that comes clearly. The first thing I remember seeing.

Red plaid jacket

Not his face. Not his voice. Not the knife. But his jacket. That worn, unwashed lumberjack pattern with its smell of cigarettes and sweat. The detail feels simultaneously trivial and vital. My handwriting is shaky, the letters uneven, but they're mine. The first concrete fact I've managed to share about him.

If I had known when I saw that flicker of red and black check in the distance what it would mean. If I had grabbed Sarah's hand right then and run in the opposite direction, would we both be safe at home now? Would Sarah be sitting in her kitchen with Joyce, complaining about homework? The weight of that moment, that simple, mundane observation of a stranger in the woods, crushes down on me. How can something so ordinary become the dividing line between before and after? Between safety and horror?

I add more words beneath the first, determined now. Still, each one takes so much effort that I wonder how I will ever write everything I need to.

Cigarette smell + BO

The details come faster, fragments of memory sharpening as I write slowly. I can almost smell that stench again: the sour undercurrent beneath the smoke. My nose wrinkles involuntarily, and Kate notices.

"That's good," she says quietly. "Your body remembers too. Trust those physical reactions."

Dog lead (tan leather - NO DOG)

That detail had bothered me from the start, like a splinter under my skin: a dog lead with no dog. It makes perfect sense now. The lead was never meant for walking a pet. It was his prop, his way in. The perfect conversation starter to make two teenage girls stop instead of walking away. *Have you seen my dog?* The oldest trick, and we fell for it.

Of course, the lead had another purpose: to bind Sarah's wrists. The image sears into my mind. I try to push it away. If I think about it too much, I won't be able to write.

The dog lead. How could I have been so stupid? That inconsistency hung in the air like a warning bell, but all I heard was a man who'd lost his pet. I stood there rooted to the spot, making polite conversation about a non-existent dog while he casually positioned himself between us and the path home. Because that's what good girls do. They're helpful, they're polite, they don't overreact.

Even as my instincts screamed danger, I ignored them. Because he was just a man looking for his dog, not a monster hunting for prey.

"Small, controlled movements," Kate says as my hands shake. "Just like the breathing exercises. Take your time."

Eventually, my muscles remember what my mind has almost forgotten. The familiar motion of writing brings other memories with it, sharper, clearer than they'd been in weeks.

"Focus on details," Kate encourages. "Anything you can recall about him. The police will need descriptions, locations, timing."

The marker squeaks against the board as I add details, then rub some out. Was his hair dark or just dirty? Did he limp, or was that just how he walked?

But something more concrete, more important channels through the pen onto the board.

Called me Maggie

Kate's expression changes, just for a moment. She leans forward slightly, studying the name.

"He called you *Maggie*?" she asks carefully. "Consistently? Not just once?"

I nod.

She makes a small note in her folder, her movements deliberate, controlled. But something has shifted in her posture. There's a new tension in her shoulders that wasn't there before.

"That's useful," she says, her tone neutral, but her eyes sharpen. "What else?"

Blind fold. Tied up. Gagged.

This time, Kate can't hide her reaction. Her breath catches, an involuntary sound barely audible but unmistakable in the quiet room. I see her throat work as she swallows, and for a second, the professional distance vanishes. She looks at me, really looks at me, with a mixture of horror and profound sadness.

"I'm so sorry, Amanda," she says softly, and I know she means it.

The simple acknowledgment nearly breaks me. So much of what happened feels unspeakable, but seeing someone else register the horror of it makes it both more real and somehow more bearable. I'm not alone in this nightmare anymore. Someone else can see it too.

When my hand starts to cramp, Kate gently touches my wrist.

"Try the communication boards for a moment. Give your hand a break."

I reluctantly set down the marker and study the police interview board. After a moment, I point to FRUSTRATED.

Kate nods. "That's normal. Your brain is working faster than your hand can write." She taps the whiteboard. "The writing is still the most important. It gives us specifics the boards can't capture. But use both tomorrow. Save your strength for the details only you can provide."

I smile, feeling the pull on my scar, but not caring. I like this woman already. She has given me a way to communicate, and she has given me a promise.

As she stacks her papers and clicks her pen closed, I urgently tap on the letter board.

S

"I promised," she says. "Focus on the interview, and I'll do my best." Then, changing the subject, as everyone does, she looks at my list with professional detachment. "This will help tomorrow. I know it's been difficult, but you should be proud of what you have achieved here."

She stacks the boards neatly on my bedside table, the whiteboard on top.

"Try to get some rest." She stands, and part of me wants to get up and hug her. "I'll be back to continue with your therapy."

I can’t say thank you, and the boards are out of reach, so I raise my hand and give her the thumbs up. Some things are universally understandable.

Kate smiles and returns the gesture before walking out of the room.

The door clicks shut behind her, leaving me alone with the silence.

Tomorrow, the police will come. They’ll ask me to relive it all; they’ll want me to drag the memories from the dark corners of my mind and spill them onto a whiteboard, piece by agonizing piece.

I need to rest. I need to be ready.

But as I lie back against the pillow, staring at the ceiling, I know sleep won’t come.

Tomorrow, I have to tell them everything.

And what if I remember something I don’t want to?

CHAPTER TWENTY

Morning brings a different kind of pain: sharper, cleaner, like a knife's edge rather than yesterday's dull throb. They've reduced my medication again, preparing me for the police interview. Each swallow feels like glass shards scraping my throat, but my mind is clearer than it's been in weeks. I need it to stay that way.

I can hear Kate's voice telling me I should be proud of what I was able to write on the board, but looking at my notes now, I wonder if they are enough.

The list mocks me with its scattered details:

Red plaid jacket (hunting jacket? lumberjack style?)
Cigarette smell + BO
Dog lead (tan leather - NO DOG)
Called me Maggie
Blindfold. Tied up. Gagged.
Truck: red/rusty???
Engine loud
Route: trees hitting roof, bumpy then smooth
????? how long did we drive ?????
Voice: Northern? Not local
Height: shorter than Paul

The question marks multiply across the board, each one a failure. A detail I should remember but can't. Or worse, details I think I remember but can't be sure of. What if I tell them something that isn't true? What if I lead them in the wrong direction?

The more I think about each detail, the less certain I become.

I close my eyes, trying to reconstruct the journey. But everything after he blindfolded me blurs together, time stretching and contracting like a rubber band. The rhythmic sway of the truck, the crunch of gravel, then smoother road. My notes say *trees hitting roof,* but was that before or after the turn? Was there even a turn? The memories slip away when I try to grasp them too tightly.

All night I've been mapping it in my head. If we turned right leaving the woods... but no, I was already blindfolded then. If the sun was still up when we stopped... but I couldn't see anything through the fabric. The blindfold slipped. I saw the red of the truck, but did I see anything else? I don't know. Every detail feels crucial, but I can't trust any of them. Except his voice. That I remember perfectly; the way he said *Maggie* like he knew me. Like he'd said it before.

When Mum appears in the doorway at 8:47am, I'm already sitting up, ready. Paul enters behind her like a shadow. His presence makes me want to hide my notes, though I'm not sure why. Something about the way he looks at the whiteboard makes my skin prickle. I don't want him to know. I don't want to share my nightmares with him. The things written on this board belong to me and Sarah, to that afternoon in the woods.

The police will be here at nine. Thirteen minutes to convince Mum I can do this. Thirteen minutes before I have to tell them everything about that day. About what he did to us.

Mum squeezes my hand. Her palm is clammy against mine, betraying her own anxiety. She's been crying. I can tell from the slight puffiness around her eyes, the way she won't quite look at me directly.

"You don't have to do this today," she says, but there's something rehearsed about it, like she and Paul practised this conversation in the car. "If you're not ready..."

I shake my head, pointing at the whiteboard with my free hand. The movement pulls at my stitches, but I ignore it. I've written as much as I can remember. Everything except the parts I know will break Mum's heart. Those details I've kept in my head, where only I can see them.

There are things I haven't written. Things I can't write. Every time I try, my hand freezes above the board. The sounds... Sarah's sounds... they're locked somewhere in my mind, trying to break free. But trying to capture them in words feels like betraying her somehow. And maybe... maybe if I don't write them down, they won't be real.

Paul moves to stand behind Mum, one hand on her shoulder like always. His eyes scan my messy writing, and I resist the urge to turn the board away.

"'Called me Maggie'," he reads aloud, and something in his tone makes me shiver. "Who's Maggie?"

Who *is* Maggie? I can only shrug, the movement sending fresh pain through my neck. It's just another detail, like his jacket or the dog lead. But Paul's question seems to hang in the air, heavier than it should be. He exchanges a look with Mum that makes my stomach twist.

"Did he..." Paul clears his throat. "Did he say anything else about Maggie?"

I shake my head, pointing at the other details on my list. The truck, what I remember about the route, things that might actually help them find him. But Paul's still staring at that name, his face pale. For once, he seems to have forgotten to maintain his usual composed expression. His fingers drum against Mum's chair in an irritating tap, tap, tap like he's counting seconds until something breaks.

"You know what this means?" Paul hisses into Mum's ear.

She shoots him a sharp look.

"Paul, let's leave it to the police. Don't start..." She waves her hands, and he gets her meaning.

I'd like to say that I haven't thought about it. That I haven't wondered about Maggie. Who she is and why he called me that name.

That I haven't wondered if we weren't the first and won't be the last.

But it was Sarah's name that I used all my strength to say. I should have written it all over this board. Sarah, Sarah, Sarah.

Where is Sarah?

Paul is still staring at Maggie's name like it holds all the answers, but he's wrong. The only answer I need is the one no one will give me. I've wasted precious space on details that don't matter.

My hand shakes as I press the marker to the board one more time, but before I can write Sarah's name, there's a knock at the door. The police are here.

I clutch the whiteboard closer, its edges digging into my palms. The smell of marker ink mingles with antiseptic, making my head swim. All night I've been preparing for this moment, forcing myself to remember things I want to forget. Now that it's here, my carefully printed notes look like a kid's homework assignment. Like something that could never capture the metal taste of fear, the sound of Sarah crying behind her gag, the way darkness felt when he pulled the blindfold tight.

My eyes flicker to the communication boards Kate left on my bedside table. Simple, colourful cards with emotions, yes/no options, and common phrases neatly organised. They seem childish compared to what I need to express, like trying to describe a hurricane with a weather emoji.

My notes. My board. That's all I have without my voice.

CHAPTER TWENTY-ONE

Three people enter; the squeak of their shoes on linoleum sets my teeth on edge. My hospital room, which normally feels too large and empty, suddenly shrinks around me. The walls seem to inch closer with each new body that crosses the threshold. A blonde officer with her hair pulled back severely, a tall male detective who positions himself near the door, and a woman in civilian clothes who makes my throat close up with everything her presence implies.

I can almost feel the oxygen thinning as they arrange themselves around my bed. There's nowhere to look without meeting someone's eyes, nowhere to escape their scrutiny. My breathing shallows as the walls press in: a physical manifestation of the pressure building in my chest. Three strangers, three new witnesses to my trauma.

"Amanda? I'm PC Winters. I'm Melanie. And this is Detective Barnes," the female officer says. Her voice is gentle but professional. The fluorescent lights catch on her badge, sending sharp reflections across the ceiling. She gestures to the woman. "This is Suki from Victim Support. She's here to help make sure you're comfortable with everything we discuss."

Victim Support. The words make me taste copper again. My fingers trace the edges of the whiteboard, following the same pattern over and over, corner to corner to corner, like if I focus hard enough on this simple movement, I won't have to think about what comes next. These facts I've written, these careful bullet points, they tell them nothing about Sarah's screams. Nothing about bleeding out into the dirt while he... while she...

Suki moves closer, creating a careful barrier between me and the police officers. The fabric of her skirt whispers against the bed rail as she positions herself like a shield. Her voice drops low, gentle.

"I'm here solely to support you through this process," she explains. "I'm independent from the police investigation. My role is to make sure your needs are met: if you need a break, if something is unclear, or if you're feeling overwhelmed at any point." She gestures to the communication boards. "You can use these to signal to me, and I'll make sure the officers understand."

She pauses, making sure I'm following.

"This is your story, Amanda. We follow your lead. If you need to stop at any time, we stop. If certain questions are too difficult right now, we can come back to them. And if you'd prefer your mother and..." She gestures almost imperceptibly, "...father to step out at any point, that's completely your decision too."

"He's not my father," I want to tell her, but I'm not going to waste space on the whiteboard with the words.

Paul shifts in his chair, the plastic creaking. "We don't... Amanda's father isn't in contact," he says, like he's confessing someone else's secret.

The words settle like dust. Dad's absence is just another fact of life, like the colour of my eyes or the way Mum takes her coffee. But now, with Paul perched on the edge of that plastic chair, trying to fill a space that stopped aching long ago, everything feels wrong.

If there was any time for Dad to show up for his family, surely it would be now.

He has no place here, anyway.

This moment, this horrible, vulnerable moment, should be just me and Mum. That's how we've always faced things. Just us. The thought of sharing what happened, of letting Paul witness the ugliest parts of my story, makes my skin crawl. It's going to be hard enough with Mum here, watching her face as I describe what the man in the red and black jacket did, even if I am writing it instead of saying it.

"Before we begin," Detective Barnes says, "we need to explain how this interview will work." He glances at my whiteboard, at my trembling fingers, leaving smudged prints along its edges. "We'll be recording everything, and we'll need to photograph your notes. Everything you can tell us is important. If you use the communication boards, I'm going to need you to show what you are pointing at to the camera."

It sounds exhausting.

I nod.

It's time.

Detective Barnes moves to close the door. The sound of it clicking shut feels like a key turning in a lock. Like a blindfold being tied. Like the moment everything changed. The walls press in closer, white and sterile and waiting for truths I'm not sure I'm ready to tell.

My list of facts fills the whiteboard in careful, cramped writing.

Safe details. Things I can share in front of Mum and Paul.

PC Winters studies my notes while Detective Barnes sets up the recording equipment. The red light blinks steadily, waiting. I focus on that instead of the weight of Paul's presence behind Mum, instead of the way Suki has positioned herself like a shield between us.

I look at Suki, catching her eye, hoping she can read my thoughts, sense my discomfort. Hoping she's experienced enough to read my tells.

It's Mum that knows me, though.

"Paul," Mum says suddenly, her voice soft but firm. "Could you give us some space?" Something passes between them - some silent conversation I can't read. "Maybe get me a coffee?"

Paul hesitates, his hand tightening on Mum's shoulder. "Abby..."

"I'll stay with her." Mum reaches up, touches his hand. "We'll be fine."

"But you..." he says, looking at the round of her belly, not her face.

It wasn't stress, it was the amnio. It wasn't your fault. I try to remind myself, but I can't help but think that this is all the last thing that Mum needs right now.

I nearly died.

I try to remind myself. I try.

But Mum is patting Paul's arm and giving him a smile that's as reassuring as she can manage.

He looks at me and hesitates. I almost feel as though he cares about me. He doesn't say anything, though. He steps towards the door, and the tall officer moves out of the way to let Paul pass.

The relief hits me so hard I nearly cry. When the door closes behind him, the room feels bigger somehow, like I can finally breathe. But now there's one less barrier between me and the memories I couldn't write down.

Mum's fingers find mine, warm and steady, joining behind Suki's back like a secret meeting.

Thank you, I think. *Thank you for hearing me, even when I cannot speak.*

The woman, Winters, sits on the PVC covered wooden chair at the head of my bed. Her smile shrinks down in the chubbiness of her face. I wonder if she has to wear her blonde hair in that gelled back ponytail for work, and realise I'm spacing out, not listening to what she's saying to me.

She's already turned her gaze to the taller man standing by the door. Barnes.

He nods towards me.

"You still with us, Amanda?" he asks in an amiable northern accent.

I open my mouth to reply, and close it again like a goldfish, instead nodding my head. My throat feels dry, scratchy, like I've swallowed sand.

I must be getting better if I'm well enough for this.

The woman tries again, shifting forward on the creaking chair. The movement makes the PVC covering squeak uncomfortably against her uniform.

"We just need to ask you a few questions, okay?" She uses that special kind of police gentleness: soft words stretched thin over steel. The kind they save for victims. Each careful syllable makes my skin crawl, like fingers walking up my spine.

"We can stop at any time if you're too uncomfortable," she adds, like she's reading from a manual.

I wonder which kind of discomfort she means. The raw fire in my neck, or the way my mind shrinks away from certain memories like fingers from a hot stove. Physical pain has measurements, scales, neat little charts with numbered faces. But how do you measure the other kind? The kind that makes you want to crawl out of your own skin when you remember.

I smile, or try to, and my fingers ghost the bandage that covers the wound on my throat.

Detective Barnes steps closer to my whiteboard, squinting at my uneven handwriting. His pen lingers over his notepad as he reads each line, occasionally nodding.

"Good instincts," PC Winters says, tapping the list with her pen. "Details like this help." She turns the board over, revealing its blank side. "But we need to start from the beginning. March 16th. Can you write about that afternoon?"

The way she says it makes it sound like a question in a history test. Something that happened long ago that she wants me to try to recall the details of. And really, that's exactly how it feels. Like trying to remember something I read in a textbook, except the memories are razor-sharp and burning behind my eyes. That afternoon in the woods, I don't know how long ago it was. Time has lost all meaning here in hospital. I don't know how long I was out, or how many times I have slipped between consciousness and unconsciousness since. I was there, and now I am here.

The marker feels heavy in my hand. Strange how something so small can suddenly weigh so much. Behind me, the camera's red light blinks steadily, recording every shaky letter I form.

Detention I write, the letters wobbling. I have to stop, adjust my grip. The effort of holding my arm up makes my muscles shake.

I never told Mum about the detention. It seemed so huge then - such a terrible secret to keep. Now it feels absurd that I was worried about it. Like being concerned about a paper cut while bleeding out. I glance at her, but all I see in her face is raw concern, lips pressed tight as she watches me struggle with the marker.

That day feels like it happened to someone else. Some other Amanda who thought detention was the worst thing that could happen to her. Some innocent version of me who didn't know how quickly everything could change.

I want to tell that other Amanda - the one sitting in detention - to run straight home. To not take the long way. To leave the bluebells where they grew. But she's gone now, that girl who thought detention was worth crying over.

Gone as completely as the flowers we left scattered in the dirt.

PC Winters's voice is steady and professional. "And after that?"

Took long way home.

My arm feels like lead, but the memories flow with terrifying precision. PC Winters waits, her practised patience making my skin crawl.

Every word I write could be used later - in court, in newspapers, by people looking to understand why it happened. Looking for someone to blame. But there's no space to explain everything, no strength to defend our choices. Only room for the facts that might help them find him.

The image flashes: his approach through the bluebells. Dog lead. No dog.

I try to turn the images into words.

Stopped for flowers.

I have to pause, letting the marker drop to my lap. My neck throbs in time with my pulse, and I can feel sweat beading at my hairline despite the hospital room's chill. The next part... Every muscle in my body tenses, remembering.

"You're doing great," PC Winters says in that careful voice. "Just take your time."

I lift the marker again, my fingers trembling so badly I have to use both hands to steady it. The bluebells. The scent of spring earth. The sound of his footsteps.

I point at the notes I wrote with Kate.

Dog lead (tan leather - NO DOG)

Then I write: He came up to us

The letters are messy now, slanting across the board. My chest feels tight, like the air is too thick to breathe. I can smell it again - that mixture of cigarettes and unwashed clothes. Taste the metal of fear in my mouth.

I pause again, marker hovering over the board. The next part... the next part is where everything changed. Where our normal afternoon turned into something else entirely. The camera keeps blinking, waiting for words I'm not sure I can write.

"Take your time," PC Winters says, but her pen is poised, ready.

Asked if we'd seen his—

The marker slips, leaving a black slash across the board. My hand is shaking too badly now. The room tilts slightly, and I feel Mum step closer to the bed.

"Maybe we should take a break," she says, but I shake my head. If I stop now, I might not be able to start again.

"You're doing great, Mandy," Barnes says, and I shudder. No one calls me that.

"Can you tell us approximately what time you first saw him?" PC Winters asks, glancing at her notes.

I lower the marker, trying to piece it together. The detention ended at 4:30. I remember watching the clock. Then the walk, the flowers... Everything after that feels stretched and distorted, like time stopped working properly.

Winters hands me the communication board with numbers on it.

I remember that I have to show the camera everything, and it makes me even more paranoid about getting something wrong.

First, I point at where I wrote Detention and then I move my finger to indicate 4:30.

"You left detention at half past four?" PC Winters clarifies, and I nod.

How long were we walking? How long did we spend picking flowers? In my memory, the sunlight was fading, the shadows stretching, but I can't pin down exactly when...

"Take your time," Detective Barnes says. "Even a rough estimate helps."

My hand wavers, uncertain. The light was dimming, but it wasn't dark. Late afternoon but not evening. I point out 5:15 and then my finger jabs the question mark.

I'm not sure. It's the best I have.

"That's still helpful," PC Winters nods, writing something. "And you left school immediately after detention?"

Something catches in my chest. No, we didn't. We stopped in the bathroom first. Sarah was fixing her hair. Such a normal moment. Such a normal day.

The memory hits me with unexpected force: Sarah leaning toward the mirror, tucking strands of hair behind her ear, laughing about something I'd said. Her reflection beside mine, both of us oblivious to what waited ahead. That last perfect moment before everything changed.

All of those thoughts come down to one point of my finger at the board:

No.

CHAPTER TWENTY-TWO

Even with my painstakingly slow writing, it doesn't take long to fill one side of the whiteboard. PC Winters carefully lifts it, angling it toward the camera's red eye. Something about seeing my shaky words captured like that, becoming evidence, makes my stomach clench.

Detective Barnes hands me a fresh board, wiping it clean with a tissue before setting it on my lap. The blank white surface seems to stretch endlessly, waiting to be filled with more details I'm not sure I can face. More memories I'm not sure I can trust.

"You're doing really well," PC Winters says. "Ready to continue with the description? Use the communication boards as much as you want to, but write what you can."

Detective Barnes carefully looks over the first whiteboard, studying the list I made with Kate. "Let's go through what you've written about him. Red plaid jacket - hunting or lumberjack style?"

Some details are carved into my memory with terrible clarity. Like the way his jacket smelled of stale cigarettes and something else, something worse. But his face... Did I even properly see his face before the blindfold?

There's nothing on the communication board for this.

I point at where I wrote Lumberjack and then, on the new board, I write Thick + fleecy.

"Good," PC Winters encourages. "What about his face? Hair colour? Eyes?"

My hand freezes over the board. I try to picture him, to see him clearly, but the memory keeps shifting like smoke. All I can really remember is the crooked smile when he first approached us, the way he showed just enough teeth to make my skin crawl.

The communication board with its generic human outline is no use to me. No use at all.

Dark stubble, I manage to write. *Red face - wind burned??*

But was it wind burn or something else? Everything before the blindfold feels like a series of snapshots. His boots in the grass, the leather lead in his hand, that terrible smile. But putting them together into a complete picture...

"Height?" Barnes prompts, checking my original list. "You wrote 'shorter than Paul'?"

I look at the communication boards again. I don't think in feet and inches; I think in terms of people I know. My hand shakes as I try to explain: *maybe Mum's height??*

PC Winters leans forward next. "You mentioned his voice in your original notes here: 'Northern? Not local?'"

The sound of him floods back - that strange accent that didn't quite fit anywhere. Or was it the way he phrased things?

Fake? I write, the letters slanting with urgency. I don't even know why I think that. Why did his voice strike me as unusual? I have no answers. I only know that there was something off about the way he spoke.

My hand is shaking harder now, but I need them to understand. *Calm. No emotion. Even when...* I stop. The memory hits like a hammer on glass. The terrible rhythmic sounds, Sarah's cries from beneath her gag, his breathing. My chest constricts as the hospital room starts to fade around the edges.

The marker slips from my hand.

I can hear it again - that wet, heavy sound of flesh against flesh. Sarah's struggles growing weaker. My blood pulsing out onto the ground while he... while he...

I force myself to reach for the marker, my vision already starting to tunnel. They need to know. Need to understand.

My eyes dart to the notes I wrote with Kate.

"Mmmmph," I say, slapping my hand over my mouth to stop my reflexive urge to speak.

Maggie. I point at the board.

Called me Maggie.

I can almost hear his voice in my head: *You don't need to see this, Maggie.*

I can't breathe. Can't focus.

Detective Barnes and PC Winters exchange a look I can't quite read. Barnes leans forward slightly.

"He called you Maggie?" he repeats, his tone neutral but his eyes sharp with new attention. "Not Amanda?"

I nod frantically, jabbing my finger at the words again. This matters. I don't know why, but I know it matters.

"Did he ask your name?" Barnes isn't looking at me; he's already looking at the communication board.

No.

PC Winters leans over her notepad. "Was it just once, or did he call you this repeatedly?"

I reach for the whiteboard again, hand trembling as I write: Always Maggie.

Barnes's face doesn't change, but I see something shift in his posture: a subtle tensing, a new alertness.

"Did he seem confused?" he asks carefully. "Like he was mixing you up with someone? Or did he seem to know exactly who he was talking to?"

The question hits something. A memory surfaces: the certainty in his voice when he said that name. Like he was speaking to someone he knew well. Someone he'd spoken to many times before.

Knew her, I write, the letters large and uneven. Not confused. Like I was her.

PC Winters is writing rapidly now, her pen scratching across the page. Barnes glances at Suki, who's remained quietly observant throughout the interview. Something passes between them, a look loaded with professional concern I can't interpret.

"Did he say anything else about Maggie?" Barnes asks. "Anything that might tell us who she is?"

I close my eyes, pushing past the wall of fear to remember his exact words. One phrase comes back with terrible clarity. I open my eyes and force my shaking hand to write:

It's that time again, Maggie.

The silence that follows is absolute. Even the monitors seem to quiet for a moment as everyone stares at what I've written.

Officer Winters breaks the silence first. "Again," she says softly. "Implying repetition."

"A pattern," Barnes agrees, his voice careful, controlled, but I can hear the tension beneath it.

Something is happening here: something beyond my understanding. The atmosphere in the room has changed, charged with a new urgency.

Suki shifts forward slightly in her chair as she exchanges a look with the detectives. I don't miss the subtle widening of her eyes, the way her hand tightens on her notebook. She quickly composes herself, turning her attention back to me with deliberate calm.

Barnes turns away slightly, already reaching for his radio. Even though he's speaking towards the door, I catch fragments of what he's saying: "...new lead... possible serial... check missing persons..."

Serial. The word lands like a stone in my stomach.

Winters is still watching me, her expression professionally blank but her eyes burning with intensity.

"Amanda, this is extremely helpful information. We need to look into this name right away."

Serial.

Serial.

The word has just filtered into my dumb head.

Serial killer? Did he *kill* Sarah?

I grab for the board again, my desperation giving me one last burst of strength. SARAH? I write, the letters shaky but clear. I point to the question mark over and over.

My message is clear: I've given you something important. Now tell me about Sarah.

Where is Sarah?

My hand barely cooperates for these last words.

The fluorescent lights blur and swim as panic claws up my throat.

"Amanda?" Mum's voice seems very far away. "I think that's enough for today."

PC Winters is already standing, signalling to someone in the hallway. "Get the nurse," she says sharply, her professional calm finally cracking.

I'm aware of movement around me: nurses rushing in, Mum's hand gripping mine. But I'm trapped in that moment, in those sounds, in my failure to help Sarah.

"Deep breaths," someone is saying, but all I can hear is Sarah's last whimper before she went silent.

As the room fades around me, all I can see is her name scrawled on the whiteboard.

CHAPTER TWENTY-THREE

When I wake, Mum's still here, sitting on the side of the bed. At first, I think it means I can't have been out for long, but the curtains are drawn now, and instead of morning sun, I see darkness seeping through the cracks.

Where are the police? Did I tell them enough? The memory of the whiteboard, my shaky handwriting becoming evidence, feels distant and unreal. Did any of it help?

"Amanda," Mum says, seeing my eyes open. She glances toward the door, then gets up to close it with deliberate care. The soft click of the latch feels ominous.

"There's something I need to tell you," she says, and my mind immediately goes to the baby.

After everything, the blood, the hospital, Paul's accusations... she must have lost it. And God help me, for one terrible moment, I hope she has. Because if that's what she needs to tell me, if that's the worst thing that's happened...

I have to stop myself from thinking about those things.

I hate myself for wishing tragedy on my unborn brother, for being willing to trade his life for the answer I desperately need.

Mum's eyes keep darting to the door, like she's about to share a forbidden secret. Like someone might stop her if they knew.

"Darling, I'm so sorry." Her voice cracks. "I wanted to tell you when you first woke up. I didn't want to lie to you. I mean, I haven't lied, but..." Her leg is bouncing, the motion jittery and uncontrolled. I don't think she even notices. "They said it might hold back your healing. You... you almost died. I thought I was doing the right thing, but..."

I know what Mum's going to say. I've known since I woke up alone in this room. Since no one would answer my questions. Since Paul's strange comment about them 'doing their best'. The knowledge sits like ice in my chest - Sarah is dead. He killed her after he thought he'd killed me. After I lay there, useless, bleeding out while he...

"Amanda," Mum's voice breaks through my spiralling thoughts. "Sarah is still missing."

The words don't make sense at first. Missing? Not dead?

Missing means alive. Missing means hope. Missing means...

Missing means she's out there.

With him.

"Neeeugh!" No. The word rips from my throat, shredding through damaged tissue. Fire explodes in my neck, but I can't stop. "Nnn..." Something hot and metallic rises in my throat as I try to force out more words, my body warring with itself - the need to speak fighting against the physical impossibility of it.

"Amanda, stop!" Mum's hands flutter over my shoulders as I choke and gasp. "You'll damage your throat!"

But how can I be quiet? How can I just lie here in this clean, white room while Sarah is missing? While he has her?

Mum pulls me against her chest, the gesture both comfort and restraint. Her heart pounds against my ear as she holds me still.

"That's why the police needed to talk to you so urgently," she whispers into my hair. "They've been waiting six weeks for you to wake up and recover enough to talk to them, hoping you might remember something that could help them find her."

Six weeks. The words echo in my head as I try to piece together how I got here. How I was found. The memories stop at blood soaking into earth, at his fingers checking my pulse, at him walking away. Everything after that is darkness.

I couldn't have left her there. I wouldn't. Even bleeding out, even dying, I would never have left Sarah behind.

Would I?

My heart races as I try to remember. Did someone find me? Did I manage to get help? The thought that I might have saved myself while leaving Sarah with him makes me physically sick.

"You were incredibly lucky," Mum says quietly, without noting the irony. "A couple driving home took a wrong turn and found you on that back road. They didn't wait for an ambulance, just rushed you straight to the hospital. They got you here at 9:13 and you were in the operating theatre before half past. The police... they searched everywhere, but there was no sign of Sarah."

How did I get to the road? The last thing I remember is lying in the dirt, feeling my life drain away. Did he move me? Did Sarah somehow...? The possibilities spiral through my mind, each one worse than the last.

Was I lucky?

Was I really?

I need to remember. Need to understand how I got away while Sarah didn't. But the memories won't come - just fragments of sensation.

My heart is beating out of my chest, but I need to tell them more. Need to remember something else that could help find her. I scrabble over the blanket, searching for a marker, a board, anything to write with.

"Baby, please," Mum says, reaching for my hands. "The police are following every lead. They're going to find her."

But all I can think about is Sarah, alone with him somewhere, probably wondering why I never tried to save her.

I picture Joyce sitting in Sarah's room, touching her daughter's clothes, waiting for news.

Did she keep making pancakes these past six weeks, setting a plate at Sarah's place?

Does she hate me for coming back when Sarah didn't?

Have I even come back yet?

The thought of Joyce breaks something in me. I try to speak, ignoring the fire in my throat. Need to tell Mum to call her, to tell her I'm sorry, that I tried, that I would trade places if I could. But all that comes out is a wet, choking sound that makes Mum's face crumple.

I know I have to stay calm, despite how I feel. If I think about her out there, I'll lose it, I know. I can't do that in front of Mum. I wasn't to blame for her bleeding before, but now? All this stress can't be good for her and the baby. Instead, I focus on the wall behind Mum's head, counting the tiny cracks in the plaster. If I look at her face, if I see the pain there, I'll break. And I can't break. Not yet. Not while she's here, watching me like I might shatter.

Thirty-seven cracks. I start counting again.

My throat burns with unshed tears, with screams I can't voice. But I keep my face carefully blank, my hands steady in my lap. Mum needs me to be okay. She needs to believe I can handle this.

I can't.

I really can't.

She's been talking for twenty minutes, filling the silence with careful explanations. Search parties. Police investigations. Dead ends. Each word is a knife, but I don't let her see me bleed.

"They're doing everything they can," she says for the third time. "They're still looking."

I nod, like this is just another conversation. Like my best friend isn't missing. Like I didn't somehow get myself to safety while leaving her behind. With him.

The thought makes bile rise in my throat. How did I get to that road? Why can't I remember?

What kind of person survives but can't remember how? What kind of friend leaves without knowing if...

No. Focus on the cracks. Thirty-seven. Thirty-eight. The paint is peeling in one corner.

How long has it been since I stared at the bruised wallpaper of my bedroom?

"Amanda?" Mum's voice breaks. "Please look at me."

I can't. If I meet her eyes, she'll see everything I'm holding back. The guilt. The horror. The crushing weight of six weeks lost while Sarah was out there somewhere, waiting for help that never came.

Instead, I reach for her hand, squeeze it gently. I'm okay, the gesture lies. I'm handling this. Don't worry.

I breathe slowly, carefully, until the heart rate monitor steadies. I've had practice hiding pain these past weeks. Physical therapy. Wound care. Each small agony carefully masked so Mum wouldn't worry more than she already does.

But this pain is different. This truth is a scar I can't hide.

Paul appears in the doorway around eight, his face drawn with concern. He manages to smile in my direction before addressing Mum.

"Abby," he says softly. "You need to rest. Think of the baby."

Mum's hand tightens on mine. "I can't leave her. Not now."

But I see the exhaustion in the slope of her shoulders, the way she keeps shifting in the hard hospital chair. She's been here since morning, and beneath her loose dress, my brother grows heavier by the day. For once, Paul is right.

I squeeze her fingers, then deliberately let go. The gesture takes it out of me, but I manage a small nod.

Go. It's okay.

I hold myself together, stay strong for her like Sarah always stayed strong for me.

"We'll be back first thing," Paul promises, helping Mum to her feet. The gentleness in his touch, the way he supports her weight - I hate that he's being kind. Hate that he's doing what's best for her. Hate that I can't hate him, not completely, not when he's making sure she takes care of herself when I can't.

The door clicks shut behind them and something inside me shatters.

Six weeks.

The thought hits me like a physical blow now that I don't have to be strong for Mum. My chest heaves as I try to gulp in air, each breath catching on the wreckage in my throat.

He took us where no one could hear us scream. And even now, weeks later, the silence holds us both: Sarah, wherever she is, and me, here. My voice trapped in my damaged throat.

He wanted us silenced. Wanted us where no one would hear.

I need to find my voice, and I need to do it soon.

CHAPTER TWENTY-FOUR

The speech therapy pamphlet Kate left sits on the bedside unit, its exercises taunting me with their methodical slowness. Just like everyone's been pretending not to say Sarah's name, the pamphlet pretends recovery can take weeks, not days.

He wanted us silent. But I won't be. Not anymore. Sarah needs my voice.

And I'm going to make myself heard.

I have to, because it's not too late to help her.

My hands shake as I open the pristine pages. The first exercises are simple: tongue placement, breath control, humming. Things Kate insists must be mastered before attempting actual speech.

But pain doesn't matter anymore. Nothing matters except finding my voice.

I run my finger down the list, past a coffee stain, to the first instruction. Breathing exercises. Control your breath. Build strength.

Shifting up in the bed sends daggers through my neck, but I ignore them. Focus on breathing the way the sheet describes. In through the nose, slow and steady. Hold. Out through the mouth. Again.

My throat protests with each controlled exhale. The wound may have healed on the outside, but inside everything feels raw, damaged. Wrong.

Like me. Damaged. Wrong. The kind of friend who somehow saved herself and left Sarah behind.

No. I push the thought away. Breathe in. Hold. Out.

The night nurse pokes her head in, and I close my eyes, pretend to sleep until she leaves. As soon as her footsteps fade, I start again.

Breathing becomes humming. Small sounds that vibrate through damaged tissue. Each attempt feels like swallowing glass, but I keep going. Have to keep going.

Somewhere out there, Sarah is waiting.

Hours blur together as I work through the exercises. My neck beats in sync with my pulse.

But slowly, something changes. The humming becomes clearer. Stronger.

I touch the bandage at my throat, feeling the vibration beneath my fingers. Sound. My sound. Trapped like a bird in a cage. I just have to learn how to open the door.

The sky outside my window shifts from black to grey as dawn approaches. My body aches from sitting up, from focusing, from fighting against six weeks of silence. But when I open my mouth again, only a strangled grunt emerges.

"Hhh."

The sound is barely there, more breath than voice. I was aiming for 'help', but it's not even close. Just this failed attempt leaves me exhausted, my throat burning like I've swallowed fire. Tears of frustration prick at my eyes. I try to swallow them back, which only makes the pain worse.

Determined, I try again.

"Fuh."

Another rasp, weaker than the first. Not even recognisable as an attempt at a word.

Help find...

I close my eyes, picturing Sarah's face. Her name forms in my mind, desperate to push into the world.

"Ssss."

Nothing but a hiss of air. My throat closes. My chest tightens.

I try again, straining every muscle in my neck. "Ssss."

This time, not even a hiss emerges. It's like my body is fighting against itself: mind willing but flesh refusing. My hand flies to my neck, feeling the frantic pulse beneath the bandage.

I slam my fist against the mattress, tears now flowing freely down my face. The sounds in my throat are nothing like words. They're guttural, animal noises of rage and helplessness. I want to scream Sarah's name, to call out for help, but all that comes are these pathetic, broken sounds that mean nothing to anyone.

The worst part is realising that Kate and the doctors were right. Medical science wins again: my damaged vocal cords won't simply heal because I want them to, because I need them to. My body follows its own stubborn timetable, regardless of my determination or desperation. Weeks, not days. The pamphlet's slow, methodical approach wasn't patronising me; it was telling the truth I didn't want to hear.

My body isn't ready, no matter how desperately my mind needs this.

The night passes in a haze of futile attempts and growing frustration. By morning, the sunlight streams through the blinds, highlighting the useless pamphlet now crumpled beside me. I must have dozed off eventually because the sound of breakfast trays clattering in the hallway startles me awake.

Nurse rounds come and go. The doctor checks my bandages, frowning at the redness around my throat but saying nothing about it. I pretend I haven't spent the night straining my vocal cords.

It's nearly eleven when a knock sounds at the door.

Kate enters, carrying her folder of exercises and a cup of what smells like peppermint tea. Her gaze takes in my rumpled sheets, the dark circles under my eyes, the crumpled speech therapy pamphlet beside me.

"You've been pushing yourself," she says, not a question but a statement. She sets the tea on my bedside table. "I brought this for me, but maybe you'd better have it."

I reach for the whiteboard, but Kate is already placing the communication boards on my lap. She's prepared for our follow-up session.

"I wanted to check how you're feeling after the police interview," she says, arranging the boards neatly. "Did our practice help at all?"

My finger jabs at BAD, then FRUSTRATING, the force of my pointing making the laminated board bounce on the blanket.

"I'm not surprised," Kate says, pulling up a chair. "Those interviews are difficult even when you can speak." Her eyes scan my face, taking in the tension, the exhaustion. "You've been up all night, haven't you?"

I nod, then tap NEED emphatically before pointing to my throat.

"You need to speak?" Kate translates, her voice gentle but professional.

My finger floats over the communication board, then points to VOICE, then WANT, then URGENT.

Kate nods. "I know. And we're going to work on that." She opens her folder, revealing new exercises. "But proper technique is crucial. Show me what you've been practising."

I demonstrate the breathing exercise from the pamphlet, inhaling slowly through my nose, holding, then exhaling through my mouth. Kate watches carefully, her eyes narrowing slightly.

"You're tensing your neck muscles," she says. "That's putting strain on the healing tissue." She gently adjusts my posture, her hands cool against my shoulders. "Like this. Let the breath come from your diaphragm, not your throat."

I follow her guidance, feeling the subtle difference. The next breath comes easier, with less pain.

"I can see you've been trying the breathing exercises," she says, watching my chest rise and fall. "But I'm concerned you might be pushing too hard. Have you been attempting to actually speak?"

I hesitate, then nod. There's no point pretending. I need Kate's help.

Her expression grows serious. "Amanda, I understand how badly you want to communicate, but your vocal cords have suffered severe trauma. Forcing speech too soon could cause permanent damage." She makes a note in her folder. "We need to focus exclusively on breathing and muscle strengthening for at least another week before attempting any sounds."

My face must show my dismay because Kate's expression softens.

"I know that's not what you want to hear," she says, her professional demeanour steady but kind. "But rushing this process won't help Sarah. You need your voice to heal properly so you can provide clear testimony later."

The implication hits me hard - not just talking to the police, but eventually testifying. In court. Facing him again. The thought of being in the same room with him, of having to look at his face while I describe what he did to us - what he might still be doing to Sarah...

Kate's hand finds mine, anchoring me back to the present.

"One step at a time," she says quietly, acknowledging my fear without naming it. "Right now, your only job is to heal."

She demonstrates, and I follow, producing a soft hum that vibrates through my damaged throat. It hurts less than I expected, and Kate nods approvingly.

It's not enough. I need to tell the police more.

My finger stabs at HELP, then POLICE.

"You want to help the police with more information," Kate translates. "And you think speaking would be faster than writing or using the boards."

I nod emphatically, but gently.

Kate sighs, tucking a strand of hair behind her ear.

"Amanda, I promise I'll do everything I can to help you recover your voice. But it's going to take time." She hesitates, then adds, "And in the meantime, your written communication is still valuable. The police told the nurses you provided several important details yesterday."

My fingers curl around the edge of the communication board, frustration building again.

"I heard they're coming back tomorrow," Kate continues. "To ask more questions."

I tap YES and point to my mouth. I need to speak.

"I understand," Kate says. "But your voice won't be ready by tomorrow. The boards and whiteboard will still help you communicate what you know." She pauses, watching me closely. "Is there something specific you haven't been able to tell them yet? Something only your voice can express?"

I hesitate, then tap UNSURE on the interview card before writing smell on the whiteboard. Every exchange is a careful balancing act: finding the least painful, least frustrating way to make myself understood.

"You remember smells?" Kate asks, leaning forward slightly. "From that night?"

My hand shakes as I write: Truck smelt of oil and cigarettes and

I pause.

I wasn't sure at the time.

I close my eyes as though that could help me remember more clearly.

Eggs

It makes no sense, and I instantly feel stupid for writing it. I rub it out, but immediately write again.

Rotten eggs

Kate reads the words silently, her professional demeanour slipping just for a moment. "You smelled eggs?" She sounds genuinely surprised. "And you're sure it wasn't your attacker? Like wind?"

She's smiling, as though it's a joke, but I can't bring myself to join her.

Kate's expression changes when she sees how serious I am. "Okay," she says. "We should pass that on to the police." She takes the whiteboard gently. "May I take a photo of this to share with them before tomorrow's interview?"

I nod.

My words come easier on the board now.

Kate pulls out her phone and takes the picture. Everything I write is evidence. Everything I point at on the communication boards. Everything could help them find Sarah.

She guides me through several more exercises, each one carefully designed to strengthen without straining. By the end of the session, my throat aches, but in a different way: the productive burn of muscles being retrained rather than the raw pain of damaged tissue.

"You're making progress," Kate says as she gathers her materials. "Much faster than I expected, actually. But please, don't try to speak during tomorrow's interview. Focus on the breathing and tongue exercises, not vocalisation."

I reach for the whiteboard, unable to conceal my frustration: When will I be able to talk?

Kate sits back down, her expression thoughtful. "I can see how determined you are, and that's going to serve you well in recovery." She leans forward slightly. "The good news is that your stoma is already beginning to close. Within a week or so, once it's healed more, you should be able to form a few words. Not many at first, maybe just two or three critical ones, but it's a start."

My eyes widen, hope rising in my chest.

"That's why I'm asking you to wait just a little longer," she continues, her voice gentle but firm. "Pushing too hard right now could damage the healing tissue and set you back weeks. But if you focus on these exercises and give your body those few extra days..." She smiles. "You might surprise both of us with how quickly you progress after that."

I consider this, the promise of actual speech, even limited, within reach if I can just be patient a little longer.

"So, what do you say?" Kate asks. "Can you work with me on this? Just focus on strengthening without straining for the next few days?"

I nod slowly, a silent promise; it's worth waiting for if it means doing it right.

"Good," she says, standing. "I'll be back tomorrow. And Amanda? I believe in your voice. It's coming back. We just need to welcome it properly."

As she leaves, I feel something I haven't in weeks: not just determination, but genuine hope. My voice isn't gone forever. It’s just waiting, healing, gathering strength for when I need it most.

CHAPTER TWENTY-FIVE

The clock on the wall reads 8:15. Forty-five minutes until the police return with questions I can't answer and expectations I can't meet. Forty-five minutes to prepare for another round of pointing at boards and scrawling partial sentences while Sarah remains missing.

The door opens, and for a moment I tense, thinking the police have arrived early. But it's Mum, carrying a small duffel bag and fresh flowers, already set in a vase.

"Morning, sweetheart," she says, her voice deliberately bright. She sets the flowers on the windowsill, not bluebells, thank God, and moves to the side of my bed. "I brought you some clean pyjamas and your hairbrush."

I reach for the whiteboard on my bedside table.

Work? I write.

"Don't worry about that," she says, waving away my concern as she unpacks the bag. "The school's being very understanding. I've got as much time as I need."

Police coming, I write, the letters sharper than I intend.

"I know," Mum says, sitting beside me on the bed. "That's why I'm here. The doctor thought it might help if I was here for your interview again." She squeezes my hand. "And I wanted to be here anyway. I couldn't let you go through that alone."

They need to find her, I write, my hand trembling slightly.

"I know," Mum says again, her voice softer now. "And you're helping them do that. But you need to take care of yourself, too."

I shake my head, frustration building. How can I explain that there's no time for taking care, no time for healing slowly? The image of Sarah, blindfolded, bound, silent, won't leave my mind. She wouldn't leave me behind, not even for a second. And somehow, I left her.

The thought makes me reach again for the whiteboard, but before I can write anything, there's a knock at the door.

"That'll be them," Mum says, squeezing my hand before standing.

The door opens to reveal Suki from Victim Support, the quiet woman who observed yesterday's interview without saying much. Today, without the police here yet, I have time to notice details I missed before: mid-thirties, dark hair pulled back in a practical bun, eyes that carry the weight of too many stories like mine. She's dressed in a beige cardigan and dark pants, professional but approachable, with a leather messenger bag slung across her body.

"Mrs Gray?" she says, extending her hand to my mother. "I'm Suki Patel from Victim Support. We met briefly yesterday, but I didn't get a chance to speak with you." She turns to me with a small smile. "Hello again, Amanda."

I nod, still unsure what to make of her presence. Am I a victim? Is that why I need victim support? Of course I am, technically, but I don't want to feel like that. There are so many negative connotations to the word. I don't want the label.

"I'm sorry I couldn't do more yesterday," Suki continues, settling into the chair beside my bed without waiting for an invitation. "First interviews can be overwhelming, and perhaps I should have stepped in more. Today will be different."

I can't help but wonder if the interview was overwhelming for *her*, if that's why she wasn't more vocal.

"You don't have to write everything," Suki says, noticing me reaching for the whiteboard. "Yes and no questions, just nod or shake your head. Save your energy for when you really need to express something complex. Remember to use the communications boards as much as possible, too."

There's something reassuring about her straightforward manner. She doesn't look at me like I'm broken, doesn't use that careful voice everyone else does. Yesterday she was nearly silent; today I'm starting to see why she's good at her job.

"I should have explained better," she says, a note of apology in her voice. "It's difficult when I don't get to meet people before the police arrive. My job is to support you during the interview. If you need a break, you tell me, tap the side of the bed, raise your hand, whatever works. If you feel like it's too much, I'll step in. You're in control here, Amanda."

The words sound hollow. I haven't been in control of anything since the moment he appeared in the woods, but I appreciate the sentiment. *Control* is a better word than *victim*.

She glances briefly at Mum before turning back to me. "I normally meet with victims outside of police interviews, too. Just to check in, help with any practical matters, answer questions about the investigation process." Her tone remains matter of fact. "I'd like to come see you tomorrow, if that's okay with you. Just us, no police."

I nod, somewhat surprised. I hadn't realised victim support extended beyond these formal interviews.

"Good," she says with a small smile. "We'll set that up before I leave today."

Mum watches from the foot of the bed, her expression a mixture of concern and relief. I think she's glad someone else is here to guide me through this, someone who isn't emotionally invested the way she is.

Another knock at the door, and this time it is the police. PC Winters enters first, her blonde hair pulled back in the same severe ponytail as yesterday. She nods at me, then at Mum, then Suki.

"Morning, Suki," she says.

I wonder how often they work together, how many people they have visited in hospital beds.

Detective Barnes follows, carrying a slim folder and the video recorder. Behind him comes another officer, a woman in her early thirties with copper-red hair. Her eyes, though professional, carry a certain intensity as she studies me.

"Amanda," Winters says, "this is Detective Reid from Major Crimes. She specialises in cases like yours."

Detective Reid steps forwards. "I know this is difficult," she says, her voice softer than I expected. "But time is critical in missing persons cases, even after several weeks."

I'm a victim. I'm a case. I wonder what other words they have to pigeonhole me with. I liked it better when I was just a daughter and a best friend. There's nowhere on my communication board that says, 'Stop treating me like I'm broken'.

Barnes sets up the recorder as Winters pulls chairs into a semicircle around my bed. The formality of it makes me jittery, like they're preparing for a performance rather than an interview. Reid's suit is impeccably pressed, but there's a coffee stain on her sleeve she hasn't noticed. I wonder if she's been up all night, looking at files of other girls who disappeared.

Other Sarahs.

Other Maggies.

"Before we start," Suki interjects, "I want to be clear that Amanda can take breaks any time. And that if a question is too difficult, we can come back to it."

She's already been through this with me and Mum, so I know this is for the benefit of the officers, to make sure they remember my needs.

Reid nods. "Of course. Our priority is finding the man who hurt you and Sarah Fairchild. I understand your mother has told you she's still missing. We're doing everything we can to bring her home."

I can't tell from the way she says it whether she is relieved that the big secret is out now, or whether Mum told me more than she was meant to. Either way, Sarah's name sends an electric jolt through me. Hearing it spoken aloud makes her real, makes the urgency real.

"Let's start with what you remember about the location," Reid says, pulling out a notepad. No small talk, no gentle lead-in. Just straight to business. I find myself appreciating her directness: no pussyfooting around, no treating me like I'm made of glass. She's here to get answers and find Sarah. It's strangely comforting.

I reach for the whiteboard, gripping the marker tightly. My hand trembles slightly, partly from weakness, partly from determination. Each letter costs me effort that sends dull pain radiating up my arm, but I push through it. Sarah would do the same for me.

Picking bluebells

Mum cuts in.

"There's a wood near where we live. It's on the girls' way home from school, or one way they can go," she says. "Joyce, Sarah's mum, used to take them there."

Used to.

The words sting like alcohol on an open wound. It seems so easy for people to speak of Sarah in the past tense now, as if they've already given up on finding her alive. As if those six weeks have already decided everything.

I nod and point at Mum as though we're playing charades.

"Perhaps you can show us where that is?" PC Winters says to Mum.

"Pull up the map," Reid tells her, without taking her eyes off me.

Winters swipes open her tablet with practised efficiency. The blue glow illuminates her face as she navigates to a detailed map of the area. I catch a glimpse of coloured pins, shaded zones, and what look like timeline markers spreading outward from a central point.

Mum leans over, jabbing her finger at the map in the same way I poke at the communication boards.

"There," she says. "This wooded area borders the reservoir behind the school. There's a path that cuts through to our neighbourhood."

I watch Reid's eyes track the location, mentally calculating something. Meanwhile, Winters zooms in, then out, taking in the surrounding terrain. I can see roads, buildings, the reservoir; places I've known my whole life, now transformed into a crime scene map.

Reid looks at me expectantly. "What happened after you entered the woods?"

I take a breath. My fingers already ache from gripping the marker too hard, but I have to try. They need to know everything.

He took us

Suki notices my struggle, leans forward slightly. "Take your time," she whispers.

in truck

My wrist cramps, but I keep going. I have to share with them everything I can remember, every detail that might help find Sarah. I point to the list I made with Kate.

Blindfold. Tied up. Gagged.

Route: trees hitting roof, bumpy then smooth

I try to remember the things I wanted to commit to memory. The things I thought that, if I survived, would help *them* find him. Now here I am with *them*, and none of it helps at all. None of it is enough to find Sarah.

Sweat beads on my forehead from the concentration and physical effort. Mum makes a small sound of concern, but I ignore it.

Taken out.

On grass.

Then nothing.

I tap the last word, summoning just enough strength to underline nothing twice. This is the gap no one seems to understand. I don't know how I got from there to the road. I don't remember anything after he took us from the truck until I woke up here in the hospital.

Apart from what he did.

I remember that.

I remember.

My arm drops heavily onto the bed, fingers still clutching the marker. The effort leaves me momentarily breathless, but I force myself to meet Reid's eyes. I need her to understand how important this is. Important enough that I'll push through pain and exhaustion to communicate it.

"The gap in your memory is normal with trauma," Reid says, recognising both my frustration and my determination. "We're working with what we have. These details about the road surface changes and trees hitting the roof are actually quite helpful."

Barnes reaches over to Winters, who hands him the tablet. After a few taps, he turns it toward me. The map has expanded, showing a larger area with various markings and annotations.

"We've been building a geographical profile," he explains, his voice slipping into the professional cadence of someone accustomed to briefing colleagues. "Based on where you and Sarah were last seen, factoring in road networks, terrain, accessibility by vehicle."

Winters points to a road I don't recognise on the screen. "You were found here," she says. The location is marked with a small red X and the notation "AG found unconscious." Not Amanda. Not even my full initials. Just AG: a case, a victim, known only by impersonal letters on a map.

I think I preferred it when I was invisible.

"The search radius has covered this area," she continues, indicating a large, shaded circle with that red X at its centre. The circle encompasses miles of countryside, countless roads, farms, buildings. The enormity of it makes my chest tighten. Sarah could be anywhere in that vast space. Or beyond it.

"Based on the timeline, from when you reported you encountered the perpetrator and when you were found, we've calculated the maximum distance he could have travelled with you." Barnes traces a wider circle with his finger. "Assuming normal driving speeds on these roads."

I stare at the tablet, willing my memory to sharpen, to give me something concrete. The truck's movement, the turns, the time it took, anything that might narrow this impossible search area. But all I have are fragments: the smell of cigarettes and that strange, eggy odour. The sound of trees scraping the roof. The sensation of gravel, then smooth road.

Water, I write suddenly, the memory surfacing from nowhere. *Heard water.*

Reid leans forward, a new intensity in her expression. "What kind of water? Ocean? River? A small stream?"

I close my eyes, straining to capture the fleeting memory. Not waves. Not the rush of a large river. Something smaller, steadier.

Brook? Stream? I write, adding a question mark because I can't be sure. The sound had been distant, background noise while I lay bleeding on the earth.

Barnes immediately turns to the map, tracing blue lines with his fingertip. "There are several creek systems in this region," he says. "If we cross-reference with isolated wooded areas..."

I see a flash of something like hope in his methodical assessment. It's a small detail, maybe insignificant, but it's something they can use. Something that might help narrow the search.

"Amanda," Reid says, her voice gentler now, "I know this is exhausting, but you're doing extremely well. These details are helping us build a picture."

I stare at the map, at the extensive areas still unmarked, unexplored. Somewhere in that wilderness, Sarah might be waiting.

Or trapped. Or buried.

The thought claws at my chest, tightening like a vice around my ribs. My fingers tremble around the marker, my pulse thudding in my ears. What if she's still with him? What if she's still alive, still enduring...

I swallow hard, nausea twisting in my stomach. My body remembers too much: the weight of him moving, the sounds, the cries.

I squeeze my eyes shut, but the images won't leave. Six weeks. If she's still out there, if she's still breathing, she's been his prisoner for six long, endless weeks.

And I've been lying in a hospital bed.

The thought makes my hands clench, nails digging into my palm. I can't fall apart now. Not when she's still out there.

I force myself to breathe, to steady my grip.

The thought gives me strength to lift the marker again.

Find her, I write, the letters shaky. It's not a detail, not a clue. Just a desperate plea.

Barnes meets my eyes, his professional detachment slipping for just a moment. "We're trying," he says. "Every day, we're trying."

The room falls silent except for the steady beep of monitors. My head pounds with effort and emotion, with memories I've been fighting to suppress now deliberately pulled to the surface. The sound of water. The blindfold tight against my face. The truck's movement beneath me. Each detail feels both vital and hopelessly inadequate.

Reid glances at her notes, then back to me. "Amanda, your speech therapist mentioned you recalled another sensory detail. Something about a smell?"

I'm still shaking from the thoughts that won't leave my head, but I know I have to focus.

In truck. Strong.

"Could it have been the man?" Barnes asks. "His body odour or breath?"

I gently move my head from side to side emphatically.

Different. Rotten egg.

He had BO, that's something I can't forget, but not the eggy kind. This was something else entirely. Inescapable, distinctive, almost industrial.

I add to the board, one word of uncertainty.

Chemical?

I watch as the officers absorb the word, the weight of it shifting the air in the room. Chemical. It lingers on the whiteboard like an unanswered question, something just out of reach.

Winters finishes her note, her gaze flicking between Barnes and Reid. Something about this detail has struck a chord, but no one says it out loud. Not yet.

I grip the marker tighter, pulse thrumming in my fingertips. It's not much, just a scent, a vague impression buried beneath fear and blood and pain. But it's something. A thread in the dark.

And if I can keep pulling, maybe, just maybe, it will lead us to Sarah.

CHAPTER TWENTY-SIX

I struggle to lift the marker again, determined to continue. The plastic feels impossibly heavy in my trembling fingers. The whiteboard wobbles on my lap.

More, I write, the single word taking all my concentration. Ask me more.

The world tilts, but I fight to stay present, to stay focused. For Sarah.

"Amanda?" Mum's voice seems to come from far away.

The marker slips from my fingers, rolling across the blanket. I try to reach for it, but my arm won't cooperate. The room tilts slightly, the surrounding faces blurring.

"She needs a break," Suki says firmly, already rising from her chair. "Ten minutes, at least."

"But..." Barnes begins.

"Ten minutes," Suki repeats, her professional courtesy masking what is clearly a non-negotiable demand. "She's pushing herself too hard."

Reid checks her watch, then nods. "We'll take fifteen. Get something to drink, stretch our legs." She glances at me, her expression softening slightly. "Take your time, Amanda. We'll continue when you're ready."

The officers file out, their voices fading down the hallway. Only Mum and Suki remain.

"Here," Mum says, holding a cup of water with a straw to my lips. "Small sips."

The water feels like heaven on my raw throat. I hadn't realised how dry my mouth had become from the effort of concentration. Suki helps me shift position, adjusting the pillows behind my back.

"You're doing incredibly well," she says quietly. "But you need to pace yourself. This isn't a sprint."

But it feels like one. Every second that passes is another second Sarah is out there with him. Another second of whatever he's doing to her.

As if reading my thoughts, Suki adds, "I know you want to tell them everything at once. But your body has limitations right now that you need to respect."

She's right, of course. My hands still tremble with fatigue, my neck throbbing where the bandage covers healing tissue. But I need them to know about Maggie. About the way he spoke to me as if I were someone else entirely. Someone he knew.

"Just focus on one detail at a time," Suki advises. "Don't try to write everything at once."

The detectives return after their brief conference in the hallway. They've changed strategy. I can see it in their posture, in the way Reid takes the lead chair while Barnes positions the recorder closer to my bed. My throat burns with words I can't speak, questions they won't answer. The whiteboard feels heavier in my lap, already smudged with my desperate attempts to communicate.

Suki offers a small nod of encouragement. "Just a few more questions," she says quietly. "You're doing really well."

Reid leans forward, her expression more focused than before. Something's shifted. Something I said has caught their attention.

"Amanda," she begins, "What you've told us so far is very helpful. There's something else I need to ask you about, though. I want to go back to something specific. You mentioned yesterday that he called you 'Maggie'. We've run that name through our databases: missing persons, criminal records, even school enrolments within a hundred-mile radius. Nothing matches the timeline or circumstances."

I stare at her, anger flaring hot beneath my skin. They still don't believe me. After everything, after the knife and the blood and Sarah's screams, they still think I might have imagined it, confused it.

Real, I write, the marker skidding across the board with the force of my emotion. The single word stands stark against the white surface, my hand trembling as I underline it twice.

Suki leans forward slightly. "Amanda is very clear about this detail," she says, her voice calm but firm. "And specific language like that is significant."

"We're not dismissing it," Reid says, though her tone suggests otherwise. "But we need more to go on. Did he say anything else about Maggie? Anything that might give us a timeframe, a location, anything?"

My fingers cramp around the marker. I've been writing for too long, my muscles unused to such sustained effort after weeks of unconsciousness. But I force myself to continue. For Sarah. Always for Sarah.

I close my eyes, trying to recall his exact words through the haze of terror and pain. Most of what he said blurs together, but a few phrases stand out with terrible clarity. When I open my eyes, the words come slowly, painfully:

Don't need to see this Maggie

The effort costs me. The marker slips in my sweating palm. I steady it with both hands to add:

Said it like routine

Reid reads this and exchanges a glance with Barnes.

"That suggests a pattern," she says quietly. "A ritual of some kind."

"Or a relationship," Barnes adds.

The word makes me shudder. Relationship. As if there could be anything that human between a predator and his prey.

Reid leans forward, her eyes narrowing with newfound intensity. "Amanda, this Maggie detail. It could be the key we've been missing." She exchanges a meaningful glance with Barnes. "Serial offenders often develop fixations, patterns they repeat."

Barnes pulls his chair closer. "We need everything you can remember about how he said that name. Was it angry? Affectionate? Did he seem confused when you didn't respond to it?"

The questions come faster now; their earlier caution is replaced with barely concealed urgency. I fumble with the marker, my cramping hand struggling to keep up.

Not confused, I write. *Certain. Like I was her.*

Reid nods, making rapid notes. "Did he say 'Maggie' as if speaking to someone familiar? Someone he knew well?"

I close my eyes, forcing myself back to that moment: the blindfold tight against my face, the smell of earth and blood, his voice above me. The memory makes my heart race.

Knew her, I manage to write.

My arm trembles with exhaustion, but I push on. If Maggie is the key to finding Sarah, I have to give them everything I can.

Said "It's that time again, Maggie", I write, the words coming slower now, the marker leaving uneven lines as my strength fails.

This catches Reid's full attention. "That's extremely helpful," she says, looking genuinely excited.

Mum shifts in her chair beside me. I can feel her tension, her fear for me, but also something else. I think it might be hope.

The detectives are talking between themselves, speaking almost in code.

"Victimology profile... signature elements... geographic clustering."

The technical language washes over me, their voices fading as exhaustion claims more of my focus. My eyelids grow heavy, the whiteboard slipping slightly on my lap.

"I think that's enough," Suki says, cutting through the detectives' discussion. "You have what you need for now."

Reid looks like she wants to argue, but Barnes nods in agreement. "We'll continue this when you've had time to rest," he says, gathering his notes. "There's plenty to work with here."

The positivity in his voice should be comforting, but something about it rings hollow. They're placing all their hope on finding a connection to someone who might have disappeared years ago, while Sarah has been missing for six weeks.

Maggie might be long dead, never real. A ghost of another girl, or a name he made up just to twist the knife deeper. Or maybe she was the one before me. Maybe she lay in the dirt like I did, thinking she was the last, never knowing that someone else would come after.

A bitter taste rises in my throat. They're searching for shadows while Sarah is out there somewhere. Flesh and blood, waiting. Enduring.

I watch them go, frustration burning beneath my exhaustion. I didn't tell them enough. Couldn't tell them enough. My throat aches with words trapped inside, important details I can't articulate through this painfully slow writing.

When they're gone, Mum exhales heavily, her shoulders slumping. "You did so well," she says, but her voice catches on the words. "So brave."

I reach for the whiteboard again, needing her to understand what I couldn't tell the police.

They're wrong, I write, my letters shaky but determined.

Mum frowns, leaning closer. "Wrong about what, sweetheart?"

Sarah not taken because of Maggie. Taken because with me.

The realisation has been forming slowly: the way he treated her, the things he did to her. She was collateral damage. Wrong place, wrong time, wrong friend.

My fault.

Tears burn behind my eyes as I struggle to explain this to Mum, to make her understand the police are looking in the wrong direction. It feels like they're hunting for Maggie instead of looking for Sarah.

My hand trembles so badly now that the words are barely legible.

Need to remember more. Need to help them find her.

"Amanda," Mum says softly, taking the marker from my hand. "You need to rest. You can't help Sarah if you collapse."

I want to argue, to insist that every minute counts, but my body betrays me. My eyelids grow heavier, the pain in my throat sharper. The monitor beside me beeps in steady rhythm, marking minutes I can't afford to lose.

There's a sharp rap on the door and Paul stands in the doorway, his expression unreadable.

"How did it go?" he asks Mum, his eyes flicking briefly to me before settling on her.

"They have new leads," she says, rising stiffly from her chair. Her hand rests protectively on her swollen belly. "Amanda gave them information about Maggie. They seemed very interested."

Something shifts in Paul's face: a flicker of recognition, quickly suppressed.

"Maggie," he repeats, the name careful on his tongue. "The name you wrote on the board. Who is she?"

I reach for the whiteboard, but it slips from my grasp, clattering to the floor. Paul picks it up, his eyes scanning my desperate scrawl.

"The attacker called Amanda by this name," Mum explains when I can't. "The police think he might have been confusing her with someone else. Someone from before."

Paul's brow furrows. "And they're focusing on finding this Maggie person? When Sarah's been missing for weeks?"

The edge in his voice surprises me. Paul has never shown much interest in Sarah, or in me, for that matter. His sudden concern feels out of place.

"They think it could lead them to Sarah," Mum says, but her tone suggests she shares his scepticism.

Paul hands me back the whiteboard, his expression unreadable. "Let's hope they're right." He turns to Mum. "Ready to go? You need rest too."

As Mum pulls on her jacket, Paul steps closer to the bed, his voice dropping so only I can hear. "These detectives, they're following protocol, doing everything by the book." His eyes meet mine, unexpectedly intense. "But books don't always have the right answers."

I stare at him, unsure what he's trying to tell me.

Before I can respond, he straightens, his usual distant demeanour returning. "We'll be back first thing tomorrow," he tells me, his hand settling on Mum's lower back, guiding her toward the door.

As they leave, I catch a fragment of their whispered conversation.

"...this Maggie thing..." Paul is saying. "The police aren't..."

The door closes, cutting off his words. I'm left alone with the harsh fluorescent light, and the whiteboard still clutched in my trembling hands.

The questions swirl as exhaustion pulls me under. My last conscious thought is of Sarah. Alone, afraid, waiting for someone to find her. And of Maggie, whoever she is, the shadow girl whose name might be the key to everything.

Or the distraction that costs Sarah her life.

CHAPTER TWENTY-SEVEN

Three days have passed since the interview. Three days of waiting, watching, wondering. The hospital room feels smaller each day, walls inching closer with every hour that passes without answers. My mind circles the same questions on endless repeat, a carousel of anxiety I can't escape: Did I tell them enough? Will they find her?

Is she even still alive?

And always, always: Where is Sarah? Who is Maggie?

These thoughts send a surge of nausea through me every time they surface, but I can't stop them from coming. My hands tremble slightly as I smooth the blanket across my lap, looking for any distraction from the crushing weight of not knowing.

Every morning, I wake with the urge to force words through my damaged throat; to demand answers, to scream Sarah's name, to voice the questions burning inside me. And every morning, I swallow those impulses back down, bitter as medicine. Kate comes to visit each day, and I'm keeping my word to her. I bite my tongue, literally sometimes, the physical pain a distraction from the deeper ache of silence. I'm banking days of restraint, saving up for when my voice might actually help find Sarah.

Suki came by yesterday, as promised. Her visit was different from everyone else's: no charts to check, no exercises to complete, no worried glances when she thought I wasn't looking. She brought updates on the investigation, though they were frustratingly vague.

"They're following leads," she told me, perched on the edge of the visitor's chair. "The chemical smell was helpful. They're looking into sites where sulphur compounds are processed: industrial facilities, abandoned plants, that sort of thing."

I might have given them some useful information.

Mostly Suki just sat with me, explaining processes, answering questions, occasionally filling the silence with stories about her rescue dog. She didn't try to fix me or rush my recovery. She was simply there, a steady presence amid the chaos, reminding me that beyond these hospital walls, people are still searching for Sarah.

Between her, Kate, David, and the rotating nurses, I'm starting to build quite the posse in here. A collection of professionals all focused on putting me back together, piece by broken piece.

Today, Mum arrives just after lunch, bringing fresh clothes and a notebook she found in my bedroom. She's working a half-day, and I get to benefit from it.

Of all my visitors, the doctors, the nurses, the specialists, the police, Mum remains my constant, my anchor to the world outside these walls. Her daily visits give structure to the endless hospital hours, something to anticipate beyond medication rounds and therapy sessions. When she walks through that door, I'm not just a patient or a victim or a case. I'm her daughter, someone who exists beyond this sterile room and the trauma that brought me here.

"I thought you might want this," she says, placing the spiral-bound journal on my bedside table. "For writing things down when you don't want to use the whiteboard."

The familiar blue cover makes something catch in my chest: it's the notebook Sarah gave me for my birthday last year. I'd only written in the first few pages, mostly random thoughts and complaints about Paul that I didn't want to say aloud. Now the sight of it brings a wave of memories: Sarah's handwriting on the inside cover, her insistence that

I should use it to *'document our eventual world domination'*.

Mum misreads my expression. "If you don't want it..."

I shake my head quickly, reaching for the notebook.

Thank you, I write on the whiteboard. Then, after a moment's hesitation: Where's Paul?

"Work," she says, settling into the visitor's chair.

I should have known this, but time seems so fluid when you're lying in a hospital bed.

Seven weeks, now. Almost eight.

Mum's hand automatically moves to her growing baby bump and I know that's something I've lost track of, too.

"I'm getting a taxi back, too," she says. "So, I can stay as long as you like. He's got some errands to run after he finishes, so..."

Seeing as I didn't need to know that, I can only assume she's telling me because she's not happy about it. There's not a lot I can say when I can't speak, but disappearing for hours seems to be his thing now.

How many weeks?

I write on the board, and point at her belly, trying to focus on something more positive, something I actually want to know.

"Oh," she says. "Nearly six months now. Well, twenty-four weeks. I'm sorry you've missed out on this."

I give her a tight-lipped smile. I'm sorry too.

"I probably shouldn't be telling you this," she says, automatically looking to see if the door is closed, "but Dr Miles says they're planning to transfer you to Oakwood Rehabilitation Centre soon. It's the next step in your recovery process, and it's much closer to home. They're looking to move you in a couple of weeks."

Oakwood.

The word sits between us like a promise or a threat. I'm not sure which.

Oakwood.

I've overheard enough conversations between nurses to know what it means: real beds instead of these mechanical hospital ones with their handheld controls and safety rails, therapy gyms instead of medical equipment, patients in workout clothes instead of hospital gowns. A place where people are expected to get better, to progress, to eventually leave.

Oakwood.

The large brick building with its manicured grounds, just fifteen minutes from our house. The word should evoke progress, but a spike of anxiety shoots through me. Being closer to home means closer to my bedroom with its bruise-coloured wallpaper. Closer to Paul at the dinner table. Closer to the path that leads to the woods, where everything changed.

Oakwood.

I swallow hard.

Am I really ready for this?

I've lost weeks in a haze of sedation and hospital routines. I don't remember arriving here, and now they expect me to leave? It feels too sudden, too soon. Like stepping off a ledge before I've learned how to stand.

If it wasn't for the scrawled date at the top of the chart of my wall, I would have no idea that we were heading into the second week of May.

I can't even talk yet. How am I supposed to face the outside world when I can't do something as simple as speak?

"We can take it slowly," Mum says, reading my expression. "They have an excellent speech therapy program, and you'll have more independence there."

Independence. Like my life hasn't already been torn apart. Like I can go back to living a normal teenage life.

Part of me wants to stay here, with David and Kate and the safety of these four clinical white walls. Part of me, the bigger part, wants to go back in time, back before any of this. I know neither of those things can happen.

Mum stays for an hour, filling the silence with gentle chatter about neighbours, house repairs, and her baby preparations. Much as I wasn't thrilled by the news originally, seeing her animatedly chat about my brother now, seeing her grow week by week, seeing the idea become a reality, I'm becoming invested.

And despite Paul's absence, he's been here for Mum. He's stayed at arm's length from me, but I don't know, something about the way he's been recently. I feel like he's finally on my side. It shouldn't take something like this, but something like this should never happen anyway.

My attention snaps back to what Mum's saying as I hear a familiar name.

"I saw Oliver Fairchild. Sarah's brother."

Like I don't know who he is.

"He asked if you were recovering well." Mum's not looking at me as she says it.

She stops there, and I sense the weight of everything she isn't telling me about their conversation. I'm here in hospital, while Sarah is missing. I left her, abandoned her.

I grab the whiteboard: How's Joyce?

Mum hesitates. "He said she's... managing. They all are. In their own way." She fiddles with her sleeve. "I don't really know how to help her."

The unspoken hangs between us: Joyce's daughter is still missing while Mum's is recovering. What comfort could Mum possibly offer? What words wouldn't sound hollow or, worse, privileged in their good fortune?

I pause, thinking through what I want to ask. Is it the right thing to do?

Could she visit? I write, the letters shaky with urgency.

"Amanda," Mum starts, her voice gentle but cautioning. "I don't know if that's a good idea right now. For either of you."

But something inside me, some certainty I can't explain, tells me that seeing Joyce isn't just something I want; it's something I need. The feeling pulses through me like a second heartbeat, insistent and impossible to ignore.

Please try, I write, underlining the words twice.

Mum sighs, but nods. "I'll try. But Amanda... prepare yourself for her to say no. She might not be ready."

I look away, blinking rapidly against sudden tears. Neither am I, if I'm honest. But what keeps running through my mind is the last thing I remember before the darkness took me: Sarah's muffled screams going silent. Her sounds of struggle suddenly stopping.

Floating in limbo, not knowing, is its own kind of torture.

And I can't shake the feeling that Joyce and I are the only two people who truly understand how that uncertainty tears at you from the inside out, moment by excruciating moment.

CHAPTER TWENTY-EIGHT

After Mum leaves, I open the notebook and begin writing everything I remember about the attack. Not the sanitised version I gave the police, edited for my mother's presence. The real version, with every brutal detail my mind has preserved.

The dog lead. The blindfold. The truck's movement.

Then the parts I've tried hardest to forget: The sounds Sarah made as he assaulted her. The way her struggles grew weaker. His calm, emotionless voice calling me Maggie as I lay bleeding on the ground.

"You don't need to see this, Maggie."

"It's that time again, Maggie."

I write down his exact words, then stare at them until they blur before my eyes. There's something important here. Something about the way he spoke, as if he'd said these exact phrases many times before. As if Maggie was someone who had heard them repeatedly. Someone who knew what they meant.

Someone he thought I was.

My hand aches, but I push through the discomfort. I draw a timeline on a fresh page, marking what I know for certain:

- Detention at school (4:30 PM)
- Picking bluebells in woods (5:15 – 5:30 PM?)
- It begins
- Truck drive (how long?)
- The worst part
- Left on road (admitted at 9:13 PM)

The gap between the attack and being brought into the hospital spans somewhere between three and four hours, depending on how long it took that couple to get me here.

Time during which, at some point, Sarah remained with him, and I somehow ended up miles away. Time I can't account for and that the police desperately need to understand.

A knock at the door interrupts my thoughts. I quickly close the notebook and slide it under my pillow.

Dr Miles enters, clipboard in hand and reading glasses perched on her nose.

"Good afternoon, Amanda. I hear you've been making excellent progress."

She's a far better judge than I am, so I accept the compliment with a small smile.

"I've been reviewing your case with the rehabilitation team," she continues, moving to my bedside. "There's been significant improvement in your wound healing, and your vital signs have been stable for over a week now. Your speech therapist says you've been working hard while following her instructions."

My smile wants to slip. Was the last sentence a borderline dig at my earlier attempts to vocalise, as Kate always puts it?

"We've got you moving around now, and you need to be up on your feet, walking confidently down that corridor soon."

It seems like a stretch. I've just about made it to the bathroom with assistance. My legs were never that into moving about and after six weeks of laziness while my body decided to live or die, they had an extended holiday.

I watch her face; Dr Miles has never been one for small talk. Thanks to Mum, I know where this is heading. Oakwood.

"We're going to be getting you off this monitoring. And... I'm sure your mother must have mentioned that we're looking at transferring you to Oakwood Rehabilitation Centre. It's closer to home, but you'll still receive all the support you're currently getting." She makes a note on her clipboard. "How do you feel about that?"

Support.

The physiotherapy.

The occupational therapy.

The speech therapy.

The *therapy* therapy.

I should get a card to stamp: collect five, win a prize. Therapy bingo.

I reach for the whiteboard: Am I ready?

She nods, though I detect a hint of reservation in her eyes. "Physically, yes. But there are psychological factors to consider as well." She sits in the visitor's chair, her posture softening slightly. "Returning to a location closer to where the trauma occurred can sometimes trigger unexpected responses."

I understand what she's saying. Oakwood is closer to the woods where he found us. Closer to the spaces Sarah and I once shared. Closer to facing a version of my life that no longer exists.

"We'll ensure the transition is handled carefully, with psychological support readily available." She studies me for a moment. "Amanda, I know you want to find out what happened to your friend."

My heart stops, waiting for what comes next.

"I want you to know that focusing intensely on the investigation is a common response to the kind of trauma you've experienced." She looks like she is trying with everything she's got to exude that bedside manner she sadly lacks. "But focusing on what the police are doing, fixating on things you can't control... It can interfere with the recovery process."

I stare at her, heat rising in my cheeks. Of course, I'm focused on the investigation. Sarah is still missing. Maggie is still a mystery. And somewhere out there, he's still free.

"I'm not suggesting you distance yourself completely," Dr Miles adds, reading my expression. "Just that you allow yourself space to process your own experience alongside your concern for your friend."

But I can't separate those things. My experience and Sarah's are intertwined, bound together by what he did to us that day. By what he's still doing to her, wherever she is.

I pick up the marker, hand trembling: Have to help find her.

Dr Miles doesn't argue, but her sigh is filled with the same gentle dismissal I've heard from everyone. The quiet assurance that they know best. That my role now is to sit and recover. To wait.

"I understand. Just promise me you'll be mindful of your own recovery as well." She stands, tucking the clipboard under her arm. "We'll schedule the transfer to Oakwood for the 22nd, a couple of weeks from now. The team there is excellent, and they're already preparing for your arrival."

The 22nd.

Two more weeks of waiting. Two more weeks of being told to focus on myself while Sarah is still out there: alone, afraid, or worse.

Dr Miles offers one last polite smile, one of those practiced, professional expressions that mean nothing. Then she turns and leaves, the door clicking shut behind her.

The next day is filled with speech therapy and gentle walks around the ward. With the lines out and monitors removed,

I can move now. As much as my body remembers how, anyway.

I should feel freer. I should feel more hopeful. But freedom is an illusion when Sarah is still missing. Each step I take around my room only reminds me of the distance between us now.

My body heals while my mind remains trapped in that moment. The doctors say I'm making remarkable progress, but they don't understand that recovering my voice will mean nothing if I can't use it to bring her home.

Paul drops Mum off at exactly five o'clock. I watch from my window as he says something to her, his hand lingering on her shoulder before he gets back into his car. Instead of driving away, he sits there, phone pressed to his ear, expression intense. He doesn't look up. He doesn't seem to realise I might be watching.

After a few minutes, he puts the car in gear and pulls away from the hospital parking lot. Not heading home; turning in the opposite direction.

Another '*errand*'.

Mum arrives carrying a bag of clothes and toiletries, her smile bright but brittle.

"I thought you might like to be out of pyjamas now you're up and about a bit more," she says.

I pull out my old jeans, a soft hoodie, the worn trainers I've had since forever. Normal clothes. The clothes of a normal girl. Not the hospital gowns I've been living in since I woke up, or the new pyjamas Mum brought that still had price tags attached.

"Do you need help to get them on?" she asks.

I shake my head, already pulling the hoodie against my chest like a shield. These clothes are from before. Before the attack, before the hospital, before everything changed.

Just holding them makes me feel like I'm straddling two different versions of my life.

Not having the monitors attached to me anymore is going to make getting dressed a lot easier.

Where's Paul going? I write on the whiteboard.

Mum blinks, surprised by the question. "Oh, he has some business in town. Employee reviews or something." She busies herself arranging my toiletries on the bedside table, not meeting my eyes. "He said he'd be back to pick me up around seven." She looks at me for a reaction. "I can stay later..." she offers, letting the sentence hang.

I shake my head. No.

Whatever Paul is doing, Mum either doesn't know or doesn't want to tell me. And right now, I have more pressing concerns.

Then I turn back to the whiteboard.

Any news? I write, which has become my standard question. Mum knows exactly what I'm asking.

"Nothing definite." She sits on the edge of the bed, her hand automatically moving to her growing belly. "Detective Barnes called this morning, but just to check how you were doing. He said there's nothing to report yet."

If there had been, I'm sure mum would have led with that as soon as she came in.

"Oh, and I spoke to Joyce," Mum adds, her voice artificially casual.

My head snaps up. I tap the board urgently: *And?*

"She said she'd try to come by tomorrow. Around lunch time." Mum folds her arms, then unfolds them just as quickly, like she can't decide what to do with her hands. "Amanda, she's... she's not doing well. I just want you to be prepared."

The warning sends a chill through me. Not doing well. What does that even mean when your daughter has been missing for almost eight weeks? Of course Joyce isn't doing well. None of us are.

But I need to see her. Need to talk to her. Even if the conversation breaks something in both of us.

Thank you for asking her, I write.

"Do you want me to come with her?" Mum asks tentatively.

I shake my head and hope that's an end to it. This is for me and Joyce.

Mum opens her mouth to speak, and I shake my head again. She nods, then changes the subject, filling the room with careful chatter about things that don't mean anything.

I listen with half an ear, nodding at appropriate intervals. My mind is elsewhere: on Joyce's impending visit, on Paul's mysterious errands, on the search grid Detective Barnes showed me. On the dreams I've been having about Sarah and Maggie, both calling to me through darkness I can't penetrate.

"Amanda?" Mum's voice breaks through my thoughts. "Did you hear what I said?"

I blink, focusing on her concerned face. I shake my head.

"I asked if you wanted me to bring anything to Oakwood when they transfer you."

The idea of leaving the hospital is both liberating and terrifying. Oakwood is a step towards normalcy, but also a reminder of how far I still have to go.

Photos, I write after a moment. *The ones from my desk.*

Mum nods, understanding.

"I'll bring them." She glances at her watch. "The physical therapist mentioned you've been doing your walking exercises in the hallway. That's good progress."

I nod. I'm on my feet more now. Small steps. From the bed to the door. From the door to the nurses' station. Each one a little easier. A little stronger.

I was in intensive care. I almost died. For six weeks, I was motionless, medicated, turned by nurses like I wasn't even there. I only know that because David told me.

The past couple of weeks, they've let me disconnect from the monitors, just for a minute at a time, to shuffle to the bathroom with help. Lazy legs, like I said. Legs that forgot how to carry me.

They're learning again.

And now, without the wires of constant monitoring to keep me down, I can choose for myself when I stand up and try to remind them further.

Want to walk in room? I suggest on the whiteboard, needing to move after sitting still for so long.

"Are you sure? You don't need to rest?"

I carefully swing my legs over the side of the bed. I stand slowly, still mindful of the dizziness that sometimes comes with sudden movements.

Mum stands by as I take a few careful steps, her hands half-raised as if to catch me should I falter. I don't. My balance has improved dramatically already, my legs growing stronger through sheer determination and the exercises I practice when no one is watching.

We complete two slow circuits of my room, Mum chatting about nothing in particular while I focus on my steps. My hand touches the wall the entire time. I'm not steady enough, not yet.

By the second lap, I'm more confident, less hesitant. My body is slowly remembering how it feels to move with purpose.

"You're doing amazingly well," Mum says, and for once the encouragement doesn't feel patronising. It's simply the truth. I am doing well, better than anyone expected. Every step, every minor victory brings me closer to answers I desperately need.

I settle back on the bed, slightly winded but satisfied with the exertion. Mum adjusts my pillows, her movements automatic, maternal.

We sit in silence, and somehow it feels like a privilege. No monitors beeping, now. No therapists, no nurses, no police; just the two of us, together.

"I haven't said this before," Mum starts from nowhere, "but I'm... it's so good to see you getting better. I thought... I thought I was going to lose you. Back when they brought you in."

I know she's telling me this now, not sooner, because I am finally healing physically. Before, with the trach tube, the monitors, the drugs, I was a shape in a bed. Now, I'm starting to feel like a version of myself. Not the person I was, but something in the same ballpark.

I'm not sure I'll ever be the person I was, but I don't tell Mum that.

I press my hand to my chest, fingers curling slightly against the thin fabric of my hospital gown. Then, slowly, I extend it outward toward Mum: a silent, deliberate motion that says everything I can't.

Her breath catches. For a moment she blinks hard, forcing back tears. Then she nods, pressing a hand to her own chest.

"I love you too," she whispers.

It's enough to break her and make the tears flow.

We hold each other, and I don't want the warmth between us to ever stop.

CHAPTER TWENTY-NINE

The next morning, as Kate sets aside the communication cards we've been working with, she pauses to look at me.

"You seem distracted today," she says. "Is everything alright?"

I reach for the whiteboard: *Sarah's mum visiting*.

"Ah." Understanding softens her face. "That must be difficult to prepare for."

Don't know what to say, I write, the words inadequate for the tangle of emotions churning inside me.

Kate considers this, her head tilting slightly. "You know, sometimes in situations where words feel impossible, simply being present is enough." She pauses. "And Amanda, remember that you're not responsible for managing her grief alongside your own."

The thought has never occurred to me. Since waking up in this hospital bed, I've carried the weight of what happened to Sarah like a stone in my chest: heavy, cold, immovable. The idea that I'm not somehow responsible for Joyce's pain feels wrong.

"Let's try something different today," Kate suggests, sensing my struggle. "Let's work on emotional expression sounds. They're often easier to produce than formal speech, especially when we're overwhelmed. We're so close to being able to try some words, but maybe today these sounds will help."

She demonstrates in noises that convey sympathy, understanding, distress. The kind of primal vocalisations that existed before language, that transcend words. I follow her lead, surprised by how natural it feels to let them slip past my damaged vocal cords. They don't hurt the way trying to form words did.

By the time Kate leaves, I've mastered a small repertoire of expressive sounds: not quite speech, but communication, nonetheless. A tiny weapon against the silence that's been imposed on me.

"You did well today," she says, gathering her materials. "And Amanda? Whatever happens with Joyce, be gentle with yourself afterward."

The words echo in my mind after she's gone. Be gentle with myself. It's difficult when all I can do is blame myself.

Just before noon, David comes in for a routine check. His movements are efficient as always as he takes my blood pressure and temperature, but today there's a carefulness to him I haven't noticed before.

"Everything's looking good," he says, noting the readings on his chart. "It's been three days since we removed the monitors, and your vitals have remained stable. We're down to checking just twice a shift now."

I nod, grateful for the increased freedom. No more wires, no more constant beeping. Small victories.

"I understand Mrs Fairchild is visiting today," he adds, his voice neutral. "Dr Miles asked me to check if you'd like someone present. For support."

I shake my head immediately. Whatever happens between Joyce and me needs to happen without an audience.

"Alright." He tucks the thermometer away. "I'll be at the nurses' station if you need anything. Just press the call button."

As he turns to leave, I catch his sleeve. When he looks back, I mouth, "Thank you."

His expression softens momentarily, and I can see he's touched. Even though I can't let the sound come with the movement yet, he gets it.

"You're welcome," he smiles.

David has barely been gone five minutes when there's a knock at my door. I don't need a monitor beside me to know that my pulse rate is spiking.

The door opens, and Joyce Fairchild steps into my room.

My first thought is that Mum wasn't exaggerating. Joyce isn't doing well.

The woman who stands before me bears little resemblance to the warm, capable mother I remember. Her clothes hang loose on her frame, as if she's been steadily disappearing inside them. The skin beneath her eyes is shadowed dark purple, her hair, usually so neat, pulled back in a hasty ponytail that doesn't disguise its unwashed state.

But it's her eyes that stop my breath. They're the same clear blue as Sarah's but altered somehow, as if whatever light once animated them has been extinguished. She reminds me so much of her daughter, my best friend. I feel my throat close with recognition.

"Amanda," she says, and her voice too is changed: rougher, like something that's been worn down by constant use. "You're looking better than I expected."

I reach for the whiteboard, hands trembling.

Thank you for coming.

She moves further into the room but doesn't sit. Instead, she stands at the foot of my bed, one hand gripping the rail so tightly her knuckles whiten.

"Abby said you wanted to see me." Her voice is carefully controlled, but I hear the tremor beneath it.

My throat constricts, not from physical damage but from the weight of what I need to tell her. What right do I have to add to her suffering? But what right do I have to withhold the truth?

I want to help find her, I write.

Joyce's expression doesn't change, but something shifts in her posture. There's a subtle straightening of her spine, as if my words have touched something vital.

"The police say you don't remember much," she says. "After you were..." She stops, searching for a word. "After what happened."

I shake my head, frustrated by the limitations of the whiteboard, by how clinical my writing looks compared to the storm of emotions behind it.

I take a breath and steel myself. I'm used to writing one or two words, but this requires more. More physical energy to hold the pen steady and more emotional energy as I write the words I've been keeping hidden away.

I remember everything until I passed out, I write.

Joyce makes a small sound, a whimper so soft it might have been the wind. She sways slightly, and for a terrible moment, I think she might collapse. But she steadies herself against the bed rail, her white-knuckled grip the only sign of her distress.

"Tell me everything you remember," she says, the words little more than a whisper. "I need to know."

I swallow hard, my damaged throat working against a flood of emotion. I've tried to prepare for this moment, tried to find words that won't shatter her completely. But there are no gentle words for what happened to Sarah.

I hesitate, the marker poised over the whiteboard. The truth is, I wasn't even sure what happened. I was blindfolded, face pressed into the dirt. I heard sounds: Sarah's muffled struggles, his grunts, his voice. Interpreting them means admitting how much I don't know, how much I only think happened.

I start to think about the sounds I heard, and my mind clouds over. It's like a photo developing in reverse, only this time it's my memories that are fading.

I was blindfolded, I write first. Then, slowly, *I think he assaulted her.*

Assault isn't the word, and I know it. I shake my head, flex my fingers, letting the pen fall onto the bedsheet where the tip touches the cotton and starts to bleed out into a black stain.

The real word, the true word, burns in my mind, but my hand won't form the letters. My fingers tremble as I pick up the marker again, but when I press it to the whiteboard, I can only manage an *R* before my hand freezes completely.

Can I not write the word because I'm not completely certain, or can I not write it because I can't face it?

I can't face what happened to her, and I can't face that I couldn't stop it.

Didn't stop it.

I furiously wipe away the single letter with my palm and try once more: *Can't be 100% sure. But the sounds...*

Joyce reads the words, her face still as stone. When she looks up, there are no tears in her eyes, only a terrible, raw fear that she's trying desperately to control.

"Was he..." She stops, unable to form the question completely. Her fingers tighten on the bed rail until her knuckles turn white. "Did he hurt her... *that way*?"

I understand what she's asking. The question she can't fully voice mirrors my own inability to write the word. I manage a small nod, feeling sick with the confirmation I'm giving her.

I think so, I write, and it's the best that I can give her.

Joyce's breath catches. For a moment, she seems to fold inward, as if physically struck. Then she straightens, her jaw tightening with a visible effort of will.

"I've been having nightmares," she whispers. "About what might have... what he might have done to her. What he might be doing to her." She presses her lips together, fighting for composure. I recognise her pain. "Part of me hoped I was just torturing myself with the worst possibilities."

I can't even let myself think about them. Somehow she is much stronger than I. Still, I have to tell her she is not alone. My hand shudders as I write:

I have them too.

She puts her hand over her mouth in a swift, sharp movement. Maybe this meet up wasn't a good idea for either of us.

I'm sorry, I write, the words painfully inadequate.

"No," Joyce says sharply. "Don't apologise. Not to me." She releases her grip on the bed rail, her hands falling limply to her sides. "None of this is your fault, Amanda."

But isn't it? If I hadn't suggested picking bluebells, if I'd run when I first saw him, if I'd managed to fight harder, to scream louder.

If I hadn't left her there.

"But Sarah wouldn't blame you either." She takes a deep, unsteady breath. "She loved you, you know. Always said you were the sister she never had."

The words break something in me: a dam I've been building since I woke up in this hospital bed. Tears spill down my cheeks, hot and relentless. I don't try to wipe them away. Don't try to hide them.

Joyce moves around the bed to stand beside me. After a moment's hesitation, she reaches out, her cool hand cupping my cheek. The touch is so gentle, so motherly, that a sob escapes me. A raw sound that seems to echo in the sterile room.

"I need to ask you something," she says, her voice steadier now. "Something important."

I look up at her through tears, nodding.

"Do you think she's still alive?"

The question hangs in the air between us, heavy with all its implications. Joyce isn't asking for comfort or false hope. She's asking for the truth, as best as I can give it.

I close my eyes, forcing myself to remember those final moments.

When I open my eyes again, I take the whiteboard and write what I believe, with all my heart, to be true:

I don't know. But she was fighting. She wouldn't stop fighting.

It takes everything I have to write the words, and then I let myself fall back into the pillows.

Joyce's expression shifts: something between pride and a heavier emotion. Maybe it's the weight of knowing just how brave her daughter had to be. Or maybe it's just another kind of pain.

"Thank you for telling me," she says. "The police... they try to protect us from the details. As if knowing could somehow be worse than imagining."

She's right. I've seen it in my own mother's face when she looks at me: the questions she's afraid to ask, the answers she's afraid to hear.

Joyce sits on the edge of my bed, the movement so unexpected that I find myself shifting to make room for her. For a long moment, we sit in silence, bound by our shared concern, our shared love.

Then Joyce speaks again, her voice changed somehow: harder, more focused. "The police think they've narrowed down the search area. Something about a chemical smell you remembered?"

I nod, surprised she knows this detail.

She stops, swallows. “We need to get her home.”

I understand completely. The not knowing is unbearable.

I want to help, I write.

“You are helping,” Joyce says firmly. “Everything you remember, every detail you give them, it all narrows the search.”

But it’s not enough. Not nearly enough. If only I could remember how I got from that place in the woods to the road where I was found. If only I could recall anything about those missing hours.

We sit together for what feels like a long time, sometimes talking, sometimes not. Joyce tells me about the support group she’s joined: parents of missing children, bound together by the worst kind of shared experience. I write about my upcoming transfer to Oakwood, about the speech therapy that’s going to give me back my voice. I use the sounds that Kate taught me, but I’m so used to the whiteboard that I rely on it now.

Neither of us mentions Sarah in the present tense. Neither of us can bear to.

When Joyce finally stands to leave, I feel the loss of her presence like a physical chill. She’s the closest connection I have to Sarah now, the only person who truly understands the weight of her absence.

“I’ll come see you at Oakwood,” she says, adjusting her bag on her shoulder. “If that’s alright.”

I nod eagerly, relief flooding through me. I hadn’t dared to hope she would want to see me again.

“And Amanda?” She pauses at the door. “Thank you. For being honest with me. For not...” She gestures vaguely. “For not trying to spare my feelings with lies.”

CHAPTER THIRTY

After Joyce has gone, I curl onto my side, exhaustion washing over me in waves. The emotional toll of the morning has left me drained, empty. But there's something else too: a strange sense of lightness, as if sharing the burden of truth has somehow made it easier to bear.

Eventually, I reach for the notebook, still tucked beneath my pillow. My fingers trace the spiral binding, catching on a loose coil of wire. I let myself read Sarah's handwriting on the inside cover.

For Amanda - to fill with all our adventures, past and future. Someone needs to document our eventual world domination. Best friends forever means I get to read this someday! Love always, Sarah

The blue ink is slightly faded but her looping handwriting is unmistakable, the words now carrying a weight they were never meant to bear. That casual assumption of a shared future seems so naïve.

I have to force myself to remember that I am sixteen years old. I am supposed to be hopelessly naïve, aren't I?

Not anymore.

I turn to a fresh page and force myself to write down everything I can remember from Joyce's visit. Not just what she said, but how she looked: thinner, her skin ashen, her eyes haunted by the same question that keeps me awake at night.

Is Sarah still alive?

I don't write my answer. Can't bear to see it in black and white, even in these private pages. Instead, I write:

Joyce deserves to know the truth.

My hand trembles over the page. The real truth. Do I even know what that is? I remember sounds. Feelings. The texture of dirt against my face as I lay bleeding out. Sarah's muffled cries. But so much is still missing. So much still hidden behind the dark curtain that fell when he cut my throat.

My thoughts are interrupted by a soft knock at the door. I close the notebook, sliding it back under my pillow just as David enters with the afternoon medication round.

"How are you feeling?" he asks, setting a small paper cup of pills on my side table. His eyes track over me, professional and assessing. "That couldn't have been an easy conversation."

I struggle to sit up, ignoring the twinge of pain in my neck. I wiggle my hand in an indication of "so-so".

David nods, checking my chart. "Dr Miles is worried about you focussing too much on Sarah and not enough on your own recovery." He glances at me, his expression softening slightly. "I... I thought seeing Joyce might help, though."

I consider lying, saying yes, it helped, everything's fine, but something about David's steady presence stops me. He's never sugar-coated anything about my condition. Never treated me like I might shatter.

I shrug and reach for the whiteboard.

She needs answers I can't give.

I pause and then below I write:

And I need answers no one has.

David adjusts something on my chart. "Recovery isn't linear," he says finally. "Not just physical recovery, but the other kind, too. Some days, you'll feel like you're moving forward. Other days..." He shrugs. "Other days, it's enough just to stay afloat."

I think of Joyce, somehow managing to keep breathing despite the crushing weight of Sarah's absence. I think of how she still holds onto hope, however fragile.

I want to get better faster, I write, underlining 'faster' twice.

"I know." David's eyes meet mine briefly. "Everyone who's been through trauma wants that. But pushing too hard can set you back."

I reach for the water glass beside my bed, swallowing my pills under his watchful gaze.

Oakwood soon.

"Soon, yes." David makes a final notation on my chart. "Your wound is healing better than expected. Speech therapy is going well. Physically, you're ahead of schedule."

Mentally? I ask. I write the word and point at my head, swirling my finger.

"That's not my department. But if you want my observation? You're a tough cookie."

He leaves me with that, his shoes squeaking softly on the linoleum as he moves to his next patient. Being tough doesn't feel like a compliment. It feels like something that's been forced on me.

The afternoon stretches ahead, long and empty. I should rest before my evening therapy session, but sleep feels impossible, with thoughts of Joyce and Sarah filling my head. Instead, I force myself out of bed, testing my legs. They're steadier than last week, though still not entirely reliable. Some days I make it to the bathroom and back without holding onto anything. Some days I wobble like a newborn deer.

It's not enough. I'm not recovering quickly enough.

I stand in the middle of the room, breathing harder than I should be. The weakness in my body feels like a betrayal. While I'm here learning to walk again, Sarah is... where?

What's happening to her while I shuffle around my hospital room like an old woman?

My legs tremble, but I push myself to keep standing. I walk to the door, to the back wall, to the window, to the bed, and repeat. I'm racing laps. I'm walking at a snail's pace.

Don't hold on to anything.

Don't be so weak.

Don't stop now.

One more minute. Then another. My muscles burn with the effort, but I welcome the pain. It's something I can control, something I can push through.

When my vision starts to blur at the edges, I finally allow myself to sink onto the edge of the bed. Too much, too soon. I know it, but I can't help it. Every minute I spend in this weakened state feels like time stolen from Sarah.

Next, I try the breathing exercises Kate taught me, forcing air deep into my lungs despite the pull of scar tissue. Then, carefully, I begin the tongue movements designed to strengthen the muscles damaged during intubation. The exercises are tedious, repetitive, but I perform them with a focused intensity that surprises even me.

Get better faster. Get better faster.

The mantra repeats in my head with each controlled breath, each careful movement. By the time I finish the full set of exercises, sweat beads along my hairline and my throat aches with effort. But I feel something close to satisfaction. Progress. Small, incremental, but real.

When Mum arrives, I'm sitting in a chair by the window. The surprise of me not being in bed makes her grin as she walks into my room.

"Look at you!" she exclaims, setting her purse down. She's wearing her teaching clothes: a simple blouse and cardigan that stretches slightly over her growing baby bump. "How long have you been sitting up like that?"

I hold one finger up.

"An hour? That's brilliant, Amanda!"

It shouldn't feel like an accomplishment, sitting in a chair like a normal human being, but it does. I want Mum to see me healing. She doesn't have to go through what Joyce is suffering. I'm not lost, but I think that at times, even though I've been lying right there, Mum has thought I am.

Mum pulls the other chair close, settling herself with the careful movements of a woman growing accustomed to her changing centre of gravity.

"How did it go with Joyce?" she asks, studying my face. "I've been thinking about you both all day."

I look out the window, watching a pair of birds chase each other across the pale blue sky.

I'm going to need the board for this.

My words from earlier, when I explained to David, are still there.

She needs answers I can't give.

And I need answers no one has.

"You've had this conversation before," she half-smiles. "Kate?" I shake my head. "David?" I give her the thumbs up. My circle of friends is small, and they are my caregivers, not my friends.

Mum's voice is gentle. "I know it must have been hard for both of you, but I hope you got what you wanted out of it."

Did I?

Maybe I just needed that connection. That one other person who might come close to understanding the pain.

Maybe she did too. Maybe that's why she agreed to the visit.

Is Sarah still alive? I write.

I meant that this is what Joyce asked me, but Mum doesn't interpret it that way.

Mum reaches for my hand, her fingers warm against my perpetually cold ones. "The police are out there searching. They are doing everything they can, and what you have told them must be helping."

What about what I haven't told them?

What about the things I can't remember?

What about the things I'm not even sure of?

I nod, not trusting myself to speak. Mum doesn't press further, sensing perhaps that I've reached my limit for difficult conversations today.

Instead, her eyes scan up the board and she points at where I wrote *I want to get better faster.*

"I want that too," she says. "But Amanda, healing takes time."

Not enough time, I write. *Sarah doesn't have time.*

Mum's eyes fill with tears, and I immediately regret my words. The last thing I want is to cause her more pain. She's already been through so much because of me.

I'm sorry

"No," Mum says. "You don't need to apologise. I understand, sweetheart. I do." She takes a steadying breath. "But pushing yourself too hard won't help Sarah. You need to be well to be useful."

The pragmatic truth of her words hits home. I know she's right, but the knowledge doesn't make the waiting any easier.

Still, I nod, and take my turn at steering away from the things we can't talk about.

Oakwood soon, I write, forcing a smile.

Something in my expression must betray my feelings, because Mum leans forward, her face serious.

"Amanda, there's a therapist who at Oakwood who specialises in helping people who have been through terrible things." Her voice shakes as she speaks those last two words, and I can hardly bear to look at her. "Dr Miles says it's important that you talk to someone about... about everything that happened. Or, you know..."

She gestures at the communication boards and the whiteboard as though the word *talk* is a faux pas.

The thought makes my stomach clench. The idea of telling a stranger about Sarah's screams, about my failure to help her, feels impossible. Whether I'm going to speak the words, write it down or draw a cosy little picture like I've seen trauma patients do in movies.

Trauma patients like me.

But I look at Mum's face and think that maybe it's necessary. Maybe it's part of getting better faster.

I'll try, I write, and I mean it.

I'll try anything that might help me get strong enough to find Sarah.

I'm still sitting by the window when Suki arrives later, her practical shoes quiet against the floor. I've been watching the sky change colour as evening approaches, tracking the gradual shift from blue to dusty rose to the deep purple that signals night is coming.

It reminds me of my wallpaper back home, and I wonder how long it will be before I see it again.

"Amanda?" Suki's voice is soft, careful not to startle me. "Is this a good time?"

I turn from the window to find her standing in the doorway, her ever-present shoulder bag slung across her body.

I bob my head, gesturing to the chair Mum vacated.

Suki smiles slightly as she settles into the chair.

"I'm just here to check in." She studies me for a moment. "I heard Joyce Fairchild visited today."

I'm about to nod again, but I feel I need to give her more of a reply.

I reach for the board point at the words I've already used for David and for Mum. Maybe I should have a set of my own communication boards with words and phrases that I have to keep repeating, questions I keep asking.

It's not actually a bad idea.

Suki's eyes have scanned the board, and she purses her lips gently at the last thing I wrote: Is Sarah still alive?

She doesn't flinch, doesn't look away. She just nods once, acknowledging the terrible weight of the question in front of us in black and white.

"You must both desperately want the answer to this question," she says. "They're doing their best to find her."

It's all I keep hearing. I tilt my head and raise the pen.

And Maggie?

Concern flickers in Suki's eyes. "They're pursuing all viable leads, including trying to identify Maggie."

It's a professional answer, carefully worded to reveal nothing while sounding informative. I've heard enough of them to recognise the pattern.

"But they haven't found anything yet," Suki holds my gaze steadily. "What I can tell you is that your testimony about Maggie was taken very seriously. Detective Barnes has teams investigating multiple angles."

They don't know anything?

"It just means exactly what I said. They're pursuing multiple possibilities." Suki is patient with my questions, and I appreciate it.

Like?

"Like whether Maggie is another victim. Or someone from his past. Or someone he's fixated on for other reasons." Suki pauses. "They're being thorough, Amanda. That's all I can say for now."

It's frustrating, but it's something. More than I've had before.

I've spent so much time thinking about those same things.

Fixating, I'm sure Dr Miles would call it.

I want to help

Suki doesn't immediately dismiss the idea, which surprises me. Instead, she considers it, head tilted slightly.

"Your primary focus here, and at Oakwood, should be your recovery," she says finally. "But the detectives will need to see you again. There's a long way to go, whatever..."

She stops herself, and I know she was going to say whatever happens. Whether Sarah is dead or alive. Whether Maggie is real or someone he made up.

All I can do is nod and try to push down the sick feeling that wants to take over my body.

When Suki rises to leave, I feel something close to regret. In a strange way, my conversations with her are some of the most normal I've had since waking up in the hospital. No careful avoidance of difficult topics. No pitying glances. Just straightforward information and realistic assessments.

"I'll see you at Oakwood," she promises, shouldering her bag. "I'm planning to be there when you arrive. Help with the transition."

I nod, grateful for the continuity she represents.

Let me know ANYTHING new

"I'll tell you what I can," she says, and I believe her.

After she's gone, I return to my bed, determined to practice the speech exercises Kate gave me one more time before sleep. Each movement, every sound is a struggle, but I push through the discomfort, focusing on the goal. If I can't form words when I get to Oakwood, how will I convince the therapist, the police, anyone, that I'm strong enough to help find Sarah? It's six days away. How far am I from speaking?

By the time the night nurse brings my bedtime medication, my throat throbs, but I've made it through the entire exercise sheet twice. It's not enough, it never feels like enough, but it's progress.

I pull out my notebook one last time before sleep, flipping to a clean page. I've been recording my progress each day, tracking improvements in mobility, speech, strength. Tonight, I add a new column: Goals.

Under it, I write:

Walk the entire hallway without stopping by Friday.

Speak a complete sentence before Oakwood.

Build enough strength to shower standing up.

Prepare questions for first session with Oakwood therapist.

Find Sarah.

I stare at the last item for a long moment. It doesn't belong with the others: practical, measurable recovery milestones. It's bigger. Harder.

But I leave it there anyway. Because in the end, nothing else matters if I can't accomplish that final goal.

I finally feel something like control returning. Not over what happened, never that, but over what happens next. Over how I move forward from here.

I close my eyes, forcing myself to breathe evenly. To rest. To heal.

For Sarah.
For Maggie.
For myself.

CHAPTER THIRTY-ONE

I wake to find my notebook still beside me on the bed where I'd fallen asleep with it. The pen has rolled into the crease of my elbow, leaving a smudge of ink on the hospital sheets. Last night's final entry stares back at me, the page slightly warped from the heat of my body curled protectively around it in sleep. My handwriting tells its own story across the page, starting with the careful, measured letters of someone trying to take control, gradually becoming more slanted, more desperate, more exhausted as I'd listed my goals. As if my determination was fighting against the limitations of my weakened body.

Five goals. Five days now until Oakwood. I don't expect to achieve one each day, but any day would be great for the last one.

Find Sarah.

Those nine letters contain my entire purpose, the reason I push through every exercise, every painful therapy session. Not just a goal, but a promise.

I trace my finger over the second goal on my list: Speak a complete sentence before Oakwood.

During our last session, Kate said we were 'so close to being able to try some words'. I've been religious about Kate's exercises, following her instructions with a precision that would have surprised the old Amanda. The one who rushed through homework, who cut corners on assignments, who thought patience was something that happened to other people.

What might have surprised her more is that I've done what I was told. I've been waiting. Following instructions. Measuring progress not in words but in small victories: reduced pain during swallowing, clearer humming, stronger breathing. The obedient patient, for once.

This new Amanda, the one who almost died on a country road with her throat slashed open, understands waiting. Understands that progress comes in whispers, not shouts.

I'm deep in reflection when David arrives with his medication tray, his usual efficiency softened by the hint of a smile.

"Morning," he says, setting down a small paper cup of pills and a glass of water. "Sleep well?"

I give a noncommittal tilt of my hand. The dark circles under my eyes probably answer his question better than any gesture could. Last night, the recurring nightmare came again: Sarah calling my name while I couldn't answer, couldn't move. I woke gasping, the phantom sensation of the blindfold still tight against my face, the sheets tangled around my wrists in a way that sent me frantically clawing for freedom.

David checks my chart, making a quick note before glancing at the notebook beside me. "Journaling again? That's good. Helps process things."

I reach for my whiteboard, the marker squeaking against the smooth surface:

Going to ask if I can try speaking today.

His eyebrows rise slightly. "That would be a big step. You've been making good progress with the exercises?"

I nod emphatically, writing again: She said we're close.

"That's great," David says, as he hands me my pills.

I can sense he doesn't want to give me too much hope. He was here when I first tried to speak, much too soon.

This is different.

Today might be the day.

David's expression remains carefully neutral, but I catch a flicker of shared optimism he's too professional to voice. "Good luck," he says simply, collecting his tray. "I'll be around if you need anything after your session."

When he leaves, I close the journal and begin my morning routine of exercises. Diaphragmatic breathing. In through the nose, expanding the belly rather than the chest, out through slightly parted lips. The scar tissue pulls with each exhale, but not as sharply as before.

Next, tongue mobility: tip to the roof of my mouth, side to side, gentle stretching. My tongue feels clumsy, under-used, but responsive. Humming follows, starting low, sustaining for five counts, progressing gradually higher until I feel the first hint of strain, then stopping. The vibration against healing tissue is a reminder of the damage, but also of the strength rebuilding beneath it.

I check the clock. Kate will arrive in thirty minutes. My heart flutters, a hummingbird trapped behind my ribs. What if she says no? What if the healing isn't far enough along? What if I've done the exercises wrong?

And worse: what if she says yes, and I fail?

I clench my fists, breathing through the wave of anxiety. Five days until Oakwood. Five days to find my voice, to become more than a whiteboard and pointing finger, to speak for myself and for Sarah.

The thought of Sarah steadies me. My impatience isn't just selfishness; it's urgency. Every day without answers is another day she's missing. Another day with him.

Before Kate comes I'm going to get up, take myself to the bathroom on the legs I'm training to carry me again. I'm going to brush my hair, clean my teeth, all the simple things that I took for granted all of my life until I couldn't do them anymore.

Like speaking.

Whoever imagines that something so essential can be ripped away?

Whoever imagines that the walk home from school is going to change their life forever?

Thirty minutes later, I'm sitting up in the chair. Dressed, clean and as confident as I can manage. When Kate enters, her expression warm but professional as she sets her folder of exercises on the table, I'm sure she already knows I mean business.

"Good morning, Amanda," she says, her eyes tracking over me with clinical assessment. "How are we feeling today?"

I reach for the whiteboard: Good. Exercises done.

She nods, pleased. "Excellent. Mind if I look at your throat today?"

I lift my chin, exposing the healing wound to her examination. Her hands are cool and confident as she gently palpates around the scar, checking for swelling, excessive tenderness. Her touch is different from the doctors', more attuned to subtle responses, watching how I flinch or relax.

Something's different about her manner today. A certain focus, an intentness that makes my pulse quicken. She's considering something, weighing possibilities.

"The stoma site is closing nicely," she says finally, stepping back. "And the overall inflammation has decreased significantly." She tilts her head slightly. "Have you been feeling any sharp pain during the humming exercises? Any burning sensation?"

I shake my head, barely daring to breathe.

Kate retrieves her file, flipping through pages of notes: my history, my progress, her assessment from days past. I watch her face for clues, for any hint of what comes next.

She closes the file and meets my eyes directly. “I think we’re ready to try a single word today.”

The world seems to stop. A buzzing fills my ears, and for a moment, I’m not sure if I’ve heard her correctly. I didn’t even have to ask.

One word. Today. Now.

I blink hard, waiting for her to retract the statement, to say it’s too soon, to tell me to keep waiting.

She doesn’t.

Instead, she sits in the chair beside me.

“This isn’t like when you tried on your own,” she says, gentle but firm. “We’ll do this with proper technique, with control. And we’ll stop immediately if there’s any sharp pain. Understand?”

I nod vigorously, barely able to contain the emotions surging through me. My hands tremble.

One word. Just one. But it’s everything.

“Let’s start with breathing,” Kate instructs, demonstrating the proper diaphragmatic breath. “Deep in through the nose, slow and controlled. Feel your belly expand, not your chest.”

I follow her lead, focusing on the rise and fall of my abdomen rather than the thundering of my heart.

“Now, think about the word you want to say,” she continues. “Form it in your mind. Feel the shape of it in your mouth without making any sound.”

There’s only one word I want, need, to say. I’ve been practicing it in silence for weeks, my lips and tongue forming its shape during sleepless nights. Sarah. The ‘S’ like a whisper, tongue behind teeth. The soft ‘ah’ in the middle. The gentle ‘rah’ finishing with open lips.

“Keep your throat relaxed,” Kate guides, watching me intently. “The air should flow easily. Don’t force it.”

I nod, concentrating on keeping my neck muscles loose. Tension will only strain the healing tissue.

"When you're ready, take a deep breath and let the sound come naturally with the exhale." Kate's voice is calm, steadying. "Remember, we're aiming for whisper-level volume. No strain."

I close my eyes, gathering myself for this moment. Eight weeks of silence. Eight weeks of Sarah missing while I lay healing in a hospital bed.

Breathe in. Belly expands.

Feel the word forming: Sarah.

Exhale gently, letting air pass through vocal cords.

"Sss..."

The first sound emerges. Not a proper 'S,' but a breathy approximation. Pain flares, hot and immediate, but different from before. Not the tearing agony of my previous attempts, but the burn of disused muscles awakening.

Kate nods encouragement, her eyes intent on my throat. "That's it. Controlled breath. Try again."

What would Sarah tell me now? She would be here by my side. She would tell me I can do it.

"Sss..." The sound comes again, clearer this time. "...aaa..."

The vowel hurts more, requires more air, more vibration of tender tissue. Tears spring to my eyes, but I push forward.

"...rrr..."

The consonant catches, rough and uneven. I can feel the strain building, the urge to push harder warring with Kate's instructions to stay controlled.

Kate watches intently, her hand hovering near my arm, ready to stop me if needed. "One more try," she says quietly. "Remember: gentle, continuous air."

I close my eyes, placing my fingertips against my throat where the bandage once was, feeling the raised line of the scar beneath. Inside that scar, inside that damaged tissue, is my voice. My truth. My power to help find Sarah.

Deep breath.

"Sarah."

It emerges as a rasping whisper, the final syllable barely audible, but unmistakable. A complete word. Her name.

My throat burns, but the tears that spill down my cheeks aren't from pain. It's the release of something I've been holding since I woke in this hospital bed: a breath I couldn't fully exhale, a scream I couldn't voice, a name I couldn't call.

The first word I have spoken since that night. The word I have been holding in the pit of my stomach, coiled tight like a snake waiting to strike.

Kate waits, giving me space to process, to breathe.

"Sarah," I say again, the word stronger now though still barely above a whisper.

Kate's professional demeanour softens into a genuine smile. "That's remarkable, Amanda," she says, her voice thick with emotion she usually keeps controlled. "That's way better than I..."

But then I can't hear what she says because I am sobbing so hard that my chest heaves, my vision blurs.

I have found one word. The most important word.

It felt like a song coming from my mouth. It felt like a prayer. It felt like

I want to say more, so much more. About Sarah, about Maggie, about what he did to us in those woods. But my throat is already aching from this small victory, my vocal cords protesting their sudden awakening.

"Let's stop there for today," Kate says, noticing my instinct to continue. "One success is enough. We need to build gradually, not push too far at once."

She's right, I know. But having tasted speech again, the silence feels heavier than before.

I reach for the whiteboard: *When can I try more?*

"Tomorrow," she says.

A full sentence before Oakwood? I write.

Kate nods. "I think that's a realistic goal now."

After she leaves, I sit in the quiet room, my fingertips still resting against my throat. I can still feel it: the vibration, the shape of Sarah's name in my mouth, the power of being heard.

CHAPTER THIRTY-TWO

Tomorrow, I leave for Oakwood. My bags are half-packed, but it's close enough. Mum will help with the rest. I have things to do.

I take twenty-seven steps down the hospital corridor without leaning on anyone. The physical therapist walks beside me, clipboard in hand, but she doesn't touch me. Doesn't need to.

I am walking on my own.

The corridor stretches ahead, fluorescent lights marking my progress in regular pools of brightness. Each step feels like a tiny rebellion against what he tried to do to me. He tried to silence me by cutting my throat. He tried to end me. But I am still here. Still walking. Still breathing. And tomorrow, I'm walking out of here on my own two feet.

Kate says I'm making unprecedented progress. Dr Miles seems surprised each time she checks my charts. David just watches me with that careful, assessing gaze, occasionally nodding like he's confirming something he already suspected.

No one knows I've been pushing myself to the breaking point every night. No one knows that every step, every word, is for Sarah. To find Sarah. To help Sarah. To make up for the fact that somehow, I escaped while she didn't.

But today, as I reach the end of the corridor, step twenty-seven, I allow myself a moment of pure selfish joy. I did this. My body did this. After everything, I am walking. Breathing. Living.

I turn back toward the nurse station, a smile breaking across my face. The first real smile I can remember since before that day in the woods.

"*Try something*," I tell my physical therapist, Emily. The words are quiet and thin, but clear.

Emily blinks, surprised by both my clarity and my initiative. "What do you want to try?"

I look at the corridor that stretches ahead of me. Another sentence is beyond me for now. I want to walk back on my own. No one beside me.

I point ahead and raise my hand in a stop sign, indicating that I want her to stay put.

She hesitates, weighing protocol against progress. "I'll be right behind you," she warns, but I can see she's going to let me try.

I nod and take a deep breath.

Then I begin the journey back. One step. Two steps. Three. The linoleum floor is cool and smooth beneath my thin hospital socks. My reflection ghosts along the polished surface: a girl growing stronger with every step. My legs no longer shake. My breathing remains steady. Six steps. Seven. Eight.

A passing nurse smiles, recognition lighting her face. "Well done, Amanda," she says, and I feel a strange lightness in my chest. Like maybe the world isn't only darkness and fear. Like maybe there's something on the other side of all this.

Halfway back to my room, I realise I'm not counting steps anymore. I'm just... walking. Almost like a normal person. Almost like the Amanda from before. Each step feels more natural than the last.

When I reach my door, a journey that would have exhausted me just a few days ago, I turn to Emily and say, "*Bit further?*"

I'm slightly out of breath, though, and my words are waiflike.

Emily laughs, jotting notes on her clipboard. "Let's not push it too far. But you're right, you absolutely could." She shakes her head, impressed. "You're determined. I'll give you that."

Determined doesn't begin to cover it.

Back in my room, I sit on my bed, not winded, not exhausted, just pleasantly aware of having used muscles that had been dormant too long. Through the window, I can see trees beginning to bloom in the hospital garden. May is fully here, the world renewing itself in defiance of all the ugliness it contains.

I'm supposed to rest before my final speech therapy session with Kate, but I'm too energised, too alive with possibility. I hope the speech therapist they assign me at Oakwood is even half as good as Kate has been. I'm going to miss her.

Instead of resting, I reach for my notebook and open it to a fresh page.

I've been keeping lists. Memories of that day. Questions about Maggie. Descriptions of his voice, his hands, the truck, everything I can possibly recall that might help find Sarah. But today I write something different.

I walked. On my own. And I spoke clearly.

I tick the items off my checklist and look at the others. I already managed the shower without the plastic chair, so there are two more goals to achieve. Neither of them seems easy.

Prepare questions for first session with Oakwood therapist.

Find Sarah.

"Amanda?"

I look up to see Kate in the doorway, her therapy bag slung over her shoulder. She's early, or I've lost track of time.

"You look cheerful," she says, setting her bag down. "Good session with your physical therapist?"

I close the notebook, a smile spreading across my face. A real smile, not the careful approximation I've been offering for weeks. "All the way," I say, pointing to the corridor behind her.

The words come out clearly, each one distinct. Not perfect, there's still a roughness, a catch on certain syllables, but so much stronger than yesterday.

Kate's eyebrows lift in surprise. "And you're speaking much more clearly today."

"Thank you," I say.

Kate pulls up a chair and sits beside me, her usual clipboard conspicuously absent. "Amanda," she says gently, "recovery isn't a race. But..." She shakes her head, impressed. "Your progress is remarkable. The human body has an amazing capacity for healing when the mind is determined."

"It is," I tell her.

"Well, since you've clearly been working overtime, let's see exactly where we are today." She reaches into her bag for assessment materials.

For the next thirty minutes, I push through every exercise Kate gives me. Consonant sounds that troubled me yesterday now flow smoothly. Words I stumbled over come naturally. My voice still doesn't sound quite like me. There's a new texture to it, slightly lower, slightly rougher, but it's getting stronger by the minute.

"This is..." Kate checks her notes, shaking her head in disbelief. "Amanda, you've compressed about three weeks of expected progress into a few days. Without risking damaging yourself. You put in the groundwork with the exercises. You should be so proud."

"Getting better faster," I say, unable to contain my happiness. I'm still choosing my words economically, but I'm choosing them. I'm speaking them.

Kate puts down her notebook. "At this rate, you'll be speaking completely normally, or your new normal, within weeks of your transfer to Oakwood. But don't rush things too much, okay? Be gentle with yourself."

I've heard those words before, and I nod. But somehow, I feel that getting better faster is being gentle with myself. Making physical progress and improving my speech makes me feel less like a victim and more like a version of myself.

My new normal, she's right.

"I need to get better," I say simply.

It's a full sentence.

It's the truth.

Kate nods, understanding more than I'm saying. "Well, you're certainly on your way." She packs up her materials, our session drawing to a close. "Same time tomorrow?"

I smile. "I have plans," I breathe. Was that my first joke in two months?

"I'm going to miss you, Amanda," she says. "If you don't mind, I might pop in and see how you're getting on over there."

I can't stop myself from grinning, even though anything more than a regular smile still hurts the scar on my neck.

"Please," I reply.

She reaches to shake my hand, and I offer my arms for a hug instead. I've done a lot of work on my own, but Kate has been amazing at keeping me on track and moving in the right direction.

I'm going to miss her too.

After Kate leaves, I stay perched on the edge of my bed, a strange energy coursing through me. For the first time since waking up in this hospital, I feel something like hope. Not just for finding Sarah, but for myself. For a future beyond these walls. Beyond the terror of that night.

I reach for the notebook again and stare at the words, a lump forming in my throat that has nothing to do with my injury. Today, I can begin to imagine a life after this. Not the same life, never that, but something worth fighting for, nevertheless.

When the lunch tray arrives, the nurse seems surprised to find me upright, alert, almost vibrant compared to my usual careful conservation of energy.

"Someone's having a good day," she remarks, setting the tray on the bedside table.

"I am," I agree. It's hard to believe that I can be positive, despite everything, but my positivity, my belief that I can get better, is necessary. I have to be better so I can help Sarah.

After lunch, I open the half-packed duffel bag Mum brought last week. I add the notebook to my bag, tucking it carefully between layers of clothing. Every detail I've written will come with me to Oakwood: the sound of the truck's engine, the feel of the blindfold, the water in the distance.

Closer to where we were taken. Closer, maybe, to where Sarah is still waiting to be found.

While I wait for Mum to arrive, I go through the final discharge checklist Dr Miles left. The hospital will sort out the array of medications I have to take to Oakwood. Appointments are already scheduled with my new therapists there. There's a map of the facility with my room marked in blue. My own room. Not a hospital room, but something closer to normal. A step toward whatever life looks like after all this. They've given me a brochure with some photos, and it looks exactly as I would imagine it: a hospital that's trying not to look like a hospital.

The bed is a shiny kind of wood that doesn't look real, and the desk and table are so basic that I'm pretty sure they have the exact same units in every single room in every single rehab centre, let alone in Oakwood. The carpet is blue, the walls are beige, and the view from my room doesn't look out over the woods.

I take a breath, steady myself, and slide the brochure into the bag.

Then I practice standing up and sitting down smoothly, without using my hands for support. Up, down. Up, down. Tomorrow when the Oakwood transport arrives, I want to walk out of here on my own power. No wheelchair. No nurse's steadying arm. Just me, standing on my own two feet, facing whatever comes next.

Voices in the corridor catch my attention: Mum's familiar tones mingled with others I can't immediately identify. She must have run into hospital staff on her way in.

I move to the door, ready to surprise her with my newfound mobility, my clearer speech. Ready to see her face light up with the same hope I'm feeling.

But when I pull open the door, the voices fall silent. Mum stands in the corridor, her face ashen, eyes red-rimmed. Beside her stands Detective Barnes, his expression carefully neutral in that way that means bad news. And beside him, Suki, clutching her ever-present shoulder bag like a shield.

Something cold slides down my spine.

"Mum?" My voice, so clear just moments ago, cracks on the single syllable.

Mum's face crumples at the sound of my voice.

"Oh, Amanda," she whispers, and reaches for my hand.

I step back, away from whatever they've come to tell me.

"No," I say, though I don't yet know what I'm refusing. Just that I don't want it. Can't accept it. Not today. Not when I've just started to feel like myself again.

Barnes takes a step forward, his voice measured but firm.

"Amanda, why don't we go inside and sit down?"

But I don't move. Can't move. My legs, so steady just minutes ago, now feel like they might give way beneath me.

"Tell me," I demand, my voice a hoarse approximation of the clarity I'd achieved earlier.

"Please," Mum says. "Sit down, love."

It's the way she says it that makes me do as she asks. The way she trembles. The way her hands clasp so tightly in front of her that her knuckles whiten. I pull myself onto the bed, tucking my knees to my chest.

She knows what's coming, but she doesn't say it.

Barnes does.

"Amanda, I'm very sorry to tell you we've found Sarah."

For one breath, one heartbeat, hope surges through me, wild and desperate. They found her.

Even though I know.

I know from the way they're all looking at me as if I'm about to shatter.

I knew as soon as they arrived, unannounced, en masse.

The world tilts sharply. My free hand finds the bedframe, gripping it for support.

"I'm so sorry," Suki says, and her voice falters.

Barnes moves closer, his hands steady, his presence solid.

"I know this is incredibly difficult..."

"No," I say again, more forcefully this time. "No, that's not... you're wrong. They're wrong."

The words are too much for me.

Mum steps toward me, tears streaming freely down her face now.

"Darling," she begins, but I cut her off.

"No!" The word tears from my throat, a scream that sends pain lancing through my healing wound.

Barnes moves closer, his hands steady, ready to catch me if I fall from the bed.

"It's wrong!" I insist, backing further into my room, away from their sympathetic faces, their terrible certainty. "It's a mistake!"

But I know.

I have always known.

Sarah didn't escape. Sarah was never going to escape. Not after what I heard that night. Not after what he did to her.

Not after what he did to me.

My breath comes in short sharp pants, and I wish I had the trach tube to do it for me again. I wish I was medicated, that I didn't have to hear this.

I look up into Barnes's sad but steady eyes.

"Where?" I ask, as if it matters. Weakly, the fight draining from me as suddenly as it came. "Where did they find her?"

These aren't the sentences I wanted to speak.

This isn't what I wanted my voice for.

This isn't fair.

"Near the old Marshall Chemical Processing plant," he says gently. "Fifteen miles from where you were both taken."

My stomach twists.

"Amanda, we wouldn't have found her without you."

The words hit me harder than I expect.

"That sulphuric smell you described. That, along with the sound of water you heard, led us to the site. Marshall Creek runs along there." He pauses, giving me a moment to process. "Your memories put us on the right track."

I grip the bedframe harder. I should feel relieved. I helped. I gave them something useful.

Then why does it feel like my fault?

The creek. The water I heard that night. He kept her close to where he attacked us. All this time, Sarah was there, just fifteen miles away from the clearing, while I lay in this hospital bed, healing too slowly.

"How?" The question scrapes my throat raw.

The detective hesitates, glancing at Mum.

"Tell me," I insist.

"The medical examiner is still determining the exact cause of death," Barnes says carefully. "Due to the time that has passed... most of the forensic evidence has been compromised. There's a lot we can't know for certain."

The meaning washes over me.

Due to the time that has passed.

It's been weeks, then. Maybe that very night.

Maybe when I was found on the road, bleeding but alive, Sarah was already gone.

I can only imagine the worst.

Sarah, alone and afraid, suffering until the very end.

A sound escapes me. Not a sob or a scream, but something more primal. A keening wail that seems to come from somewhere deep inside, somewhere untouched by weeks of careful therapy and recovery.

Mum wraps her arms around me, pulling me against her. Her tears fall into my hair as she rocks me like a child.

"I'm sorry," she whispers, over and over. "I'm so sorry."

But her comfort can't reach me. I'm falling through space, untethered from everything I thought I knew. From the hope that had been growing inside me all day. From the future I had just begun to imagine.

Sarah is gone.

Sarah has been gone all along.

All my determination, all my progress, all my desperate attempts to recover quickly enough to help find her. None of it mattered. I was too late from the very beginning.

PART THREE

CHAPTER THIRTY-THREE

"Amanda, we've been sitting here for forty minutes, and you've said exactly twelve words."

I stare at the geometric pattern in the carpet, counting the blue diamonds that form imperfect rows across Dr Harriet Craig's office. Forty-two diamonds from the door to the window. Twenty-seven from her desk to the sofa where I'm sitting. Her voice is gentle but firm, the same tone she's used for the past eight weeks.

Eight weeks at Oakwood.

Eight weeks of staring at different walls, different carpets, different concerned faces.

Five weeks since Sarah's funeral.

"Amanda, I've noticed you're speaking less than you could be," Dr Craig continues. "Your speech therapist tells me you're physically able to talk more than you have been. I'm wondering if there's something else holding you back?"

I raise my eyes briefly to meet hers, then return to counting diamonds. Dr Craig is probably in her forties, with short black hair that frames her face in a neat bob. She wears minimal makeup and simple jewellery; today it's small pearl earrings and a silver watch. Nothing flashy. Nothing distracting. Everything about her is precisely calibrated to create an environment of calm focus.

I hate it.

I hate the calculated serenity of her office, with its tasteful watercolour landscapes and strategically placed plants.

I hate the way she watches me with patient expectation.

Most of all, I hate that I'm here at all, working through exercises that no longer have any purpose.

Every breathing technique, every carefully constructed sentence, every step down the hallway without my legs giving out. All of it was meant to help me get strong enough to find Sarah. To save her. To bring her home. That was the only thing that mattered, the only reason to push through the pain and the fear and the endless, exhausting work of recovery.

But Sarah is gone. She's been gone all along. All those weeks of fighting to get better, of forcing words past my damaged throat, of telling myself that every small victory brought me closer to finding her. It was all for nothing. She was already dead while I lay in a hospital bed, dreaming of rescue. While doctors patched me up and therapists coaxed me back to life, Sarah was cold in the ground, beyond anyone's help.

So, what's the point of any of this now? The breathing exercises. The coping strategies. The meaningless milestones.

They were stepping stones to finding Sarah, and now they lead nowhere at all.

"Would you prefer to write today?" she asks, sliding a notepad toward me.

"No." Thirteen words now. My voice still carries that raspy quality, like sandpaper over stone, but it doesn't hurt anymore. Not physically, at least.

Dr Craig waits, her stillness a kind of pressure. She's good at this, the strategic silence that pulls words from reluctant patients. Usually, I break first. Today, I match her stillness with my own.

After what feels like an eternity, she sighs quietly. "Amanda, I understand that Sarah's death has changed how you view your recovery. The purpose you had before is gone. That's a devastating loss on top of an already traumatic experience."

I flinch at Sarah's name. Two months isn't enough to blunt that particular pain.

Maybe she's a psychic as well as a psychologist. She can just read my mind, write down whatever broken thoughts she finds there, and we can both stop pretending this is helping.

She could skip straight to the diagnoses, the labels, the neat little boxes to file me away in. Traumatised. Damaged. Survivor with no reason to survive.

"But refusing to engage with therapy isn't honouring her memory." Dr Craig doesn't let up. "It's not helping you process what happened. And it's certainly not helping catch the man who did this to both of you."

My fingers dig into the soft material of the sofa. She knows exactly which buttons to push. In our early sessions, when I was still raw from the funeral, still numb with shock, I'd told her how I couldn't understand why I survived, and Sarah didn't. How unfair it felt. How guilty I felt, even though logically I knew it wasn't my fault.

"I'm tired," I say. Fifteen words now.

"I know you are." Dr Craig's voice softens slightly. "Grief is exhausting. Trauma is exhausting. Recovery is exhausting. But you've been at Oakwood for two months now, and we're making very slow progress."

I raise my eyes to meet hers again, longer this time. "So what?"

Dr Craig holds my gaze. "So, the recovery arc we initially projected has stalled. Your physical therapy is progressing, but psychologically, you're stuck."

"Maybe this is just who I am now." Eighteen, nineteen, all the way up to twenty-five words. I'm on a roll.

"No." Dr Craig shakes her head firmly. "This isn't who you are. This is who trauma has temporarily made you. There's a difference."

I look away, focusing on the window behind her desk. The grounds of Oakwood Rehabilitation Centre spread out in carefully landscaped perfection: manicured lawns, flowering shrubs, winding paths where patients practice walking again, talking again, living again. From Dr Craig's second-floor office, I can just see the edge of the woods that border the property to the east.

Woods. My chest tightens, throat constricting. I force myself to look away.

"The police have asked about interviewing you again," Dr Craig says casually, too casually. "They have some new information they want to discuss."

This catches my attention despite myself. "What information?"

"I don't have those details." She makes a note on her pad. "But Detective Barnes specifically requested to speak with you. I told him I'd need to assess whether you're ready for that kind of conversation."

"And am I?" The question comes out sharper than I intended.

"Are you?" Dr Craig returns. "An interview would require engagement, Amanda. Active participation. Verbal communication. It would be difficult."

"I can handle difficult." Twenty-nine words now. No, wait, thirty. I've lost count.

"Can you?" She leans forward slightly. "Because from what I've observed over the past eight weeks, you've been avoiding *difficult*. You've been going through the motions in physical therapy, attending your sessions here but barely participating, keeping interactions with other residents to a minimum."

Each observation lands like a small slap. True, all of it, but still painful to hear.

"That's not fair," I say, my voice catching. "I talk to Ellie."

Ellie, my one friend at Oakwood. Seventeen, recovering from a traumatic brain injury after a car accident. She doesn't push, doesn't ask questions. Doesn't look at me with pitying eyes. Just sits with me sometimes, sharing silence that doesn't feel like drowning.

"Yes, you do," Dr Craig acknowledges. "Which tells me you're capable of more connection than you're allowing yourself."

I pick at a loose thread on my sleeve. The clothes Mum brought from home hang off my body now. I haven't been eating enough. Another failure to add to the list.

"Amanda," Dr Craig's voice gentles further, "when you first arrived at Oakwood, you were still in shock from learning about Sarah. No one expected you to jump into therapy then. But it's been two months, and you've built walls instead of bridges."

I close my eyes, suddenly tired in a way that's beyond physical. I remember the early days after the funeral: the numbness, the disconnect, as if I were watching myself from a great distance. I remember Mum's worried face, Paul's awkward attempts at comfort. Joyce, hollow-eyed and diminished, reaching for my hand at the graveside.

"I don't know how to do this," I whisper, the admission slipping out before I can catch it. Thirty-seven words now. "I don't know how to get better when she can't."

Dr Craig doesn't immediately respond, giving the words space to exist between us. When she finally speaks, her voice carries a different quality: less clinical, more human.

"Recovery isn't a betrayal, Amanda. Sarah wouldn't want you stuck in this halfway place."

"You didn't know her," I say, a flash of anger cutting through the fog. "You don't know what she'd want."

"You're right, I didn't know her," Dr Craig agrees. "But I know something about survivors. And I know that honouring those we've lost rarely means sacrificing our own lives."

"I'm not..." I start to protest. But isn't that exactly what I've been doing? Not living, just existing. Going through the motions without purpose or direction.

"The police believe your testimony could still help the investigation," Dr Craig says after a moment. "The information you provided before, about the chemical smell, about him calling you Maggie. It's led to new leads."

Maggie. The name hits me like cold water. Maybe because it's the only part of that night that still feels like a mystery.

"What did they find?"

Dr Craig shakes her head. "I don't have those details. But if you want to find out, you'll need to be ready for that conversation." She glances at the clock. "Our time is almost up for today. For the next session, I'd like you to think about what recovery might look like if you separated it from Sarah."

I frown. "What does that mean?"

"It means finding a reason to heal that isn't about her. Something just for you." She closes her notebook. "We'll talk about it tomorrow."

As I stand to leave, legs steadier than they were weeks ago, voice stronger, but spirit still broken, Dr Craig adds, "And Amanda? You spoke almost eighty words today. It's not much, but it's more than the last session. That's progress, whether you want to acknowledge it or not."

I don't respond. I don't tell her I've been counting, too.

Outside her office, the corridor stretches long and bright, windows alternating with doors to other offices, other therapy rooms. My room is in the east wing, a five-minute walk from here. I've memorised the layout of Oakwood the way I once memorised the pattern of bruise-coloured wallpaper in my bedroom at home. Mapping spaces has become a habit, a way to feel control in an uncontrollable world.

"Amanda?"

I turn to see Ellie leaning against the wall, clearly waiting for me. She's pulled her dark curls back in a messy ponytail that makes no attempt to hide the still-healing scar running along her left temple. There's something both unsettling and admirable about how she displays her trauma so openly. Meanwhile, I've been collecting scarves. I have fifteen now, in various patterns and materials; not my style, but I need something to cover the six-inch scar he left on my neck.

Ellie smiles, the expression slightly asymmetrical because of the nerve damage on one side of her face.

"Hey," I say. "You didn't have to wait."

"Group got out early." She shrugs. "Thought we could walk back together."

Ellie doesn't talk about her therapy sessions, and I don't talk about mine. It's our unspoken agreement: we exist in the present tense only, no past, no future. Just now, just here.

We walk in companionable silence down the corridor, past the tall windows that overlook the grounds. It's July now, high summer. The world bursts with colour and life outside these walls.

It would have been Sarah's birthday next week. She never made it to seventeen. When I did, a week after her funeral, I didn't feel like celebrating.

"You okay?" Ellie asks, noticing my expression.

"Just thinking," I reply.

She nods, not pressing further.

We do this. We think. There's a lot to think about, and a lot to avoid thinking about.

Ellie tries to change the subject.

"They put up the schedule for movie night. Some superhero thing."

"Not really in the mood," I say automatically, the same response I've given to every invitation for the past eight weeks.

"Yeah, figured." Ellie sounds resigned but not surprised. "Offer stands, though."

We reach the fork in the corridor where our paths separate. Her room is in the west wing, across from the common area where residents sometimes gather in the evenings. I've avoided those gatherings. I'd rather be alone in my room.

"Thanks," I say, meaning it. Ellie's quiet companionship has been the only thing that makes Oakwood bearable.

She gives me a small wave and heads left while I turn right, continuing alone down the hallway that leads to my room. Each door I pass belongs to someone else working through their own recovery: from strokes, accidents, violence. We're all broken in different ways, all trying to find our way back to some version of normalcy.

My room at Oakwood is nicer than the hospital room: a single bed with a blue coverlet, a small desk beneath the window, a dresser for my clothes, and an attached bathroom I don't have to share. The walls are painted a soft beige instead of institutional white. There are enough personal touches to make it feel less transient: photos from home, books on the nightstand, the blanket Mum brought from my bedroom.

But it's still not home. Still not where I should be.

I sit on the edge of the bed, looking at the framed photo of Sarah and me that Mum placed on my nightstand when I first arrived. We're laughing, heads tilted toward each other, her arm slung across my shoulders. It was taken last summer, before everything changed. Before the woods and the knife and the darkness.

I pick up the frame, tracing Sarah's face with my fingertip. She looks so alive, so present, her smile bright enough to light the darkest corners. How can someone so vital just be gone? How can the world keep turning without her in it?

"Amanda?"

It's Deborah, one of the nurses from my floor. She's not quite David from the hospital, but there's a similar steadiness to her that makes the transition a little easier.

"You have visitors."

I frown. It's early for Mum and Paul. Mum's not starting her maternity leave until the end of the week, when school breaks up for summer. She could have finished weeks ago, but with all the time she took out when I was first... Just after the...

With all the time she missed, she didn't want to leave the school short-staffed at the end of the year. And with the baby not due until the end of August, she insisted she could manage until summer break.

They still come every evening. Both of them, even though Paul sometimes just drops Mum off at the entrance. When he does come in, he hovers at the edges of conversations, his hands in his pockets, eyes darting around the room like he's searching for an escape route. After all these months, he still doesn't know how to talk to me, and I still don't know how to let him.

I wonder about the what ifs more often these days. If none of this had happened. If Sarah and I had just gone straight home that afternoon. If I'd never spent weeks with a tube breathing for me, learning to communicate all over again. If things had been different, would Paul and I have figured each other out by now? Would we have found some common ground, some language that didn't feel like we were translating from different native tongues? Or were we always destined to be awkward satellites orbiting Mum's world, connected but never quite touching?

The irony isn't lost on me. I've spent months focused on finding my voice again, on making myself heard and understood. Yet here we are, Paul and I, perfectly capable of speech but still communicating in shrugs and averted gazes, in sentences that trail off into silence.

Joyce is my only other visitor. She's been a handful of times. I'm sure seeing me is still difficult for her, a reminder of what she's lost while I survived. Each time she walks through that door, I watch her steel herself, see the way her eyes linger on whatever scarf I've wrapped around my throat before finding my face. Even so, she comes, and I appreciate it. I look forward to it in a way that surprises me, this connection forged in the worst kind of shared experience.

One time Oliver came with her, but I don't think it was helpful to any of us. He stood in the doorway, hands shoved deep in his pockets, looking everywhere but at me. He's struggling hard. I could see it in the hollows beneath his eyes, in the bitten-down nails, in the way he flinched when his mother touched my hand.

But we all are. Struggling. Surviving. Finding our way through a world that looks exactly the same as before but isn't. Not for any of us.

So, which of my unexpected visitors is it today?

"Who is it?" I ask, setting the photo back on the nightstand.

"Detective Barnes and another officer," Deborah says. "And Suki. They're in the visitors' lounge. Dr Craig approved the meeting."

My heart rate picks up. She approved it? After our conversation earlier? After telling me I wasn't engaging enough?

"I'll let them know you need a minute," Deborah continues when I don't immediately respond.

"Wait," I say, standing up. The decision forms even as I speak. "I'll come now."

Deborah looks surprised but nods, stepping back to let me pass.

I glimpse myself in the small mirror on my wall: hollow-eyed but steady, hair pulled back. My scarf has slipped slightly, revealing just a hint of the raised tissue beneath, and I quickly adjust it higher around my neck. I look like someone who could handle whatever news is waiting. I hope I am.

Following her down the corridor, my mind spins through possibilities, each one more urgent than the last. My pulse quickens with each step, blood rushing in my ears like ocean waves.

What new information could they have?

Has there been another attack?

Have they found him, the man who took everything from Sarah and nearly destroyed me?

For the first time since learning of Sarah's death, I feel something crack through the protective numbness I've wrapped around myself. The sensation is almost painful: a sharp, insistent emotion breaking through scar tissue I thought was permanent. It takes me a moment to identify the feeling as it spreads through my chest, bright and dangerous.

Hope.

And behind it, like a shadow stretching long in the afternoon sun, fear. Because hope is the thing that hurts most when it's taken away. Hope is what I had before they told me Sarah was gone.

But I keep walking. One foot in front of the other, toward whatever waits in the visitors' lounge. Toward whatever truths they've brought me today.

CHAPTER THIRTY-FOUR

The lounge is designed to feel casual and comfortable: overstuffed armchairs, coffee tables stacked with magazines, potted plants in sunny corners. They've blocked it off for my meeting with the police today, which makes it feel less homey. Still, the lounge has a different vibe to the stark hospital setting where I last spoke with Detective Barnes.

Barnes sits near the window, his posture tense despite the setting. He rises slightly to shake my hand as I arrive. With him are Detective Reid from Major Crimes, who I met back on the ward, and Suki from Victim Support, who I've seen every couple of weeks since I moved here.

Suki has been checking in on my progress, but always without updates on the case. Our sessions have developed a rhythm: careful questions, measured responses, reassurances that the investigation is 'ongoing'. Empty words that have come to mean nothing is happening. Week after week, time suspended in the limbo of not knowing. But today is different. The police wouldn't arrange this formal meeting, wouldn't record our conversation, if something hadn't changed.

"Amanda," Barnes says, genuine warmth in his greeting. "I'm going to pop the tape recorder down on the table here to record our conversation, if that's okay. Thank you for agreeing to see us."

I haven't really agreed to anything, but I don't correct him. Instead, I take a seat in an armchair, positioning myself so I can see both the detectives and the door. It's a digital voice recorder, this time, not a video device. In a way, it's a sign of how things have changed. Still, I raise my hand to my scarf to make sure everything is covered up.

“You remember Detective Reid,” Barnes continues, gesturing to the redhead.

“It’s good to see you, Amanda,” Detective Reid says, her voice gentler than I remember. “How has your recovery been progressing?”

“I’m fine,” I say automatically. It’s become my default response to everything.

Barnes clears his throat and gets straight to business. “We have something specific we’d like you to look at.”

My pulse quickens as Barnes reaches down beside his chair and lifts a sealed evidence bag onto the coffee table between us. The plastic crinkles as he carefully positions it. It’s opaque, larger than a carrier bag, smaller than a bin bag. My mind is already racing, trying to guess what’s inside it.

Something sick inside me thinks it’s a dead animal. A dog, a fox maybe. I don’t know why that’s where my mind goes, and I hope above hopes I’m wrong. It’s an irrational thing to imagine and I try to reassure myself.

Suki must recognise the shock on my face as she puts her hand on my arm.

“It’s okay,” she says, even though she can’t read my mind and see the dumb ideas that worry me.

Thanking her is all I can manage.

Reid is getting comfortable, so I brace myself for a long, or maybe very serious, session.

My eyes remain fixed on the bag, my heart hammering against my ribs. Whatever is inside connects to my attack, to Sarah’s death, to the mysterious Maggie. I can’t look away, can’t focus on anything else while that sealed package sits between us like a bomb waiting to detonate.

Reid brings me back to the room with the next two words she speaks.

“Sarah’s body was found on the grounds of the old Marshall Chemical Processing plant, as you know, a facility that's been abandoned for about five years now. That sulphuric smell you described is consistent with chemicals they used to process there."

Sarah's body.

Everything inside me locks up. My vision tunnels. The room, the voices, the crinkle of the evidence bag, it all fades. Two words. Just two words, and suddenly she isn't Sarah anymore. She's a piece of evidence. A name on a report. Something to be catalogued, examined.

I gasp, even though I've known for weeks now that she's gone. Something about hearing Reid say it so matter-of-factly makes it all suddenly, brutally real again. The weight of it presses down on my chest, and for a moment I can't breathe, can't think, can't do anything but feel the crushing grief I've been learning to live with.

I can only focus on the package in front of me.

"What's in the bag?" I ask, my voice steadier than I expected.

Reid and Barnes exchange a glance, and then Reid leans forward slightly.

"We've discovered some former employees of Marshall Chemical moved to a new company when the plant shut down. We're focusing our investigation on that group. We need to pin down as much evidence as we can to support our operation. As part of the investigation, we've impounded several trucks from the new factory. Since the tyre tracks at the scene could match the type of trucks used there, we're conducting a forensic examination on all of them to rule them out. Or in."

"And in the process," Barnes says, "we believe we've recovered a jacket like the one you described."

Reid continues. "Red plaid, lumberjack style. We need you to confirm if it's the same one before we proceed with forensic testing."

My stomach drops. The jacket. His jacket. The one he was wearing when he lured us in. The one I see in every nightmare.

Barnes speaks carefully. "Once we test it, we may not be able to recover everything. Some forensic processes, like chemical treatments for touch DNA, can degrade trace evidence. That's why your confirmation matters."

"Amanda?" Suki's voice pulls me back again. "Are you okay with this? We can take a break if you need time?"

"No," I say quickly. "I'm okay. Show me."

Barnes nods. He reaches down to a bag I hadn't noticed before and pulls out a pair of matte black gloves. Snapping them on, he opens a small, sterile packet and withdraws a crisp sheet of forensic paper, laying it out carefully on the table. Only then does he slice through the seal on the evidence bag.

"I should warn you, we've preserved it exactly as we found it, which means..."

He doesn't finish the thought. Instead, he grips the edge of the jacket with tweezers and slides it free. The smell hits instantly. A wave of stale cigarettes, sour sweat, and that same eggy stench I'd described. It's all there, curling into the air, heavy and unmistakable.

It's repulsive and compelling at the same time.

Suddenly, I'm not in the visitors' lounge at Oakwood. I'm standing among bluebells, hearing Sarah's voice beside me, seeing that flash of red and black through the trees.

"Amanda?" Suki says, her voice shaking. "Do you need a moment?"

I force myself to focus, to breathe through my mouth instead of my nose.

"I'm fine," I manage, but my voice betrays me, cracking on the second word.

The jacket lies between us. Red and black plaid, worn at the elbows, exactly as I remembered. My eyes trace the fabric, confirming every detail I'd given them. The collar is frayed slightly. The cuffs are stained darker than the rest.

Then I notice something I hadn't remembered until this moment: the right pocket is torn along the seam, clumsily repaired with thick black thread. A detail I never mentioned because I hadn't consciously registered it.

"That pocket," I say softly, pointing with a trembling finger. "It was torn. Fixed with black thread. I remember, now."

Barnes leans forward, his expression sharpening. "You never mentioned that detail in your statements."

"I only just remembered," I admit. "But seeing it..."

Reid is taking notes, her pen moving quickly across her notepad, even though they're recording everything I say. "This kind of specific detail is extremely helpful, Amanda. Is there anything else about the jacket that stands out to you now?"

I force myself to look more carefully, fighting against the smell that keeps threatening to drag me back to that day. The smell that is both repulsive and compelling in its certainty.

"This is his jacket," I say, the words ringing with a finality I can feel in my bones. "I know it."

"We were uncertain because..." Barnes pauses, as if there's anything he could say that could make me feel worse. "...there are no traces of your blood. Despite the wound to your neck, which would have created, uh, a large release, potentially directly in the attacker's direction."

My breath stutters in my throat and I'm back there again with blood bubbling in my airway.

"He..."

I stop.

I've never said it.

Can I tell them now?

Can I finally speak the word?

"He..."

I look at Suki, and she holds my hand carefully.

"I think he took some of his clothes off. I think he..."

My hand reaches out in a strange, instinctive movement. I'm reaching for the whiteboard that I haven't had for weeks.

I'm looking for a way to write the word I don't want to say.

Barnes's eyes lock with mine.

"If you can tell us...?" she says.

"He raped her."

I finally say it, but it doesn't feel like a relief. It feels like a betrayal.

She never got to choose whether anyone knew what happened.

My mouth feels dirty.

Reid and Barnes look at each other again, something shifting in their expressions. I see it register. This new information, this detail I was never certain of, but feared was true.

But in this moment, something clicks. I know. I don't just suspect. I don't just fear. I know. The truth has been there all along, buried under my own denial.

Suki squeezes my hand.

"Amanda," Barnes says carefully, "this is very important. Given the condition of Sarah's remains when we found her, after so many weeks outdoors... we couldn't determine this from physical evidence."

The word *remains* makes me gag, and Suki pulls in closer to me. I had imagined her lying in her coffin, looking exactly as she had when she was alive. Hearing Barnes say '*Sarah's body*' was bad enough. This word floors me.

I know she's gone.

I know she's dead.

But that's just another word I don't want to say.

Then realisation hits me in the face. All this time, I've been afraid to say that he raped her, afraid to make it real. I *heard* those sounds, those terrible subdued cries, but part of me hoped I was wrong. That maybe it wasn't what I thought. That I'd misunderstood what was happening in those moments before I lost consciousness.

I didn't want to believe it, like I don't want to believe she is dead.

But now I understand: if I don't speak this truth, no one will ever know what happened to Sarah. Her body can't tell them. Only I can.

I give Suki a small nod, showing that I want to continue.

"You heard him rape Sarah?" Reid asks quietly. "During the attack?"

I nod, the weight of responsibility settling heavy on my shoulders. My testimony is all Sarah has now. My voice is her only chance for justice.

The thing I couldn't tell them. The darkest truth that I've carried. Sarah deserves for them to know, even if speaking it feels like reopening a wound.

"But then, don't you have his DNA? From Sarah's..." I can't finish the sentence. The words stick in my throat.

Barnes's expression softens slightly.

"After weeks out in the open, any DNA was too degraded to be useful. The rain, heat, and animal activity broke down anything we might have recovered."

Animal activity.

The room tilts. My stomach lurches violently, and for a second, I think I might be sick. My ears start to ring, drowning out the hum of conversation.

Not Sarah. Not her body. Not her skin, her hands, her face.

I squeeze my eyes shut, but the images come anyway: scattered remains, clawed at, dragged through the dirt, left out there like nothing.

She wasn't nothing. She was Sarah. She was my best friend.

A sharp gasp rattles from my throat. Suki presses a cool hand against mine, grounding me. I force myself to breathe.

And all this time, I'd assumed science would provide the answers, would speak for Sarah when I couldn't.

When I finally open my eyes, Barnes is watching me carefully. His voice is gentler when he speaks again.

"That's why your testimony about what you heard is so crucial. And why this jacket..." he gestures to the evidence bag, "...could be our best lead."

Reid adds, "Now that you've positively identified it, we'll send it straight to the lab. If we recover DNA, yours, Sarah's, or his, it will be the most direct forensic link tying him to the attack."

He glances at Barnes, who nods. "Regardless, we're building a strong case. The tyre tracks, your testimony, and the partial fingerprint we recovered from the dog lead: it all fits together."

"The print was degraded, so it's taken time to process, but we're closing in. If we can extract enough data points, it will strengthen our case against him," Barnes says.

I stare at the jacket, my stomach twisting. They might find DNA. They might not. Either way, my words, my memories, might be the strongest evidence they have.

"And your testimony about the sexual assault is particularly important," Barnes adds quietly. "Without that, we wouldn't have known to look for certain kinds of evidence or patterns."

I frown, trying to understand. "So, you know who he is, and you're 'closing in'?"

Barnes hesitates just for a moment before answering. "We need this case to be airtight."

There's something in the way he says it: careful, measured. Like he already knows but isn't ready to tell me yet.

A new determination flows through me, cutting through the fog that's surrounded me since Sarah's funeral. I'm not just surviving anymore. I'm fighting.

"What else do you need from me?"

Reid exhales, measuring her words. "We'll need a more detailed statement, if there's anything you haven't previously been able to tell us."

Not that I didn't want to. Just that I couldn't.

Until now.

They're close. Closer than I realised.

All these weeks, I've been drifting, lost in grief and guilt, while the investigation kept moving without me. But now I see it. Now I understand.

Barnes observes me. "We're still processing evidence," he says, his voice measured but certain. "But your help has been invaluable."

"We may need you to look at some images, possibly for a photo lineup," Reid says, her tone careful. "If we go ahead with it, we'll bring the photographs here, so you can review them in a controlled environment. You wouldn't have to go to the station, and you absolutely would not have to see him in person."

Suki's hand finds my arm again, grounding me. I'm glad she's here. Glad I'll be able to talk to her about what's to come.

I nod, straightening my shoulders. "I'll do whatever you need."

Reid's voice softens. "Amanda, we understand this is difficult. You've been through unimaginable trauma, and you're still recovering. We don't want to push you beyond what you're ready for."

I lift my chin. "I'm ready."

And I mean it.

I mean it as strongly as I did when I wrote those words on the board, but now, I am stronger.

"I need to do this." My voice doesn't waver. "For Sarah."

After they leave, I remain in the visitors' lounge, staring out the window at the manicured grounds. The scent of that jacket lingers in my nostrils, a phantom presence I can't quite shake. But instead of dragging me back into a traumatic memory, it now fuels something different.

They're close to nailing him. Close to making sure he never hurts anyone else the way he hurt Sarah. The way he hurt me.

I feel a renewed sense of purpose. A determination that feels almost foreign after weeks of simply existing.

I have no illusions about what comes next. I know it won't be easy. But I'll do it.

For Sarah.

For myself.

CHAPTER THIRTY-FIVE

After missing the police interview, Mum was insistent on being here for my next therapy session. I know she feels guilty about taking time off work, but she had a midwife appointment this morning, so she arranged to come straight here afterward.

"It's all going well," she says with a smile. "Six weeks to go, and everything looks perfect. Last few days at work, then I'm officially on maternity leave."

Six weeks. That doesn't feel like much time at all. By then, she'll be bringing my baby brother home, settling into life with him. I wonder if I'll be home too, or if I'll still be here, stuck in limbo while life moves on without me.

I've missed her entire pregnancy, first in the hospital, then here.

He took that from me, just like he took Sarah.

It's not often Mum comes with me to therapy, but I don't mind so much. Today, I'm actually grateful. A part of me thinks maybe it could help her as much as it helps me. Maybe more.

"You've been more engaged these past few days," Dr Craig says, leaning forward slightly in her chair. "Ever since the detectives brought in that jacket. And after you could finally verbalise what happened to Sarah."

I tense immediately, my shoulders drawing up toward my ears. Even now, I can feel the shame and guilt washing over me at the memory of saying those words out loud. Rape. I've finally said it.

"How did it feel," Dr Craig asks gently, "to speak about the sexual assault after keeping it inside for so long?"

I count the blue diamonds on the carpet. I can't look at her. Not now. Mum shifts uncomfortably beside me.

"Like I was betraying her," I say finally, my voice barely above a whisper. "Like I was sharing something private that she never got to choose."

It takes me a lot of effort to speak, and not because of my injury.

"Something that belonged to her." My words are almost inaudible.

I tug at the polka dot scarf I chose for today, feeling the chiffon rub between my fingers.

Dr Craig nods slowly. "And yet it was also something you witnessed: something that traumatised you as well."

"It wasn't the same," I insist. "It happened to her, not me. And I only heard... I wasn't even sure."

But I was, wasn't I? I always knew.

"Witnessing violence against someone you love creates its own trauma," Dr Craig says, undeterred. "Especially when you felt powerless to stop it."

I swallow hard against the lump forming in my throat. "I should have done something."

"Amanda," Mum says softly, her hand finding mine. "You were injured. Bleeding."

"But being able to say it now," Dr Craig redirects gently, "to name what happened. Has that changed anything for you?"

I consider this, surprised to find that it has. "It feels... less like a secret. More like evidence." I pause, then add, "But I still feel guilty for saying it."

I shift on the sofa in her office, aware of my mother beside me. Dr Craig pauses, sensing I have more to say.

"I guess it has, though," I admit. Speaking still doesn't come easily, but the words flow better than they did a week ago. "Helping with the investigation feels like... doing something."

"As opposed to just healing?" Dr Craig asks. She makes inverted commas in the air around the word '*just*'.

I nod. "Healing feels passive. Like I'm waiting for time to pass." I glance at Mum. "But identifying that jacket felt like I was actually making a difference."

"You are," Mum says softly. "The detectives said your help has been invaluable."

Dr Craig makes a note on her pad. "That's a significant shift in perspective, Amanda. Seeing yourself as an active participant rather than just a victim."

The word '*victim*' still makes me flinch. I hate it, how it reduces me, defines me by what happened to me. But Dr Craig has been trying to help me reclaim the narrative, to see survivorship as an active process rather than a passive state.

"I want him in prison," I say simply. "For Sarah. For her family."

Mum reaches over and squeezes my hand. Her eyes are bright with unshed tears.

"Joyce called yesterday," she tells Dr Craig. "She's... well, as well as can be expected. She asks about Amanda every time."

Dr Craig nods. "And how do you feel about Amanda's involvement in the investigation?" she asks Mum. "As her mother, that must bring up complicated emotions."

Mum takes a deep breath. "I'm proud of her strength," she says. "But terrified of what it costs her. Every time she has to relive that..." She trails off, unable to finish.

"I need to do this," I tell her, squeezing her hand back. "I'm the only one who can."

"I know," she whispers. "That's what scares me."

There's a moment of silence as Dr Craig observes our interaction. She's been cataloguing these moments of connection, pointing them out as evidence of healing. Not just mine, but our family's.

"And what about Paul?" Dr Craig asks. "How has he been handling Amanda's recovery process?"

Mum looks away briefly. "He's been... supportive. Distant lately, but that's just his way. Always running errands, keeping busy."

I can't help the small snort that escapes me. Mum gives me a look but doesn't contradict me. It's the closest we've come to acknowledging the elephant in the room; Paul has never known how to deal with me, especially now.

"We're working on it," Mum says finally. "He's trying, in his way."

Dr Craig nods, making another note. "Supporting someone through trauma recovery can be challenging for family members. They often don't know what to say or do."

"He could start by being present," I mutter.

As much as I'd like to complain about Paul, though, I still can't help but remember that my own father hasn't shown his face through all of this.

"Amanda," Mum says, but there's no real rebuke in her tone.

Dr Craig checks her watch. "Our time's almost up, but I want to acknowledge the progress you've been making, Amanda. Your willingness to engage, both with therapy and with the investigation, shows remarkable resilience."

I don't feel resilient. I feel like I'm holding myself together with tape and string. But I nod anyway, accepting the compliment because it seems important to Dr Craig that I do.

As we step out of her office, Mum touches my arm. "Lunch in the common area today?" she asks, hopeful but casual. "Before I go?"

It's a small thing, but I know what she's really asking. Every meal I eat outside my room is a small victory in her eyes. A step toward something resembling normalcy.

"Sure," I say. "Why not?"

The common area at Oakwood feels like an upscale café rather than an institutional dining space. Tables of various sizes scattered across a room with tall windows overlooking the gardens. At this hour, it's about half full. Mostly residents and visiting family members. The lunch crowd.

Ellie waves from a table by the window as we enter. I hesitate only briefly before steering Mum in that direction.

"Hey," Ellie says as we approach. Her hair is pulled back again today. I wish for a moment that I could be more like her. "You must be Amanda's mom."

"Abby," Mum says, shaking Ellie's hand. "Nice to meet you. Amanda's mentioned you."

"All lies," Ellie says with a smile. "Except the part about me being devastatingly charming. That's one hundred per cent accurate."

Despite everything, I find myself smiling. Ellie has a way of cutting through the darkness without dismissing it. She understands. Not what happened to me, specifically, but what it's like to have your life cleaved in two by a single event. Before and after.

We collect our lunch trays, soup and sandwiches, nothing fancy, and settle at the table. Mum asks Ellie polite questions about her recovery, her family. Normal conversation that feels both foreign and comforting.

"So," Ellie says, turning to me after a while. "You seem different today. Less... zombie-like."

"Ellie," Mum starts, but I wave her off.

"It's fine. She's right." I take a sip of water. "I've been helping the police with the investigation."

Ellie's eyebrows shoot up. "Seriously? That's intense."

"They brought in evidence for me to identify," I explain. "A jacket that belonged to him." Just saying it aloud makes my throat tighten, and I have the urge to reach up for my scarf, but I push through. I can at least try to be more like Ellie. "It helped narrow down their suspects."

"That's really brave," Ellie says simply.

"Or really stupid," I counter.

"No," she says firmly. "Brave. There's a difference."

Before I can respond, a staff member approaches our table. "Amanda? Your presence is requested in the visitors' lounge. Detectives Barnes and Reid are here to see you."

My pulse quickens. "Now?"

"Yes. They said it's important."

Mum and I exchange a glance. We haven't expected them back so soon after the jacket identification. Something must have happened.

"We'll be right there," Mum says, already standing. "Thank you."

Ellie gives me an encouraging nod as we leave. "Let me know if you need anything," she calls after us.

CHAPTER THIRTY-SIX

The visitors' lounge has been cleared again for our meeting. It feels as though it's becoming my own personal suite. Barnes and Reid are waiting, along with Suki, who gives me a small smile as we enter.

"Thank you for coming so quickly," Barnes says, gesturing for us to sit. "We need your help with something important to the investigation. It couldn't wait, I'm afraid."

It couldn't wait.

Those words send my mind racing with possibilities. I sink into an armchair, suddenly very aware of my breathing, of the way my hands automatically reach for the scarf around my neck.

Mum takes the seat beside me, her expression tense. Suki moves deliberately, positioning herself on my other side rather than across from me. The subtle shift in her usual seating choice doesn't escape my notice.

"Before we begin," Suki says, her voice calm, "I want to remind you that we can take this conversation at whatever pace you need, Amanda. If at any point you want us to pause, or if you need a break, just signal me." She places a bottle of water on the small table within my reach. "Whatever reaction you have today is completely normal."

Something in her careful preparation makes my heart beat faster. My mouth goes dry.

"What is it? Have you found something?"

Barnes and Reid exchange a look. Then Barnes turns to me, his expression carefully controlled but unable to fully mask his excitement.

"We've had a significant breakthrough," he says. "Your identification of the jacket, combined with the chemical smell you described, confirmed that we were looking in the right place."

Reid leans forward slightly. "We told you we recovered a partial fingerprint from the dog lead found with Sarah. Our forensics team has finally managed to extract enough usable points. Enough to match it to one of the men we've been investigating."

My breath catches. This is it. After all these weeks, actual physical evidence confirming that the man they suspected is the one who did this. The one who hurt Sarah. The one who nearly killed me.

"What we need from you today," Barnes continues, "is to look at some photographs. We'd like you to tell us if you recognise the man who attacked you and Sarah."

The room seems to tilt slightly, then right itself, listing like a ship in a storm. My vision narrows, focusing on Barnes's face.

Suki's hand rests lightly on my forearm. "Take a deep breath, Amanda," she murmurs. "In through your nose, out through your mouth."

I follow her instructions automatically, the simple technique anchoring me when I feel like I might float away from the shock.

"We'd like you to look at a lineup of six men," Reid says, removing a folder from her briefcase. "The person who attacked you may or may not be among these photographs. Take your time, and don't feel pressured to make an identification if you're not certain."

Mum rubs her thumb across my knuckles. "Are you up for this?" she asks quietly.

I nod, suddenly unable to speak. After all these weeks of nightmares, I might finally see his face again. Deliberately this time, not in fragments of traumatic memory.

Reid opens the folder and places six photographs on the table in front of me. Six men, similar in age and general appearance, all with the same neutral expression staring back at the camera.

My eyes move across them mechanically. The first. No. The second. No. The third.

My heart stops.

There he is. The red, stubbled face, the pale eyes that looked at me with such emptiness. His face is burned into my memory.

My finger trembles as I point to the third photograph.

"That's him."

Barnes and Reid exchange a glance.

"How confident are you that this is the same man?" Barnes asks.

"One hundred per cent," I say, my voice steadier than I feel.

Reid makes a note, her pen scratching across her notepad. "Thank you, Amanda. This is incredibly helpful."

"What happens now?" Mum asks, her voice shaking slightly.

I stare at the photograph, at the face that has haunted me for months. He looks so ordinary. Not a monster, just a man. How can someone capable of such cruelty look so normal?

"Your identification is an important piece of evidence," Barnes explains. "But we need more before we can make an arrest. We're fast-tracking DNA results from the jacket you identified. Once we have a match, that will be enough to move forward."

Reid hesitates. "There's something else. We have searched the suspect's home."

My mind spins, catching on a detail I almost missed. "You already searched his place? While he's still... out there?" The thought sends a chill through me. "What if he figures out you're on to him?

"It was a limited search," Barnes clarifies. "He has no idea we suspect him. Officers conducted surveillance while a small team executed the warrant when he was at work."

"Limited?" I echo, my pulse quickening.

Reid nods. "At this stage, we can't conduct a full search of his home without stronger forensic confirmation, but we can seize specific items tied to the case."

Barnes's voice lowers. "And we did."

He reaches into his briefcase and removes an evidence bag. Inside is what appears to be a photograph in a simple wooden frame.

"We found this in his bedroom," Barnes says, his eyes fixed on my face. "It appears to be a photograph of you, Amanda."

A cold wave crashes over me. My breath catches in my throat. "What?"

Barnes carefully removes the photograph from the evidence bag, holding it by the edges. He places it on the coffee table between us.

"This could be significant to establishing motive," Reid says quietly. "He had it displayed prominently on his bedside drawers. We believe it might explain why he specifically targeted you."

I lean forward, my heart racing. My fingers instinctively reach for my scar, tracing its length through my scarf. The photograph shows a teenage girl with light brown hair and pale skin. She's standing in front of what looks like a lake or reservoir, smiling awkwardly at the camera. She's wearing a plain blue t-shirt and jeans, her arms crossed self-consciously across her chest.

I stare at the image, unable to make sense of what I'm seeing. It's like looking into a mirror, but something's not quite right. The setting is unfamiliar. The clothes aren't mine. The girl has my face, my colouring, my build, but something is off, like seeing yourself in a dream.

I've never posed for this photograph.

"I don't..." I begin, but the words die in my throat.

My mind races, desperately trying to place when this could have been taken, where this could have been taken. But there's nothing. No memory, no recognition, just an uncanny sensation of wrongness that makes my skin crawl.

"When was this taken?" Barnes asks gently. "Do you remember?"

Before I can answer, Mum reaches for the photograph, her movements stiff with tension. Her hands are shaking visibly as she lifts it for a closer look. She studies it intensely, her expression morphing from confusion to something else, something that would have made the monitors back at the hospital go wild if they were connected to me right now.

Time seems to slow as I watch her face. I know every minute shift in her expressions, have catalogued them all my life. This one, this wide-eyed, pale-faced shock, is one I've rarely seen. My pulse pounds in my ears, drowning out everything but the sound of my own ragged breathing.

"Mrs Gray?" Reid prompts. "Do you recognise when this might have been taken?"

The room falls silent as Mum continues to stare at the photograph. When she finally looks up, her face is pale, her eyes wide with shock.

She looks from the photograph to me and back again, as if confirming something unbelievable.

"This isn't Amanda," she says.

The detectives exchange confused glances.

"Are you certain?" Barnes asks. "The resemblance is..."

"This isn't my daughter," Mum says again, her voice firmer now, filled with an absolute certainty that silences everyone in the room.

CHAPTER THIRTY-SEVEN

The words '*This isn't my daughter'* hang in the air, so definitive they seem to alter the atmosphere of the room.

Barnes and Reid exchange bewildered glances.

"Mrs Gray," Barnes says carefully, "the resemblance is remarkable."

"I'm her mother," Mum says, her voice unwavering. "I think I would know."

"Detective," Suki says, her voice calm but firm, "We need to take Mrs Gray's identification seriously. I think we need to explore what this means for the investigation, if the photograph is of someone else entirely."

I stare at the photograph again.

"It *must* be her," I whisper. "Maggie."

Suki's eyes meet mine with sharp understanding.

"The name he called you," she says, not as a question but as confirmation.

I nod, unable to take my eyes off the photograph. The girl at the reservoir, smiling awkwardly, arms crossed, looking so much like me it's unsettling. So much like me that a killer confused us.

A horrible thought forms in my mind, one I can barely bring myself to voice. "Is she... do you think she's dead too?" I ask, my voice barely audible.

Suki leans forward at this, her posture alert, but she remains silent, letting the detectives address the question while carefully monitoring my reaction.

Barnes shifts uncomfortably. "We don't know, Amanda. There's no missing persons report matching her description, which is unusual but not impossible in certain circumstances."

"We've been looking into any record of someone named Margaret or Maggie since you first mentioned the name,"

Reid adds, making a note on her pad. “There are no missing persons and so far, we haven’t found any records of a daughter, niece, or any female relative or associate in the suspect’s background.”

“What do you mean?” Mum asks, finally looking away from the photograph. “There’s no one with that name that’s missing? Out of all the people that go missing...”

Barnes shakes his head. “No one that would fit the profile. And we’ve done a thorough background check on the suspect. Never married according to public documents. No children listed in any official capacity.”

“If this girl is Maggie, it’s a lead,” Reid says, tapping the photograph with her pen. “We’ll be interviewing neighbours, coworkers, anyone who might have known the suspect personally rather than just on paper. And we can use the image to help us search the databases. Even with an older photograph, modern systems can account for ageing and still identify potential matches in driver’s licence and passport databases.”

My mind struggles to process this information. The girl in the photo is real. She existed, she stood by that reservoir, she smiled for that camera. But somehow, she’s managed to leave no trace in any system the police can access.

“The reservoir?” I ask. “Couldn’t you...”

I wonder if I’ve watched too many detective shows. On television, they would feed the photograph into a computer, and it would tell them exactly where and when it was taken. Real life, it seems, is far more complicated.

“There’s a chance. We will certainly be following that line of enquiry now that we know the person in the photograph is not you.”

“This changes the profile of the case,” Reid says, returning the photograph to its evidence bag. “We initially believed the ‘*Maggie*’ reference might have been to a previous victim, or possibly a fixation from the suspect's past. Now we have evidence of a real person who bears a striking resemblance to Amanda."

"Which suggests his attack on you wasn't random," Barnes adds, his expression grave. "It's possible you were targeted, Amanda, because of your resemblance to this girl."

The knowledge settles on me like a physical weight. All this time, I've believed we were simply in the wrong place at the wrong time. That Sarah and I had the terrible luck to cross paths with a predator. But if Barnes is right, if I was targeted specifically...

Suki watches me carefully, clearly noting the shift in my breathing as I process this revelation. She doesn't speak, but her presence is steady, grounding: a silent reminder that I'm not alone with this terrifying new information. Mum grasps me more tightly.

"What about Sarah?" I ask, my voice barely audible. "Was she just... in the way?"

Barnes and Reid exchange another look, and I can tell they've already considered this possibility.

"We couldn't possibly say that," Reid says gently. "But we need to find this girl."

"How does this change things?" Mum asks.

"We'll continue building our case," Barnes explains. "As soon as we get the DNA results from the jacket, we'll know whether we can move to an arrest."

"And we'll be investigating this new lead," Reid interjects. "Attempting to identify the girl in the photograph and determine her relationship to the suspect."

"If you remember anything else about what he said regarding Maggie, anything at all, please let us know," Barnes adds, looking directly at me. "Even small details could help us understand this connection."

I nod, though I can't think of anything beyond what I've already told them: how he called me Maggie, how he spoke to me as if I were someone he knew.

"We should get back," Suki says, speaking for the first time since Mum's revelation. "Amanda's had a lot to process today."

The detectives stand. Barnes carefully secures the evidence bag containing the photograph.

"We'll keep you updated on any developments," he promises.

Without even thinking about it, I blurt out, "Could I have a copy of the photo?"

The request catches everyone off guard. Barnes freezes, his hands still on the evidence bag. Reid and Suki exchange a look I can't quite interpret.

"I'm sorry, but that's not possible," Barnes says, his voice taking on that formal police tone. "It's evidence in an active criminal investigation."

"I know, but..." I falter, suddenly unsure why I asked. Why do I need to see this girl's face again? This stranger who looks so much like me, but isn't me? "I just thought it might help me remember something. About what he said that night."

Mum's expression is somewhere between concern and confusion. "Amanda. Maybe it's best if you don't..."

"Actually," Suki interjects, her voice measured, "we should consult with Dr Craig before making that decision." She turns to me. "Your psychologist would be in the best position to determine if having access to the image would be beneficial or potentially harmful to your recovery process."

Barnes nods, looking relieved at the suggested protocol. "That makes sense. We'll speak with Dr Craig and follow her professional recommendation."

"If she approves," Reid adds, "we can provide a controlled copy with appropriate documentation." Her expression is sympathetic but professional. "We understand your interest, Amanda, but we need to ensure we're not compromising either the investigation or your well-being."

I want to argue, to insist, but I can't form the words. Of course they'd need to consult my psychologist. Of course, there are protocols. Still, disappointment sits heavy in my chest.

"We'll let you know what Dr Craig says," Suki promises, her eyes meeting mine with understanding. "If she approves it, we'll arrange for you to receive a copy."

I nod, trying to hide my frustration. "Thank you."

Barnes glances at his watch. "We should get going. Thank you both for your time today." He looks at me directly. "Try not to dwell on this too much, Amanda. Let us handle the investigation."

After they leave, Mum and I sit in silence for a long moment. The visitors' lounge feels cavernous now, too big for just the two of us.

"Are you okay?" Mum asks finally.

"I don't know," I admit. "It's all so..."

"Overwhelming," she supplies.

"Yeah."

She stares out the window, her expression distant.

"They caught him," she says, almost to herself. "After all this time, they've actually caught him."

"Or at least they almost have," I say.

Mum nods. "And because of you. You identified his jacket. You told them about... what happened to Sarah." She turns to me, her eyes shining with unshed tears. "I'm so proud of you, Amanda. So proud of your strength."

But I don't feel strong. I feel confused, disoriented. The narrative I've constructed about that night has shifted, leaving me unmoored. I wasn't just a random victim. He saw something in me, a resemblance to this mysterious Maggie, that made him single me out.

And because of that, Sarah is dead.

Mum hesitates, then asks quietly, "How did it feel? Seeing his face again?"

I inhale sharply, my fingers tightening around the fabric of my scarf. I don't answer right away. I want to tell her the truth, but I don't want to shatter whatever fragile sense of relief she's holding onto.

How did it feel?

Like my stomach turned inside out. Like the room shrank and expanded at the same time. Like I was back there, with his hands on me, his breath in my ear. Like Sarah was still screaming. Like the blood was pumping out of the slit in my throat.

I swallow hard.

"It felt like looking at a nightmare that never ended," I say finally. "He's still out there, breathing, walking around like a normal person. After everything he did."

Mum nods slowly, but I see her hands curl into fists in her lap.

"I hate that he still has this hold over you," she says, her voice tight.

I let out a bitter breath. "He doesn't. Not anymore." I don't know if that's true not. But I say it anyway.

"I think I need to lie down," I tell her.

Mum looks concerned. "Of course. Should I stay?"

"No, it's okay. You should get home. Rest." I gesture vaguely toward her baby bump. "You know, for him."

She hesitates, clearly torn between staying with me and taking care of herself. "I'll come back tomorrow," she promises.

I nod again, though my mind is already spinning with questions about the girl in the photograph. Who is she? Where is she now? And why, of all the people in the world, does she look so much like me?

Back in my room, I lie on my bed, staring at the ceiling. The white plaster offers no answers, no matter how long I search its blank expanse. Outside my window, dusk is falling, casting long shadows across the grounds of Oakwood. In another life, my life before, I might have been at home now, finishing homework, arguing with Mum about what to watch on TV, pointedly ignoring Paul.

Instead, I'm here, trying to make sense of a photograph of a girl who shares my face but not my identity. Trying not to think about the photograph of the man who murdered Sarah.

A soft knock at my door interrupts my thoughts.

"Come in," I call, expecting a nurse with my evening medication.

Instead, Ellie peers around the door, her expression uncertain. "Hey," she says. "Thought I'd check if you're okay."

I push myself up on my elbows. "Define 'okay'."

She slips inside, closing the door behind her. "That bad, huh?"

"I had to identify him," I say. "The man who... who killed Sarah."

Ellie's eyes widen. "Holy shit," she breathes, crossing to sit on the edge of my bed. "That's... wow."

"Yeah. It was a photo line-up, but... I think they're going to arrest him soon."

"How do you feel about it?"

I consider this. "Relieved? Scared? I don't know." I sigh, dropping back against my pillow. "It's complicated."

"I bet," Ellie says. She doesn't press for details, doesn't ask the questions most people would. It's the thing I appreciate most about her. She understands some experiences defy simple explanation.

We sit in comfortable silence for a while, the room gradually darkening around us.

"You should turn on a light," Ellie says eventually.

"Probably."

Neither of us moves.

"They found a photograph," I say suddenly. "At his house. Of a girl who looks exactly like me."

Ellie turns to face me, her expression sharpening with interest. "What do you mean, *exactly* like you?"

"Like... could be my twin. My mum had to tell them it wasn't me."

"That's seriously creepy," Ellie says. "Who is she?"

"That's the thing. They don't know. The police haven't found any records of her. But during the attack, he called me by another name. Maggie."

Ellie is quiet for a moment, absorbing this. "You think this is her? And he targeted you because you look like this other girl?" she says finally. "That's... that changes things, doesn't it?"

"Everything," I agree. "All this time, I thought it was just bad luck. Wrong place, wrong time. But now..."

"Now you're part of something bigger," Ellie finishes for me. "Something you don't understand yet."

I nod, grateful that she gets it without me having to explain further.

"What will you do?" she asks.

"What can I do? The police are investigating. They'll figure out who she is, what her connection is to him."

Ellie nods, but there's a scepticism in her expression that mirrors my own feelings. The mystery of Maggie feels personal in a way I can't quite articulate, like her identity is somehow tied to mine, her story interwoven with my own.

"Just be careful," Ellie says. "This whole thing sounds... messy."

"Messy," I repeat. The word is so inadequate it almost makes me laugh. "Yeah, I guess it is."

When Ellie leaves, I finally turn on the lamp beside my bed. The warm light pushes back the darkness but does nothing to dispel the shadow of questions hanging over me. I reach for the notebook Sarah gave me, flipping past pages of earlier entries: fragmented memories, therapy observations, details about the investigation.

On a fresh page, I write a single name:

Maggie.

Then I stare at it, as if the letters might rearrange themselves into answers if I look hard enough. But they remain stubbornly unchanged, a name without a face, or rather, a face without a story.

Somewhere out there is, or was, a girl who looks like me. A girl whose existence changed the course of my life in the most horrific way possible. A girl whose identity remains a mystery despite being captured in a photograph.

I close the notebook, suddenly too tired to think anymore. Tomorrow will bring new information, new questions, perhaps even answers. For now, all I can do is try to sleep, knowing that the man who hurt Sarah and me is finally in custody.

But as I drift off, the image of the girl by the reservoir follows me into my dreams: a mirror reflection that isn't quite right, a version of myself that never existed, a mystery waiting to be solved.

I couldn't save Sarah, but perhaps Maggie is still out there. Perhaps I can help her.

CHAPTER THIRTY-EIGHT

Three days later, I'm sitting across from Dr Craig in our regular therapy session. She's been different since I identified the suspect: more focused, more direct in her questions. Less willing to let me retreat into silence.

"I've spoken with Detectives Barnes and Reid," she says, setting her notepad aside. Her tone is carefully neutral, but I can sense something beneath it. "They told me about the photograph."

My pulse quickens. "And?"

"And they asked for my professional opinion on whether providing you with a copy would help or hinder your recovery." She studies me, eyes calm but watchful. "What do you think my answer should be?"

It's a typical Dr Craig move: turning the question back on me, making me articulate my thoughts rather than simply telling me hers.

I take a breath. "I think... I think understanding what happened is part of getting better. And understanding why he targeted me means understanding who Maggie is." I hesitate. "If this girl... if the girl in the photograph is Maggie... I need to know."

Dr Craig nods, neither agreeing nor disagreeing. "And why do you need the physical photograph to do that?"

"Because..." I struggle to explain something I don't fully understand myself. "Because I need to really look at her. To see if there's something there, something beyond just physical resemblance."

Dr Craig taps her pen lightly against her pad.

"Amanda, you identified the suspect, but you've barely spoken about him since. You saw his face again after all this time, but you haven't told me how that made you feel.

Instead, your focus has been on the girl in the photograph. Why do you think that is?"

I stiffen. "Because she's important."

"More important than the man who attacked you?" Her voice is gentle but firm, a steady pull toward something I don't want to name.

A deep ache coils in my stomach. I don't want to talk about him. I don't want to think about his face, his voice, his breath hot against my skin.

Thinking about Maggie is easier. It doesn't hurt the same way.

Dr Craig watches me, waiting. "How do you think the photo will help you?"

"I don't know," I whisper.

"Amanda, sometimes trauma survivors become fixated on certain details because it helps them feel in control of what happened," Dr Craig says, her voice even. "Trying to understand every piece of the puzzle can be a way of avoiding the reality that some things may never fully make sense. Like trying to find a girl in a photograph. Or trying to find a reason you survived and Sarah didn't."

The impact of her words is instant, like stepping off a curb and finding nothing beneath my feet.

"But I need to understand," I say, gripping the photo tighter. "If I can just figure out who she is, then maybe... maybe everything will make more sense."

"Or maybe Maggie gives you a distraction from the parts that feel too painful to face." She watches me closely. "The guilt of surviving when Sarah didn't. The questions that have no answers." She pauses, letting her words sink in. "Maybe you'll never know who she is. The last thing I want is for you to focus on this instead of your healing. You're doing so well. This could set you back."

I look away, unable to meet her eyes as the truth settles over me. It's easier to obsess over a stranger's face than to confront the weight of being the one who made it out alive.

It's like Dr Miles all over again.

She's going to say no.

"However," she continues, "in this case, I believe there could be therapeutic value in allowing you to process this connection at your own pace." She reaches into her desk drawer and removes a manila envelope. "Which is why I told the detectives I support your request, with some caveats."

Relief floods through me as she places it on the table between us.

"Detective Reid dropped this off yesterday," Dr Craig explains. "She asked me to emphasise that this is a copy provided solely for your personal recovery process. It shouldn't be shared or distributed in any way."

I nod, barely hearing her as my eyes fix on the envelope. "I understand."

"I'd like us to look at it together," Dr Craig says. "So I can help you process your reactions."

Part of me wants to snatch it and run. To examine it alone in my room, where no one can see whatever emotions it might trigger. But I restrain myself, knowing Dr Craig is offering something valuable: a safe space to confront whatever this photograph might stir up.

"Okay," I agree.

She slides the envelope across the desk. My hands tremble slightly as I open it and remove the glossy photograph.

And there she is again. The girl at the reservoir. The not-me.

When the detectives showed it to me, I only caught a glimpse before Mum's declaration that this wasn't me had changed everything.

Now, I can truly study her.

Her hair falls the same way mine used to, before everything. But her eyes are spaced differently: wider, somehow more vulnerable. Her jawline is sharper than mine. It's not noticeable on first glance, but if you really look, you can tell we are ever so slightly different. Her stance is similar to mine, arms crossed protectively over her chest, but there's something in the set of her shoulders that speaks of a kind of wariness.

Maybe I have that too, now.

I have one hand on her photograph, and one toying with the folds of the scarf around my neck.

"What do you see?" Dr Craig asks quietly.

"She looks like me, but..." I trace the outline of the girl's face with my finger, careful not to smudge the photo. "She's not me."

"No, she's not," Dr Craig agrees. "She's her own person, with her own story."

"A story connected to mine somehow," I murmur. "Through him."

I turn my attention to the background, the lake or reservoir stretching behind her. The shore is rocky, with dense trees visible on the far bank. The lighting suggests late afternoon, the sun catching on the water's surface. There's something at the edge of the image, just out of shot, but I can't tell what it is. A sign, maybe. Something wooden? I squint, but it doesn't help me see any better. I want to zoom out, to see more, but it's an old school, real-life, tangible photograph, not a digital image on a screen.

"Do you recognise the location?" Dr Craig asks, noticing where my focus has shifted.

"No. Maybe. I don't know." I frown. "There are a dozen lakes like this within fifty miles of here."

As I continue studying the photo, I'm struck by the girl's expression. Not quite a smile, more like she's tolerating the photograph rather than enjoying it. There's a distance in her eyes that resonates with me on a level I can't articulate.

"She looks sad," I say finally.

"Does she?" Dr Craig asks, neither confirming nor denying my interpretation.

"Or maybe not sad exactly. Just... resigned. Like she's not posing by choice."

Dr Craig makes a small note on her pad. "The photograph tells us she existed, but not much else. Not her relationship to your attacker, not what might have happened to her."

"But she was important to him," I say. "Important enough that he kept her picture by his bed. Important enough that when he saw me, he saw her. It must be Maggie. It must be."

"Important, yes," Dr Craig agrees. "And that gives the investigators a critical lead. They'll be trying to find out if this is Maggie, that's for sure."

"And where she is, if she's still..."

I don't finish the sentence. Instead, I slide the photo back into the envelope, suddenly exhausted. The brief examination has drained me in a way I didn't expect. But beneath the fatigue is something else. A sense of purpose I haven't felt since picking out photograph number three.

"May I keep this now?" I ask.

Dr Craig studies me for a long moment, then nods. "Yes. But I'd like you to be mindful of how much time you spend with it. It shouldn't become an obsession, Amanda."

I nod, but we both know I'm lying.

I will obsess over this. I need to.

Because if I can figure out who Maggie is, then maybe I'll finally understand why this happened.

And if I understand why, then maybe I can make peace with the fact that it did.

Dr Craig glances at her calendar before I leave. "Before you go, Amanda, I wanted to mention that we'll be starting discharge planning discussions next week. You've met most of your physical recovery goals, and your speech has improved dramatically."

The words catch me off guard. "You mean... going home?"

"That's the idea. We'd transition you to outpatient therapy. You'd still see me twice a week, but you'd be living at home." She studies my reaction carefully. "How do you feel about that?"

I'm not sure how I feel. Part of me craves the familiarity of my own room, my own things. But Oakwood has become a sanctuary of sorts: structured, safe, removed from the world where Sarah died, and I nearly did.

"I don't know," I admit. "With everything that's happening... waiting to hear about the arrest, the photo..."

Dr Craig nods. "It's a lot to process. And that's exactly what we'll discuss in our planning session. We won't send you home until you're ready, Amanda. But it's something to start thinking about."

I nod, suddenly overwhelmed by the prospect of returning to normal life, whatever *normal* means now.

Going home means facing my bruise-coloured wallpaper, the woods at the end of our street, Paul's awkward attempts at connection.

"Okay," I say finally. "I'll think about it."

Back in my room, I pull out the notebook Sarah gave me. The pages are creased now, filled with my cramped handwriting: memories, questions, fragments of dreams that might be real or imagined. I flip past all of it to the list I made weeks ago, shortly after arriving at Oakwood.

GOALS, the heading reads in careful block letters.

I checked them off one by one as I completed them:

✓ Walk the entire hallway without stopping by Friday.

✓ Speak a complete sentence before Oakwood.

✓ Build enough strength to shower standing up.

✓ Prepare questions for first session with Oakwood therapist.

Find Sarah.

My hand hovers over that last unchecked item. Find Sarah. The only goal I can never accomplish. We found her, yes, but not in the way I'd meant when I wrote those words. Not alive. Not waiting to be rescued.

I trace my finger over her name, feeling the indentation in the page from how hard I'd pressed the pen. I can't bring myself to cross it out. Can't bear to draw a neat checkmark beside it like the others, as if her death is something to be ticked off a to-do list.

Instead, I reach for my pen and add a new line below it:

Find Maggie.

I stare at the photograph again, taking in every detail. The girl's uneasy stance. The reservoir stretching behind her. The resemblance between us is undeniable. She could be my sister, my cousin, maybe even my twin. But Mum is right. She isn't me. The differences are subtle but unmistakable. Her eyes, her jawline, the set of her mouth. All slightly different from mine. And yet, similar enough that a killer could see me and think I was her.

I should be thinking about *him*. About the man I picked out of a lineup, the man the police are waiting to charge. About the DNA results that could prove, without a doubt, that he's the one responsible for Sarah's death. That he's the one who took everything from me.

But I'm not.

Instead, all I can think about is *her*.

The girl in the photograph. The girl who might be Maggie. The girl I don't know, but who feels like a missing piece of my story.

Why?

Why does she feel more important than the man who hurt me? Why does staring at her face feel more urgent than knowing whether he'll be locked away forever?

Thinking about him means thinking about what happened. The blood. The weight of his hands. The moment my life split into before and after.

But Maggie is still a mystery. A puzzle. She is something I can still solve.

Maybe finding her could give meaning to what happened. Maybe understanding why he targeted me, why he called me by her name, will make the senseless make sense.

As I drift toward sleep, it's not *him* I see behind my closed eyelids, it's her.

Maggie. The girl with my face, standing by a reservoir, waiting for someone to save her.

I slip the photo between the pages of the notebook, closing it carefully before tucking it under my pillow.

The police are waiting for DNA results.

I'm waiting for answers of my own.

CHAPTER THIRTY-NINE

Going home. The words have been circling in my mind since Dr Craig mentioned discharge planning yesterday. Going home to my bruise-coloured wallpaper, to the silence that hangs between Mum and Paul, to a house that sits too close to the woods where everything changed.

The thought of leaving Oakwood twists my stomach into knots. Not because I love it here, the institutional routine, the bland food, the careful voices, but because it's safe. Predictable. Here, no one expects me to be the Amanda from before. They only know this version of me: the one who flinches at sudden movements, who tugs on the scarf around her neck when she's anxious, who speaks in sentences measured like medicine doses.

I don't have time to wallow in my thoughts, as there's a sharp knock on the door.

I already recognise it, just as I used to know who was about to enter my room back in the hospital. David and Kate became such a part of my life there, and now they are just parts of my past. They'll be helping other patients now, and I can't help but wonder if they even give me a passing thought. Will it be like that when I leave here? Will Ellie forget me too?

"Come in," I call, my voice stronger now than it was a week ago. No longer a rasp, just a slight roughness around the edges.

Ellie pokes her head in, already dressed for physical therapy in loose track pants and a faded university sweatshirt. "Morning, sunshine. They've got French toast in the cafeteria. The actual good kind, not the soggy disaster from last week."

I force a smile. "Thanks. I'll grab some later."

Something shifts in her expression; there's a subtle tightening around her eyes. She steps fully into the room, closing the door behind her. "Okay, what's up? You've been weird since yesterday. And not regular Amanda-weird. Extra weird."

"Nothing's up," I say, the lie slipping out automatically. "Just tired."

Ellie crosses her arms, her scar catching the light as she tilts her head. "Bullshit."

"What?"

"You heard me. Bullshit." She slumps into the chair by the window. "You've been avoiding me since your therapy session with Craig. Did something happen? Is it about the arrest?"

I look away, focusing on a spot on the wall. "Dr Craig mentioned discharge planning."

"Ah." A single syllable loaded with understanding. "Going home scary, huh?"

"I'm not scared," I snap, the words coming out harsher than I intended.

"Sure you're not." Ellie doesn't take the bait. "Just like I wasn't scared when they told me I could start overnight visits with my family. I only cried for, what, three hours straight?"

I glance at her, surprised. "You cried?"

"Like a baby. Locked myself in the bathroom so my parents wouldn't hear. Institutions suck, but they're safe. Predictable. Home is..."

"Not the same anymore," I finish for her.

"Yeah." She offers a small smile. "Plus, you know, then you have to figure out who you are now. What your new normal looks like."

Normal.

Everyone keeps using that word, as if I could ever be normal again. As if there's a version of me that didn't watch her best friend die, that didn't feel blood pulsing from her own throat into the earth, that didn't hear her own name replaced by a stranger's as she lay dying.

"I'm not sure I want to find out what normal looks like now," I admit.

Ellie nods, unsurprised. "Yeah, well, welcome to the club. We don't have jackets, but the emotional baggage is free."

I should laugh, or at least smile. It's what she wants, what she expects. But something in me has gone cold, distant. I can feel myself pulling away from her, bricking up the small openings I'd allowed in our friendship.

She'll still be here after I'm gone. Still walking the same hallways, eating in the same dining room, seeing the same therapists. And I'll be... where? Back home, trying to be someone I'm not sure I can be anymore, while Ellie continues the slow work of putting herself back together here at Oakwood.

It feels like abandonment. Like I'm leaving her behind, just as I somehow left Sarah behind.

"I should get going," I say, not meeting her eyes. I can't think of a lie quickly enough to give her, though.

Ellie stands, recognising the dismissal. "Right. Well, the French toast will probably be gone soon, so..." She trails off, awkward in a way she's never been with me before. "See you later?"

I nod, but I know it must look uncertain.

At the door, she pauses. "You know, the nice thing about not being normal anymore is that you get to decide what your new normal looks like. It's kind of liberating, in a fucked-up way."

Then she's gone, leaving me with a hollow feeling in my chest that has nothing to do with hunger.

I sit on my bed, staring at the blank wall, feeling the absence she's left behind like a physical thing. Another goodbye, another person walking away. Another reminder that however much I try to connect, there's always distance now. Always a gap between me and everything else.

I don't know how long I sit there, empty and alone, before another knock comes at my door, softer this time, hesitant.

"Come in," I call, automatically smoothing my scarf higher around my neck.

Mum pokes her head in, her expression tense.

"Amanda, sweetheart." She steps inside, closing the door partially behind her. "I need you to stay calm, okay?"

My heart immediately kicks into a higher gear. Nothing makes you less calm than someone telling you to stay calm.

"What's wrong? Is it the baby?"

It's almost the due date. Surely nothing can go wrong now. Please, not that.

"No, no," she says quickly. "The baby's fine. It's just... the police are here. Detective Barnes. He says they have news about the case."

I sit up straighter. "What news?"

"I don't know exactly." She doesn't look me in the eyes. "They asked to speak with you directly. Paul drove me over when they called."

My mind races through possibilities: They found more evidence. They lost the evidence they had. They need me to look at more photographs. They found Maggie.

I know, though.

I already know what's happened.

"Are you okay with seeing them?" Mum asks, studying my face. "I can tell them to come back later if you're not up to it."

"No," I say firmly. "I want to see them. Now."

Mum nods, though I can tell she's concerned. She opens the door wider and gestures to someone in the hallway.

Detective Barnes steps in.

"Amanda," Barnes says with a nod. "Hope you don't mind the unexpected visit. Suki's just..."

As he says her name, my Victim Support friend hurries into the room.

"What's happening?" I ask.

"We have news," Barnes says. "Important news."

He pulls the chair by my desk over and sits facing me. "The DNA results came back from the jacket."

My breath catches. "And?"

"We have a match," he says, his voice steady but his eyes bright with victory. "It's him."

"You found Sarah's DNA?" I ask.

Barnes's face changes then, softening from professional satisfaction to something more personal.

"We found *your* DNA on the jacket, Amanda. It wasn't quite what we expected, but it was there. And it is enough. It proves that you were with him that night, that he's the one who attacked you and Sarah. It places him at the scene, directly connecting him to what happened in a way he can't explain away."

"I don't understand. I never touched his jacket..."

I stop, remembering the blindfold, the way it rode up. How my face pressed against his chest as he carried me over his shoulder to the truck.

Had blood from my neck soaked into the fabric?

"My blood?"

No.

He wasn't wearing it then, was he?

When the knife sliced across my neck and stole my voice.

There was no blood on the jacket I identified.

"No," Barnes shakes his head. "Not blood."

"I don't understand," I say.

"Tears, Amanda. You were crying. Your tears soaked into his jacket when he was carrying you."

"My... tears?" The words don't make sense at first. Of all the evidence they could have found, blood, skin under fingernails, hair, my tears seem so insignificant. So weak.

"Tears contain epithelial cells," Barnes explains, his tone shifting into something more clinical, steadier. "They're microscopic cells that shed from the surface of your eye. When you cry, these cells carry your unique DNA signature, and they transferred to his jacket. The fabric absorbed and preserved them, like a time capsule of evidence that he never thought to destroy."

"He was careful not to get your blood on him," Suki adds quietly. "But he didn't consider your tears."

The realisation hits me. I had felt so powerless, so completely at his mercy. Blindfolded, gagged, bound at the wrists, unable to save Sarah or myself. My tears had seemed like the ultimate symbol of my helplessness in that moment.

But they weren't.

They were evidence. They were power. They were the very thing that would eventually condemn him.

"Your tears placed you with him, definitively," Barnes continues. "Combined with your identification of both the jacket and the suspect, plus the partial fingerprint from the dog lead, it's airtight. He's not getting away with this, Amanda. Not after what he did to you and Sarah."

There's a roaring in my ears, blood rushing through my body in great surging waves. I'm dimly aware of Suki's hand still holding mine, of Barnes watching my face carefully.

"How?" I finally manage. "After all this time, how were my tears still... still there?"

"I guess he never washed it after that night, just tossed it in that truck. It's only been a few months, so the DNA was still viable despite some degradation," Barnes says.

I shake my head, remembering the stench that clung to him that night. "I'm not surprised he didn't wash it. The man reeked of BO when he attacked us." I wrap my arms around myself. "He probably thought he was being careful. He didn't get blood on the jacket, so he thought it was safe."

Suki nods. "That's often how they get caught. They're careful about the obvious evidence, blood, fingerprints, but overlook things like tears, skin cells, fibres. Even leaving the tyre tracks was careless."

I don't want to think about him pulling that jacket back out, using it again, the fabric where my tears had soaked in pressed against his body as he went about his life like nothing had happened. Like he hadn't destroyed Sarah's life and nearly ended mine.

"He thought he was so careful," I whisper. "He thought he took everything from me. My best friend. My voice. My sense of safety." My fingers drift to my scarf, to the scar beneath it. "But he missed this. He missed my tears."

"He never considered them evidence," Suki says softly. "He never thought your vulnerability could be strength."

"You can arrest him now?" The words come out in a whisper.

"We already have," Barnes nods. "We brought him in two hours ago."

Everything inside me goes still. The man who killed Sarah, who cut my throat and left me to die, who haunts every nightmare. He's in custody.

He's caught.

Suki's hand finds mine, squeezing gently.

I look up at Barnes, suddenly desperate to know more. "Will he go to prison? For how long? Will I have to testify?"

"One step at a time," Barnes says, his voice gentle but firm. "Right now, we're building the strongest case possible. With the DNA evidence and your testimony, he's looking at life without parole. As for testifying, that's a conversation for another day. Today, I just wanted you to know that we got him. And that it was because of you."

Barnes stands. "I should get back to the station. There's a lot of paperwork when we bring someone in on charges this serious. But I wanted you to know. You helped us catch him, Amanda. You should be proud of that."

Proud. The word settles strangely in my chest. Am I proud? I don't know. Relieved, certainly. Vindicated, maybe. But proud implies I did something heroic, something brave. All I did was cry. All I did was survive.

"What about Maggie?" I ask suddenly. "Have you found out who she is? Does he have her too?"

A shadow crosses Barnes's face. "We're still investigating that angle. He's not talking, but we're searching his house more thoroughly now that we have him in custody. If there's anything to find about Maggie, we'll find it. The investigation doesn't end just because we've made the arrest."

I nod, unable to form more words past the tightness in my throat.

Suki stands. "I'll stay for a bit, if that's alright with you, Amanda?"

"Yeah," I manage. "That's... that would be good."

After Barnes leaves, my room falls into a thick silence. The detective's words hang in the air, almost visible: *We got him. It was because of you. Your tears.*

Mum sits on my bed, her face a complicated mix of relief and concern. One hand rests protectively on her belly, the other reaches for mine, squeezing gently.

"Amanda," she whispers, her voice thick with emotion. "They caught him."

"I should feel better," I whisper. "Relieved. Happy. Something. But I just feel... empty."

Mum smiles sadly. "That's... that's normal, I think. After everything you've been through."

Suki nods. "It is normal. When survivors finally get news of an arrest, sometimes it doesn't bring the closure or relief they expected. It's just one more step in a very long journey."

"What happens now?" I ask, my voice stronger.

"Now there will be legal proceedings," Suki explains. "Arraignment, bail hearing, though with these charges, he won't get bail. Eventually, a trial. Unless he pleads guilty."

"Will he?" I ask. "Could he?"

Because I know that really, it isn't over yet.

Not until I've given my testimony.

Not until he's been convicted.

Suki's expression becomes more careful.

"It's impossible to predict. Some do to avoid a trial. Others fight every step of the way, even with overwhelming evidence."

Mum squeezes my hand again. "Whatever happens, we'll be with you through all of it. You don't have to face any of this alone."

"And Maggie?" I ask, returning to the question I asked Barnes. "What about finding her?"

"The investigation continues," Suki says. "Now that they have him in custody, they can search more thoroughly. They'll look for records, correspondence, anything that might lead to her identity or whereabouts."

"Do you think she's alive?" The question bursts from me with an urgency that surprises even me.

Suki hesitates. "I honestly don't know, Amanda."

"He thought I was her. He called me by her name while he..." I stop, unable to finish the sentence. "Finding her matters."

"Of course it does," Mum says. "If it matters to you, it matters to us. Maybe we should focus on the good news. On moving forward."

"Forward to what?" I ask. "Going home? Pretending to be normal again?"

Mum flinches as if I've slapped her. I immediately regret my tone, if not my words.

"I'm sorry," I say. "I just... I don't know how to feel about any of this."

"That's okay," Mum says, reaching for my hand again. "You don't have to know yet."

Her fingers are warm against mine, and I'm struck by the sudden realisation that she's been carrying this too: the fear, the guilt, the helpless waiting for news. For the first time in months, I really look at her: the new lines around her eyes, the tension she carries in her shoulders, the careful way she watches me, as if afraid I might break.

"Joyce should know," I say suddenly. "About the arrest. Has anyone told her?"

"Detective Reid and one of the other Victim Support workers, the lady who has been with Mr and Mrs Fairchild, are with the family now," Suki says.

I try to imagine Joyce receiving the news. Will it bring her comfort? Or will it just remind her of everything she's lost? Sarah can never come home the way I did. There's no rehabilitation centre for the dead.

"I'm going to give you some time alone to process what has happened," Suki says, standing. "I can come back tomorrow if you'd like to talk more."

"Thanks," I say, meaning it. "I'd like that."

After Suki leaves, Mum moves to sit closer on the bed, and I lean my head against her shoulder the way I used to when I was small. It doesn't fix anything. It doesn't answer the questions still swirling inside me. But for now, in this moment, it's enough.

My tears caught him. My humanity, the very thing he tried to take from me, is what brought him down.

And somewhere out there, Maggie is waiting to be found. I'm sure of it. What I don't know yet is whether she's waiting for rescue, or whether, like Sarah, she's only waiting for justice.

Either way, I'm going to find her.

CHAPTER FORTY

The morning after they arrest him, I wake before dawn, my mind oddly quiet. I lie in the semi-darkness, staring at the ceiling, waiting for the rush of relief, of triumph, of vindication. Some emotional tsunami to mark the seismic shift in my reality.

He's in custody. Behind bars.

Because of my tears.

The thought replays like a news ticker across my consciousness, factual but distant. Somehow, I expected to feel different today. Lighter. Freer. Instead, I feel hollow, as if something vital has been scooped out, leaving an empty space where purpose used to be.

I wonder what they're saying about him on the news, if they're showing his face, printing his name, and I realise I never asked Barnes what it was. It didn't seem to matter.

It doesn't matter.

He's the man who left me to die

The man who called me Maggie.

The man who killed Sarah.

And then I think about Joyce, and how she is taking the news. Knowing that they have him won't bring Sarah back. Nothing will. All we can have now is justice. But even justice feels like an empty promise: a consolation prize when the real prize, Sarah, alive, is forever out of reach.

Mum's maternity leave has started now. I know she didn't want to go home yesterday, after hearing the news of the arrest. It was too much for her, never mind for me. I can't believe she has managed to get through this pregnancy so well with everything that's happened.

And to think that Paul said I stressed her out all those months ago.

This is how you *really* do it.

I almost smile to myself.

Things have changed.

Everything has changed.

And now, it's almost time for me to go home.

Does it make it easier for me, knowing that he won't be out there? Knowing he's in custody now?

I still don't know.

What I do know is that this isn't over. I'm still going to have to testify in court. I'm still going to have to relive that evening. I still want to find Maggie.

When Mum arrives, we talk about everything apart from the things that matter most.

I pick at a feather, sticking through the cotton that covers my pillow. Jab the sharp end against my finger, just because.

Mum's eyes narrow, and she purses her lips in disapproval.

"Have you...?" Whatever she's about to ask, she changes her mind.

"Yeah," I reply anyway.

"Been thinking about...?"

I nod.

I know it must be on her mind, but she doesn't know how to talk about it. She doesn't have the professional focus of Suzi, or the probing nature of Dr Harriet Craig. She's my mother, she loves me, and sometimes that makes it impossible to talk.

"I know they've got him now," I say, "But everyone keeps talking about getting back to normal. Going back to school. Coming home. Like I'm just supposed to pick up where I left off. But that girl is gone, Mum. The Amanda from before, she died in those woods. She's not coming back."

I don't know where it comes from, and I can't stop the words pouring out. Like the blood that pumped from my neck onto the earth, they are unstoppable.

Mum's eyes fill with tears. "I know that, sweetheart. I do. I just... I want to help you move forward. Find your way to whatever comes next."

"What if there is no '*next*'? What if this is it?" I gesture to myself: the covered scar, the too-thin frame, the shadows under my eyes. "What if this is all I get to be now?"

"Don't say that." Her voice breaks. "Please don't say that."

The silence that follows is heavy with all the things we don't know how to say to each other. How do you tell your mother that you don't know who you are anymore? That sometimes you're not sure you want to find out? That you feel like a ghost haunting the edges of your own life?

"I'm sorry," I say finally. "I just... I don't want you to expect too much. I don't want to disappoint you when I can't be who I was before."

"Oh, Amanda." She leans forward, taking my hands in hers. "You could never disappoint me. I'm just grateful you're alive. That you're here. Everything else can wait until you're ready."

I want to believe her. Want to trust the sincerity in her eyes, the gentle pressure of her fingers against mine. But there's a distance between us now that wasn't there before. A gap filled with the things she can't understand, and I can't explain.

"Being home means you'll be around when I have the baby," Mum smiles, trying to change to subject.

"Do you know if it's definitely a boy?" I ask, grateful for the safer topic.

"The scan was pretty clear." She smiles, that maternal glow returning. "Paul's already talking about football and camping trips."

"Where is he today?" I ask, noticing his absence. "Another mysterious errand?"

Mum's smile tightens slightly. "He's picking me up later. He's been busy lately. Work, and some other things."

"Things like not visiting me?"

She sighs. "Amanda, please. He's trying. In his way."

"Is he? Because from where I'm sitting, it looks like he's doing everything possible to avoid being here."

"That's not fair."

"Isn't it?" I know I should stop, should let it go, but something in me can't. "He's barely been. Always some excuse, some *errand*, some reason he can't make it. Just like Dad. I mean, come on, I almost died. I'm going through a lot of shit and Dad hasn't even been in touch."

The moment the words leave my mouth, I regret them. Mum flinches as if I'd slapped her.

"Paul is nothing like your father," she says, her voice suddenly hard. "Your father left us. Paul is here. He's building a nursery. He's planning for our future. He's just... *struggling* with all of this."

"While you've been dealing with everything alone."

"I haven't been alone," she protests weakly. "I have you."

The irony of that statement, that she's leaning on me, her traumatised daughter, for support, is so painful I almost laugh.

Instead, I squeeze her hand.

"It's fine. I'm not his responsibility anyway."

"Amanda..."

"No, really. It's fine." I force a smile. "Tell me more about the baby plans. Have you picked a name yet?"

For the next hour, we talk about safer things; the routine conversational dance of a mother and daughter pretending everything is fine. When her phone buzzes, she checks it with a small sigh.

"That'll be Paul. He said he'd pick me up on his way home."

"Is he actually coming in this time?"

"Amanda." Her voice carries a note of warning. "Please."

She taps on her phone and I'm pretty sure she's telling him not wait in the car. I'm not sure I want to see him, really. I just want the idea that he cares. Still, I can't be bothered to have the argument again.

She stands, smoothing her dress with hands that aren't quite steady.

"I need to use the bathroom before he gets here. I'll be right back."

After she slips into my en suite, I wait, a headache building behind my eyes. I should feel guilty for pushing her, for adding to the stress she doesn't need in her condition. But all I can think about is Paul, disappearing when things get difficult, leaving Mum to handle everything alone while he goes off to do whatever it is he does.

Just like my father.

I reach under my pillow for the notebook, needing to look at Maggie's photo again. Her face grounds me somehow, reminds me that there's a purpose beyond all of this.

I'm so focused on the photograph that I don't hear the door open. Don't realise I'm not alone until a shadow falls across the bed.

"Amanda? Where's..."

Paul stops mid-sentence, his eyes fixed on the photo in my hands. Something shifts in his expression, a subtle change I might have missed if I hadn't been watching so carefully. Recognition, followed quickly by confusion.

"What's that?" he asks, his voice casual but his posture suddenly tense.

I slide the photo deep into the notebook, an instinctive movement.

"Nothing."

"Doesn't look like nothing." He takes a step closer, and I resist the urge to back away. "May I see?"

"No."

His eyebrows rise at the sharpness of my refusal. "I was just asking."

"And I'm just saying no."

We stare at each other, the air between us heavy with mutual distrust. This is the longest conversation we've had in weeks, possibly ever.

"Where's your mother?" he says finally. "We should get going soon. Traffic's going to be bad with the construction on Wells Road."

I don't respond. I have nothing to say to him. But his eyes dart to the notebook still clutched in my hands.

"When were you at Lacey Point?" he asks, as though it's a casual question.

My heart skips.

"What?"

"In that photo." He gestures at the book that holds the image. "You were at Lacey Point, weren't you?" His brow furrows as he leans closer. "When did you go there? It's not exactly easy to find."

He says it as though it's an accusation, as though I was somewhere I shouldn't be.

"I've never been there," I say, my voice sounding strange, distant.

I take the photo out, trying to stop my hand from trembling, and show it to him.

If he thinks he knows where this is, it could help me... it could help *the police* find Maggie.

I've stopped thinking of any other possibilities.

To me, that's definitely who the girl is.

Maggie.

Paul's eyes narrow as he studies the photo more carefully, then my face, then the photo again.

"That's... not you?" He reaches for the photograph, but I pull it closer to my chest.

"No," I say firmly. "And you can't have it."

He should be grateful that I'm even letting him see it.

Paul straightens, something unreadable flickering in his eyes.

"She looks exactly like you. And that's definitely Lacey Point. Most people don't even know it exists. It's completely isolated, hidden on the far side of the reservoir. There aren't even any proper roads. It's about a half hour hike from the nearest access point."

His gaze is now intense, searching.

"If that's not you," he continues, "who is it? And how did you get the photo if you weren't there? I don't know what it is with you, Amanda. I'm just..."

He stops, silent for a moment.

"Never mind," he says.

I shake my head, unable to form words as my mind races to process this information.

Why would Maggie be at a place so remote that Paul claims few people know about it? A place he apparently visits?

And why does he seem so disturbed by the existence of this photograph?

He stares at me for a long moment, then adds, "I found that spot two or three years ago, back when I was exploring some old logging trails. Been back a few times since. It's... peaceful. Private." His voice lowers slightly. "No one really goes there anymore, not since they tore down the boathouse last year. You can just about see the edge of it in the photo there."

It's not something I would have noticed unless it was pointed out to me. It looks like a green line at the edge of the frame. The line that I thought was a sign, perhaps.

A *boathouse*?

Paul studies the photo more carefully. "That's definitely Lacey Point. Half the roof of that boathouse blew away in that big storm two winters ago. Then the county condemned it and tore it down about eight months later."

He's talking for talking's sake, filling the awkward space between us. What he doesn't know is that this time, I'm actually hanging on his every word.

He points to something else in the background.

"And look, you can see they haven't started clearing the trees for the new conservation project. That happened last spring."

There's a lot to take in, but this narrows it down precisely. The photo must have been taken after the storm damaged the roof, but before they started clearing trees. That's a window of just a few months, less than two years ago.

I can't even make out a roof. I guess you have to know what you're looking for to be able to see it. Just like Mum and I knew that the girl standing beside it was not me.

"So, this photo was taken when? A year and a half ago?" My voice sounds strange even to my own ears.

Not some old picture from another lifetime, but recent. Maggie was at Lacey Point while I was sitting in biology class, complaining about homework. While Sarah was alive. While everything was normal.

Before Paul can respond, Mum steps out of the bathroom.

"Ready to go?" she asks, glancing between us, sensing the tension. "Is everything okay?"

"Fine," Paul says smoothly. "Just chatting about old fishing spots."

Mum smiles, relief evident in her face at this supposed moment of bonding. "That's nice. We should get going, though. I promised Joyce I'd stop by this afternoon."

Joyce. Sarah's mother. Another bolt of lightning, another connection I'm not ready to make.

But Mum has stopped, her face frozen. Paul's words took time to sink in, but now they're embedded firmly.

"Fishing spots?" she asks, backtracking. "Since when is Amanda interested in fishing spots?"

I hold up the photo of Maggie.

"Since *Maggie* was photographed by one," I say, watching Paul's face for signs of recognition.

"Maggie?" he asks.

I know from this that either Mum isn't racing home with details about the case or that Paul hasn't been paying attention. It could be either.

"The police left it for me," I say in a record-breaking conversation with Paul. "It was... or at least the original was... with the killer's belongings. They thought it was me."

"So did I," Paul says. "She could be your sister. Your twin."

"Yeah, I've got enough trauma to deal with, thanks," I say without a smile.

Paul looks at Mum and she tightens her eyes.

"What?" she asks. "You're not seriously asking?"

Paul raises his eyebrows. "Of course not. So have they found her?"

Mum really isn't feeding him the news updates.

"No," Mum says.

"The fishing community is pretty tight-knit," Paul says. "If your Maggie has been around there, someone will know her."

Your Maggie.

My Maggie.

I've never met her, but still, I feel a connection beyond words.

"Detective Barnes needs to know about this," Mum says suddenly, reaching for her phone. "If you recognise the location..."

"Of course," Paul agrees readily. "It could be important." He turns to me. "It's an odd coincidence, but maybe it'll help them figure out who she is."

His straightforward response catches me off guard. I'd expected... what? Resistance? Evasion? Instead, he seems genuinely willing to help.

"Mum's right," I say, watching his face carefully. "Detective Barnes should know."

Paul nods.

For once, we all seem to want the same thing. The three of us frozen in this strange moment of alignment. Mum, Paul, and me, all suddenly focused on a photograph of a girl who looks like me but isn't. A girl whose name I know but whose story remains a mystery. A girl who might still be out there somewhere, waiting to be found.

As Mum reaches for her phone, I realise that for the first time since waking up in the hospital, I feel something breaking through the numbness: purpose.

CHAPTER FORTY-ONE

Paul stands motionless beside me, his expression unreadable as he watches Mum's fingers scroll through her contacts. This call could change everything: for the investigation, for finding Maggie, for understanding why he targeted me.

Mum presses call and puts the phone to her ear, her free hand instinctively moving to her belly in that protective gesture I've grown used to seeing. When Detective Barnes answers, her voice is steady, determined.

"Detective Barnes? It's Abby Gray, Amanda's mother. I think we might have some information about the photograph you showed her. The one of the girl we think is Maggie."

Her words aren't lost on me.

She said, 'the girl *we* think is Maggie.'

As she talks, Paul moves closer, his attention on the photo I'm still holding.

"It's strange," he says, his voice low enough that it won't interfere with Mum's call. "The resemblance is really remarkable."

"We wondered whether that was why he... targeted me," I say, but quickly change the subject. "Do you think she could be local?" I ask.

Paul considers this. "Hard to say. Stewart Reservoir draws people from several counties. Hikers, fishermen, nature photographers. But if she was at Lacey Point specifically..." He pauses, thinking. "Like I said, that's off the beaten path. You'd need to know it was there, or at least be willing to explore beyond the main trails."

There's nothing suspicious in his manner, just someone trying to be helpful, thinking through possibilities.

Mum's voice breaks through our conversation.

"Yes, that's right. Lacey Point at Stewart Reservoir. Paul recognised it immediately." She pauses, listening. "Yes, he can... Of course. We'll wait for you." Another pause. "Thank you, Detective."

She lowers the phone, turning to Paul. "They want us to wait here. Barnes is sending a car to pick you up. He wants to show you some more photographs, see if you recognise any other locations."

"No problem," Paul says easily. "Anything I can do to help."

"They'll be here in twenty minutes." Mum glances at me, then back to Paul. "Joyce will understand if we're late."

An uncomfortable silence settles over the room, but not because of Paul, but because of the weight of what this might mean. I clutch the photo of Maggie, studying it again with new understanding. The boathouse that Paul recognised stands partly visible behind her left shoulder, weathered green wood against the darker water. Only visible to someone who knows it's there.

It was demolished a year ago. But in this photo, it seems it was definitely still standing.

"Can I see it again?" Paul asks.

This time I hand him the picture, and he studies it with genuine interest.

"Have you ever seen her there?" I ask. "At the reservoir? At Lacey Point?"

Paul shakes his head. "No, never." He passes the photo back. "It's not exactly a busy place. Most times I've been there, I haven't seen another soul."

"Why do you go there?" I ask, curious now rather than suspicious.

"Honestly? Just to think. Get some space." His expression is open, thoughtful. "With everything that's happened... sometimes I need to clear my head. Find somewhere quiet where I can sort through things." He glances at Mum. "It's been a lot to process."

For the first time, I consider how all of this might have affected Paul. He'd barely entered our lives when violence tore through it. A new relationship, a baby on the way, and suddenly his girlfriend's daughter is attacked and nearly killed. No wonder he's been disappearing on solitary hikes.

"I understand," I say, surprising myself with the words.

Paul looks equally surprised, but he nods in acknowledgment.

"Maybe this will help them find her," he says, gesturing to the photo. "This Maggie. If knowing the location gives them something to work with."

Twenty minutes. The police will be here in twenty minutes, and Paul will tell them everything he knows about Lacey Point. It's not much, but it's something. A starting point. A place where Maggie once stood, looking so much like me, it's frightening.

I need to know why. Why she was there. Why she mattered to that man. Why he saw me and thought of her.

"Thank you," I say to Paul, the words feeling strange on my tongue. "For recognising the place."

He nods, and for the first time since I've known him, there's no awkwardness between us. Just a shared purpose, however temporary.

Finding Maggie.

The door closes behind Mum and Paul, leaving me alone with my racing thoughts. My fingers trace the edge of the photograph, following the outline of the boathouse visible behind her shoulder.

The boathouse. The reservoir. Maggie.

The pieces feel like they should fit together, but I can't see the pattern yet. I slide the photo back into the notebook, tucking it safely beneath my pillow. If I stare at it any longer, I'll drive myself crazy with questions I can't answer.

A knock at the door breaks my spiral of thoughts.

"Come in," I call.

Ellie pokes her head in, her expression a mixture of curiosity and concern. "Hey. So, your mum and Paul just got escorted out by someone who seemed very much like a police officer. Should I be worried or entertained?"

I almost smile. "Entertained, I think. They aren't being arrested, if that's what you mean."

"Ah." Ellie steps inside, closing the door behind her. Her eyes narrow slightly as she studies my face. "You've got that look."

"What look?"

"The one where your brain is going a million miles an hour." She drops into the chair by the window, pulling one leg up beneath her. "Spill. What's happening in that head of yours? What's going on with the olds?"

I hesitate, but only for a moment. After shutting her out yesterday, I owe her something.

"That photograph the police found with my attacker's belongings," I say.

"The girl who looks like you?"

"Yeah," I shudder. "Well, it turns out she was at this place called Lacey Point. It's by some reservoir. Paul recognised it. Knew exactly where it was."

Ellie whistles softly. "That's... intense. Does that mean they might find her? This girl?"

"Maybe. I hope so. I need to know who she is. Whether she is Maggie. Whether she's okay."

There's a moment of silence before Ellie speaks again, her voice gentler than usual. "You know it's not your job to solve this, right?"

The question catches me off guard. "What?"

"Finding this girl. Solving the case. That's not on you." She watches me carefully, as if gauging my reaction.

"If not me, then who?" The words come out more defensive than I intended.

"Um, the actual police?" Ellie raises an eyebrow, and her scar shifts along with it. "The ones with badges and forensic labs and salaries?"

"They don't understand the connection," I insist, sitting straighter. "They can't feel it like I do."

Ellie's expression softens. "The connection to this girl? Or the connection to Sarah?"

My breath catches. "What do you mean?"

"Just... I wonder if you're transferring some of what happened with Sarah onto this Maggie person. Like maybe if you can save her, it'll make up for not being able to save Sarah."

The words hit with unexpected force. I open my mouth to protest, but nothing comes out. Ellie doesn't push, doesn't press the point. She just sits there, concern written across her face.

"You don't understand," I finally manage.

"Probably not," she agrees easily. "But I do know what it's like to feel responsible for something you couldn't control." She gestures vaguely toward the scar on her temple. "In the car accident, my boyfriend was driving. He didn't make it."

I stare at her, this vital piece of information reframing everything I thought I knew about Ellie. "I didn't know."

"Not something I lead with." She shrugs, but the casual gesture doesn't match the darkness that crosses her face.

"For months, I kept thinking that if I'd done something different, asked him to slow down, suggested an alternative route, anything, he'd still be alive."

"I'm sorry," I whisper.

"Yeah. Me too." She meets my eyes. "But eventually I realised that no amount of 'what ifs' was going to change what happened. And no amount of trying to save other people is going to bring him back."

The parallel isn't subtle. I look away, fixing my gaze on the window beyond her shoulder.

"This is different." My voice sounds tiny.

"Is it?" Ellie asks but doesn't wait for an answer. She stands, stretching. "Anyway, I should go. Got physical therapy in ten. Just wanted to make sure you weren't all being arrested or something."

"Thanks," I say, my mind still churning with her words.

At the door, she pauses.

"For what it's worth, I think it's good they might find this Maggie person. I just don't think it has to be your crusade."

Then she's gone, leaving me with a seed of doubt I didn't have before.

Dr Craig notices the shift in my energy the moment I enter her office for our afternoon session. Her eyes track my restless movements as I settle into the chair across from her, my fingers drumming against my knees.

"Something's happened," she says.

It's not a question.

"Paul recognised the location in Maggie's photo." The words tumble out in a rush. "It's a place called Lacey Point at Stewart Reservoir. He's with the police now, telling them what he knows."

Dr Craig leans forward slightly, her expression carefully neutral. "That's a significant development. How are you feeling about it?"

"Hopeful. Anxious." I force myself to sit still. "It might help them find her."

"And why is that so important to you?" she asks, her tone gentle but probing.

"Because it's connected to everything," I reply, frustration creeping into my voice. "To what happened to Sarah. To what happened to me. I have to find her. I mean *they* have to find her."

"Why does this have to be your responsibility?" Dr Craig's question echoes Ellie's from earlier, but with a different weight.

"Because I survived for a reason," I say, the words emerging with surprising force. "Because she's connected to me somehow. Because if I don't find her, who will?"

Dr Craig doesn't flinch from my intensity. "The police will. They have resources, expertise, authority that you don't."

"But they don't have my connection to her," I insist.

"What exactly *is* your connection to Maggie?" Dr Craig asks, her voice still calm. "Beyond a physical resemblance and the fact that your attacker called you by her name. This girl in the photograph, Amanda. You have to be open to the fact that it might not even be Maggie. You know that, don't you?"

I open my mouth to answer, then close it. I don't know. There is no real connection, just the one I've created in my mind: the one I need to believe exists to make sense of everything that's happened.

And what if it isn't her?

What if Maggie is never found?

What if Maggie never existed?

Why does this thought bother me so much?

"Amanda," Dr Craig says softly, "I want to ask you something difficult. Is this about Maggie, or is it about Sarah?"

My throat tightens. "What do you mean?"

"I wonder if you're trying to save Maggie to make up for not saving Sarah."

The words knock the air from my lungs. For a long moment, I can't speak, can't even breathe properly. Dr Craig waits, her silence an invitation rather than a demand.

"I couldn't save Sarah," I finally whisper, the admission raw and painful. "I lay there while he... while she... I couldn't do anything to help her."

"That wasn't your fault," Dr Craig says firmly. "You were injured, bleeding. There was nothing you could have done differently."

"But there must have been something," I insist, heat building behind my eyes. "Some way I could have stopped him, or warned her, or..."

"Amanda." Dr Craig's voice cuts through my spiral. "Sometimes terrible things happen that are completely beyond our control. What happened to Sarah, what happened to you. None of it was your fault."

"Then why did I survive?" The question tears from my throat, ragged and desperate. "Why am I here when she isn't?"

"I don't have an answer for that," Dr Craig admits. "But I do know that survival doesn't automatically come with an obligation to solve mysteries or right wrongs. Sometimes survival just means healing. Finding a way forward."

I shake my head, unwilling to accept the simplicity of it. "But Maggie..."

"Is not your responsibility," Dr Craig finishes gently. "The police will search for her. They'll investigate the connection. But you? Your only responsibility right now is to focus on your own healing."

I sit with that for a long moment, the resistance inside me slowly giving way to something else, something that feels strangely like relief. The thought that I don't have to find Maggie, that I don't have to solve this mystery, is both terrifying and liberating.

"What if they never find her?" I ask quietly.

"Then that will be difficult," Dr Craig acknowledges. "Unanswered questions are hard to live with. But learning to exist alongside uncertainty, that's part of healing too."

By the time I leave her office, my mind is swirling with contradictions. Part of me still insists that finding Maggie is essential, that it's the key to understanding everything. But another part, quieter but growing stronger, wonders if Dr Craig and Ellie might be right.

CHAPTER FORTY-TWO

Back in my room, I pace the small space between bed and window, my thoughts circling like vultures. Dr Craig's questions echo inside my head, challenging everything I've told myself about Maggie, about my role in finding her.

"Is this about Maggie, or is it about Sarah?"

I don't know anymore. The lines have blurred; the connections have tangled until I can't separate one from the other. Sarah, who I couldn't save. Maggie, who I somehow need to find. Both of them reflecting parts of myself I can barely recognise.

I stop at the window, pressing my forehead against the cool glass. Outside, people move along the paths: patients, staff, visitors, each carrying their own invisible burdens. Their own unanswered questions.

The memory of Sarah surfaces suddenly. Not from that night, but from before. Her smile as we walked home from school, her shoulder bumping mine as she told some ridiculous story about her brother. The easy comfort of her presence.

And then, unbidden, the other memory. Sarah's muffled cries. The helplessness as I lay bleeding. The terrible silence that followed.

"You couldn't save Sarah. That wasn't your fault."

But it feels like my fault. It always has. As if, in some way I still can't identify, I should have done more. Been stronger. Fought harder. And in the absence of that possibility, I've latched onto the next best thing: finding Maggie. Saving her, at least. Making sense of the senseless.

"Are you trying to save Maggie to make up for not saving Sarah?"

The question cuts too close to a truth I've been avoiding. I sink onto the edge of my bed, suddenly exhausted by the weight of my own expectations. The responsibility I've placed on my shoulders feels crushing now that I've named it.

I couldn't save Sarah. And the terrible, liberating truth is that I can't save Maggie, either. I don't even know if she needs saving. I don't know anything about her beyond a photograph and a name that isn't even certain.

For the first time since learning about Maggie's existence, I allow myself to consider the possibility that finding her isn't my purpose. That perhaps my survival doesn't come with this specific obligation attached.

The realisation brings both grief and relief, tangled together in a knot I'm not sure how to unravel.

A soft knock at my door interrupts my spinning thoughts.

"Amanda?" Mum's voice calls. "Can we come in?"

We. Not just Mum, but Paul too. The shift doesn't escape my notice.

"Yes."

The door opens, and Mum enters first, her expression a mixture of exhaustion and barely contained excitement. Behind her, Paul steps in, not staying at the threshold as he usually does, but actually entering my space. He looks unexpectedly drained, with dark circles under his eyes I've never noticed before. There's something different about his presence, a purposefulness that's replaced his usual awkward distance.

For months, he's found every excuse to avoid my room, my recovery, anything connected to what happened. Now he's voluntarily here, looking like he's been through a battle of his own.

Is it some kind of macabre fascination with the case? Or has he finally found something useful to do, a concrete way to help that doesn't require talking about feelings or facing the damage done to me?

"You've been with the police all this time?" I ask, directing the question at both of them but finding myself looking at Paul.

He nods, running a hand through his dishevelled hair, hair that's usually meticulously styled, with not a strand out of place.

"Four hours of looking at maps and photographs. I never thought my hiking obsession would be useful for something like this."

Mum perches on the edge of my bed while Paul takes the chair by the window, maintaining a respectful distance but no longer avoiding my gaze entirely.

"They believe the picture was definitely taken in the last two years," Mum says, her hand automatically moving to her belly. "Everything Paul said about the boathouse and the tree clearing gave them a specific timeframe."

"The forensic tech showed me how they can analyse the seasonal growth patterns," Paul adds, a hint of genuine interest breaking through his usual reserve. "Apparently they can date outdoor photos within a few months based on vegetation alone."

I lean forward. "Can they use this to identify her? Is she definitely Maggie?"

Mum and Paul exchange a glance I can't quite read.

"They're not certain of anything yet," Mum says carefully. "But they're showing the photo to everyone connected to the reservoir: park rangers, maintenance crews, even regular visitors who might recognise her."

Paul shifts in his chair. "I gave them contact information for some of the local fishing groups. There might be people who were around Lacey Point during the timeframe the police are looking into."

The image of Paul willingly spending hours with the police, drawing maps and offering contacts, doesn't align with the distant figure I've known. This Paul seems engaged, invested. It's almost as if he actually cares.

"Have they questioned *him* about the photograph?" I ask. They know who I mean.

Mum and Paul exchange a quick glance before Mum answers.

"They showed it to him during the initial questioning," she says carefully. "Barnes told us he had a... strong reaction to it."

"What kind of reaction?" I lean forward, suddenly alert.

Paul shifts in his chair. "Apparently he just stared at it for a long time. Wouldn't say a word about it, but his body language changed completely. Barnes said it was the only time during the interrogation that he seemed genuinely rattled."

"But he didn't say anything?" I press.

"Not a word," Paul confirms. "They're building their case methodically. Barnes said sometimes it's better to let a suspect stew before pressing for answers."

Heat rises to my face, and I don't know if I'm more angry or frustrated.

"Standard procedure," he adds, surprising me with his knowledge. "They've only had thirty-six hours with him. They've searched his house, but processing all that evidence takes time."

"What Barnes did say was that the photograph is particularly interesting to them now, given his reaction," Mum continues. "They did an initial sweep of his home yesterday, and so far they haven't found any personal items from Sarah in his possession."

"Or from you," Paul adds, then clears his throat awkwardly. "Sorry, I mean, they didn't find anything of yours either. Which is unusual for someone like Matheson."

"Matheson?" I repeat, the unfamiliar syllables feeling strange on my tongue.

The name hangs in the air between us.

Matheson.

The man who killed Sarah. The man who tried to kill me.

I've never heard his name before.

Now he has a name that sounds so ordinary, so human. Three simple syllables that suddenly make him real.

My throat tightens unexpectedly. My fingers find their way to my scarf, pressing against the raised scar tissue beneath the fabric. For a moment, I hear his voice again. '*It's that time again, Maggie.*' Feel the blade against my skin, taste blood filling my mouth.

Matheson.

Paul freezes, his eyes darting to Mum, who looks equally startled. "I..." he begins, then stops, swallowing hard. "Sorry. It's been all over the news since yesterday's press conference. I didn't think..."

"I don't watch the news," I say, my voice sounding hollow even to my own ears. "No one told me his name."

Matheson.

I roll the name silently in my mind, trying to make it fit with the face I identified, with the man who wore that red plaid jacket, who held the knife, who called me Maggie.

It feels both too mundane and too powerful: a name that could belong to a teacher or a neighbour, not a monster.

I store the name away; I'll deal with it later. Right now, I can't let it consume me. Right now, there's Maggie to think about. There are more questions to ask.

"Why would he have our things?" I ask, deliberately steering the conversation away from his name.

For a split second, I wonder what happened to our backpacks, abandoned in the clearing with the bluebells.

"Well, from what I've seen on those true crime shows," Paul begins, "serial offenders almost always take trophies from their victims. If he kept a photograph of one victim by his bed, he'd likely have similar items from others."

Mum rolls her eyes. "You watch too many episodes of Forensic Files, Paul."

"What? It's relevant," he says defensively, a slight flush creeping up his neck.

"But that's just it," I say, suddenly realising something. "If he is a serial offender, wouldn't they have found more than just this one photograph? Other trophies? Other victims?"

"That's... actually a good point," Paul admits. "Barnes mentioned they were surprised they didn't find anything else during their search. No hidden collection, nothing from Sarah or you. Just this one photograph, displayed openly. Maybe they're rethinking the whole case."

I flash him a sharp look when he says that last word.

Case.

It still feels like such a simplification of something so much bigger, so much more significant than a four-letter word can convey.

"So maybe he's not a serial killer at all," I say, the thought forming as I speak. "Maybe this is about something else entirely."

This.

If Paul can simplify what I've been through and what happened to Sarah, so can I.

"The fact that he only had this one photograph tells them something important about the girl's relationship to him," Mum says thoughtfully.

Maggie's.

"Anyway, maybe it means the girl in the photograph isn't a victim," Mum says, bringing the conversation back to steadier ground. "At least not in the same way as..."

She doesn't finish the sentence. She doesn't need to.

"So, who is she, then?" I ask, voicing the question that's been haunting me since I first saw her face. "If she's not a victim, who is Maggie to him?"

"That's what they're trying to figure out," Paul says. "Barnes thinks that photograph is the key to understanding him. Understanding why he targeted you specifically."

"I hope she's okay," I whisper, almost to myself.

Paul leans forward, elbows on his knees. "I'll be going back tomorrow to help them map out some of the more remote areas around the reservoir. Places that wouldn't appear on standard maps."

I look between them: Mum, exhausted but hopeful, Paul, awkwardly earnest in a way I've never seen before. Both of them here, bringing me information, including me.

But instead of bringing more answers, they've just given me more to think about.

What if Sarah and I were his only victims?

What if it was because of the girl in the photograph?

What if she is Maggie?

What if she's not?

After Paul tells me about helping with the maps tomorrow, a heavy silence falls over the room. Mum shifts uncomfortably on the edge of my bed, one hand supporting her lower back. She glances at Paul, who immediately notices her discomfort.

"Are you alright?" he asks.

"Just tired," she says, rubbing her belly. "Would you mind getting the car? I don't think I can face that long walk to the lot right now."

Paul hesitates, looking between us as if sensing there's more to her request. "Of course," he says after a moment. "I'll bring it round to the front entrance."

He stands, and for a second, I think he might reach out to touch my shoulder or say something else. Instead, he just nods awkwardly. "See you tomorrow, Amanda."

"Yeah. See you tomorrow." I smile at him, and I mean it. Even feeling drained and confused and whatever else is making me feel like I want to throw up, I appreciate what he has done. "Thanks, Paul."

Once the door closes behind him, Mum relaxes slightly.

"He seems different," I observe.

"He's trying," she says simply. "In his own way."

I'm sure I've heard her say that before, but now it feels more believable.

I look down at my hands, at the notebook hidden beneath my pillow. Matheson's name circles in my mind, refusing to settle.

"I saw your reaction when Paul mentioned his name," Mum says, watching me closely.

I can't meet her eyes. "Matheson," I say, forcing myself to say it aloud, as if testing how it feels in my mouth. "It sounds so... normal."

"I know." Mum's hand finds mine. "That's what makes it so hard, isn't it? Monsters should have monstrous names."

I trace the edge of my scarf with my fingertips. "All this time, I've been so focused on Maggie. On finding her. Like somehow that would fix everything."

Mum watches me, something shifting in her expression. "You know, when your father left, I did the same thing."

"What do you mean?"

"I became obsessed with fixing the gutters on the house." She smiles ruefully. "Of all things. They'd been leaking for months, and suddenly it was the only thing I could think about. I spent hours researching, comparing materials, calling contractors."

"Gutters?" I can't hide my surprise.

"Ridiculous, isn't it? But I couldn't control him leaving. I couldn't control how it was affecting you. So I found something I could control." She squeezes my hand. "Sometimes when the big things are too painful to face, we fixate on smaller puzzles."

"This isn't the same," I protest, but even as I say it, I hear how defensive I sound.

"No," Mum agrees. "She's important. She's a person. But finding her won't bring Sarah back. And it won't heal what he did to you."

The truth of her words hits me with unexpected force. For months, I've been channelling all my fear, my grief, my anger into finding Sarah, finding Maggie, as if doing that would somehow undo everything else.

"I just want to do something," I whisper. "I feel so... useless."

"I know, love." Mum's voice catches. "But the most important thing you can do right now is heal. Detective Barnes has an entire team working on finding Maggie. Which means you don't have to."

I watch her, really see her, for the first time in months. The dark circles under her eyes, the careful way she holds herself, the mixture of exhaustion and determination in every movement. All this time, I've been so wrapped up in my own trauma that I haven't fully acknowledged what it's been doing to her.

"You know who I was thinking about earlier?" I say, surprising myself with the random thought. "Officer Winters. That police officer who came at the very beginning, when I still had to use that stupid communication board."

Mum tilts her head. "The blonde one?"

I nod. "I thought she was going to be a major part of the investigation. She was there for that first interview, taking all these notes, asking all these questions. Then Barnes and Reid took over, and I never saw her again."

"I wonder what happened to her," Mum says.

"That's just it. I keep wondering if she still thinks about the case. If she still itches to get involved. It's weird to be so invested in something and then just... have to let it go."

Mum studies my face, understanding dawning in her eyes. "I suppose that's part of her job. Knowing when to step back and let others take over."

"Yeah," I whisper. "I just... I don't know if I could do that."

"You mean with Maggie?" Mum asks gently.

I look away, caught in my transparency.

"With all of it. The investigation. Finding Maggie. Everything."

"It doesn't mean she stopped caring," Mum says. "Officer Winters, I mean."

The parallel doesn't escape me, and from Mum's careful tone, it doesn't escape her either.

We let the idea hang in the room, just like Dr Craig does in our sessions.

"When are you due again?" I ask, changing the subject.

"Only a few weeks now." A smile softens her face. "Though the doctor thinks it might be sooner. Your brother's already dropped into position."

"I want to be home when he arrives," I say, the decision forming as I speak.

"Really?" Hope brightens her eyes. "I thought you were nervous about coming home."

"I am. But..." I trail off, trying to find the right words. "I can't hide here forever. And I want to be there for you. For him."

Mum's eyes fill with tears. "Oh, Amanda."

"I need to do it," I say. "Like jumping into cold water. The longer I wait, the harder it gets."

Mum wraps her arm around my shoulders, pulling me close. "You don't have to figure everything out at once, you know. Healing takes time."

"I know." I lean against her, allowing myself to accept the comfort she offers. "But I need to start somewhere. And I think being home, being with you and... and Paul... when the baby comes. That's where I need to be."

She hesitates, then adds, "Detective Barnes promised to call if they learn anything about Maggie. You don't need to let go of wanting to know. Just maybe let others do the looking for a while."

"I'll try," I say, and I mean it.

Mum's phone buzzes. "That's Paul. He's waiting outside." She stands, a little awkward with her growing belly. "Will you be okay?"

I nod, surprised to find it's not entirely a lie. "Yeah. I think I will be."

After Mum leaves, I open my notebook. Not to look at the photograph, this time; instead, I flip through the pages, filled now with memories, questions, fragments of my attempts to understand what happened that night. I keep turning pages until I reach the list.

✓ Walk the entire hallway without stopping by Friday.

✓ Speak a complete sentence before Oakwood.

✓ Build enough strength to shower standing up.

✓ *Prepare questions for first session with Oakwood therapist.*

Find Sarah.

Find Maggie.

I run a finger over "*Find Sarah.*" I still can't bring myself to cross it out or mark it complete. It feels like a betrayal, an abandonment. Yet Sarah has been found. Not alive, not as I'd hoped, but found, nonetheless.

Below it, the newer addition: "*Find Maggie.*" Written in the same determined hand after I first saw her photograph. After I decided it was my responsibility to understand the connection between us.

I stare at the two lines, these missions I've assigned myself. One impossible, one perhaps beyond my reach. Both driven by a desperate need to control something, anything, in a world that's proven how little control I actually have.

Slowly, deliberately, I pick up my pen. But instead of marking either of the previous items, I add a new line below them:

Find myself.

The words look strange on the page, almost embarrassingly earnest. But they feel right. True, in a way the others aren't. Because this is a search I can actually conduct. A person I might actually be able to find.

I close the notebook, determination coursing through me. Not happiness, not by a long shot. But something steadier. More grounded.

I stand, decision made, and leave my room to find Ellie. Before I walk to the door, I unfurl the scarf from around my neck and let it fall to the floor.

CHAPTER FORTY-THREE

The last day at Oakwood arrives with the strange combination of anticipation and apprehension that seems to mark every transition in my life now. Sunlight streams through the half-open blinds, casting striped shadows across my nearly empty room. My bags are packed, personal items carefully folded and tucked away.

I'm just about done when Dr Craig knocks at the door.

"Ready for your final in-house session?" She asks, her calm presence filling the doorway.

I nod, following her to her office one last time.

We've spent countless hours in this room, dismantling and rebuilding my understanding of what happened that night in the woods.

"So," Dr Craig says, settling into her chair, "how are you feeling about going home today?"

"Nervous," I admit. "Excited. Scared. All of it at once."

She smiles slightly. "That's normal. Transitions are hard, especially after trauma."

"I keep thinking about my room at home." I trace the scar on my neck, a habit I'm trying to break. "Everything will look the same, but nothing will be the same."

"Including you," Dr Craig points out. "You're not the same Amanda who left that house months ago."

I consider this. "No, I'm not. I'm not sure who I am now, but... I'm ready to find out."

Dr Craig nods, making a small note on her pad.

"That's significant progress. Throughout your recovery, you've been focusing on finding Sarah, and then on finding Maggie. Now you're ready to find yourself."

It's almost as though she's been reading my journal. So close to the truth, in fact, that I wonder for a brief, paranoid second if she has.

"I'll still think about them," I say, feeling strangely defensive. "I'll still care about what happens with the investigation."

"Of course you will," Dr Craig agrees. "But there's a difference between caring about the outcome and making it your responsibility. Between honouring Sarah's memory and being defined by her loss. Between being curious about Maggie and needing to find her to validate your own survival."

Her words settle over me, articulating something I've been feeling but couldn't quite express. "I think I understand that now."

"That's why you're ready to go home," she says. "Not because you've forgotten or moved on, but because you've learned to carry it differently."

The session continues with practical matters: my outpatient therapy schedule, coping strategies for difficult moments, warning signs to watch for. Through it all, I feel a growing certainty that this is the right step, however terrifying.

"Before we finish," Dr Craig says, "is there anything else you want to discuss? Any concerns about the transition home?"

I hesitate, then reach into my bag and pull out the notebook, opening it to Maggie's photograph. "I've been wondering if I should give this back to the police. If keeping it is... I don't know, unhealthy."

Dr Craig studies the photo, then me. "What do you think? Does looking at it still trigger the same obsessive thoughts? The same need to solve the mystery?"

I consider this. "Not exactly. I'm still curious, still hope they find her. But it doesn't feel like my mission anymore."

"Then it might be okay to keep it," she says. "As a reminder of your journey, not as an assignment."

I slip the photo back into the notebook. "That makes sense."

But still, my fingers linger on the image of the girl at Lacey Point. The place Paul recognised. The place I've thought about more and more as my discharge date has approached.

As our session ends, Dr Craig stands and extends her hand. "You've done remarkable work here, Amanda. Remember that progress isn't linear. There will be setbacks, difficult days. But you have the tools to handle them now."

I shake her hand, suddenly overwhelmed by the formality of the gesture after weeks of intensive therapy. "Thank you. For everything."

She smiles. "You did the hard part. I just provided the space."

Outside Dr Craig's office, Ellie is waiting, leaning against the wall with practised casualness that doesn't quite mask her emotions.

"Final goodbye time?" she asks, pushing off the wall.

"Not goodbye," I correct. "See you later."

We walk together toward my room, our footsteps echoing in the familiar corridor that once seemed endless but now feels almost too short.

"You're going to crush it out there," Ellie says, bumping my shoulder with hers. "Don't forget, I expect full reports." She stops at my door. "And visits. Lots of visits."

"Promise." I hesitate, then add, "And you'll text me? Let me know how you're doing?"

"Obviously." She rolls her eyes, but I can see the emotion beneath. "Someone has to keep you updated on the Oakwood gossip."

We stand there awkwardly for a moment, neither quite knowing how to say goodbye to someone who has seen you at your most broken without making it weird.

"Oh, for God's sake," Ellie finally says, pulling me into a quick, fierce hug. "Take care of yourself, Amanda Gray."

I laugh, the sound still slightly strange to my ears.

"I will. And you too."

"Going home isn't the end of the story," she says, her expression suddenly serious. "It's just the next chapter."

The words stay with me after she has left the room. The next chapter. Not the final one. Just the next step in a longer journey.

When Mum arrives to pick me up, her eyes are bright with a mixture of happiness and concern.

"Ready to go?" she asks, reaching for one of my bags.

I take one last look around the room that has been my sanctuary and prison for the past ten weeks. The bed where I've stared at the ceiling for countless hours. The window where I've watched the other residents come and go, walking their own paths to recovery. The small desk where I've written my thoughts, memories, fears, and hopes.

"Yeah," I say. "I'm ready."

In the car, Mum chatters about preparations at home: Paul's work on the nursery, the new couch in the living room. Normal, mundane details that somehow feel precious in their ordinariness.

"Paul wanted to come today," she says as we pull away from Oakwood. "But I thought... I thought maybe just us would be better for the first day home. Was that right?"

I think about Paul recognising Lacey Point, about his willingness to help the police, about the possibility that he's been trying in his awkward way all along.

"Actually," I say, "I wouldn't have minded if he came."

Mum's eyes widen slightly before returning to the road. "Really? That's... that's good to hear, Amanda."

As we turn onto our street, I feel my chest tighten. The familiar row of houses, the trees at the edge of the neighbourhood, the way the late afternoon sun catches on the windows. It's all exactly as I remember and somehow completely different.

Mum pulls into the driveway and cuts the engine. For a long moment, we both sit in silence, staring at the house.

"Home sweet home," she says finally, her voice soft.

I take a deep breath. "The next chapter," I whisper, echoing Ellie's words.

Then I open the car door and step out, ready to face whatever comes next: not as a victim, not as a saviour, but as myself.

Whoever that turns out to be.

CHAPTER FORTY-FOUR

Home is both exactly as I remembered and completely different. The hallway seems narrower, the ceilings lower, as if the house has somehow shrunk during my absence. Or maybe I've grown in ways that have nothing to do with physical space.

Paul stands in the doorway between the hall and living room, his uncertainty matching my own.

"Welcome home," he says, his voice carefully upbeat.

"Thanks." I set my bag down, studying the changes Mum mentioned during the drive and some she didn't. New couch. Different arrangement of the photos on the wall. Small adjustments that make the familiar slightly strange. "It's good to be back."

"Well, I'll let you get settled. There's lasagna for dinner whenever you're ready," he says. Still that same old awkward Paul, but as with everything else, it's the same, but different.

"Thanks," I say again. "You didn't have to... But I appreciate it."

As he retreats to the kitchen, Mum catches my eye, her expression a mixture of surprise and hope.

"That was nice," she says quietly.

I shrug. "He's trying."

"Yes, he is." She touches my arm lightly. "We all are."

Upstairs, I pause outside my bedroom, my hand on the doorknob. The bruise-coloured wallpaper that haunted my thoughts along my journey waits on the other side of this door. Those purple-blue swirls have become a symbol of everything that happened: my life before the attack, Sarah's death, my recovery.

I take a deep breath and push the door open.

The room that greets me is unrecognisable. The walls are now a soft, warm grey: not institutional, not sterile, but clean and calm. My furniture has been rearranged, the bed now beneath the window rather than against the wall where it used to be. My photos and posters have been carefully preserved, arranged in a new configuration that somehow makes sense.

"Is it okay?" Mum asks from behind me. "If you hate it, we can change it back. I just thought..."

"It's perfect," I say, meaning it. "Thank you."

She smiles, relief flooding her face. "Paul did most of the work, actually. He researched which colours are supposed to be calming. Spent a whole weekend in here with paint samples."

The revelation catches me off guard. I picture Paul painstakingly painting my room, trying to create a space where I might feel safe again.

"That was... thoughtful of him," I manage.

"He wants this to work, Amanda." Mum's hand rests briefly on her rounded belly. "All of this. The four of us."

I nod. The lump in my throat feels like gratitude mixed with shame for how I've treated him, mixed with lingering resentment that isn't quite ready to dissolve completely.

"I'll let you unpack," Mum says, sensing my emotional overload. "Take your time. Dinner whenever you're ready."
Once I'm alone, I begin the process of reclaiming the space. I unpack slowly, deliberately, each item a small piece of myself being re-implanted here. Clothes in the dresser. Books on the shelf. My notebook on the nightstand.

The sight of my laptop gives me pause. After a moment's hesitation, I open it and power it on. The background photo appears: Sarah and me at the beach last summer, laughing into the camera. My fingers freeze over the keyboard. I'd forgotten about this photo, this moment from what feels like another lifetime.

I can't bear to look; I'm not ready for that particular memory yet. I slam the lid down and push the laptop away from me across the desk. I wanted to open up a search window, see what I could read about the investigation, about the arrest, but most importantly to me, what I could find out about Lacey Point.

Instead, I sit here, my hand still resting on the laptop's closed lid, and picture it: the threads, the amateur sleuths, the speculative posts dissecting every last detail. I already know what they'd be saying. I've seen it before, on other cases. How people piece together a timeline from scraps of information. How they analyse grainy images, latch onto rumours, pore over case files.

They'll be arguing over why we went that way home. Whether I fought back. Whether I should have known better. They'll compare me to other victims. They'll call me lucky or stupid, maybe both. They'll swap theories about my state of mind, like they can extract the truth from a handful of news articles and speculation.

And I realise: I would have done the same thing.

Before this happened, I read those threads. Watched the documentaries. Followed cases like they were serialised stories, as if each new piece of information was an episode drop, leading to some grand resolution. I was one of them, the obsessives, the ones who zoomed in on the details, who speculated and analysed from behind the safety of a screen.

The realisation sits in my stomach like a stone.

If I were anyone else, if this had happened to someone else, I'd already be deep in the search results, clicking through crime blogs, reading every half-baked theory. I'd be scrolling through forum posts, watching grainy TikTok recaps with ominous background music, listening to a podcaster dissect the details like it's some abstract puzzle rather than someone's life.

I would have wanted to know everything.

And now? Now I *do* need to know everything.

I'm no better than them. The first thing I wanted to do the second I got home was open my laptop and type *Lacey Point* into the search bar.

I need to read what's been written, comb through every detail, look at it from every angle, just in case I've missed something. Something that could make sense of what happened. Something that could make it feel less senseless.

I tell myself it's different for me. That I have a right to this obsession. That I lived it, that I survived it, that Sarah *didn't*, and that gives me the right to dig, to analyse, to collect every scrap of information like I can piece her back together again. So that I can find out where Maggie is.

I'm meant to be letting this go.

I'm meant to be moving on.

I'm meant to be healing.

But all I want to do is play sleuth in my own true crime story.

I want to, and at the same time I can't even bring myself to look at that picture of me and Sarah, let alone the horrors that wait for me on the internet.

I can't do this. Not now.

The pale, alien walls of my room feel too close, the air suddenly too thick. I need to move. I need to do something, anything, before I spiral all the way down.

I stand up too fast, my chair scraping against the floor. My legs feel unsteady, like I've been sitting in one position too long, my body unsure of itself. I move toward the mirror without thinking, just to ground myself, to prove I'm still here.

My skin looks sallow under the dim light, my eyes too wide, too hollow. My hair, once effortlessly styled, is dull and limp around my face. The scar across my throat has faded some, but I can still see it, a thick red line, evidence of how close I came to never coming home at all.

I press my hands to the dresser, breathe in deep. I can't go back downstairs like this.

I'm home. Things should be better.

I should be better.

I force myself to stand up straighter, roll my shoulders back, shake out my hands like I can loosen the tension wound so tightly inside me.

Breathe.

I smooth down my sweater, brush my fingers through my hair, pinch my cheeks to bring some colour back into them. I practice a small smile in the mirror.

I take one last steadying breath, then open the door, step out of my room, and start down the stairs.

By the time I reach the bottom, I've carefully pieced myself back together.

Or at least I hope I look like I have.

I pause at the kitchen door, listening to the soft clatter of plates, the low murmur of my mum and Paul's voices. A normal, domestic sound. A world I was a part of before, one I'm supposed to slip back into now, like nothing's changed.

I push a smile onto my face, square my shoulders, and step inside.

Dinner passes in a strange mix of ordinary conversation and careful navigation around difficult topics. Paul talks about work at the accounting firm. Mum talks about birth plans. I offer snippets about Oakwood that feel safe to share: Ellie's sarcastic commentary on the food, the view from my window, the books I read during my stay.

Safe topics, just like I've been used to for the past few months when the real conversations are too hard to face.

The words flow around me, warm and familiar, but I feel detached from them, as if I'm watching the scene play out from somewhere just beyond my own body. Home-cooked food. The low hum of the TV in the background. The scrape of cutlery against plates. It should be comforting. It should make me feel safe.

But the air in here is different now.

I am different now.

Home is the same as it ever was, but I don't fit inside it the way I used to. The walls feel off-kilter, like they belong to someone else's life, and I'm just an intruder slipping into their seat at the dinner table.

I go through the motions, chewing, swallowing, responding when necessary. But my mind is elsewhere, stuck upstairs in my room, in the glow of the laptop screen.

Even now, I can feel it. The pull. The gnawing, restless need to know.

CHAPTER FORTY-FIVE

When I wake the next morning, for a moment, I can't place where I am. Everything looks different. My brain struggles to make the connections. Not hospital with its clinical white. Not Oakwood with its reassuring, non-challenging beige.

Home. I'm home.

The bruise-coloured walls are grey now, but I'm home.

I slept fitfully, dreams crowded with fragments that don't quite connect: Sarah laughing on a beach; the sound of water somewhere nearby; a boathouse I've never seen but can somehow picture perfectly.

The house is quiet. I check my phone: 8:13am. Too early for anyone else to be up. It's Saturday morning; even Paul will be asleep for another hour or so. No work today.

For the first time in months, I have true privacy. No nurses, no scheduled check-ins, no roommates down the hall. Just me and a sleeping house.

I slip out of bed, pull on a hoodie and jeans, sit at my desk and look at my laptop. My heart thunders so fast I can almost hear the phantom echo of hospital monitors tracking each beat.

All I need to do is lift the lid.

But I can't.

I have so many questions, there's so much I want to know. I could type **Matheson**. I could type **Sarah Fairchild**. I could type my own name, and I'm sure I'd get enough hits to keep me reading until after the baby is born.

I can't face it.

I don't want to read filtered responses, news reports, amateur sleuthing. I need something real.

I need to see Lacey Point.

I want to stand where she stood. Feel what she felt.

The idea forms slowly, then all at once, blooming like one of those time-lapse videos of a flower unfurling. It makes perfect sense.

Paul knows the location.

He's been there multiple times.

He could take me.

I pull out the photograph of Maggie, study it in the morning light. The boathouse is just visible behind her left shoulder, exactly where Paul pointed it out. I hadn't even noticed it until he mentioned it. What else might I see if I were actually there?

I imagine standing in that exact spot, looking out at the water, breathing the same air she breathed. Maybe then I'd understand why he kept her photograph. Why he saw me and thought of her. Why Sarah had to die.

The questions circle, familiar and incessant as vultures.

I check the time again: 8:28am. The idea has taken root, and I'm already calculating how long it would take to get there. Which bus routes would take me closest. Whether I could afford a rideshare for the rest of the way.

But even as I strategize, my heart rate picks up. Public transportation. Strangers. Open spaces with no controlled exits.

The closest I've been to the outside world since March is the monitored, enclosed, *safe* garden at Oakwood, and now we're sliding into August.

The thought of standing at a bus stop, exposed, vulnerable, makes my palms start to sweat.

What if someone recognises me from the news?

What if they stare at my scar?

What if I panic halfway there, trapped on a bus with nowhere to escape?

The tightness in my chest feels too familiar. The last time I ventured into the woods with Sarah, I came back in an ambulance, fighting for my life. Sarah didn't come back at all.

Getting on a bus alone suddenly seems impossible. Even contemplating a rideshare with a stranger makes my throat close up.

New symptoms to discuss with Dr Craig when I go for my first outpatient appointment. Not even nine o'clock and we're already expanding my collection of post-trauma issues. Fantastic.

So, I can't go alone.

I need Paul to take me.

Not just because he knows where Lacey Point is, but because I'm not ready to face the world alone yet. The realisation is humiliating, but undeniable. For all my progress, I'm still afraid.

But I can't let him see that fear. Better to approach this as a practical issue, his knowledge of the area, the difficulty of the hike, than admit the truth: that navigating the world without a buffer terrifies me.

By 9:15, I can't wait any longer. I hear movement downstairs: the quiet rhythm of breakfast preparation, the soft murmur of voices. I take a deep breath and head down to the kitchen.

"Morning," I say, aiming for casual and missing by a mile.

"You're up early," Mum says, smiling. "Sleep okay?"

"Fine," I lie, pouring myself a cup of coffee. The normalcy of the moment feels surreal, like I'm acting in a play about everyday family life. "What are your plans for today?"

Paul sets down his phone. "Thought I might finish that shelving unit for the nursery." He glances at Mum. "Unless you need me for something else?"

I brace myself. "Actually, I was hoping you might take me somewhere."

They both look at me with identical expressions of surprise.

"Oh?" Mum's voice is carefully neutral, but I can see the instant tension in her shoulders.

She's only had me home for one night after months of wondering if I'd survive, and now I'm already talking about leaving again. The protective instinct flashes across her face before she can mask it. That same look she wore in the hospital when nurses came to take my vitals, as if she wanted to stand between me and the entire world.

"I want to go to Lacey Point."

The words land with a weight that seems to alter the atmosphere of the room. Paul's coffee mug freezes halfway to his lips. Mum's spoon clatters against her breakfast bowl.

"What?" Paul asks, setting his mug down slowly.

"Lacey Point," I repeat. "Where Maggie's photo was taken. You know exactly where it is. I want to see it."

Paul and Mum exchange a glance, having one of those silent conversations that always makes me feel left out.

"Amanda," Mum begins carefully, "I'm not sure that's a good idea."

"Why not?" I pull out the photograph, smoothing it on the table. "The police haven't found anything yet. But what if I could see something they've missed?"

"If the police haven't found anything, why would you?" Mum says, and it sounds like the first excuse that comes to her mind. "They're professionals, Amanda. They know what they're doing. Leave it to them."

I stare at her, stunned by the dismissal. "So I should just sit here and do nothing? After everything that's happened to me?"

Paul looks at me with a look somewhere between concern and fear.

"It's not an easy hike," he says, shifting to practical objections. "At least a half hour from the access point, and that's if you know where you're going. Parts of the trail have completely overgrown since they demolished the boathouse last year."

"That's why I need you to take me." I lean forward. "Please, Paul. It's important."

"No." He says it simply, definitively. "I'm sorry, Amanda, but no."

The refusal hits harder than I expected. "Why not?"

"Because it's absolutely out of the question," he says firmly. "You're barely twenty-four hours out of rehabilitation. Your doctors specifically said to avoid stressful situations or physical exertion."

"And because we almost lost you once," Mum adds, her voice tight with emotion. "I'm not letting you wander off into some isolated woodland where..." She stops abruptly, hand moving protectively to her belly.

"But don't you see?" I press. "People might recognise me. Not as the girl who was attacked, but as someone who looks exactly like her. If local fishermen or hikers saw me there, it might trigger their memory of seeing Maggie. It could help the investigation."

"Amanda," Mum says, her voice firmer now, "the answer is no. Not today, not tomorrow, not next week. Let the police handle their investigation. You are focusing on recovery. That's all."

"You're just saying that because he is." The accusation flies out before I can stop it. "You always take his side. Always."

Hurt flashes across Mum's face. "That's not fair."

"None of this is fair!" I push back from the table, the chair scraping against the floor. "Sarah is dead. I nearly died. And all I'm asking is to see the place in this photograph. But no. That's too much to ask. Can't let Amanda do anything but sit at home like a good little victim."

"That's enough." Paul's voice is quiet but firm. "This isn't about controlling you. It's about making sure you're safe."

"Safe?" I laugh without humour. "Where was all this concern for my safety before? When you were blaming me for stressing Mum out? When you couldn't even be bothered to visit me in the hospital for weeks?"

Paul closes his mouth and stares at me, and for a moment, I feel a vicious satisfaction.

"Amanda, stop." Mum pushes herself up from the table, one hand at her lower back for support. "This isn't helping anything."

"Nothing helps!" The words tear from my throat. "Sarah is still dead. Maggie is still missing. And I'm still stuck here, trying to put the pieces together while everyone tells me to just move on!"

"No one is telling you to move on," Paul says, his voice steady despite the pallor in his face. "We're asking you to focus on healing."

"I can't heal without answers!" I slam my hand on the table, making the mugs jump. "I need to understand why this happened. Why he picked me. Why Sarah had to die and I didn't!"

"And you think going to Lacey Point would give you those answers?" Paul asks, rising from his chair, his voice quiet with concern rather than accusation. "Amanda, after everything you've been through... I just don't think returning to an isolated spot in the woods is what you need right now."

The gentle way he says it somehow hits harder than anger would have. I hadn't even made the connection until now, but he's right. Lacey Point is isolated. In the woods. Just like where Sarah died.

"It's different," I insist, but my voice wavers.

"Maybe," Paul says, his eyes meeting mine with unexpected compassion. "But I'm worried about what being there might trigger for you. The memories, the trauma... I'm not sure it's worth the risk."

"I wouldn't be in danger if I was with you!" I counter, sharper than he deserves. "Unless you're admitting you can't protect me either!"

He recoils slightly, pain flashing across his face, and I know I've hit a nerve.

Good, I think, then immediately feel guilty for deliberately hurting him.

"Why don't you ask my psychiatrist whether it's *good for my healing* or not?" I snap, the sarcasm dripping from my voice. "Since you both seem to know what's best for me."

Mum looks at me steadily, her voice calm. "And what do you think she would say, Amanda?"

The question stops me cold. I can almost hear Dr Craig's voice.

Sometimes trauma survivors become fixated on certain details because it helps them feel in control...

Your only responsibility right now is to focus on your own healing...

Finding Maggie is not your responsibility.

The truth of it leaves me speechless. Mum's eyes fill with tears, but she doesn't look away.

"I'm not taking you there," Paul says again, his voice firmer now. "End of discussion."

"Since when do you get to decide what I do?" I demand, anger and frustration boiling over.

The words form on my tongue. '*You're not my father.*' It's such an obvious, teenage cliché that I almost cringe at myself for even thinking it.

But some ugly part of me wants to say it anyway, wants to see the hurt on his face.

Instead, I just glare at him, letting the unspoken accusation hang in the air between us. He seems to hear it anyway, his expression shuttering, that careful mask slipping back into place. Mum's tears spill over, running silently down her cheeks.

"I'm sorry, Amanda," he says quietly. "I can't help you with this."

Paul stands, moving to Mum's side. He puts his arm around her shoulders, comforting her without a single accusatory glance in my direction.

"Fine," I say finally, grabbing the photograph. "I get it. You both want me to just stay here and be a good little invalid."

"Amanda..." Mum starts, but I cut her off.

"Don't worry, I'm not going anywhere," I say, and we all hear the bitterness in my voice. "I know the thought of me leaving the house terrifies you both. Heaven forbid I actually try to do something useful."

The words are deliberately cruel, and I can see they hit their mark, even though they are only a cover for the truth that leaving the house terrifies me too.

I storm out before either of them can respond, taking the stairs two at a time despite the twinge in my legs. In my room, I slam the door hard enough to rattle the new pictures on the wall, the ones Paul so carefully arranged.

My breath comes in ragged gasps as I pace the small space, hands clenched into fists.

How dare he?

How dare he act like he's protecting me when all he's doing is controlling me?

He's keeping me from the one thing that might actually help make sense of everything.

I pace until my legs ache, until my anger burns itself out, leaving only exhaustion in its wake. I sink onto the edge of my bed, the photograph still clutched in my hand.

Maybe they're right. Maybe there's nothing to find at Lacey Point. Maybe I'm just grasping at straws, desperate for anything that might make sense of the senseless.

But I can't shake the feeling that Maggie is the key to everything: to understanding why I was targeted, why Sarah had to die, why I survived when she didn't.

I stare at the ceiling. The grey paint is flawless, not a single streak or bubble. Paul did this. He spent hours making this room a haven where I wouldn't have to stare at bruise-coloured walls and remember.

The realisation softens something in me, but only slightly. He might have painted my room, but he still won't help me.

Five months. That's how long I've been trapped in one room or another. First the hospital, then Oakwood, and now here. Five months of people telling me to rest, to heal, to be patient. Five months of fighting to find my voice, only to be told not to use it.

This doesn't feel like progress at all.

As I drift toward sleep, I think about the look on Paul's face when I almost called him *not my father*. The hurt. The resignation. As if he'd been expecting it all along. He must have, because he knew. I know he knew.

It shouldn't matter. He's not my father. He's just the man my mother chose, the man who's about to be a father to my brother.

But somehow, it does matter. And the knowledge that I've hurt him, that I meant to hurt him, settles in my chest like a stone.

I think of Sarah, of Maggie, of all the questions still unanswered. Of the woods, the reservoir, the boathouse that no longer exists.

I can't stay trapped in yet another room. Not after everything.

I have to do something.

CHAPTER FORTY-SIX

I don't know how long I've been asleep when a soft knock on my door pulls me back to consciousness. The light in my room has shifted, shadows stretching across the floor. My phone says it's just past noon.

"What?" I call, my voice thick with sleep.

"Can I come in?" It's Paul's voice.

I sit up, wiping at my eyes, suddenly conscious of how I must look.

My hand reaches to straighten the scarf I don't wear anymore.

"Why?"

"I want to talk to you." A pause. "Please, Amanda."

The "please" catches me off guard. Paul doesn't beg. Paul doesn't even ask, most of the time. He tells, or he retreats.

"Fine," I say, swinging my legs over the side of the bed. "It's open."

The door creaks slightly as he pushes it inward, hesitating at the threshold as if unsure whether the invitation extends beyond the door itself. The circles under his eyes are darker than they were this morning.

"Can I sit?" he asks, gesturing to the chair by my desk.

I shrug, trying to look indifferent. "I guess."

He enters cautiously, closing the door behind him with a soft click that feels unnervingly final. For a horrible moment, I wonder if this is it. If he's come to tell me that my outburst this morning was the last straw. That he's done trying. That Mum needs to focus on the baby and not her troubled daughter.

"I'm not here to fight," he says, as if reading my thoughts. He settles into the chair, his posture unusually tense. His hands rest on his knees, knuckles white with tension.

"Then why are you here?" I keep my voice neutral, even as my heart picks up speed.

"I wanted to explain why I said no." He looks at me directly. "And..." His voice catches as he continues. "I wanted to apologise."

"Apologise?" The word comes out sharper than I intended. "For what?"

"For a lot of things." He takes a deep breath. "Starting with what I said to you that day. Before... before the attack."

The memory surfaces: *This is what happens when you stress her out.*

My throat tightens. "I don't need your apology."

"Maybe not. But I need to say it." His eyes drop to his hands, still clenched on his knees. "What I said to you that day was cruel and untrue. Your mother's bleeding had nothing to do with you. But I blamed you anyway."

He pauses, swallowing hard. "And then you were gone. And we didn't know if you were coming back."

The words hang in the air between us, heavy with an implication he doesn't voice, but I hear anyway: *And those might have been the last words I ever said to you.*

"I didn't know how to face you after that," he continues. "In the hospital. When you were first there, I'd see you lying with that tube in your throat, and all I could think about was what I'd said. How I'd blamed you."

He turns his eyes downwards. "The truth is, even before the attack, I wasn't... I wasn't really there for you. Not in any way that mattered. I was so focused on my relationship with your mother that I never made a real effort to connect with you. I told myself I was giving you space, that you didn't want me around, but really, I was just avoiding the hard work. I wasn't ready to be any kind of father figure. I wasn't sure I wanted to be."

He clears his throat. "And then when you were in hospital, I told myself more lies. That I was staying away so I wouldn't upset your mother. So I could focus on practical things: painting your room, building furniture for the baby. But I was a coward. I didn't know how to say I was sorry."

I look around the room: the walls he painted, the photos he arranged. All these months, he'd been trying to apologise without words, while I'd been fighting to find mine. There's something almost poetic about it. Me, learning to speak again, and him, struggling to say the things that mattered. Both of us looking for a voice that worked, a way to be heard.

"You could have just said it," I tell him. "Just said you were sorry."

He laughs, a short, self-deprecating sound. "I know. Seems simple, doesn't it? But I kept thinking about how close you came to..." He stops, unable to say the word.

"Dying," I finish for him. "You can say it. It's not a secret."

"Right." He nods, a muscle working in his jaw. "I kept thinking about how close you came to dying. How Sarah didn't make it. How your last memory of me might have been me blaming you for something that wasn't your fault. And somehow, saying sorry felt... inadequate."

For the first time, I notice the redness around his eyes. Has he been crying? I've never seen Paul cry. Never even imagined him capable of it.

"So, you avoided me instead," I say, unsure whether I'm accusing or just stating a fact.

"Yes." He doesn't try to defend himself.

The honesty of his response disarms me. I expected excuses, justifications. Not this raw admission of cowardice.

"When I first met your mother," he continues after a moment, "the idea of being a father terrified me. I'd never thought about having kids. Never pictured myself in that role. And suddenly there was this ready-made family: a partner I loved, a teenage daughter I didn't know how to talk to, and a baby on the way."

He shakes his head, a rueful smile touching his lips. "I had no idea what I was doing. Still don't, most of the time. But I know enough to recognise when I'm making the same mistake twice. And sending you back into isolated woods, back to a place connected to the man who hurt you. That would be a mistake."

His words strike a chord in me, one I didn't expect to resonate.

"I'm not asking you to be my father," I say quietly. "I'm asking you to help me understand why this happened."

"I know." His voice softens. "But Amanda, going to Lacey Point won't give you those answers. It won't bring Sarah back. It won't erase what happened. It will just reopen wounds that are barely starting to heal."

"So, I'm just supposed to, what? Forget about it? Pretend it never happened?" I can hear the edge creeping back into my voice, that familiar anger rising.

"No. Not at all." Paul leans back in the chair, his posture still tense, but his expression softening. "You're supposed to grieve. To heal. To eventually find a way to live with what happened, even though it will never make sense. But chasing after Maggie, thinking if you just see where she stood, you'll somehow unlock some great mystery. That's not healing. That's staying stuck."

The words hit with unexpected force, echoing what Dr Craig tried to tell me. What Ellie tried to tell me. What Mum has been trying to say all along.

"It's not your responsibility to solve this, Amanda," Paul says gently. "It's not your fault that Sarah died. It's not your fault that you survived. None of this is your fault."

The words break something loose inside me: a dam I've been building since that night in the woods. Since I woke up in the hospital and learned Sarah was still missing. Since they found her body and I learned she had been dead all along.

"But I was there," I whisper, my voice cracking. "I should have done something. I should have helped her."

"You couldn't." Paul's voice is firm. "You were injured, bleeding. There was nothing you could have done differently."

"You don't know that," I argue, but the fight has gone out of my words.

"The police know that. The doctors know that." He pauses. "Sarah would know that."

The mention of her name sends a fresh wave of grief washing over me. I picture her face, not as I last saw her, terrified and gagged, but smiling, laughing, alive.

"I miss her," I admit, the words barely audible.

"I know." Paul doesn't try to offer platitudes or false comfort. He just sits there, a steady presence, allowing me the space to feel what I've been trying so hard not to feel.

"It's not fair," I say, knowing how childish it sounds.

"No. It's not." He agrees without hesitation. "Nothing about this is fair."

We sit in silence for a long moment. For the first time since the attack, I feel something loosen in my chest, not healing, not yet, but the beginning of something like it. The faintest possibility that there might be a future beyond this moment, this grief.

"Your memories, your statements. They helped catch the man who did this. They found Sarah. They're still looking for Maggie. But you can't solve this alone. You have to let yourself heal."

"How?" The question comes out small, vulnerable.

"One day at a time," he says simply. "By letting people help you. By not blaming yourself for things you couldn't control."

He hesitates, then adds, "And by forgiving yourself for surviving when Sarah didn't."

The words strike at the heart of what I've been carrying: the crushing guilt of being the one who lived. The constant, nagging sense that it should have been me instead of her.

"I don't know if I can," I whisper.

"You can," he says with unexpected certainty. "Not today. Maybe not for a long time. But eventually, you'll find a way to live with it. To make it mean something."

"Is that what you did?" I ask. "With the guilt about what you said to me?"

He nods slowly. "I'm trying. It's why I painted your room. Why I stayed up nights researching trauma recovery. Why I'm sitting here now, finally saying the things I should have said months ago."

I study his face: the lines around his eyes, the tension in his jaw, the awkward sincerity with which he's trying to reach across the gulf between us.

"I don't expect to replace your father," he says after a moment. "I know I can't. But I do care about what happens to you, Amanda. I want to be someone you can count on, even if I'm still figuring out how to do that."

The admission seems to cost him. His discomfort with emotional vulnerability is clear in the way he shifts in his chair, unable to meet my eyes directly.

"I think you're doing okay," I say, surprised to find I mean it. "Better than my actual father, anyway."

A ghost of a smile touches his lips. "Low bar."

"Still." I shrug, feeling suddenly awkward. "Thanks. For talking to me. For apologising."

"Thank you for listening." He stands, clearly ready to leave. "Your mother's worried about you. About this morning."

"I know. I'll talk to her. Apologise."

He nods, moving toward the door.

"Paul?" I call as his hand reaches for the knob.

He turns. "Yes?"

I take a deep breath. "Do you think they'll ever find her? Maggie?"

He considers the question. "I don't know," he says honestly. "But if they do, it won't be because you put yourself in danger. It will be because professionals who are trained for this are doing their jobs."

I nod, accepting the answer even as part of me still yearns to do more, to understand more.

"Detective Barnes said he'd call if there were any developments," Paul adds. "I know waiting is hard, but it's the safest option right now."

"I need to focus on getting stronger," I say, surprising myself with how much I mean it. "There are more important battles ahead."

As the door closes behind him, I pick up Maggie's photograph one last time. Her face stares back at me, so familiar yet so strange. I made finding her my mission, my purpose. The thing that kept me going when everything else felt pointless. When I could no longer put all of my energy into thinking about Sarah and how I had let her down.

But now Matheson is in custody. The man who called me Maggie, who killed Sarah, who cut my throat and thought I was dead. He's locked away, awaiting trial. And that's where my focus needs to be.

I think about what's coming. The trial. The testimony. Looking him in the eye and telling the world what he did to Sarah. What he tried to do to me.

I touch my scar, feeling the raised line of tissue beneath my fingertips. My voice, the one he tried to take from me, will be Sarah's voice now. I'll speak the words she can't. I'll tell her story when she can't tell it herself.

But to do that, I need to be stronger than I am now. I need to heal. Not just physically, but deep down, where the nightmares live. Where the guilt festers. Where Sarah's screams still echo.

"I'll be ready," I whisper, a promise to myself. To Sarah.

I carefully slide the photo back into my notebook, looking at Maggie's face one last time. Her eyes seem to hold secrets I'm still not ready to understand. Questions I'm not ready to answer.

"Not forgotten," I tell her quietly. "Just not now."

With deliberate movements, I stand and cross to my bookshelf, finding a space between my old, dog-eared copy of *To Kill a Mockingbird* and a battered *Harry Potter*. I place the notebook there, spine out. Not abandoning the search, but setting it aside for something more immediate, more vital.

Justice for Sarah.

For months, I've been searching for answers outside myself: in the investigation, in Maggie's face, in the mystery of why he chose me. But maybe what I need most right now is the strength to face him in court. To look him in the eye and not shatter. To say the words that will help lock him away forever.

Outside my window, a car pulls into the driveway: Mum returning from a quick grocery run. I watch as Paul hurries out to meet her, his hand automatically moving to support her back as she climbs out, laden with bags. The tenderness in the gesture, the care it reveals, would have gone unnoticed by me before today.

In less than a month, the baby will be here, our family will change again. The trial date will approach. I'll need to prepare, to strengthen myself for what's coming.

But for now, in this moment, I focus on what's in front of me. This house. This family. The slow work of gathering my courage.

Of using the voice it took me so long to recover.

Matheson may have marked me, but he hasn't defined me. He took Sarah's life, but he doesn't get to take my future too. And he doesn't get to silence either of us.

Not as a victim.

Not as a saviour.

Just as Amanda, learning to carry both my scars and my determination into whatever comes next.

When the trial comes, I'll be ready.

When they find Maggie, if they find Maggie, I'll be ready for that too.

But first, I need to heal.

PART FOUR

EIGHT MONTHS LATER

CHAPTER FORTY-SEVEN

"He's doing it again," I say, leaning against the kitchen doorway. "Just sitting there, staring at you like you hung the moon."

Paul looks up from where he's cradling my seven-month-old brother, his expression that unique blend of exhaustion and wonder that seems permanent since Thomas's arrival. "What can I say? The kid has excellent taste."

I watch them, this tableau of father and son that once would have filled me with resentment, but now feels like a small miracle of ordinary life. Thomas's chubby fingers reach for Paul's nose, his delighted gurgle filling the kitchen with impossible lightness.

Eight months since I came home from Oakwood.

Eight months of rebuilding, of therapy sessions Dr Craig that help me process the fragments of trauma without reliving them, of nightmares that come less frequently now.

Eight months of learning to exist in this new version of our family: Mum, Paul, Thomas, and me. The four of us, finding our way toward something that feels increasingly like normal.

"Want to hold him while I finish dinner?" Paul asks, already standing.

I nod, accepting the warm weight of my brother against my chest. Thomas immediately grabs a fistful of my hair, his grip surprisingly strong for someone so small.

"Ouch, T," I murmur, gently disentangling his fingers. "We've talked about this. Hair is not a toy."

He responds with a solemn blink, then promptly reaches for my necklace instead: the small silver pendant Ellie gave me for Christmas.

We still text almost daily. She's going home full-time next month, transitioning to outpatient therapy like I did. We have plans to meet at the coffee shop halfway between our houses. Neutral territory for two people still learning to exist in the world outside institutional walls.

I'm looking forward to having a friend to talk to who isn't from school, where I've returned part-time to finish my coursework. Everyone there tries too hard, either treating me like I'm made of glass or pretending nothing happened. At least Ellie understands.

"He's got your determination," Paul observes, stirring something on the stove that smells promisingly like the curry Mum and I love. "Once he decides he wants something, that's it."

"Poor kid," I say, but there's no bite to it. Just the gentle self-deprecation that's become possible as I've made peace with parts of myself I once hated.

"It'll serve him well," Paul counters. "Determination got you here." He gestures vaguely, encompassing the kitchen, the house, the life we've patched together from broken pieces.

He's right, though I'm still learning to accept compliments without flinching. Determination gets me through the days when the scar on my neck feels like it's burning, when memories surface without warning, when survivor's guilt threatens to pull me under.

And determination brought me here, to this kitchen, holding my brother while my once-enemy, now-ally, makes dinner for our family.

"Earth to Amanda," Paul says, his voice pulling me back. "You okay?"

I nod, shifting Thomas to my other arm. "Just thinking."

"Dangerous habit," he teases, then sobers. "Your mum should be home any minute. She texted that her appointment ran over."

The therapy sessions are ongoing for both of us. Mum's dealing with her own trauma: the near loss of her daughter, the complex emotions around Thomas's birth during such turbulent times. Dr Craig recommended a colleague for her, someone who specialises in family therapy. It helps, I think. We're all helping each other in ways I couldn't have imagined.

"I'll set the table," I offer, carefully transferring Thomas to his bouncy seat. He protests briefly, then becomes entranced by the dangling toys overhead.

Paul and I move around each other with the easy choreography of people who've shared a kitchen for months now. Not best friends, not even close, but something like family. Something I never expected to feel with him.

"How was your therapy yesterday?" he asks, the question casual but attentive.

"Good." I arrange forks beside plates, considering. "We talked about the anniversary coming up."

Paul nods, giving me space to continue or not. One year since that evening in the woods. One year since Sarah died, and I almost did. The date looms ahead like a shadow on my calendar, growing longer as it approaches. Dr Craig says anniversaries often trigger a resurgence of trauma symptoms: nightmares, hypervigilance, flashbacks. She's been helping me prepare for it, develop strategies for when the memories inevitably intensify.

"I've been wanting to talk to Joyce about it," I add, setting down a glass harder than I intended. "About how we both might handle that day. It might be easier to face it together than alone."

Paul pauses, stirring the curry thoughtfully. "Joyce might find comfort in sharing that day with someone who truly understands. And I think you might too." He doesn't add platitudes about closure or moving on. He's learned better than that.

"Yeah." I smooth a non-existent wrinkle from the tablecloth. "I'm nervous about it."

"Understandable." He turns down the heat under the curry. "But you and Joyce have built something important. I think it would be good for both of you to share those feelings, even the hardest ones."

My relationship with Joyce has been one of the unexpected gifts of the past months. We started with awkward visits, neither sure how to navigate the reality that I survived, and Sarah didn't. But over time, the shared grief has become a connection rather than a divide. Now we meet regularly. Sometimes just to sit together, sometimes to talk about Sarah, sometimes to talk about anything but.

Last week, she brought photo albums I'd never seen: Sarah as a gap-toothed seven-year-old, Sarah playing football with her brother despite hating sports, Sarah in the blue dress she wore to our school dance. We cried together over those images, but it was cleansing somehow. Proof that Sarah existed beyond the horrific night that took her, beyond my fractured memories of blood and darkness.

"Yeah," I agree. "Dr Craig says I should trust my instincts more now. That they're becoming reliable again."

Paul nods, understanding without making me explain further. It's one of his better qualities, I've discovered, his willingness to let things be difficult without trying to fix them.

The front door opens, followed by the sound of Mum's keys dropping into the bowl by the entryway. Thomas immediately perks up, his legs kicking excitedly.

"Hello, my loves," Mum calls, appearing in the doorway. Her cheeks are flushed from the early spring chill, her hair windblown. She looks tired but present in a way she wasn't during those dark months after the attack.

"Perfect timing," Paul says, moving to kiss her. "Dinner's ready."

She smiles, squeezing his arm before crossing to Thomas, who is now bouncing with enthusiasm. "And how's my little man?" she coos, lifting him from the seat.

I watch them, this family that feels both mine and not-quite-mine, familiar and strange. Eight months of rebuilding, and still moments when I feel like an observer of my own life.

For a fleeting moment, I catch my reflection in the window, my face overlaid against the darkening evening. Something about the angle, the fading light, triggers a memory: another face, so like mine but subtly different. Maggie's face in that photograph I haven't looked at in months. I wonder where she is now, if they'll ever find her, if I'll ever know why he called me by her name.

The thought passes quickly, and I return to setting the table, pushing away the familiar prickle of unease that accompanies thoughts of her.

Dinner unfolds with the comfortable rhythm we've established. Thomas contributes by attempting to feed himself curry and mostly decorating his face with it instead.

It's so normal it almost hurts, this glimpse of what life could have been without the woods, without the knife, without the blood and loss and grief.

Later, after Thomas's bath (a two-person job that leaves both Mum and Paul drenched but laughing), I volunteer to put him to bed. These quiet moments with my brother have become sacred, a time when the world narrows to just his breathing and mine. His innocence and my complicated heart.

"Hey, T," I whisper as I lower him into the crib. "Ready for a story?"

He blinks up at me, his eyelids already heavy with sleep but his gaze attentive. I've been reading to him since he came home from the hospital. First just to give Mum a break, but eventually because these moments ground me. Remind me there's still goodness in the world.

"Once upon a time," I begin, the familiar words settling something inside me, "there was a girl who lived by the sea."

It's a story I've made up for him, about a girl who finds a magical shell that lets her breathe underwater. She explores the ocean depths, discovering a world more beautiful and stranger than she could have imagined. And when she returns to shore, she brings that magic with her, using it to heal and protect.

"The ocean was dark sometimes," I continue, watching his eyes grow heavier. "Full of currents that pulled and creatures with sharp teeth. But the girl learned to navigate those waters. She learned which currents would help her, which would harm her. She learned when to swim and when to be still."

It's only as I speak I realise how much the story reflects my own journey through trauma. Learning to breathe through the panic, to find beauty even in dark places, to move at my own pace through treacherous waters. Maybe that's why I tell it, night after night, not just for Thomas, but for myself.

"And she was brave," I whisper as his breathing deepens, "even when she was afraid. Especially then."

Standing over his crib, watching the gentle rise and fall of his chest, I'm struck by a sudden, fierce protectiveness.

What would I do if anything happened to him? The thought forms before I can stop it, opening a door to darkness I try to keep closed.

I would do anything. Everything. I would tear the world apart with my bare hands.

But nothing will happen to him, I remind myself firmly. Not like that. Not like Sarah.

I can't think that way. I can't live expecting tragedy around every corner. Dr Craig calls it *catastrophising*, this tendency to imagine the worst possible scenarios. A normal response to trauma, she says, but not one that serves me well now.

"Sleep tight, little brother," I whisper, adjusting his blanket one last time before slipping out of the nursery.

Downstairs, I find Paul alone in the living room, his laptop open but his attention on the rain now pattering against the windows.

"Where's Mum?" I ask, curling into the armchair opposite him.

"Shower," he says. "Thomas got her good with the bath water." He closes his laptop. "He went down okay?"

I nod. "Story about the ocean girl. Works every time."

Paul smiles. "You're good with him."

The compliment warms me unexpectedly. "He makes it easy."

"Not all siblings would..." He hesitates, clearly searching for the right words. "Given the circumstances, I mean. You've been amazing with him."

I shrug, uncomfortable with praise I'm not sure I deserve. "He's innocent in all this. It's not like he asked to be born into the aftermath of..."

I still struggle to name it directly. The attack. The tragedy. The thing that divided my life into before and after.

"Still," Paul says. "You've been a rock for your mother. For both of us, honestly."

I don't know how to respond to that, so I don't. Instead, I pick up the book I left on the side table: a collection of essays Dr Craig recommended about survivors of various traumas. I'm only a few pages in when the doorbell rings.

Paul and I exchange glances. It's almost nine, too late for casual visitors.

"I'll get it," he says, already rising.

Something tightens in my chest, an old fear I've never quite shaken. The doorbell ringing at unusual hours still triggers a flash of panic, a momentary certainty that bad news waits on the other side. My fingers automatically rise to my throat, tracing the raised line of scar tissue beneath my sweater's neckline.

I hear Paul's voice in the hallway, then another, more familiar one. I hear a woman's voice, too. Softer, measured. Footsteps approach, and Detective Barnes appears in the living room with Suki from Victim Support right behind him, Paul following them in.

"Amanda," Barnes says, his expression a carefully neutral mask I've come to recognise. "Sorry to stop by so late."

I set my book aside, my heart suddenly pounding. "What's happened?"

"Nothing bad," he assures me quickly. "Is your mother around?"

"I'm here," Mum says, appearing in her bathrobe, hair still damp. "What's going on?"

Barnes glances between us. "I wanted to update you in person," he says. "It's about Maggie."

CHAPTER FORTY-EIGHT

My ears ring. The room seems to collapse around me. I'm instantly transported back to that terrible day in the hospital: Barnes standing there with that same careful expression telling us they'd found Sarah's body.

"Is she alive?" The question tears from my throat before I can stop it, my hand instinctively flying to my scar. "Have you found her?"

Suki leans forward, her calm presence a stark contrast to the electric tension that's suddenly filled our living room. "Yes, Amanda. She's alive."

My vision tunnels, black edges creeping in as the oxygen seems to vanish from the room. Alive.

Relief floods through me, followed immediately by confusion at my reaction. Why should I care so deeply about this stranger? But I do.

Paul and Mum exchange bewildered glances, and Mum moves across to sit beside me. Her hair will dry wrong if she doesn't brush it, but she doesn't seem to care. Everyone is invested in this news.

"Where?" I manage, my voice a rasp that sounds too much like those first days of learning to speak again. "Where was she?"

Barnes's mouth tightens. "Actually, we didn't *find* her. After all these months that we've been looking for her, she walked into the station yesterday morning."

I stare at him, the words not quite computing. "She just... showed up? At the police station?"

"Walked right through the front door," Barnes confirms.

The implications hit me in waves. She's been out there all this time. Aware. Hiding. She could have come forward months ago.

I feel like I'm underwater, sounds muffled, thoughts sluggish. For months, finding Maggie was all I could think about. Her photograph became a talisman, her mystery the thread I clung to when everything else unravelled. I convinced myself that understanding the connection between us would somehow make sense of what happened to Sarah, to me.

But now?

Relief wars with a surge of something darker. Anger? Betrayal? Or maybe just the disorienting sensation of having a ghost suddenly materialise in flesh and blood.

It almost feels like an anticlimax.

"Why now?" The words come out sharper than I intended. "Why wait so long?"

Barnes exchanges a glance with Suki before choosing his words carefully. "She had reasons for not coming forward straight away, but she has shared some information with us about the case. I can't tell you much more about that, but Maggie has made a statement."

She wasn't *there*. She didn't see what he did to us. How can she make a statement?

For just a moment, I'm back in those woods, the taste of blood filling my mouth as he calls me by her name. Maggie. Was she there watching? Did she know what was happening to us? The thought sends a surge of nausea through me, so powerful I have to swallow hard against the acid rising in my throat.

"What reasons?" Mum asks, as she gently strokes my hand.

Barnes's expression shifts, almost imperceptibly. "That's... complicated."

'*Find Maggie*' was on my list of goals, but I never expected it to be anything like this. I don't feel satisfied, or elated, or even happy. I'm just confused.

"So, she just appeared out of nowhere after a year?" I press, frustration edging into my voice. "And you can't tell me why, or what she knows, or where she's been this whole time?"

Barnes exchanges a glance with Suki. "I understand your frustration, Amanda. But there are protocols we need to follow."

My fingers drum against my thigh. Every instinct tells me Barnes is holding something back. Something significant.

"Protocols," I repeat, the word tasting bitter. "While I've been in therapy, she's been... where exactly? Living her life? Watching from a distance?"

"We have interviewed her, and she's agreed to come back and help us as much as she can," Barnes says.

He hesitates, then continues. "She's asked to meet with you, Amanda."

As Barnes speaks, my heart pounds so violently I can feel each beat in my fingertips, my throat, behind my eyes. The familiar sensation of unreality washes over me—*derealisation*, Dr Craig calls it. The living room seems to recede, as if I'm suddenly viewing everything through the wrong end of a telescope.

"Amanda?" Mum's voice sounds distant. "Are you okay?"

I can't answer. My tongue feels too large for my mouth, my breathing shallow and rapid. The room is too bright, too loud, too everything.

The girl whose face I share, whose name was on his lips as I lay bleeding.

The girl who might hold answers to questions I've been asking for months.

The girl who might unravel everything I've worked so hard to rebuild.

"Why?" Paul asks, his voice carrying a protective edge. "Why does she want to meet Amanda?"

Barnes lets out a deep breath, as though it's taking everything he has to adhere to protocol.

"Some of the information she shared with my colleagues," he says, "is rather sensitive. And some of it was very personal to Maggie." He looks at Suki, as though asking her to throw him a lifeline.

"What sort of information?" Mum's voice is tight and tense. "Can't you stop talking in riddles and tell us exactly what's going on?"

Barnes straightens, his expression serious. "What I can tell you is that Maggie has provided information that could be crucial to building our case against Matheson. Information that connects directly to Amanda."

"What does she know about me?" I whisper, a tremor running through me. "How does she know anything about me at all?"

Barnes's gaze is steady, measured. "That's something Maggie would like to explain to you herself."

I stare at him, thoughts racing. After all these months of searching for Maggie, of obsessing over her connection to what happened, she's found me. Or at least, she's ready to be found.

"And is this *protocol*?" I ask, unable to keep the bitter edge from my voice.

Barnes clears his throat, shifting uncomfortably. "Not quite. Ordinarily, we'd keep potential witnesses separated. But we need more from Maggie, and she..." he hesitates, "she said needs to talk to you. She's been quite insistent about it."

"What does that mean?" Paul asks, his protective instinct clearly on high alert. "You're bending the rules because she demands it?"

"It's more complicated than that," Suki interjects gently. "Maggie has shared some information, but we think she's holding back some critical details."

"So, you want to use Amanda to make her talk? It sounds like manipulation to me," Paul mutters.

All these months I've tried to move forward, to accept that some questions might never be answered. I've learned to live with the mystery of Maggie, to let go of the desperate need to understand why he targeted me. And now, just when I've started to build something stable, she appears. A living, breathing connection to the worst night of my life.

Part of me wants to refuse. To tell Barnes I'm not interested, that I've moved on. That I don't need her explanations or her intrusion into the careful peace I've constructed.

But another part, the part that still wakes gasping from nightmares, the part that still jumps at unexpected sounds, the part that has never stopped wondering. That part needs to know.

I look at Mum, whose face reflects my uncertainty. At Paul, whose protective stance by the door suddenly seems comforting rather than controlling. I think about Thomas sleeping upstairs, about the life we've built from the wreckage of that night in the woods.

All this time I've committed to healing. The therapy and nightmares and small victories. The effort of learning to live with unanswered questions.

And now, Maggie.

"When?" I ask, the decision forming even as I speak, even as my pulse races and my palms dampen with sweat.

Barnes studies me for a moment. "We could arrange it for tomorrow, if you're willing."

Mum starts to object, but I squeeze her hand.

"I'll do it," I say firmly.

"Amanda," Paul begins, concern evident in his voice.

"I need to," I explain, surprised by my certainty. "I've been wondering about her for so long. Imagining who she is, why she looks like me, what she knows." I meet Barnes's eyes. "I want to know who she is, but I'm also terrified of what she'll tell me. What if her story changes everything? What if..." I stop, swallowing hard. "But I need to hear what she has to say. I need to know."

Barnes nods, something like respect in his expression. "I'll arrange it for tomorrow afternoon. Four o'clock?"

"I'll be there," I promise, even as anxiety churns in my stomach. Whatever Maggie knows, whatever she wants to tell me, I need to face it head-on.

After he leaves, the three of us sit in silence, the rain providing a gentle backdrop to our unspoken thoughts.

"Are you sure about this?" Mum finally asks, her voice careful.

I consider the question, examining my feelings with the techniques Dr Craig has taught me. The anticipation, the fear, the curiosity: all present, all valid. But beneath them, a steady certainty.

"No," I say honestly. "I'm not sure at all. But I need to do it anyway."

Paul moves from the doorway, sitting across from us.

"Then we'll be there with you," he says simply. "Whatever happens."

Later, in my room, I take my notebook from my nightstand drawer where it's been for months. Opening it feels like peering into a past life: the desperate lists, the half-formed theories, the photograph of Maggie still tucked between its pages. I haven't looked at her face in so long, and now, knowing I'll see it in person tomorrow, my hand trembles as I pull it out.

The girl at Lacey Point stares back at me, her expression somewhere between resignation and defiance.

Tomorrow, I'll meet her. Tomorrow, I'll hear what she has to say. Tomorrow, the mystery that's haunted me for almost a year might finally have answers.

Two words at the bottom of the goals list stare out at me from the notebook's final page. I can't tick them off, not yet.

Find myself.

I've been working on that one, slowly but steadily. Finding pieces of the new Amanda, assembling them into someone I'm beginning to recognise. Someone I might someday learn to fully embrace. Sometimes I catch glimpses of her: when I'm reading to Thomas, when I'm sitting with Joyce, when I'm in class and manage to focus on something beyond survival. But she's still forming, still becoming.

But there, above it, the uncrossed items still wait:

Find Sarah.

Find Maggie.

Finding Sarah, the truth of what happened to her, where her body lay for those terrible weeks. That brought only a different kind of pain. Not closure, not peace, just confirmed grief.

Will finding Maggie be any different?

CHAPTER FORTY-NINE

The police station feels smaller than I remember, less intimidating. The last time I was here was shortly after coming home from Oakwood, giving an additional statement about the attack. I'd been nervous then, fragile, uncertain of my own memories. But I spoke, used my own voice to describe the things I could only write on a whiteboard when I was first questioned. Now, eight months later, I walk through the front doors with a steadier step, Mum and Paul flanking me like guards.

Detective Barnes meets us in the lobby, his expression professional but kind. "Amanda, Abby, Paul." He nods to each of us in turn. "Thank you for coming."

"How is she?" I ask, surprising myself with the immediate concern for Maggie's welfare.

"Anxious," Barnes admits. "But cooperative. She's been giving us information about Matheson's activities that could help build an even stronger case against him. I should tell you something before we go and meet her, though," he says.

"What?" I'm instantly on guard.

Barnes looks me dead in the eye, and without dropping a beat, he says, "Maggie is Matheson's daughter."

I let out a gasp, as though I've been punched in the gut, even though part of me knew it was a possibility.

This was one of many scenarios that have floated through my mind. Victim. Family. Target.

Daughter.

I let it sink in.

"How awful for her," I say. The words come to my mind and out of my mouth before I can think. I'm glad that Barnes told me here and now, because I'm not sure that this is the response I should have had in front of Maggie. I don't know what went on between her and her father. I don't know anything.

"Well, quite," Detective Barnes says. "Look, we're really not going by the book here, but I thought you should know, and she consented to me telling you."

My mind races, struggling to reconcile the image of the girl in the photograph with the monster who haunts my nightmares. How could someone who shares my face be connected to him by blood? The thought makes my skin crawl. If she's his daughter, was the attack somehow about her? Was I targeted specifically because I resembled her? Questions pile up faster than I can process them, each one more disturbing than the last.

Suki steps out into the hallway in front of us, and I'm glad for the interruption. I'm going to have a lot to process after this meeting. My next visit to Dr Craig's clinic should be interesting.

"Hi, Amanda," she says, nodding to Mum and Paul. "I was asked to be here today, but how we do this is up to you. If you would like to have a chat with me first, or if you would like me to come in with you... it's all your decision."

"I can be with her," Mum says.

I look from Suki to Mum and back again.

"I want to meet her on my own," I say. "If that's okay?"

"Okay," Mum says, quietly, protectively.

I smile and turn my attention back to the Detective.

"Has she said why she wants to meet me?" I reach up to my neck to fiddle with a scarf that isn't there.

Barnes shakes his head. "Only that it's important. That she owes you an explanation."

Explanation. The word carries weight: the promise of answers, understanding, perhaps even closure.

"We'll be in the observation room," Barnes continues, gesturing down a hallway. "Maggie is aware of that arrangement and has agreed to it. You can leave at any time if you feel uncomfortable. We won't listen directly to your conversation, but we need to make an audio recording, with your consent. Maggie has already agreed."

I nod, glancing at Mum, whose face is a carefully composed mask of support that doesn't quite hide her concern.

"Yes," I say. "Of course."

Then I turn back to Mum.

"I'll be fine," I tell her, finding that I believe it. Months of therapy has given me tools I didn't have before: ways to ground myself, to stay present even when memories threaten to pull me under.

"We'll be right there," Paul says, his hand briefly touching my shoulder. "Just on the other side of the glass."

The interview room is exactly as movies and television shows have trained me to expect: plain walls, a simple table, two chairs facing each other. Nothing to distract from the conversation about to take place.

Maggie is already seated, her back to the door. All I can see is her hair, brown like mine, but cut shorter, falling just below her shoulders. She's wearing a simple flannel shirt, the pattern reminiscent of the jacket her father wore that night in the woods. The similarity makes my stomach clench briefly before I push the reaction aside.

Officer Winters stands nearby, and for a moment, it jars me to see her. I assumed she had moved on, gone on to other cases. I thought I would never see her again, but here she is. She nods at me as I enter, then slips out the door, leaving us alone but undoubtedly watched through the one-way mirror.

Maggie turns at the sound of the closing door, and for a moment, we simply stare at each other.

I'm staring at my own face, but not. It's like looking into a mirror where the reflection has a mind of its own, moving independently, existing separately. The uncanny valley of recognition floods me with a dizzy disorientation so profound I have to grip the back of the chair to steady myself. My brain struggles to process the cognitive dissonance. This is me but not-me, familiar yet foreign, known yet completely unknown.

Her eyes widen as she experiences the same jolt of recognition, her hand reflexively rising to her throat, the same gesture I make when anxious, except where my fingers find scar tissue, hers touch only smooth skin. The identical movement from both of us creates a surreal moment of synchronicity that makes my heart race.

The resemblance is unmistakable: the same high cheekbones, the same slight widow's peak, the same curve of our upper lips. But as my initial shock fades, the differences emerge like a developing photograph: her eyes are wider set than mine, her jaw slightly sharper, the hollows beneath her cheekbones more pronounced. The resemblance is unmistakable, but not identical. Not twins, not even sisters. Just an uncanny echo that feels like staring into some alternate version of myself.

She sits with a rigidity that speaks of years of hypervigilance: shoulders slightly hunched as if perpetually bracing for impact, right hand automatically positioned to protect her left side, eyes constantly tracking between me and the door as if calculating escape routes. Even her breathing follows a pattern I recognise from my own early days of recovery. Deliberately controlled, never fully filling her lungs, always ready to hold her breath at the first sign of danger.

The thought strikes me that she looks like what I might become in a few years: a slightly older version of myself with edges hardened by experience. I study her face, finding traces of my own in her expression, in the way she holds herself.

And suddenly, unexpectedly, I wonder what Sarah would have looked like at nineteen, twenty-one, thirty. All the ages she will never be. How her smile might have matured, what she might have done with her hair, whether the laugh lines around her eyes would have deepened. But I'll never know. Sarah is forever sixteen, frozen in time at the moment he took her future away. No matter how many years pass, how many birthdays we mark without her, she will never age beyond the girl I knew.

The realisation aches deep in my chest. This finality, this irreversible truth. I can imagine my future, can even see a version of it sitting across from me in Maggie's face. But Sarah's future exists only in memory and imagination. All I can do is love the friend I knew, carry her with me as I continue forward into years she'll never see.

"Amanda," she says, her voice higher than I expected, with a slight tremor that betrays her nervousness.

"Maggie," I respond, moving to the chair opposite her.

Up close, the differences between us become more apparent. She's thinner, her face holding the sharp angles of someone who's known hunger.

There's no scar on her neck.

Not like mine.

"Thank you for coming," she says, her fingers twisting together on the table until the knuckles whiten. She hunches forward slightly, unconsciously making herself smaller in the chair. "I wasn't sure you would."

"I've been wondering about you for a long time," I repeat, settling into the chair. "Ever since..." Since he called me by your name. Since he raped my friend. Slit my throat. Destroyed my life.

Maggie flinches, a full-body response that goes beyond mere facial expression: her shoulders contract, her head ducks slightly, her hands momentarily clench before deliberately relaxing. It's the practiced response of someone who has learned to make herself smaller, less noticeable, in moments of threat or stress.

"I know what happened," she says, a muscle twitching involuntarily along her jaw. "That's why I needed to see you. To explain. To apologise."

"Apologise?" The word catches me off guard. "For what?"

She takes a deep breath, her gaze dropping to her hands. "For everything. For what he did to you and your friend. For not stopping him sooner. For running away instead of going to the police."

Her words tumble out, raw with a guilt I recognise too well. I've carried my own version of it for months. The belief that I should have done something more, something different. That Sarah's death was somehow my fault.

"You think it was your responsibility to stop him?" I ask quietly.

She looks up, her eyes bright with unshed tears. "I knew what he was. What he did. And I did nothing. For years." She pauses, swallowing hard. "Your friend wasn't the first. There were others."

"Others?" I repeat.

Maggie nods, her fingers tracing an invisible pattern on the table. "I was aware of at least seven over the years. Maybe more when I wasn't around."

Seven. The number echoes in my head, each repetition bringing fresh horror. Seven lives ended. Seven families shattered. And Sarah makes eight.

I recall now fragments of conversations between Barnes and Reid in the hospital: hushed tones, cryptic references to ‘MOs’. Barnes had mentioned once that they were looking into other missing persons reports, but they never confirmed anything to me. Never had proof. Never found bodies. Maybe now they can.

The thought creates a strange, conflicted feeling in my chest. On one hand, these families deserve answers, closure, the confirmation of what they likely already suspect but can’t fully accept without proof. On the other hand, that closure comes at a terrible price: the final extinguishing of hope, the concrete knowledge that their loved ones aren’t coming back.

“They suspected,” I say, my voice barely audible. “The detectives. They thought there might be others, but they never said anything definitive to me.”

The pain in her voice is so familiar it aches. I see myself in her guilt, in her certainty that she should have prevented something beyond her control.

“Tell me,” I say, settling back in my chair. “From the beginning.”

CHAPTER FIFTY

Maggie nods, takes another steadying breath, and starts talking.

"My mother died when I was six. Cancer. After that, it was just me and him. We moved around a lot. He never kept jobs long. I wasn't enrolled in school. He said he was homeschooling me, but mostly I just read whatever books I could find."

I try to imagine it. A childhood of constant movement, of isolation, with only Matheson for company. The thought makes my skin crawl.

"When I was about eight, he started taking me to parks, trails, places where people went hiking or walking," Maggie continues. "He'd tell me it was a game. I was supposed to run ahead, act lost or confused. When someone stopped to help me, I'd tell them I couldn't find my dad."

Her voice catches, and she pauses, visibly collecting herself.

"They'd always try to help. Always. Sometimes they'd hold my hand, take me back down the trail looking for him. But he'd be watching, following. He'd direct me toward isolated spots, and then he'd appear, all relieved to have found his 'lost daughter'." The bitterness in her voice is palpable. "People trusted him because of me. Because what kind of monster brings his little girl along to..."

She can't finish the sentence, but she doesn't need to. I understand with sickening clarity what she's describing. The perfect cover. The perfect way to appear harmless to potential victims.

Like a man looking for a lost dog.

A man with a lead on a country path.

A man talking to two girls who are just collecting bluebells.

"You were a child," I say, the words emerging with more force than I intended. "You didn't know what he was doing."

"Not at first," she agrees, wiping at her eyes. "But as I got older, I started to understand. I'd hear noises in the night. Once, I saw him dragging something heavy into the woods behind a motel we were staying at." She swallows hard. "I think it was a woman. Or a girl. I was eleven."

The horror of her childhood unfolds before me. Not a single traumatic event like mine, but years of slow realisation, of growing understanding of the monster who called himself her father.

"I tried to run away when I was thirteen," Maggie continues. "Got picked up by the police in this burger place near Davistown. Told them my dad hurt people. That he was dangerous." She laughs, a bitter sound without humour. "They called him to come get me. Said I had an 'active imagination.' That night, he..."

She trails off, absently touching her right shoulder. "He made sure I understood what would happen if I ever tried to tell anyone again."

My throat tightens with emotion: anger at Matheson, at the police who didn't listen, at the world that failed to protect this girl who shares my face.

A strange thought hits me as I hear Maggie describe her childhood with Matheson. My dad had simply disappeared, while hers had remained, a constant, destructive presence. Two different types of abandonment: one through absence, one through abuse. Yet somehow, we've both ended up here, carrying wounds that shape us in similar ways.

Not that I'm comparing my dad leaving us to what Matheson did, not at all. We're inverse reflections: she, running from a father who wouldn't let her go; me, forgotten by one who left without looking back

"When I was seventeen, I finally got away," Maggie continues. "After a particularly bad night. He'd been drinking more than usual. Brought a woman back to the cabin we were staying in. I heard her screaming. I was too old then to use as bait, so he'd tell me to stay home, keep quiet..."

She stops, her hands trembling visibly on the table.

"I knew he'd kill her. Like the others. But this time, I had my backpack ready. I'd been planning for months, saving what little money I could find around the house. While he was... busy... I slipped out. Started walking and didn't stop until I reached the next town over."

"How did you end up at Stewart Reservoir?" I ask, thinking of the photograph, of Paul recognising the boathouse.

"Walking, mostly. Then hitchhiking," Maggie says. "I had no plan. I ended up in Henderson, that small town near the reservoir, and then down in the boathouse. They pulled it down, so I guess you could say I was evicted. Was sleeping behind the grocery store when an old man found me."

I don't get it. It doesn't make sense.

I tilt my head for the cross examination. "Wasn't it risky to stay somewhere he had a photo of? Somewhere he might look for you?"

"I chose it specifically. *Because* he had that photo next to the bed, you know. He took that photo before..."

She swallows hard and picks the glass of water off the table, downing it in one long gulp. Her throat works visibly with each swallow, her fingers gripping the glass so tightly I fear it might shatter.

"Before one of the times..."

She looks at me, and I nod in understanding. I'm trying to keep my face as straight as possible, trying to conceal the horror.

"I kind of knew that if he'd been there, if he had used that spot before, he wouldn't go back. He was... obsessive about his patterns. Never returning to a location after he'd used it for... for one of his victims. It was like a rule for him."

She turns her gaze to the ground.

"And I bet on the fact that he wouldn't expect me to go there either, after what he did. I suppose as well, there was always a chance that if he ever got caught, that they should catch me too."

"Catch you?" Her words shock me, and I blurt out the repeat.

"I helped him," she says, flatly. "I was an accomplice. For a long time, I wanted to be caught. I wanted *them* to make me pay for what I've done." She nods her head towards the mirror on the wall that we both know separates us from our audience.

Tears stream down her face from eyes that look like mine. I reach over and pass her a tissue.

"It wasn't your fault," I tell her. "You were a child. There was nothing you could have done differently. You were a victim too, Maggie. A child used as bait, then a teenager running for her life. The only person responsible for what happened is Matheson. Your dad."

She looks up, clearly surprised by my vehemence.

"I used to think it was my fault too," I continue, the words coming easier than I expected. "That I should have saved Sarah somehow. That I let her die while I survived. But that's not how it works. We didn't choose what happened to us."

"But I knew what he was," she insists. "I could have stopped him."

"At what cost?" I lean forward. "You said yourself the police didn't believe you when you tried to tell them. He hurt you for trying to run away. What do you think he'd have done if you'd kept trying?"

She has no answer for that.

"My therapist talks about the difference between responsibility and blame," I say, drawing on months of sessions with Dr Craig. "Like how we can acknowledge the reality of what happened without taking on blame that isn't ours to carry."

Maggie studies me for a long moment. "You sound like you've done a lot of work to get to that place."

"Shitloads of therapy," I admit with a small smile. "And I still have days when I don't believe it myself. When the guilt feels too heavy to put down."

"How do you bear it?" she asks, the question vulnerable and genuine. "Knowing what happened to your friend?"

I consider this carefully. "I honour Sarah by living," I say finally. "By trying to find joy again, by being present for the people who love me. By refusing to let that night define the rest of my life."

The words surprise me with their clarity, their certainty. Somewhere in the past year, without my fully realising it, I've begun to believe them.

Maggie nods slowly, absorbing this. "I've been running for so long," she says. "Always looking over my shoulder, always waiting for him to find me again. Even knowing he's in custody now, I can't quite believe I'm safe."

"I understand that too," I tell her. "The hypervigilance, the constant feeling that danger is just around the corner. It gets better, though. Not gone, but... manageable."

"I hope so." She hesitates, then asks, "Do you still have nightmares?"

"Yes," I admit. "Less frequently now, but they still come. Especially around significant dates or when something triggers a memory."

"I dream about the woods," she says quietly. "Always the woods. In my dreams, it's always trees and darkness and knowing he's somewhere behind me."

The image resonates so strongly with my own nightmares that, for a moment, it's hard to breathe. This is what connects us: not just our similar appearances, not just the man who harmed us both, but the psychological aftermath. The dreams, the fear, the constant work of rebuilding a life around the wound.

"What will you do now?" I ask. "After all this is finished?"

Maggie looks surprised, as if she hasn't considered a future beyond giving her statement, beyond confronting the past. "I don't know," she admits. "I've never really had a normal life. Wouldn't even know what that looks like."

"One day at a time," I suggest. "That's what Dr Craig, my therapist, always says."

She considers this, her fingers tracing patterns on the table. "The police psychologist mentioned art therapy might be a good fit for me." She shrugs but can't quite hide the flicker of interest in her eyes. "Drawing's always been the one thing that helped when things got bad. When I needed to escape."

I recognise her expression, that cautious reaching toward possibility, toward a future that might contain more than fear and running. I've seen it in my own mirror over the past months.

"You could try," I tell her with conviction. "You're more than what he made you. You have to find yourself."

She blinks rapidly, clearly fighting tears. "That's what scares me the most, I think. Figuring out who I am without him. Without being defined by running or hiding or being afraid."

"It's terrifying," I agree. "But worth it. I'm still on the journey."

"Finding myself," she repeats softly, as if testing how the words feel. "I like that." A small smile touches her lips. "Maybe I'll start with the art therapy. See where that leads."

"That sounds like a good first step."

For a moment, we sit in silence, two girls connected by trauma but finding something like understanding in its aftermath. I study her face. The face that so resembles mine but carries its own unique story. The weight of shared experience settles between us, neither fully comfortable nor entirely unwelcome.

"I should go," I say finally. "My mum's probably worried sick."

Maggie smiles faintly. "Must be nice to have someone worry about you like that."

The casual observation strikes me with its loneliness. Maggie has no one waiting anxiously for her return, no family creating a protective circle, no home to go back to after all this is over.

"What about now?" I ask, the question forming even as I speak it. "Do you have anyone? Anywhere to go after all this?"

She shakes her head. "The police mentioned victim services, maybe some kind of temporary housing while the trial preparation continues." Her attempt at nonchalance doesn't quite mask the uncertainty beneath. "I'll figure something out. Always have."

I hesitate, then make a decision I hope I won't regret. "Give me your number," I say. "If you want to talk sometime. About any of it. Or about nothing at all."

Surprise flashes across her face, followed by something that might be hope. "You'd want that?"

"I think we could both use someone who understands," I say simply. "Someone who gets it without needing explanations."

She nods slowly, then accepts the pen and paper I slide across the table. Writes down a number, then passes it back.

"I might be moving on," she warns. "After the trial, you know. I'll be here for that. I'll tell them everything I can to make sure he goes away and stays away. And then... a fresh start somewhere else."

She could have moved further away before now.

I wonder for a moment if she stayed because of the glimmer of an idea that one day she might have to walk into a police station and tell them what she knows.

I'm glad she did.

"It's okay," I assure her. "No pressure either way."

As I stand to leave, Maggie looks up at me, her expression serious. "Thank you," she says. "For listening. For not hating me."

"I could never hate you," I tell her, and know it's true. "We're both survivors of the same man, just in different ways."

At the door, I pause, looking back at this stranger who shares my face, who carried guilt I recognise, who has lived a life I can barely imagine.

"Take care of yourself, Maggie," I say softly.

"You too, Amanda," she replies. "And thank you. For finding me when I couldn't find myself."

The words echo my own journey so precisely that for a moment, I can't respond. Then I nod, acknowledging the strange synchronicity of our paths. Two girls with the same face, both lost, both found. Both still finding their way forward.

CHAPTER FIFTY-ONE

Outside in the hallway, Mum and Paul are waiting, their expressions a mixture of concern and relief. Mum immediately pulls me into a hug.

"Are you okay?" she whispers against my hair.

I nod, surprised to find that I am. The conversation with Maggie was difficult, painful in places, but also healing in ways I hadn't anticipated.

"What did she tell you?" Paul asks as we make our way toward the exit.

I think about all that Maggie shared: her childhood, her escape, her years in hiding, her guilt. The complex, terrible story of a life shaped by the same man who nearly ended mine.

A thought crosses my mind, and I try to unthink it. When he sliced my throat, did he think I was her? Would he have done that to her if she had stayed?

I wonder if she has thought about that too.

"Everything," I say simply. "She told me everything."

Detective Barnes catches up to us at the front desk

"Thank you for coming in," he says.

I nod, thinking of Maggie sitting alone in that interview room, preparing to formally testify against the man who both raised and terrorised her.

"What happens to her now?" I ask.

"We're arranging temporary housing," Barnes explains. "And victim services are working on a more permanent solution. She's agreed to testify at the trial, which likely won't be for several months. After that, she'll have options: victim relocation programs, identity protection if needed."

"She's all alone," I say, the reality of it settling heavily. "No family, no friends, no support system."

Barnes's expression softens slightly. "We're doing what we can within the system. But yes, her situation is... complicated."

I think about Maggie's face when I offered to stay in touch. That flicker of surprise, of cautious hope. About her words: '*Must be nice to have someone worry about you like that.*'

In the car heading home, I sit silently in the backseat, processing all that I've learned. Mum keeps glancing at me in the rearview mirror, clearly concerned but giving me space. Paul stares straight ahead, but I know he's listening attentively to any sound I might make.

"She was a victim too," I say finally, breaking the silence. "All those years, he used her as bait. Made her complicit in his crimes without her understanding or consent. And when she finally escaped, she felt responsible for everyone he hurt afterward."

Mum's knuckles whiten on the steering wheel. "That poor girl."

"She was just a child," Paul says, his voice tight with anger. "How could anyone do that to their own daughter?"

I think about Thomas, about the simple, pure love that surrounds him. About the way Paul's face softens when he holds him, the way Mum's entire body seems to curve protectively around him. The concept of using your own child as a tool to harm others is so alien to our family that it's almost incomprehensible.

"She blames herself," I say. "For not stopping him sooner. For running away instead of going to the police. For Sarah."

"That's not her fault," Mum says firmly.

"I know," I say, believing it. "That's what I told her."

The irony doesn't escape me: offering Maggie the same absolution I've struggled to grant myself. The same truth

Dr Craig has been patiently, persistently helping me accept, that survivor's guilt is natural but not rational. That we are not responsible for the actions of others, even when we survive them.

The rest of the drive passes in contemplative silence. By the time we reach home, the sun is beginning to set, casting long shadows across the yard where, in a different lifetime, Sarah and I once played. The house waits, solid and familiar, Thomas undoubtedly awake from his nap and being entertained by our favourite babysitter, Joyce.

As Mum pulls into the driveway, I make a decision. Not dramatic or life-changing, but significant, nonetheless.

"I'm going to text her," I announce. "Maggie. Just to check on her. Make sure she's okay after today."

Mum and Paul exchange a glance I can't quite interpret.

"If that's what you want," Mum says carefully.

"It is." I open the car door, stepping out into the fading afternoon light. "She deserves to know someone cares what happens to her."

Inside, Joyce greets us with Thomas on her hip, his face lighting up at the sight of his family returning. I take him from her, breathing in his baby-powder scent, feeling his solid warmth against my chest.

"How was he?" Mum asks.

"Perfect as always," she assures us. "Slept for an hour, then we read every book in his room at least twice."

"Will you stay for dinner? It's pizza night." Mum offers, but Joyce is already shaking her head.

"I told Oliver we would watch the game tonight," she says. "Next time, though, I promise."

As she passes me, she looks at me for a few extra seconds, as she always does. The look always ends in a smile, and I like to think she sees traces of Sarah in me. Not in the same way that Maggie and I have that physical similarity, but the way that Sarah and I had similar souls. The bond, the love, and the way that Sarah is so deeply ingrained in my heart. Now, then, always.

"See you soon, Joyce," I tell her.

As Mum sees her out, thanking her profusely, I carry Thomas to the living room, settling with him on the couch.

Paul sits across from us, his expression thoughtful. "You okay?" he asks quietly. "Really?"

I consider the question, bouncing Thomas gently on my knee. "Yes," I say finally. "It was hard, hearing everything she went through. Everything he did. But it helped, too. Knowing the whole story."

He nods, understanding without needing me to elaborate. It's one way our relationship has evolved over the past months, this ability to communicate without every thought requiring full articulation.

Later, after Thomas's bath and bedtime story, I retreat to my room and pull out my phone. The piece of paper with Maggie's number sits on my nightstand, the digits unfamiliar and somehow momentous.

I type, delete, and retype a message several times before settling on simplicity:

This is Amanda. Just wanted to check how you're doing after today. It was a lot to process.

I hit send before I can overthink it further, then set my phone aside and pull out my notebook.

After a moment's hesitation, I pick up a pen and draw a careful checkmark beside Find Maggie. Not because I solved the mystery myself, not because I tracked her down or unravelled her connection to Matheson. But because I've found something I wasn't expecting: a kind of understanding, a shared experience that transcends the horror that connected us.

My phone buzzes with an incoming message. Maggie's response:

Still processing everything. Thank you for listening. For understanding. It means more than I can say.

I smile, typing back,

One day at a time, right?

Her reply comes quickly:

One day at a time. I like that.

I set the phone down, a strange sense of peace settling over me. Not closure. I've learned there's no such thing, not really. Life doesn't tie itself up in neat narrative bows. But something like acceptance. Something like hope.

There are things I will never know. Gaps in my memory that protect me from the things my traumatised mind cannot process. I'll never know how I got from where he attacked us to the road where I was found. But now, I don't care. It's enough to know I made it.

Tomorrow, I'll wake up and continue the work of healing. Continue helping Mum with Thomas, navigating my evolving relationship with Paul, rebuilding a life that isn't defined by trauma.

But today, I've found Maggie. And in doing so, perhaps found another piece of myself as well.

EPILOGUE

The morning of Sarah's birthday dawns bright and clear, sunlight casting dappled shadows through green-leafed trees that edge the cemetery. I adjust Thomas on my hip, his weight solid and reassuring as we follow the familiar path to her grave. He's getting too heavy to carry for long, but today feels like a day for holding close the people we love.

Ahead of us, Joyce walks with Mum, their voices too low to hear but their body language comfortable, familiar. They've forged a friendship I never expected: two mothers connected by loss and survival, by the strange, terrible intersection of their daughters' lives.

Paul trails slightly behind with Oliver and Sarah's dad. Their conversation flows more easily than I would have imagined a year ago, when the wounds were fresher, the grief rawer.

I pause at the crest of the small hill, taking in the scene below. Sarah's grave is already decorated with flowers. The headstone is simple, elegant, carved from pale marble that catches the morning light. Around it, wildflowers have pushed through the grass, small bursts of colour against the green.

Thomas squirms in my arms, reaching toward the ground.

"Down," he demands, his vocabulary expanding daily now. "Walk."

He's just short of a year old and finding his voice - and his feet - early. This is a boy who knows what he wants.

"In a minute, buddy," I say, pressing a kiss to his dark curls. "We're going to see Sarah first."

He doesn't understand, of course. To him, Sarah is just a name, a person in photographs, a story I sometimes tell when we're alone. The good parts. The things we loved to do together. Everything I adored about her. Someday, when he's older, I'll explain. I'll tell him about my best friend, about how brave she was, about how much she would have loved him.

As we reach the grave, Joyce turns, her arms opening automatically to accept Thomas. He goes willingly, always happy for attention from his extended family of not-quite-relatives but more-than-friends.

"He's getting so big," she says, bouncing him gently.

"And heavy," I agree, rubbing my arm. "Started climbing out of his crib last week. Mum found him in the hallway at midnight, looking very pleased with himself."

Joyce laughs, the sound easier than it once was. For months, her laugh was a rare, fragile thing, but now it comes more frequently, though never without a shadow of what she's lost.

We gather around the grave, our small circle of mourners and celebrants. Today would have been Sarah's eighteenth birthday. An age she never reached; a milestone forever marked by absence rather than presence.

Oliver steps forward first, placing a small arrangement of roses and a small teddy bear on the marble ledge.

"Hey, little sister," he says softly. "Happy birthday."

Joyce follows, with her husband by her side. He looks so solid beside her still fragile frame. Still fragile, but still standing. Her hand trails over the carved letters of her daughter's name.

Finally, it's my turn. From my pocket, I withdraw a black sandstone heart, perfectly smooth, heavy and solid. As soon as I saw it at the market, I knew it was meant for Sarah.

"Happy birthday, S," I say, propping the gift against her headstone. "Miss you every day."

The grief rises, familiar but no longer overwhelming. I've learned to live with it, to carry it alongside joy, to let it be part of me without defining me. Dr Craig calls it integration: weaving trauma and loss into the fabric of life without allowing them to distort the whole pattern.

We stand in silence for a moment, each lost in our own memories. Then Thomas, impatient with the solemnity, lets out a delighted squeal as a butterfly floats past his face.

Joyce laughs, the sound mingling with tears. "Sarah would have loved that," she says. "She never could stay serious for long."

"Remember when she started giggling during Christmas service?" Oliver asks, smiling at the memory. "Dad was so embarrassed."

Mr Fairchild grins and pulls his son in towards him for a hug.

"She had the most infectious laugh," I add, the memory warm rather than painful. "Once she started, you couldn't help joining in."

This is how we honour her now. Not just with silence and flowers, but with stories. With remembering who she was in life, not just how she was taken from us. With allowing ourselves to laugh even as we mourn.

After a while, we make our way back to the cars. The day stretches ahead, starting with brunch at Joyce's house. A celebration of her life rather than a memorial of her death.

As we drive, my phone buzzes with a text message. I check it at a stoplight, already knowing who it's from.

Thinking of you today. Hope it went okay. M

Maggie and I have maintained our tentative connection over the past months since we met: text messages, occasional phone calls, a handful of video chats. She's settled in Sandhill now, part of a victim relocation program that provided a new identity, a small apartment, educational opportunities. She's taking community college classes, working part-time at a bookstore, seeing a therapist twice a week.

Rebuilding a life that was never really built in the first place.

I type back quickly:

It was good. Hard but good. Thanks for checking in.

Her response comes almost immediately:

One day at a time.

I smile at our shared mantra, tucking the phone away as we pull into Joyce's driveway. The house is decorated with streamers and balloons. Not for a party, exactly, but for a gathering that acknowledges both grief and joy, both absence and presence.

Inside, Joyce serves Sarah's favourite foods: strawberry pancakes, despite the late morning hour, and the chocolate chip cookies she used to bake whenever Sarah was sad. The dining table is set with Sarah's photos positioned between place settings; her presence acknowledged in this intimate celebration of her life.

Thomas is immediately the centre of attention, toddling between adults, accepting cuddles and snacks with equal enthusiasm. I watch him from the kitchen doorway, this little brother who has never known a world with Sarah in it but who embodies the possibility of joy after devastation.

Paul appears beside me, two mugs of coffee in hand.

"You okay?" he asks, offering one to me.

I accept the coffee, considering his question.

"Yes," I say finally. "Not perfect. But okay."

He nods, understanding the nuance.

"That's all any of us can ask for, I think.

Our relationship has evolved into something I never expected. Not quite father and daughter, but something steadier, more trusting than what we had before. He makes mistakes, as do I. But we're both trying, both committed to building something that works.

As I've got to know Maggie these past months, I've come to understand something about fathers. Mine disappeared when I needed him most; hers remained to inflict unimaginable harm. Two different brands of betrayal. Paul isn't perfect. Sometimes he still doesn't know what to say or how to help, but he tries. Every day, he tries. And I'm learning that sometimes showing up imperfectly is the most anyone can do. My father never even managed that. For Thomas, I hope Paul continues to be the father neither Maggie nor I ever had: present, protective, and kind.

"Where's Mum?" I ask, noticing her absence from the living room.

"Helping Joyce with something upstairs," Paul says. "Photo albums, I think."

I nod, sipping my coffee. Through the window, I can see Oliver in the backyard, setting up the croquet set Sarah always insisted on playing at family gatherings despite being terribly, hilariously bad at it.

"We're going to play," I guess, a smile touching my lips.

"Joyce's idea," Paul confirms. "Said Sarah would want us to, especially since she always lost spectacularly."

The afternoon unfolds in a gentle rhythm of food, games, and stories. We play croquet on the lawn, Thomas "helping" by occasionally stealing the balls and running in random directions. We look through photo albums, pointing out favourite memories, laughing at Sarah's unfortunate fashion phases and terrible school pictures.

"I can't believe she wore that hat to the school dance," Oliver groans, pointing to a picture of Sarah in an enormous, feathered monstrosity she'd found at a thrift store. "She was so proud of it."

"It was a statement," Joyce says, her tone mock defensive. "She said she wanted to be memorable."

"Well, it worked," I say, smiling at the image of Sarah beaming beneath the ridiculous hat, utterly unconcerned with looking cool or fitting in. "No one who saw that would ever forget it."

As the day winds down, I find myself alone with Joyce in the kitchen, helping to pack leftovers. She moves with the efficiency of long practice, containers neatly labelled, portions carefully distributed.

"Take some for Ellie," she says, handing me an extra container of cookies. "I know she loves these."

Ellie, now fully recovered from her injuries, has become an unexpected addition to our extended family. She and I meet weekly for coffee, text daily, share the unique bond of trauma survivors who found each other at their most vulnerable. She's starting university in January, studying psychology with a focus on rehabilitation services.

"She'll be thrilled," I say, accepting the cookies. "Last time she visited, she mentioned missing your baking."

Joyce smiles, pleased. "Bring her next time. She's always welcome here."

I nod, touched by the invitation. "I will."

Joyce pauses in her task, studying me with the gentle directness that's become characteristic of our relationship.

"How are you really doing, Amanda? With everything?"

I consider deflecting, offering the same reassurances I give most people who ask. But Joyce has earned honesty. Has earned the truth in all its complexities.

"Most days are good now," I tell her. "I still have nightmares sometimes. Still jump at unexpected noises. Still have therapy twice a month." I arrange cookies in the container, focusing on the simple task. "But I'm living, not just surviving. That feels like progress."

"It is," she agrees quietly. "Enormous progress."

"I still miss her," I admit, the words catching slightly. "Every day."

"So do I." Joyce's hand finds mine across the counter, a brief squeeze of shared understanding. "But I think she'd be proud of you. Of all of us. For finding ways to keep going. For finding joy again."

I think about Sarah: her laughter, her loyalty, her unwavering belief that things would work out in the end.

"She would," I agree. "She always said we were stronger than we knew."

Later, back home with Thomas asleep in his room and Paul and Mum dozing in front of some movie, I step into the back garden. The evening is warm, the air carrying the scent of flowers from the garden. A year gone, an entire revolution around the sun without Sarah.

But not without growth. Not without healing. Not without new connections forming in the spaces grief left behind.

My phone buzzes with another text from Maggie:

Professor approved my art therapy project. Starting with kids next month. Scared but excited.

I smile, typing back:

You'll be amazing. They're lucky to have you.

Maggie's path toward healing has taken its own shape: art therapy. Not just as a recipient, but now she's also in training herself, working with children who've experienced trauma, using drawings to help others process what words cannot express. Finding purpose in the very skill she developed during her years of isolation and fear.

Another message arrives seconds later:

Just heard from Detective Barnes. Trial date is confirmed for September. Are you ready?

The trial. The words still send a small tremor through me, though not the paralysing fear they once did. Soon I'll sit in a courtroom and face Matheson for the first time since that night in the woods. I'll speak the truth of what happened, what he did to Sarah, what he tried to do to me. And Maggie will do the same. Testifying against her own father, breaking the silence she maintained for so long.

As ready as I'll ever be, I reply. **We'll get through it together.**

The prosecution is confident. DNA evidence. The jacket. The partial fingerprint. My testimony. Maggie's account of years of witnessing his patterns. All the things she heard him do. Everything she saw. The connections to other cases they've since linked to him.

Detective Barnes called it "airtight" during our last preparation session, though I know enough now to understand that justice is never guaranteed.

But whatever the outcome, the truth will be spoken. Sarah's name will be in that courtroom. What happened to her will be acknowledged. And that matters, even if nothing can bring her back.

I will be heard.

Maggie will be heard.

And although she can't be there to speak for herself, Sarah will be heard.

One day at a time, Maggie texts back, our shared mantra.

I take a deep breath, set the phone down. The trial looms on the horizon, but it no longer defines my days. It's just one more step in a journey that continues forward, never erasing what happened but refusing to be controlled by it. One more chapter in a story that belongs to me now.

Before heading upstairs, I pull a blanket over Mum and Paul on the sofa and smile at the vision of normal family life.

My normal life.

In my room, I open the notebook that I haven't written in since the day I met Maggie. Today feels important, worth recording.

I flip to a fresh page and write the date, then pause, pen above the paper. After a moment, I begin:

Happy birthday, Sarah. We celebrated you today—not your absence, but your presence in our lives. The way you changed us, shaped us, loved us. The way you continue to do so, even now.

I wish you could see Thomas, how he laughs with his whole body, just like you used to. How he approaches the world with the same fearless curiosity you always had. I tell him about you, even though he's too young to understand. Someday he will.

I wish you could see how your mum finally smiles more now. How all of us carry pieces of you forward in ways I don't think any of us expected.

I'll sit in that courtroom and be your voice. I'll make them hear what happened to you, what he took from you, from all of us. I'm terrified, but I'll do it anyway. For you. Because your story deserves to be told, and I'm the one who can tell it. The one who survived to speak your name aloud.

I wish you could see me—not perfect, not "fixed," but healing. Living. Finding my way forward while keeping you with me.

I miss you every day. I think I always will. But I'm learning that grief and joy can exist together, that one doesn't cancel out the other. That life continues, changed but not ended by loss.

Wherever you are, I hope you know how loved you still are. How remembered. How important.

Thank you for being my friend. For showing me what courage looks like. For being part of the person I'm still becoming.

It's the most I've ever written in a single entry, and writing comes so easily now. I can't believe that it once took every ounce of strength to write one word, that it was once too difficult for me to say her name.

"Sarah." I speak her name loudly and clearly. "Sarah, Sarah, Sarah."

I close the notebook gently, setting it back on the nightstand.

"I love you, Sarah," I say, hoping that somewhere she can hear me.

As I prepare for bed, I catch my reflection in the mirror. The scar on my neck is now a thin line, visible but no longer angry and raw. A permanent marker of what happened, what changed, what was lost. But not the only thing that defines me.

I touch it lightly, thinking of all the invisible scars I carry as well. The ones no one can see but that have shaped me just as surely. The weight of survivor's guilt that still sometimes presses down in the darkest hours of night.

But I am not defined by these scars alone. I am Amanda Gray. Daughter. Sister. Friend. Survivor. I am visible now, seen and known by the people who matter most. No longer the girl who whispered "I am invisible" like a mantra, disappearing into herself even before the attack made her disappear from the world for those six long unconscious weeks and many more months of recovery.

I think back to the motto carved above the school entrance, words I passed beneath every day for years without truly understanding their meaning: *Nulli soli, omnes uniti*. No one alone, all together.

Back then, I felt alone, even surrounded by others. Now I understand that being seen, truly seen, by just a few people who matter is worth more than any crowd of casual observers.

Joyce sees me. Ellie sees me. Maggie, in her unique way, sees me. Even Paul, with his awkward attempts at connection, sees me now. And I see them in return: their struggles, their strength, their humanity beyond their relationship to me.

Tomorrow will bring its own challenges, its own small victories and setbacks. The journey of healing isn't linear, doesn't follow a predictable path. Some days will still be hard. Some memories will still hurt.

But tonight, I feel a quiet peace. A sense that I'm exactly where I need to be on this winding road toward whatever comes next. Not alone, not lost, but surrounded by people who love me. Supported by connections forged in both joy and pain.

I am still finding myself, one piece at a time. Still discovering who Amanda Gray is after everything that happened. Still learning to carry both grief and hope, both memory and possibility.

But I am here. I am alive. I am still me.

And I am no longer invisible.

For tonight, that is enough.

AUTHOR'S NOTE

Thank you for spending time with Amanda and her story. As you've walked alongside her from those first terrible moments in the woods to the healing journey that followed, you may have noticed something about the way this story unfolds.

In crafting "Where No One Can Hear You," I made a deliberate choice to focus on Amanda's experience rather than her attacker's. Too often, our cultural narratives about violence centre the perpetrators, their motivations, their backgrounds, their psychology, while relegating survivors to secondary characters in their own stories.

I wanted to write a different kind of thriller.

This novel isn't about understanding Matheson. It's about witnessing Amanda as she reclaims her voice, rebuilds connections, and discovers who she is after trauma. It's about Sarah, whose life mattered immeasurably more than the manner of her death. It's about Maggie, whose survival was an act of quiet heroism long before we met her. It's about all the people who help piece together what violence shatters: Joyce, Ellie, Mum, and even Paul in his awkward way.

In real life, survivors don't get to know all the answers. They don't receive neat explanations for why they were chosen or why others weren't. What they do get is the chance to decide what happens next. How they carry their experiences, what meaning they make from suffering, and who they choose to become.

That's the story I wanted to tell.

I hope that as you close this book, you carry with you not the shadow of Matheson, but the light of Amanda's resilience, Sarah's memory, and the profound truth that even in our most invisible moments, we matter. Our stories matter. And we are never as alone as we sometimes feel.

With gratitude,

JE Rowney

Made in the USA
Columbia, SC
02 April 2025